Futuristic Romance

Love in another time, another place.

PRISONER OF PASSION

"Come into the pool, Thea," Galen ordered quietly. Several more paces and he stood before her seated form. "You obviously came for a bath. I have no desire to deny you that pleasure."

Thea could only look up at him, aghast. She swallowed hard. "No...I want...I came looking for you." The steamy air seemed to be filled with the scent of his closeness. She looked away, unable to think straight with him standing so near.

"Thea," he whispered. Long, tanned fingers worked through the thickness of her hair to cup her chin and turn her face toward him. "Do not be embarrassed. Take my hand."

Thea watched in awe as his fingers closed around hers. She squeezed her eyes shut, willing away the waves of pleasure his touch evoked. This was not right. Not possible. She couldn't love him. It would be unthinkable! He was her prisoner, held to portray her stepbrother in a charade to save her home and his.

Galen reached forward slowly and drew her to his chest. His lips smothered her whimper of protest when he tightened his embrace. His mouth moved forcefully, possessively, over hers. His tongue reclaimed her sweetness.

D1413373

TRUDY THOMPSON

Prisoner of Passion

LOVE SPELL **NEW YORK CITY**

LOVE SPELL®

January 1995

Published by

Dorchester Publishing Co., Inc.
276 Fifth Avenue
New York, NY 10001

Copyright © 1995 by Trudy Thompson

The name "Love Spell" and its logo are trademarks of Dorchester Publishing Co., Inc.

Printed in the United States of America.

With love to my husband, J. D., for his support in turning my dreams into reality, and my daughters, Theresa and Michelle, for their encouragement along the way.

Special thanks to my agent, Natasha Kern, for her generous assistance and guidance, and to Lesley Kellas Payne, for putting me back on course whenever I strayed.

Prisoner of Passion

Prologue

Gustoff climbed stone stairs, higher and higher up a decrepit passageway much used over time. The lumalantern he firmly held caused flickers of ghostly light to creep up the ancient walls. Smoke and ash teased his nostrils as he gained the top of the stairs. With aged fingers, he reached out from beneath overly long purple sleeves to tug off his cowl. Heavy silver-gray locks tumbled loose and fell to his slumped shoulders.

He set the lantern on a dust-covered table, bent to place several more small *picea* sticks on a fire in the pit at room's center, then hovered over the rim of the cauldron to inhale a whiff of steam as it rose into the cold night air.

Shaking his head, he walked across the tower to a barrel beside the far wall. He filled a battered bucket with water, returned to the cauldron, and added liquid to that already bubbling over the pit. He gazed up, following the steam that mingled with smoke near the ceiling before escaping through the opening in the stone created for its release.

Gustoff took a seat in a huge wooden chair beneath the lone tower window to await the appointed hour. As he waited, his thoughts traveled back over time and gathered strength from his memories. He had made a mistake in discharging his duties as Guardian. Had he destroyed the emerging evil force when he had the opportunity, he might have prevented the destruction foretold and altered the path of Fate over the next decade.

Instead, tonight marked the beginning of events that would eventually complete the task he had forsaken. His Guardianship would end, and a younger, more agile being would finish the battle he had fought for 58 of his 70 winters.

Alert for a noise he knew to be forthcoming, Gustoff's senses were charged in a manner lacking for many winters. Eyes raised, he watched fingers of flame dance and stroke the black cauldron hanging over the pit, the shadows entwining along the stone walls, twisting and turning as beasts of the night.

Returning his gaze to the window above his head, he studied the full moon. It cast lonely slivers of white down through the opening to intermingle with sparks of fire, smoke, and beads of steam that glistened as fireflies, sparkling in the chamber as the hot water frothed and spilled over the grate.

With arthritic fingers, he absentmindedly stroked the beard covering his chin, following its silky length downward to touch his breastbone. The shuffle of footsteps disturbed his silent musing. He tilted his head. A smile creased his face. The chamber grew brighter as approaching footsteps brought another lantern and a tiny figure covered in gray from head to foot. The figure paused on the top step and, with eyes cast in darkness by the hood of a cape, searched the chamber.

"Gustoff?" A soft whisper pierced the silence as the covered head turned from side to side. "Gus, are you here?"

"Enter, my child." The head shifted in his direction. Gustoff's smile widened as the figure edged forward and paused before his chair. The old man squinted briefly as his eyes grew accustomed to the light of the lantern held suspended from the sleeve of gray.

"Is it time?"

"It is time, my child," he answered. He stood slowly, and hovered above the figure. He extended his hand to rest upon the shoulder before him, then raised it higher to push back the cowl and expose the trusting face. He grasped an offered hand.

"Everything you have been taught has had its purpose. Tonight you will learn the reasons. Come with me."

Gustoff lead the figure into the light. The glow of the fire caught shafts of russet and sent flares of gold around her still-bent head. Tendrils of long, dark hair escaped the gray cape and cascaded forward over the cape ties, falling to where the evidence of budding breasts was hidden beneath the folds of wool.

"Sit, my child," he ordered, and pointed to a stool beside the warmth of the fire. Knowing she would do his bidding without question, Gustoff turned to a table against the wall and removed one candle. He dipped the wick in the pit and shielded the gathered flame with his hand as he placed the candle in a holder at the center of the table.

"Hold out your hands, my child."

He waited until her slender hands were cupped, palms up, before him. He reached back to the table and drew the candleholder into his left hand, and with his right captured the flame in his fingers. The fire continued to flicker as it danced on the tips of his fingers, not charring his flesh, but becoming a part of his extended hand.

Gustoff closed his eyes and mumbled words in a tongue familiar only to the Ancient Ones. When he opened his eyes, the tiny flame had grown into a blazing white sphere that covered the palm of his hand. The sphere pulsed with life and energy, grew in intensity until its luminescence flooded the tower.

Reaching forward, he placed the Sphere of Light into the girl's upturned hands, stepped back, and whispered yet another incantation as he placed his hand on the top of her head.

"A hundred centicycles past, long before the *Articles* by which we now live were written, the Ancient Ones ruled our world. In their time there was no separation of peoples. All lived as one. But there were devious men among the populations. Men dissatisfied with the teachings of the Ancient Ones. Those men sought to undermine the Ancient Ones and gain power for themselves.

"Their words caused great unrest. Soon revolution spread. War followed. Blood ran like water into the sands of Solarus, through the jungles of

Borderland, and froze in the tundra of Glacia. Still the usurpers were not satisfied. They killed hundreds of thousands of people, destroyed everything in their path, and finally met the Ancient Ones on the field of battle.

"Because the Ancient Ones held the Sphere of Light and their powers were far beyond the knowledge of the men who thought to destroy them, the battle lasted but one moonrise. All of the leaders who sought to obliterate peace were executed.

"Ten centicycles passed. Then another, Queen Shakara of Borderland, sought disharmony. The Ancient Ones were called upon again to destroy the forces working against world peace. Because their numbers were few and the distance they ruled far, the Ancient Ones elected a Council of Elders to help govern so they might be forewarned of any upheaval taking place in the world before such destruction took place again.

"The Elders became more accessible to the general populace and, after a few decades, grew in power. They disagreed with the Ancient Ones on how the world should be ruled. In order to prevent another revolution, the Ancient Ones relinquished rule to the Elders and assumed the position as Guardians of the Sphere.

"The Elders then designed the *Articles* and split our world into three different regions, believing climate would be deterrent enough to hold harmony over the masses. They chose hundreds of Messahs to go forth over the three regions and teach the knowledge of the *Articles* to all people.

"The people of Glacia and Solarus were eager to accept the Elders' teachings and abide by the *Articles,* but the warriors of Borderland, staunch supporters of their deceased queen, Shakara, refused the Messahs admittance into their lands.

"Centicycles passed, and the Ancient Ones, being mortal men, gradually decreased in number, unheeded and ignored by the populace. Yet the Sphere of Light burned on. To protect the Sphere, the remaining Ancient Ones selected the most worthy of their members and entrusted Guardianship of the Sphere to his keeping. Over the cycles that followed, protection of the Sphere has been passed through the dwindling numbers until now only a few may control it.

"As the Elders passed and were replaced by new generations, interpretations of the original *Articles* were altered until laws of docile neutrality and male supremacy, to prevent another female leader from gaining enough power to create a revolution, were firmly established in the lives of all who followed the Elders' teachings.

"Now, as we enter into a new decade, warned by the Ancient Ones that it will be filled with death and destruction, the gentle society the Elders have created will be powerless to prevent their own demise. Once again, through the Guardianship of the Sphere of Light, the Ancient Ones will be called upon to save our world from disaster."

Thea opened her eyes and watched the Sphere pulse between her fingers. Its glow did not burn, but reassured as its power enfolded her. She studied the Sphere, seeking its source, finding no logical explanation for the object she held in her hands. In an attempt to examine its composition, she moved her fingers back and forth. They passed through what had appeared to be solid. If she closed her hands, the Sphere engulfed her

14

flesh and remained intact. She raised her gaze to Gustoff's.

"Explain the Sphere to me, Gus. Tell me why I can feel it in my hands, yet it bears no weight or substance."

Gustoff's gaze dusted over her childish face as she stared up at him in awe. "In due time," he whispered. He had seen the future, knew what trials she would face. His heart ached at the pain she would suffer, but he could not change what was now predestined. He touched her forehead with two fingers.

"Close your eyes." Russet lashes immediately fanned her cheeks. "Evil will once again spread over our world like a pestilence, Thea DeLan. Blood will flow like water over the snows of Glacia, the sands of Solarus, and the jungles in between. The Sphere of Light holds our salvation. I have kept it safe from those who would use its power adversely since it was passed to me when I reached two and ten. Now, on the eve of your second and tenth winter, I pass its safekeeping to you."

Gustoff closed his eyes. "The passing of the Sphere of Light gives you the knowledge of the Ancient Ones to be hidden in the depths of your mind until the demand for such knowledge surrounds you. When needed, a voice will come, whispered through thousands of years by generations. You will seek wisdom and find allies in the most unlikely places. Comrades will guide you along your chosen path. The heritage passed to you from your forefathers will find victory in our cause.

"But know this: The task is for you as the last of the Ancient Ones. No one will be able to assist you over the threshold, nor be able to assume your responsibilities, though there are those who will try. Trust only those who earn your trust. Confide only in those trusted, and remember, while not in physical form, I will always remain at your side.

"Take this Sphere into yourself, my child. Keep it safe until the time comes for its next passing. Cherish the truths and faiths you have been taught, for if you allow doubts and uncertainties to fester and grow, the power of the Sphere will weaken. Bless you, Thea, daughter of the Ancient Ones."

Gustoff then spoke the words told to him many years before. He opened his eyes as Thea repeated the words, and watched as the Sphere of Light grew smaller until it finally disappeared. Satisfied the Sphere had diffused itself into Thea's body, he lifted the two fingers still on her forehead and placed his hands on her slim shoulders.

"Open your eyes, Thea." She stared at his face, entranced. "You will go on with your life as it was meant to be until the special powers within you are needed. I will continue to help you control the gifts you possess till I am called to join the Ancient Ones. Go with love, my child."

A flash of light appeared, then disbursed.

Gustoff stood alone in the tower.

Chapter One

A Decade Later . . .

Exhaustion threatened to collapse his aching lungs, but Galen Sar ran on, forcing his cramped legs to take another step after dense jungle undergrowth slapped him across the face, stung his eyes, and drew blood from the many welts on his cheeks, chest, and arms. Still he ran, ducking low limbs, hurdling small boulders and fallen trees.

He did not see the ravine ahead until it was too late to change direction. Tumbling headfirst into the ditch, he scraped more skin from his arms and chest, felt twigs and branches gouge the flesh of his back. He struggled to his feet.

The harsh clang of metal against metal combined with cries of the injured, shouts of battle, and the woeful wail of mourning, playing a dreadful symphony inside his head. His people were in danger. His skills, and those of the 20 warriors with him, were desperately needed. Adrenaline surged, giving another burst of energy to his depleted muscles.

Galen glanced at the men standing near, then gazed quickly around to avoid another mishap that might slow their pace. He signaled for his warriors to spread out, then began to run again.

Sweat beaded on his brow, accumulated dirt from the smudges covering his face, and dripped into his eyes. Not breaking stride, Galen used his shoulder to wipe away the salty mixture blocking his vision. He slapped at a web of the poisonous *feringe* spider, ignoring the huge black creature that unfolded legs as long as his arm.

He stumbled, righted himself, pushed on. A half mile. Another quarter. The terrain beneath his feet became rockier, the vegetation more sparse, the air cooler. The city of Cree lay beyond the next bend.

"Galen! Behind you!"

Galen turned to find a warrior cloaked in robes the color of sand poised to strike a lethal blow with his broadsword. The warrior's fierce cry echoed through the jungle. With no time to draw the sword belted to his waist, Galen sprang forward, blocked the downward thrust of the warrior's arm, and deflected his sword.

Shorter by several hand spans and lighter by at least two stones, the warrior stumbled, then fell beneath the force of Galen's blow to his midsection. Galen straddled his prone foe, forced the sword from the warrior's hand, and used the interloper's own weapon to end his life.

"Ahheeeee!"

Galen turned at the alien war cry. Three more warriors blocked his path. He lunged, locking sword hilts with the first warrior. Kajar, his second in command, was soon at his side, blade flashing in the slivers of waning sunlight that filtered down through the dense jungle foliage. A third Creean warrior joined the battle, but his opponent turned and ran back toward the city.

Quickly dispatching his charge, Galen kicked the body of his victim aside. "That soldier will warn of our approach."

Kajar wiped the blood from his sword on the side of his leg. "Perhaps we should—"

A woman screamed.

Thoughts of strategy scattered. Running head-long, Galen and the 20 warriors of Cree rounded the bend and entered the city.

Galen could barely contain the stampede of emotions that pounded through him. Hundreds of his people lay dead or dying in the clearing that formed the main thoroughfare of Cree. The smell of fresh blood and burning flesh hung in the air as thick as the smoke that billowed from the houses lining the avenue. Enemy warriors, perhaps 50, looted and pillaged the buildings that remained, strewing clothing and household articles in their wake as they moved from one abode to another.

"Galen!"

Galen pivoted at Kajar's warning in time to ward off the blow of the pike aimed at his head by a warrior he had not heard approach. He stepped back, stumbled over the body of another foe who had been defeated by one of his warriors, and deflected the oncoming blow by raising his foot and kicking his attacker in the stomach. Kajar

19

finished the man and Galen pressed forward.

"Gaaalen!"

His mother's voice reached him over the din of battle. Galen turned to discover his father lying on the steps of the temple, his body covered with blood and dirt, his golden head cradled against his mother's breast. Galen stumbled toward them, but another member of the invading army blocked his path. The warrior attacked viciously, swinging his bloody sword like a club. Galen dropped to one knee and thrust his own blade upward, burying it beneath the warrior's breastbone, plunging it in to the hilt.

A movement from the corner of his eye caught Galen's attention. Turning, sword raised, he found Kajar had stepped to his flank. Kajar now engaged a charging foe, clearing the way for Galen to make his way to his parents.

"Gaaalen!" His mother's garbled scream tore at his innards.

A warrior was at his mother's side gripping her hair, holding her head back to expose the tender white flesh of her throat, sword poised, prepared to strike.

Less than 50 arm spans separated them, but it might as well have been 500. Galen ran, fighting the agony that crushed his heart, knowing he'd never reach her in time. He hurdled blood-covered bodies of children, slipping and sliding in the sticky wetness that soaked into Borderland's fertile soil.

"Ahhheeeee!"

The warrior's battle cry echoed in Galen's ears. A bloodied sword raised high in one hand, his mother's head in the other, the warrior of the desert had but one second of triumph before Galen's sword ripped into his midsection and punctured his heart.

Galen fell to his knees before the mutilated bodies of his parents. Tears slipped unchecked down his cheeks. He reached out, disentangled the dead warrior's fingers from his mother's platinum hair, then closed her eyelids with trembling fingers. He clasped his father's lifeless hand and brought it to his cheek.

"I swear I will avenge you both. I pledge this with every beat of my heart, each breath I draw into my body."

A hand touched his shoulder.

"Galen, by the Gods, I'm sorry."

He looked up into the deep blue eyes of his trusted friend. "Why?"

"The invaders have been defeated, Galen, but several escaped into the jungle. We were able to capture one. He told us that all this was Berezan's doing. Berezan sent his armies to Borderland in search of some mysterious Sphere of Light."

Galen closed his eyes. He trembled with grief and rage. For many sunrises he had warned his father not to ignore the rumors of unrest and violence from Solarus, had insisted that the warriors of Cree remain home instead of leaving the populace vulnerable while they went on their semiannual hunting trip. But Omar Sar had cast aside Galen's worries, maintaining that the rumors from Solarus were only rumors, that Berezan would never be foolish enough to attack Borderland.

The senseless murder of his parents, his people, might have been prevented if he had been stronger, more insistent.

Kajar saw the pain in his friend's eyes. "Don't blame yourself, Galen. You could not have foreseen this." Kajar bent and slipped a golden chain from Omar Sar's neck. He held it out to Galen. The bronzed sun-shaped medallion suspended from the chain glistened in the last afternoon light. "The warriors who escaped may bring back reinforcements."

Galen pushed Borderland's symbol of leadership away. "We need to bury our dead, help the wounded, and see that the survivors are taken to our hiding place." Galen rose, wiped the blood from his sword on the beige robe of the fallen warrior at his feet, then sheathed his weapon.

"Galen? Take this." Kajar held out the bronzed medallion. "It is your place to lead."

Galen shook his head. He lifted his father's body from the temple steps. "I have no right to accept the emblem of leadership nor the position of *regis* until I have avenged our people's deaths. Come. There is much to do before I depart."

"Don't be foolish, Galen. After our people are seen to safety, your warriors will go with you."

"No, I won't wait. Berezan is mine."

The pounding of equox hooves and the angry shouts of Galen's pursuers somehow penetrated his brain over the loud drumming of his heart. He couldn't let Berezan's henchmen capture him again. He couldn't stand any more torture. Galen shook his head to ward off the wooziness. With an effort, he pushed away from the tree trunk that lent support, almost sagged to his knees, recovered his balance, then stumbled forward.

The center of his world became the effort it took to place one foot in front of the other. Galen was nearly oblivious to the cold white powder beneath his booted feet, the rising wind that whipped over his bare arms and chest.

He had no idea how long it had been since he'd last eaten. Thirst dried his mouth, making it impossible to draw a deep breath. He panted, gasping for what little oxygen he could force into his lungs, and continued.

Another mile. Two. His teeth chattered. Fever burned his brow. Chills shook his body.

Galen cursed his own stupidity. He should have heeded Kajar's counsel, stayed, taken his place as *regis*, and seen to the welfare of his people.

Instead, he had followed the fleeing members of Berezan's army. Alone. And he had fallen into their trap.

Pain had obliterated his sense of time. How long had it been since he had heard his mother's pitiful cry of anguish as she held his dying father in her arms?

Galen shook his head to clear the memories. He looked around. He was in the middle of nowhere. Blinding whiteness glared at him from every direction. Cold penetrated so deep his blood felt sluggish. He could no longer feel his legs, could not force his feet to move.

His last coherent thought before he fell to the snow-covered ground was that he going to die and there was nothing he could do about it.

A Mooncycle Later . . .

"Please, let him be the one."

The faint rustle of her long silken robes whisked through the moonless night to blend with the soft tattoo of impatient feet. A blustery wind shifted the light snow that capped the chest-high stone wall of the balcony and sent white powder skittering over the frozen floor. Whiffs of smoke and ash rose from chimneys a hundred spans below. Tinkling sounds split the near-quiet when an icicle broke free from the edge of the roof high above and crashed onto the stone walkway surrounding the governing house of Glacia.

Thea DeLan turned, drew a deep breath, and released it slowly. The thick tapestries shielding the arched entrance to the balcony parted. A sliver of light crossed the floor. Between the parted tapestries stood her mentor, Gustoff, the glow from the chamber outlining his deep purple robe, but hiding the features of his aging face.

She placed her hand upon his arm. "Were you successful?"

"Be patient, child. Come," he whispered, then backed into the chamber.

After Thea entered the room and made sure the tapestries were closed, Gustoff nodded. "Be comfortable and listen carefully. There is not much time."

With a motion of his withered hand, he pointed to the chaise and waited while she took a seat. "Your lessons serve you well, Thea. Only a few short winters ago, you would have bombarded me with impatient questions."

"It's not easy," she confessed. "Please." She patted the side of the chaise next to her and took Gustoff's hand as he seated himself. "Don't make me wait."

Gustoff closed his eyes and sighed. "His appearance is similar, but I cannot attest to his mental abilities."

Thea tapped her foot. Gustoff had a way of prolonging explanations. She had loved him her entire life, but she had never learned to tolerate this annoying habit. "Please, Gus. I'm trying, yet my patience has almost expired. Does he or does he not look enough like Alec?"

Gustoff raised his hand to stroke the white whiskers on his chin. "He has the same light eyes and golden hair. His height is sufficient, or so my sources tell me. Yet . . ."

"Yet what?"

"His physical condition as well as his mental stability are somewhat in question."

"Why?" she prodded. Gustoff would get to it eventually, but she couldn't wait.

"He is a Creean warrior."

"And?" The fact he was Creean gave her a mental picture of the man under discussion. Born of the Borderland jungles, the Creeans were the fiercest race of people to inhabit their world. Men and women grew to towering heights and were well known for their physical prowess and stamina. However, this man's capacity seemed to be in serious doubt.

"He was found wandering alone in the tundra a mooncycle ago, near frozen and with no memory of how he arrived. He has been held at Dekar Facility in the lower ward."

Thea inhaled sharply. "With no memory?"

"Precisely."

"I wish to see him."

Gustoff gained his feet slowly, walked across the huge chamber, and opened the door of an ancient wardrobe. He removed two heavily furred, hooded capes, handed one to Thea, then folded the other over his forearm. "Put these on," Gustoff said as he piled a bundle of coarse clothing into her outstretched arms. "I will be back in one moment."

Thea did as Gustoff instructed. She closed the last clasp on her cape as he returned.

"I have arranged suitable conveyance. Come."

Thea placed her hand in Gustoff's. A flash of light appeared; then the chamber stood empty.

Chapter Two

Snow-covered mountains jutted high into the black sky that was now lit by a full moon just beginning to climb. Not a wisp of cloud marred the star-studded beauty. The ground glistened with a new coat of snow as the moon rose higher, sending long furrows of light across the pearly surface. Dark shadows hid most of Glacia, but tiny dots of light blinked in clusters from the cliffs a thousand spans above her head.

Thea adjusted the fur cape around her body to ward off the chilled Nordic night, then cast a hurried glance at Gustoff, expecting to find him faring far worse. Yet Gustoff, even with all of his years, seemed impervious to the cold. As if he sensed her perusal, he looked in her direction.

"Why didn't we transport directly to Dekar? It seems more efficient than riding in that." Thea

27

pointed to the rickety coach drawn by a pair of equally old mulus.

"Trust me. It is important we arrive thusly to support the ruse I have perpetrated to gain the man's freedom—should he meet our specifications."

Thea nodded. Gustoff always had valid reasons for the things he did. Whatever they were this time, she would not question him further.

"We will reach Dekar Settlement in a short while. Pull that hood over your head and keep it there. Should anyone recognize us sneaking about like thieves in the night or entering the Facility, and report our activities to the Elders, our mission will be exposed before we have the opportunity to place your plan into action." Gustoff waited while she covered her head, then took her hand and assisted her into the coach.

Thea drew back the *lepus* fur on the window and gazed out at the frozen valley. Located at the foot of the mountains four miles north, Dekar and its surroundings were a part of her country she knew little about, except that most of the villagers who lived beyond the fortress walls made their livelihoods working for the Facility, either by cultivating foodstuff consumed by those within the walls or by furnishing ironworks for implements the likes of which she had never seen used.

A shiver ran the length of Thea's spine. The Settlement around Dekar was as dark and forbidding as the Facility itself. Gustoff told her families of persons working inside the enormous fortress inhabited ramshackle dwellings in the shadows.

Could the man she needed possibly be found

in such a place? Did she have a choice other than accept him if he was? She was desperate to the point of recklessness. Time grew shorter and shorter with each turn of the wheels that buoyed the old coach.

Forcing down the lump that rose to her throat, she reached to turn up the fur flaps of her heavy boots. The wooly clothes Gustoff had borrowed from one of her servants chafed against the tender flesh of her legs. With a sigh, she reached for the thickly lined gloves that rested in her lap and drew them snugly onto her fingers. Gustoff tapped on the roof as a signal for the driver to halt.

"How are we going to get inside?"

"It was not easy to find a guard I could bribe. Only the late eve watch was approachable. A greedy chap named Moog was obliging enough to offer us entry for ten crystals." He clasped her hand.

Thea gasped at the enormous amount her mentor had paid to gain entry to an establishment she should have been allowed to inspect freely. Should have—*if* she were male and permitted to legally assume the position she had secretly held for almost two mooncycles. She pushed away the anger that always followed such thoughts and looked around.

Inside the Settlement bright fires burned in huge metal vats. Sparks rose like geysers into the darkness. Around each blaze, clusters of people hovered for warmth. Others milled idly on slippery roadways. A haunting melody filled the air, but it sounded more like twangs and moans than the light strains that floated gently over the rest of Glacia.

"It is not a long walk." Gustoff assisted her down from the coach and aided her balance as she steadied her footing on the slippery surface.

Out of nowhere, two children almost collided with them, nearly causing Thea to lose her balance. Thea drew a determined breath to ward off the chill of fear that stung more deeply than the prickling cold. She wrapped the thick fur closer to her face and held tightly to Gustoff's arm, stabilizing him as he steadied her. They moved to the far side of the roadway, out of the flow of bustling dwellers.

They paused to rest momentarily and stood in awe, heads held back to study hundreds of icicles dangling from heights almost 30 hand spans overhead, each reaching just a little closer to the ground until some, at the edge of the building, formed tiny pools of ice beneath their feet.

Thea turned away from the beautiful spectacle that seemed foreign to a place so decadent. She stomped her booted feet and raised her gloved hands to rub her cheeks. Exhaling a frosty breath, she said, "I'm near frozen. How much longer must we wait?"

Gustoff bowed his hooded head. "I think sufficient time has passed. We will proceed, but I must warn you again. Do nothing to give away who you are. Do not look directly into the guard's eyes nor utter a sound. I will speak for us."

"But . . ."

Gustoff raised his hand into the air to stay her comment. "He will not deal with a female."

The warning was perfectly clear. The Elders believed a female incapable of controlling power and had decreed that a woman's place in society should be subservient. Because of this ridiculous notion, she had always been shunned whenever she attempted to offer her opinion or answer a question, except by her staff and Gustoff. Everyone else treated her with the reverence due her family, but entirely discounted her as an individual. Anger once again threatened to surface, but Thea held it back. It would accomplish little. With a reluctant nod, she agreed.

"Come."

Within moments they huddled inside a tiny guardroom. The lone luma bar on the debris-strewn table cast little light to brighten the stone structure. For this one occasion, Thea was glad. It didn't take much imagination to know what made the skittering sounds she heard streak across the floor, nor guess at the condition of the surface beneath her feet. She resisted the urge to reach down and lift her skirts higher, and forced her attention to Gustoff and the man behind the table.

After a few grumbled exchanges and the obvious sound of crystals being placed upon the dirty table, the guard stood and preceded Gustoff through a heavy metal doorway. Gustoff cast another glance at her over his shoulder. The light of the luma defined with shadows each line on his face, every year of his advanced age, and his deep concern for her.

Thea made sure her hood shaded her face and walked slowly toward Gustoff. He turned. She followed.

They traveled cautiously down a long, dark corridor. Thea gazed from side to side and up tall walls of hot, rough stone. The guard explained to Gustoff that, centicycles past, the stone had been cut high in the mountains surrounding Glacia and hauled down rutted roadways by the very inmates who inhabited the structure as each section was completed. As they proceeded, the small group sidestepped enormous webs of the poisonous *feringe* spider, which according to the guard were brought from the Borderland jungles to deter escape. They also made numerous detours around debris, accumulated over years of neglect, and around odd objects Thea could not identify.

She was hot—hotter than she had ever been in her life. Perspiration dripped from her forehead to distort her vision. Reluctant to expose more of herself, yet unable to take another step in blindness, Thea discarded the heavy gloves into a pocket on the side of her cape and wiped at the moisture. Her eyes burned for several moments until her sight cleared.

Before her lay an enormous stairway leading down even farther into the hellish pit. Down, down, winding, turning and twisting, then down again. She could hear the sound of running water. Steam rose from the bottom of the stairway. Moog stepped back to avoid two other huge guards as they approached and passed.

Thea's heart pounded in her ears. She panicked, fearing the questions that would have to be answered if their identity was discovered, but a calm presence filled her as Gustoff touched her mind. She was not alone.

She blinked when Moog shoved aside an enormous wooden door, opening to a dank chamber. A lone luma gave little light to the stone floor and the solitary figure huddled on a tiny cot at the far side of the chamber.

Closer! Touched by her thoughts, the guard stepped forward across the floor until he paused about four spans away. *More light, please!* Time appeared to stretch as the guard moved the lumalantern until she could see the man clearly.

"This him, Messah?"

Thea's gaze shifted quickly to Gustoff's face. *You told the guard you were a member of the Elders' staff? Oh, Gus, what would the Messahs possibly want with a prisoner?* His gaze met hers. Gustoff shook his head.

"This is he," Gustoff whispered. The guard stepped back against the door to allow a better look.

Thea followed Gustoff's concerned gaze. She suddenly stared into beautiful eyes fringed with gold-tipped lashes that met her gaze without seeing. A glaze covered the surface, distorting the color of the iris so she couldn't determine if his eyes were actually blue or gray. Thousands of questions pushed into her mind. Again, the gentle presence touched her. Gustoff understood and would answer everything later.

Breaking the hypnotic trance, she studied the prisoner's face. A thick beard covered the contours of his jaw and cheekbones. His nose was straight, classic, but his upper lip was covered by more hair that hid his mouth completely. Heavy, matted hair swept his shoulders. She knew his hair to be of a light color because some of the wisps that clung to his forehead were almost golden in the light, yet the rest was so dirty. . . .

Her gaze slipped to his broad, hunched shoulders, then the strange fur vest that hung open on his chest. She contemplated his slumped body and counted each band of muscle that stretched across his broad chest. Weakness engulfed her. She swallowed and searched lower, noted the corded mass of his long legs and the condition of the dark leggings that covered his frame.

A gentle hand took her elbow and tugged. "I will send word within two moonrises," Gustoff advised the guard.

The guard nodded and replaced the luma. Thea and Gustoff hurried back ahead of the guard, not bothering to wait for his assistance.

As soon as they were safely ensconced in the coach, Thea blinked, shook her head, and stared into the light reflected from the two tiny lumas attached to each side of their dilapidated transportation.

"I had no idea such horrible conditions were possible. Was my father aware such things go on inside Dekar?"

"Dekar was erected by your forefathers at the direction of the Ancient Ones after the bloody wars that resulted in the split of our world into three alien regions. Its original purpose was to house the hostiles who fought against the lasting peace the Ancient Ones sought. Over the years, I fear, it became a place our rulers, your father included, used to confine those deemed unfit to reside in Glacia's docile society."

"Are there others like that warrior?" Thea tore her gaze from the light to meet his.

"Many," Gustoff confessed sadly. "But only the lower levels of Dekar are occupied. The majority of the fortress is empty."

"We must do something about Dekar, Gus. We cannot condone people being treated worse than animals."

"In due time."

"This cannot wait. We must act now while we are still able to use Alec's name."

Gustoff stroked his beard. "What do you suggest?"

Thea lifted the fur at the window and gazed outside. "You saw the living conditions in the Settlement. We must order the empty chambers of Dekar to be refurbished and opened to house these people. We must also see that the remaining prisoners are given proper nourishment, ample exercise, and cleaner living quarters."

Gustoff nodded. "I will prepare a directive for Dekar immediately. It will be delivered as soon as we return to Glacia."

He touched Thea's hand. "Our most pressing problem at the moment is Berezan. The Creean does not seem to be the answer. He is barely alive. For moon after moon, he has been forced to swallow food and kept drugged to stop him from doing harm to himself. He has not spoken a word since they placed him in the chamber. Before that, he ranted and raved like a wild beast, threatening anyone who came near. He had no idea what he was doing. No idea who or what he was."

Thea shook her head. "The trip to Glacia might kill him."

"This will be your decision, Thea. I do not wholeheartedly agree with your plan, but at this point, I feel desperate enough to try anything. If Berezan discovers we have deceived him . . ."

Chills raced along Thea's spine. She turned from Gustoff's kind face to stare out into the darkness of the passing countryside as the coach rumbled onward, nearer and nearer to her mountain home, high above the atrocities she had witnessed.

"I must rethink this plan, Gus. There are too

many things that could go wrong."

"We have only a matter of days. Time is also our enemy. Berezan comes soon, and we have much to do. Do not allow sentiments to distract you."

Thea rose from the chaise and crossed to the tapestries that shielded the balcony. Parting them slowly, she stepped outside into the darkness. She brushed aside a light dust of fresh snow, placed her hands on the edge of the balcony wall, and lowered her head to offer a silent prayer for guidance.

By the next full moon, she would reach her twenty-second winter. Gustoff, her father's advisor, had been her constant companion since her mother died giving her birth. He had been her nursemaid, her teacher, and avid cultivator of the fledgling powers she possessed.

Over the years of her life, Gustoff had guided her, employing his vast knowledge to hone her skills. She was special, he would say. Chosen. One of the few remaining who possessed the abilities of the Ancient Ones: the capability to transport physically from place to place, to touch another's thoughts by weaving her own consciousness gently through theirs, and most important by her measure, to heal another's hurts by absorbing their ailments into her body, then diffusing harmless energy into the air.

Because of these gifts, she had been sheltered, her talents carefully hidden until the day they were needed. By Gustoff's own words, that day fast approached.

Her deep breath billowed into a frosty exhale. Thea shivered. Her layered silk robe held back the cold. Tonight she felt not the blistering Nordic air, but the chill of fear at what she must do.

Centicycles past, after the great war of Shakara had divided their world into three parts, delegates were elected from each sector, and the Council of Elders formed to create laws that would maintain world harmony. Ruling houses were established in each region to administer the Elders' laws. The Elders also chose Messahs to go forth over the world and convey their words to the masses, to work closely with the ruling houses to preserve the peace proclaimed in the *Articles* all agreed to live by.

Thea looked down at the village. The ruling house of Glacia sat on the mountainside, overlooking the majority of the city on the plateau below. The houses scattered over the frozen wonderland were dark at this late hour. The huge urns that burned on each cobbled street corner gave the only illumination to the ice-covered roadways.

She thought about the people of Glacia sleeping cozily in their beds, unaware of the danger fast approaching. Glacians were gentle people— hydro farmers, ironsmiths, stone craftsman, and weavers. The Glacians had never been warriors, but had relied first on the Ancient Ones, and now the Elders to keep their land safe so they could raise their families in peace. They had no defense against Berezan's evil, none of the special powers she and Gustoff possessed, no abilities beyond those passed on from their parents to make a good life for their children.

But evil once again threatened their world.

Two mooncycles ago Thea's father had died. Alec, her stepbrother, had been summoned by the

Elders from his home high in the mountains surrounding Glacia to rule in their father's place. A mooncycle past, Thea and Gustoff received word from a private messenger that Alec had met with an unfortunate death on his journey to Glacia. By telling the people of Glacia Alec had been delayed in his travels, Thea and Gustoff had been able to rule in Alec's place by relaying messages to the Messahs in his name.

But they couldn't keep up the ruse indefinitely.

Thea blinked back a tear. Word had come from Solarus that Berezan planned to visit Glacia within two mooncycles. Berezan had already overthrown the House of Japier, leaders of Solarus, to claim the deserts of the south as his evil domain. With Alec dead, Thea, the surviving heir, a woman, could not succeed to power under the stipulations of the *Articles* drawn because of Shakara's war. Moreover, the *Articles* had been drawn forbidding the citizens they governed to participate in violence, and this precluded the Elders from any act of revolution. Therefore, Berezan could seize control of Glacia by placing his appointee in office to rule as Berezan himself commanded.

In desperation, she and Gustoff had undertaken a frantic search to find someone who could impersonate her stepbrother long enough for Gustoff to go to the Borderland and try to form a secret alliance with the rulers of the jungle against Berezan.

"After ignoring Glacia for years, why has Berezan sent word he will come now? Unless, of course, he's learned of Father's death." Thea groaned, raised her eyes to the black night sky, and whispered, "Help me."

She turned and entered the chamber to find Gustoff on the chaise awaiting the decision she had postponed for two moonrisings.

"Is there any way we can keep Berezan from coming to Glacia?" she asked, pacing impatiently while Gustoff stroked his white beard. She felt her heart sink when he finally shook his head.

"We knew from the beginning our secret could never continue. We only bought time for Glacia by withholding word of Alec's death. As soon as Berezan arrives and discovers—"

"Bring the warrior here immediately!"

Chapter Three

"You cannot bring that *creature* into this chamber!"

The three servants struggling with their heavy burden paused at Nola's declaration.

Thea directed a glare at her waiting woman. The servants believed the man they were transporting to be Alec and that he had met with an accident on the way to Glacia. Nola knew the truth, but unless she kept her silence, their secret would be out. "Ignore her! Place him on the bed and stoke the fire! He's near frozen!"

Thea hurried across the room, threw back the thick fur on the huge poster, and fluffed the pillows to extra fullness. She eased around the bed, tying the heavy tapestries open with gilded cords so the warmth of the fire could penetrate the interior.

"Thea, you cannot do this!" Nola challenged again.

"Hush," Thea hissed. "I *know* what I'm doing," she said, adding silently, "I hope."

A loud thump drew her attention as one of the servants dropped the man's leg and his booted foot hit the floor. "Be careful! He's not a sack of grain."

"Oh, please. Listen to me," Nola begged, tugging lightly on Thea's robe sleeve. "He's—"

"Enough!" Thea's sharp command stifled the woman's words. "We'll discuss this later," she whispered. More loudly for the benefit of the other servants, she said, "Prepare Alec's bed and make him comfortable. Now!"

Nola's frightened gaze circled the chamber. "This is wrong, Thea. Very, very wrong. That creature should be placed in one of the lower rooms. Not in Master Alec's bed," she argued softly.

"Thea!"

Nola's lips pressed into a satisfied smile as she studied the man leaning against the doorjamb.

"Gustoff! Hurry, I need help," Thea cried, looking first to Nola, then to the three men bustling to do her bidding. She gestured to them to finish quickly, and watched Nola cast a reproachful glance over her shoulder as she brushed by Gustoff and left the chamber. As soon as the servants deposited their heavy burden in the middle of the bed and stoked a fire, they hurried after her.

Gustoff pulled himself from his position against the jamb. His deep purple robe flowed softly around his legs as he walked. He paused beside the bed and gazed at the man sprawled there unconscious. "Why did you bring him here? We should have kept him hidden until we were sure he would recover."

"I can't trust his well-being to healers, Gustoff. I must tend him myself. This way I'll be sure he receives every possible care."

"Thea." Gustoff's raspy voice carried a warning tone.

"Please. We've searched so long to find him. I can't take a chance something will go wrong."

"He is Creean, Thea. He could awake at any minute, discover you hovering over him, and become violent."

Thea worried her bottom lip with her teeth. Her gaze swept slowly over the blond giant huddled in a bed so large it dwarfed the room. His body filled it almost to capacity. She studied the grayish pallor of his skin, the dark circles under his eyes. Reaching forward, she pulled the thick fur from the bottom of the bed and spread it over his body, across his wide shoulders, until it reached his chin.

"The fact he's Creean could aid our cause, Gus. If I can convince him our goals are the same, perhaps he will help us persuade the Creean rulers to join our fight against Berezan."

Gustoff's hand settled on her shoulder and gave a weak squeeze. "He is your enemy, too, Thea DeLan. The success of an alliance is doubtful. The Creeans do not trust the people of Glacia any more than they trust Berezan's followers. This warrior will try to kill you at his first opportunity."

Thea's body trembled at Gustoff's words. "He's also Berezan's enemy. If he'll only give me time to explain—"

"This man is a son of the jungle, a savage. He

will not allow you time to explain your dilemma or request his assistance. He will strike as soon as he realizes where he is being held."

"He's not to be treated as a prisoner. He's been through too much already," she whispered, remembering the conditions she had witnessed at Dekar.

She reached across the bed to place her hand upon his brow. "I have touched his body, Gus. Using all of the knowledge I possess, I could not reach him. I could not get past the black void that encloses his mind." With a gentle swipe of her warm fingers, she pushed a blond lock from his forehead. "He's our only hope, but until all of the narcotics they have given him at Dekar are out of his system, I cannot help him."

Gustoff grasped her hand and pulled her fingers from the man's hair. "Come, child. The alterants in his system weaken by the hour. Since he is no longer under sedation, only his physical condition holds him bound." With a gentle tug he led her across the chamber and pulled her down next to him on the chaise.

"This warrior could mean more trouble than good. He might resemble Alec, but it will be near-ly impossible to turn a half-wild beast into a gen-teel man who can impersonate your stepbrother," he whispered. "I am sorry I brought him here. I may have doomed us all."

Thea ignored Gustoff's comments. Her thoughts clung to an entirely different pattern. "What would a man of the tropic region be doing in Glacia? The difference in climate should have killed him long ago, especially dressed as he is." She recalled the taut dark leggings that hugged his long limbs, the strange fur vest that clung to his chest and shoulders and left his massive arms bare.

Gustoff rubbed his bearded chin thoughtfully. "We may never know his reason. If he dies, the reason for his journey may be forever secret."

Thea gasped. "He won't die. He can't!" She stood abruptly and turned to look down into Gustoff's eyes. "He's the only hope we have to overcome Berezan's wrath."

She hurried back to the bedside and gazed down upon the warrior. "You can't die," she whispered. "You must become my stepbrother so control of Glacia will remain in my family until other arrangements can be made." A strange tightness gripped her chest. Using another person was something she abhorred. It went against everything she'd been taught, all she believed in. But desperate circumstances bred desperate choices. Her homeland was in danger. His, too. They could help each other. "I won't give up, warrior. You *must* help me."

Thea climbed up on the tiny stool that made access to the high bed easier, and took a seat on the side of the thick mattress.

She stroked the warrior's brow. "Your fever is down. The herbal brew I have forced into you has replenished the fluids lost during your stay at Dekar. Your color is a little better. I wonder how much longer you will sleep."

Servants had bathed the warrior's huge body, shaved the growth from his cheeks, washed his blond hair. The image the man now presented was nothing like the dirty miscreant she had seen in the dark chamber of Dekar. His skin still held a strange pallor, but Thea knew from the darkness of his flesh that normally his complexion was bronzed by the sun. She suspected the fierce jungle sun had also lightened the streaks of near-white in his hair. His arched brows were several shades darker than the hair on his head. The gold-tipped lashes that fanned his high cheek-bones darkened until they were almost black near his lids.

Closing her eyes, Thea remembered his eyes when he had stared blankly at her in the chamber of Dekar. A warm flush crept to her cheeks when she recalled her inability to await his waking to find out if those beautiful eyes were blue or gray. She couldn't have helped herself had she tried when she'd gently lifted his lids to discover eyes of the palest blue she had ever seen.

Thea now opened her eyes to gaze upon his handsome face. The straightness of his nose, the strength of his jawline, the firm chin that bore a slight cleft—all beckoned her fingers. She held her hand rigid at her side.

"You're too perfect, warrior," she whispered. "Alec was a handsome man and similar to you in coloring, but his face bordered on frailty. He was tall, but his shoulders weren't this wide." A glance from shoulder to shoulder across his wide chest confirmed her statement. "The people of Glacia have not seen Alec in many mooncycles. Will they accept that Alec could have grown into someone who looks like you?"

Suddenly, the warrior's eyes opened and he appeared to stare right at her.

Thea held her breath and willed her thundering heart to slow. She dared not twitch or make a sound until she was sure the warrior posed no threat. His blond head turned from side to side as he apparently studied the room. She relaxed by degrees. He either didn't see her, or had decided to ignore her presence until he understood more of his situation.

He *had* to know she was within reach. Thea took a slow step backward and bumped into the post, jarring the tapestry loose to swing against the mattress. He tilted his head, listening. Thea eased away from the concealment of the tapestry until she stood in full view. The warrior's eyes never moved.

Frozen under the warrior's light gaze, Thea struggled to draw breath into her aching lungs. His eyes bore through to her soul, yet he gave no indication he was aware of her presence. Chills raced along her spine, and an inner voice warned her to be cautious. Ignoring the voice, Thea stepped forward. Her fingers shook as she raised her hand. He didn't blink until she touched his cheek.

He reached out, grabbed her arm.

"Warrior, please!" Thea concentrated on the pain in her wrist, and used her mind to strengthen her bones so the pressure of his fingers didn't crush her arm. "Don't hurt me." She sighed when the hold on her arm loosened slightly.

She moistened her lips with the tip of her tongue. "I can help you, warrior. I mean you no harm. Do you understand me?"

"Who are you, and why do you hold me in darkness?" He tightened his grasp.

Thea gritted her teeth to withstand the pain and replayed his words in her mind. His voice was deep, somewhat gruff, but she judged his vocal cords were suffering from lack of use and probably thirst. "I mean you no harm, warrior. Please release me." His grip eased, but he did not release her. Instead, his light eyes sought her voice. The expression on his handsome face showed this time he understood.

"Who are you?"

A weak smile lifted Thea's lips. He was still partially under control of the drugs that had been administered at Dekar. Possibly those drugs had altered his thought processes. She also remembered Gustoff saying the warrior had not spoken a word since he was brought to Dekar. The fact he had spoken to her gave her hope. Thea raised her free hand to stroke his cheek. "I am Thea, warrior. I would like to know your name."

He drew a deep breath. A deep growl passed parted lips as he pulled Thea forward until she was almost in his lap.

"What have you done to me?" He relinquished his brutal grip on her arm to grab her around the back and hold her so tightly Thea could hardly breathe.

"I haven't harmed you, warrior. You—"

"Silence! Answer now!" Both arms moved and he grasped her against his chest. "Why do you hold me in darkness and steal my memory?"

Thea gasped. Her ribs felt as if they were about to puncture her lungs. She feared at any moment she would black out from lack of oxygen. "P-please, I m-must have air."

As light-headedness engulfed her, Thea remembered Gustoff's warning about the Creean warrior. The warrior would kill her without giving her time to beg his assistance. She did the only thing she could think of that would disorient him enough to release her so she could breathe.

She kissed his bare chest.

He pulled back. The pressure on her ribs eased, and she could breathe freely. Thea raised her hands to gently massage the muscled expanse of his chest. She caressed his breastbone, his collarbone, the fluttering indentation of the pulse at his throat. Thea reached higher, up toward the massive cords in his thick neck.

She inched her fingers across the top of his shoulder, buried them into his long hair, then slid them slowly upward until they rested in the hollow behind his earlobe. She heard him moan as she placed a soft kiss on the shell of his ear, and closed her eyes and heart to the fluttering that stirred to life within her own body. She pressed her index finger firmly against the tiny hollow and instantly immobilized him.

Thea pulled away, splayed her hands against his breastbone, and shoved. He fell unconscious against the mattress. "I'm sorry, warrior," she whispered to his sleeping form. "I had no other way to defend myself against your strength."

With a sigh, she scrambled down from the bed and walked to the fire, stared into the flames for the hundredth time in three days. "He's blind!"

Thea chewed the inside of her lip as tears slipped slowly down her cheeks. "My *only* hope, and he's blind. Gustoff warned me about his memory loss and his physical condition, but neither of us could have suspected this!"

Thea risked another glance toward the warrior. She tried to visualize what he had looked like before Dekar. She could imagine the bulging muscles in his body springing to life, flexing with each move he made, the proud swagger he would have when he walked. With those long, muscular legs it could be no other way. The vision of him standing tall, his head at a proud tilt, that glorious hair falling about his wide shoulders . . .

Thea walked back to the bed and stared down at the handsome man sprawled across its softness. She licked her lips as memories of the taste of his warm flesh rekindled the strange sensations she had felt inside as she kissed him.

With an unsteady hand Thea drew the heavy fur coverlet up until it draped over his chest, and tucked it snugly under his chin. Unable to resist another stolen touch, she raised her hand and traced her finger over his full, parted lips and his brow, then brushed the fan of his lashes.

"Even perfection is flawed, warrior." Another tear slipped down her cheek. "Obviously you weren't always blind, but I have no idea what's causing your condition." She pressed her fingers against his temple. Closing her eyes, she concentrated on thoughts buried deep in his subconscious to awake them from the effect of the drugs. After several seconds, her eyes flew open.

"How you must have suffered," she said. "I have no idea what has caused so much anguish. I can't make sense of the jumbled thoughts in your mind, but I detect something very painful." Thea climbed up on the stool and sat on the edge of the bed. She watched him sleep. "I suspect whatever happened caused you to wander alone in the tundra. Are you blocking out thoughts too painful to experience?"

Memories of her plight resurfaced to tug at her heart. "I need you, warrior—Glacia needs you." Thea sighed. "I can help you if you'll allow it, but in order to do so you must trust me. I don't know how I'll gain that trust. You already think

I've done something to take away your memory. You'll be doubly hostile when you realize you are sightless."

She touched his cheek. "I can use the gifts I possess to help you regain your memory, but I cannot restore your sight." She brushed his brow. "Glacia and Borderland must prevail over Berezan, warrior. We must place our people before anyone and everything even if I must force your cooperation. I don't want to, but if it's my only option, I will."

He opened his eyes slowly to study every little nook, each shadow or fire-brightened corner of the chamber, before he focused on a chaise before the blaze. He tried to bring his hand to his eyes to wipe away the vision that hovered on that chaise, but found his wrist restrained by a thick coil of rope. He arched his shoulders, only to find his other wrist also secured. He shifted his buttocks on the soft mattress and attempted to pull himself into a sitting position. His ankles were tied, too.

He dropped his head back to the fluffy pillows and closed his eyes. Why would someone have gone to the trouble to bind him when he could snap the coils with one flex? The situation demanded study. He opened his eyes, and drew a quick breath when he discovered the vision that had rested peacefully on the chaise now stood at his side, looking at him with an expression that bordered on concern.

Shadows covered his face. He took advantage of his placement upon the bed and watched as she reached forward to rest her slender fingers upon his chest. He didn't count on his heart nearly jumping through his ribs when she caressed his breastbone.

"Alec," she whispered.

He resisted the urge to pull away from her tender touch. *Who is Alec?*

"You must get well."

Her voice was like the gentle wind that rippled through the trees surrounding his home. At the thought of home, he wondered again where he was, how he'd gotten here. Her fingers worked their way upward, closer to the pulse he knew thudded in his neck. His thoughts scattered.

"I need you." She placed her hand against his jaw, touched the area beneath his lashes, then glided her finger along the cleft in his chin. The mattress sagged as she sat upon the bed.

Fire coursed through his body, along with the urge to snap the futile binds and pull this enticing creature beneath him to appease the needs she spoke of. But he did nothing more than close his eyes when her fingers rose higher to stroke the planes of his cheek.

"I want you well, Alec. I want you to regain your memory, to find your sight. Sightless, you won't be able to help me."

He wondered at her strange words. He might feel weak, but he was in no way helpless. He could remember every little detail of the past three mooncycles. Berezan's murderers had invaded his homeland, killed his parents, his people, and . . .

He shoved the thoughts away. For now, he was in no position to act on the anger that flushed through him. It took all of his strength to remain still while the beautiful creature beside him worked strange magic on his flesh with her warm fingers.

"Alec," she whispered. Then she touched his lashes again.

He stopped breathing. Did she believe him to be this Alec? That he was blind? He almost chuckled. Hadn't he gazed at her most thoroughly while she lay upon the chaise? Certainly he hadn't dreamed the abundance of burning hair that flowed over the side of the chaise until it pooled in thick auburn waves against the floor. He couldn't have imagined the look of concern on her face as she neared the bed and cast her thick-lashed brown gaze upon him.

What strange game was this she played? His name was not Alec. He was Galen Sar, descendent of Shakara, and now that his father had been murdered by Berezan's warrior, *regis* of Borderland. He sensed danger, but he couldn't fathom what harm could befall him at the hands of this enticing female.

Galen made a silent vow to learn all he could about his situation before he acted, to continue to be exactly what she thought him to be until he knew all of the facts.

Chapter Four

Solarus . . .

Berezan discarded his heavy gloves on a table at the end of the long dark hallway, unclasped the golden closure at his throat, and threw his dusty emerald cloak into the arms of a waiting servant. He did not pause to pay heed to the dozen or so soldiers who had returned before him from Borderland and now sat around the table in front of the cold hearth. He shoved aside the servant struggling with his cloak, turned to the stone stairway at his right, and began a hurried ascent.

Hardly winded after climbing the hundred stone stairs, he pushed open the wooden door at the zenith with a force that caused it to bang loudly against the inner tower wall. Several brisk strides brought him to the room's center and an elderly man huddled over a table, working diligently on a scroll spread across the table's width.

"One more false prediction and you will draw your last breath, Elsbar!" Berezan slammed his fist down upon the scroll, spilling a small bottle of ink. "I've wasted six mooncycles on another of your foolish assumptions and have nothing to show for my efforts."

The old man lifted his head slowly, ignoring the black discoloration that slid over the calculations he'd spent years completing. His eyes, clouded with cataracts, watered. He raised his ink-stained hand and wiped gnarled, swollen fingers across his lids to remove the moisture caused by endless hours working in faint tallow light. "Borderland was the logical hiding place for the Sphere. *Naro*, the burning mountain of Cree, is the only force I know of powerful enough to shield the Sphere's energy."

Fury darkened Berezan's face and made his brown eyes flash. "Borderland has felt my power. I've all but annihilated the Creean race, searched every conceivable hiding place, and have come away empty. We have waited long enough to confront Gustoff. Your foolish assumptions and predictions have caused us to lose valuable time."

Elsbar paid little heed to Berezan's ravings as he watched the younger man turn from him and stride toward the tower window. Elsbar studied Berezan's tall frame, noted the tenseness in his muscular body, and felt the aura of fury that flowed around him like static electricity. He shook his head at his pupil's impatience. That was the one lesson of discipline Berezan had never been able to master.

Elsbar had raised the young man from a lad of six summers. In fact, he *owned* him if all accounts were to be settled, for he had given six crystals to purchase the boy from the servant woman who had all but abandoned the child in the fierce desert sun.

Elsbar had been alone then, living out his life in exile in a cave at the border, banished because the previous rulers of Solarus had abided by the dictates of the Council of Elders and outlawed his practice of the arts of the Ancient Ones.

Berezan's arrival had given Elsbar's life purpose. The servant woman had boasted that Gustoff himself had paid her to dispose of the lad, and when touched by Elsbar's mind probe, had inadvertently revealed the secret she'd sworn to go to her grave protecting: The child was the true heir to Glacia, Arlin DeLan's only son, betrayed by Gustoff's magic and, unknown to Glacia's ruler, cast off when Gustoff glimpsed the evil waiting to be awakened within the young boy.

Elsbar had seen traces of what the lad could become with the proper tutoring. He had spent the last 25 summers teaching the young Master all he needed to know to overthrow the rulers of Solarus, to become proficient in the skills necessary to meet and defeat Gustoff, and eventually to rule all denied him by Gustoff's act.

Through careful manipulation, Elsbar's own deep-seated lusts had driven Berezan's ambitions. Revenge had become a deadly game, the quest for power as necessary as breathing. Restoration of his honor, the reclamation of his heritage, his own brand of justice against those who ousted him— those were the driving forces within the younger man, as they were Elsbar's.

Berezan believed he needed only the Sphere of Light and the knowledge to wield it to attain his goals; Elsbar knew differently. He had not taught Berezan all there was to know. Berezan sensed that, thereby making futile the threats hurled at Elsbar in anger.

Elsbar blinked and clasped his crippled hands together in front of him on the table. He watched Berezan march back and forth for several moments.

"Gustoff would not be foolish enough to hide it within his person or in his domicile," Elsbar said. "No other host would be successful in cloaking the Sphere unless they were highly trained in the arts of the Ancient Ones. To my knowledge, there are only the three of us left."

Elsbar closed his eyes and brought his fingers up to press them against his wrinkled temples. "Glacia is the only place left to search, my son, but great danger awaits you there. You must finally meet Gustoff. I see death and destruction, yet the visions are not clear."

"I'm not afraid of Gustoff, old man. I'm younger, far stronger, and with your help, wiser. Defeating the aged one will be simple. I'm already one step ahead of you. I have sent a messenger to Glacia to announce my intended arrival. As suspected, my intentions were not welcomed." A deep chuckle filled the tower. "*Father* is dead. Dear stepbrother Alec thinks to rule Glacia in my place. *My place!*

"Gustoff and the Elders will be shocked when brother Alec welcomes me into Glacia with open arms." Another devious laugh echoed off the stone tower walls. "Gustoff will rue the day he changed the path of my destiny, Elsbar. He will rue the day."

"Even if you locate the Sphere, you may not be able to control it," Elsbar warned.

"Glacia and the right to possess the Sphere are mine!"

A flash of light appeared, then disappeared, leaving Elsbar alone in the tower.

Chapter Five

Galen shifted to ease the ache in his shoulders. The pain persisted. He tried to raise his arms above his head so he could stretch his muscles, but he was still secured to the bed. He raised his buttocks off the mattress, and used the muscles in his thighs to push himself higher and relieve the tension in his lower back. He drew his hands into tight knots and willed all of his strength to break the ropes that held him prisoner.

Something tickled his stomach. Galen forced himself to relax, and opened his eyes to find sunlight flooding through the parted tapestries. Bright light cut a wide path across the chamber, up and over the side of the bed to his prone form. He followed the path of light until his perusal ended at a length of rich auburn flowing over his abdomen. He studied the highlights that glistened in that thick mass. Red, yellow, gold, and white combined with brown to sparkle like gems against his flesh. He followed the length of one long strand to the top of a head cradled against his side.

Galen almost groaned when the silk-covered bundle stretched her leg against his and sent his blood into a frenzied flow. What was she doing in bed with him? The last thing he remembered was her beautiful hair as she leaned over him and touched her warm fingers to his skin.

The need to touch her was uncontrollable. Galen tightened the muscles in his arms, bunched his fists, then pulled with all of his strength. The posts groaned in protest, but held firm as the ropes that bound his wrists strained, frayed, then snapped.

Galen wanted to roll his aching shoulders, to raise his arms above his head to flex out the stiffness, to rub his raw wrists. But he resisted the urge to do any of those things. Unexpected movement on his part might wake the sleeping goddess sprawled half across his body.

She moaned again and stretched her leg, bringing it in direct contact with his throbbing hardness. Heat bolted through his body. Galen gritted his teeth, and resisted. He drew several breaths, reached forward, and grasped her about the waist. He tugged her pliant body forward, and eased her up and over his chest until she lay on top of him, her head nestled into the side of his neck, her firm, full breasts pressed against his chest with nothing separating his flesh from hers but a thin layer of silk, her woman's mound perfectly positioned above his staff.

Need grew powerful within him. It had been many sunrises since he had taken a female to his furs, but Galen forced himself to wait, cautioned himself to remember she believed him to be weak and blind.

Galen buried his nose in her hair. The scent that filled his mind was sweet, alluring, unfamiliar. His circumstances were still unknown. He had no idea where he was or who this tempting morsel heating his body to a fevered pitch might be. He resisted the urge to raise his hips and rub his length against her woman's heat, to test her body's reaction.

He wondered how she could sleep so deeply she would not respond to his touch, then pushed the thought away when she sighed again. Galen could no longer deny temptation. He cupped her face. His large hands covered the sides of her head completely. He raised her face just high enough to study her features. Exquisite. Flawless skin as white as the snow that covered the ground just past the border of his jungle home held his gaze. Her small nose turned up just a bit at the end. Her cheekbones were high, marred only by the dark smudges beneath the fan of her thick lashes, lashes that matched the color of her hair.

Galen eased the thumb of his left hand across her cheek to touch the darkness beneath her eye. She had been awake last eve, hovering over him. How many other moons had she been by his side? Why? Did she truly believe him to be this Alec she had spoken of at his last waking?

His chest tightened. Galen found himself wondering just who this mysterious Alec might be. A lover? Mate? The idea of this beautiful female sharing herself with another annoyed him, but he shook away the feeling with memories that he was someone's captive, as evidenced by the ropes that had bound him to the bed. Whose? Hers? The idea seemed ludicrous, but he couldn't discount the facts he had already gathered.

She wiggled again in her sleep. Her curves melded with his and brought the blood in his veins to a heat that matched the burning rock of *Naro*, the flaming mountain that sheltered his home. Galen drew a deep breath and held it until his lungs burned. He exhaled slowly. His breath raised the tiny curls that framed her forehead. He finally looked at her mouth. Her lips were full, pink, and so inviting they made his mouth water. He pulled her closer, felt each time she inhaled, drawing air over his face. He closed his eyes as his lips found hers.

Galen used the tip of his tongue to moisten her mouth from corner to corner, the fullness of her bottom lip, the softness of the top. He tasted her. Nipped at her sweetness. Licked and sucked her mouth, forgoing the instinct to sink his tongue deep into the tantalizing depths of her and brand her with his need.

She wiggled against him again. Galen almost broke the binds that held his ankles when he strained against the effect she had on his body. She moaned, accepting him against her lips, applying light pressure of her own until Galen thought he would explode. Her soft hands crept upward, buried themselves into his hair, and entwined his locks about her fingers. Her lips parted. Galen took advantage of the offer.

Thea resisted the urge to open her eyes and escape the deep, rejuvenating sleep she required after exercising her *gifts* and the dream that had taken her to unexplored heights. Heat catapulted through every nerve in her body, soothing and relaxing each muscle until she felt liquid. A firmness had settled against her lips, warm and searching. Something enticed her to meet this firmness, to test herself against the warmth, to bask in its glow. Fire engulfed her, burned her body, yet magically called her nearer until she became a part of the flame. She stretched, sighed, melted. She couldn't seem to get close enough.

Something invaded her mouth. Something slick, hot, and wonderful. It glided slowly over her teeth, around her tongue to capture even the small moans of pleasure that escaped her throat. Her senses came alive. Taste, touch, smell warred with her unwillingness to open her eyes and allow sight to explore the wonders taking her to a pinnacle she had never reached.

A deep groan reached through the fog that clouded her brain and brought her sense of hearing and self-preservation to full alert. She forced her eyes to open and discovered herself held tightly in the warrior's embrace, his arms covering her back, his lips and mouth doing strange things to her equilibrium. She sucked a deep breath and pulled away.

Thea wiggled out of the warrior's embrace until she sat upon his stomach. Her cheeks burned fiercely, but she pushed past that feeling in an attempt to understand why she was in his bed, atop his body, making such a fool of herself by taking advantage of the warrior's weakness. She held her breath for several seconds, recited every lesson of self-control Gustoff had ever taught her. Nothing helped.

She finally stared down into his eyes. The gold-tipped lashes were open wide. His beautiful blue eyes were clear and bright. She studied his forehead. Tiny drops of perspiration dotted the smooth surface. Her gaze dropped to his nose, followed its length, then slipped to his lips. She closed her eyes when she remembered the feel of his mouth against hers. She didn't expect his touch upon her cheek.

Galen had given away the fact he was unbound when he raised his hand, but he couldn't help himself. The need to touch her was too great. He skimmed the tips of his fingers across her lips, swollen and lush from his kisses. At that moment, he wanted and needed her more than he had ever wanted or needed anything in his life.

"Alec?"

The softness of her voice, that man's name, caused his fingers to freeze in place. Galen forced his gaze to remain upon her face and wished for a second he was Alec, the Alec who had the right to bury his body deep within the folds of her flesh and keep her one with him forever.

He did blink when he noticed tears in her eyes. Galen fought for all of his faculties. He needed every wit he possessed if he was to carry off his intended ruse. She thought he could not see her staring down at him. She believed the flush of her cheeks and the hurt in her eyes went unheeded. It was all Galen could do not to follow the path of her hand as she reached out for something. Galen jerked when her soft fingers clasped his wrist. He forced his muscles to go limp and offered no resistance when she raised his arm. Pain shot up his forearm as she ran her fingers over the raw spots on his flesh where the rope had burned him.

"I *told* Gustoff not to bind you. Now look what's happened."

Galen's mind worked at a frantic pace. How would a blind man react to her touch? Should he try to pull away? He made a weak effort, but she reached forward to touch his cheek with her other hand, immediately stopping his actions.

"I won't hurt you, Alec. You must believe me."

Galen watched as she leaned her cheek to press it against the injuries on his wrist, being careful not to let his gaze follow the motion. Her dark lashes dipped. The fingers that were resting so gently against his cheek disappeared beyond his limited line of vision. He felt her wrap her small hands around his wrists.

Her body became rigid. Her chest rose and fell rapidly with each breath until she was panting. Galen studied the expression on her face, saw her teeth grip the flesh of her bottom lip, her brows furrow as if she were in pain. It was everything he could do not to shake loose of her hold and bring her into his arms to sooth away the agony she felt.

She sighed and relaxed. Her expression changed instantly from one of pain into one of bliss. Galen had to hold his breath to keep from acknowledging her action. He flinched, however, when her soft mouth touched his wrist.

"There," she said with a smile.

Galen was glad when she brought his wrist within view because he couldn't move a muscle on his own. Miraculously, the raw spots on his flesh had disappeared, leaving no trace of an injury. He subdued his urge to ask how she had cured him. She leaned over and grabbed his other wrist. Within seconds it was also free of injury.

Studying her, Galen knew she had pushed aside the incident of their kiss only moments before. He wished he could erase the effect she'd had on him as quickly. He groaned when she slipped off his body and scrambled to the side of the bed. Galen didn't count on the sight of her lean thigh being exposed when the silken gown she wore hiked up as she moved.

Galen watched her carefully as she paced about the chamber. The white gown she wore flapped over in front and was secured by a golden cord that accentuated her tiny waist and the swell of her hips. The silky fabric clung to her body and glided seductively over his skin when she moved. Heavy locks of burnished hair cascaded over her shoulders, teasing the fullness of her buttocks. Her bare feet left tiny prints in the thick gold carpeting as she tread the floor.

Her face was flushed. She fidgeted with the tie of her robe. Not once did she gaze in his direction. That she was embarrassed by her actions made him realize she had never been intimate with Alec. The thought made him uncomfortable and dashed any hope of easing the fullness in his loins. He groaned purposely to see if she would return to the bed. She cast a timid glance in his direction before she hurried toward the chamber door.

Galen inhaled, then exhaled slowly in an effort to fight the effect she had on his body. He prayed for the strength he needed to resist the temptation she offered. He flopped back against the mattress when sounds came to him from the direction of the closed doorway. He cursed the strange weakness that overcame him when he tried to reach his feet and take the bindings from his ankles.

He couldn't remember the last time he had eaten, and his empty belly told him he wouldn't regain all of his strength until it was filled. He considered asking the female for something to eat. Maybe if he allowed her to believe he thought he was Alec . . .

"Hurry."

Her soft voice floated over him. Galen closed his eyes and waited, knowing he couldn't stop his gaze from following her about the chamber. He grimaced when he realized this act he undertook would be one of the hardest things he had ever done. It could even prove fatal. He didn't hear her approach the bed, and couldn't help himself when he tensed as her warm fingers traced his brow.

"His wrists are free, Thea."

Survival instinct came upon Galen with full force when a raspy, male voice issued those obvious words.

"Yes. Remove the bindings on his ankles immediately. I have already had to heal the burns on his wrists. I told you I would not have him treated like this, Gustoff."

So, she was in command of his fate. But just how far would the unknown male go to appease her?

"Remove the binds," the male voice said.

The fur lifted from his feet. Cold air crept up his legs. Galen discovered himself to be naked under the fur. Memories came back to him with a shattering force. The entire time the beautiful woman lay upon him, he had been bare as the day he was born, except for the fur and the thin silk that hid her body from his view. His loins jerked. It took every drop of his willpower to hold himself still upon the bed.

Several pair of hands worked frantically at the ropes around his ankles. Galen fought the desire to stretch out his feet and ease the cramps in his toes.

"Alec, wake up."

Her fingers dug through his hair. Galen couldn't hold back the groan that slipped from his throat.

He forced his eyes open slowly. His body stiffened when he discovered her face only a few inches above his own. He focused on her eyes. It was the only thing that kept him from jumping up when she was suddenly pulled away from him.

"Get back, Thea. He may harm you."

Thea. Galen repeated her name several times. Alec should know her. *Thea.* Her name was as lovely as she was. A protective instinct charged to life when she was far enough away he could see a hand upon her shoulder, restraining her. He watched as she shrugged away from the old man's grasp.

"He won't harm me, Gustoff."

Her warm hands were firm on his shoulder. "Gustoff, Nola, stack his pillows."

Two figures hovered on the other side of the bed. Galen was thankful he had good peripheral vision. He scooted back until he was cushioned by a mountain of soft pillows. Thea climbed up on the step and sat down on the side of his bed. Alec's bed.

"Thea, Alec needs nourishment to recover his strength."

Galen fought the urge to strangle the man who had spoken those words. Thea shook her head, almost as if she remembered herself, then slid away from him.

"Gustoff will heal the rope burns on your ankles," she said.

Galen almost jumped up off the mattress when he felt cold hands grasp his feet. One ankle, then the other came under Gustoff's care. In a matter of only minutes the old man moved away.

"Nola is bringing something hot for you to eat," she said.

Galen turned his head and found himself staring into the gaping neckline of her robe, the fullness of her breasts less than inches from his nose. The sound that left his lips was half groan, half growl. Thea pulled away.

"I think you should try to get out of bed, Alec. Mardus and Elijah will help you."

Two men paused beside Thea. Only a few inches taller than she, neither male seemed dangerous enough to offer resistance if he decided to overpower them. Galen tucked that thought away when Thea leaned near the foot of his bed to gather something into her arms he hadn't noticed before.

"I hope this robe still fits you. It's been a long time since you've worn it." She shook out the creases in a luxurious jade satin robe. "I'll help you slip it over your shoulders."

His control was precarious at best, and the last thing Galen needed was Thea touching him again. "I'm not an invalid, Thea. I can dress myself." He hadn't meant for the words to be so gruff, nor had it been his intention to hurt her feelings, but judging from the stricken expression on her face, he had. His conscience argued for him to take back his harsh words, to ease her distress.

But a blind man could not see any pain he might inflict.

Until Galen had answers, he had to do everything in his power to hold Thea away. If it took cruelty to make her keep her distance, so be it. "Give it to me." He held out his hand.

Chapter Six

Thea draped the silken cloth across his out-stretched arm and backed away.

"Where are the two servants who are to help me?" Galen dropped his legs over the side of the high mattress. The fur slipped away, exposing his flesh to the cool chamber air. Galen looked down at his bare body. He glanced at Thea, and watched her gaze drop to his groin, then jerk away. She turned to busy herself with setting up his tray, but not before Galen noticed the redness that stained her cheeks.

The two male servants stepped forward. Though it galled to pretend helplessness, Galen gritted his teeth and endured as the men paused at his side and assisted him as he stood. One of the servants grabbed the silken robe from his hand and shook it out before he slid one sleeve over Galen's hand. Every muscle in Galen's body tensed as the garment was draped over his shoulders, flapped partially over his exposed chest, then tied at the waist with a cord.

"Help him to the chaise. Carefully," Thea ordered.

Galen closed his eyes briefly and damned himself for the charade he perpetrated. He wanted to shout at Thea he wasn't some weakling she needed to coddle, but he tensed his muscles and endured. The circumstances he found himself in were partially his own fault. If he'd never begun this ruse, he wouldn't be in this predicament.

Galen took several slow steps toward the chaise, guided gently by a pair of hands on each of his forearms. He made a concentrated effort not to look at Thea as he walked across the floor, studying instead the far chamber wall. He paused when pressure on his arms redirected his thoughts, and sat as instructed on the chaise he'd seen Thea use as a bed.

"I've had something filling prepared for you, Alec." He tried to assess the expression on her face as she tucked a smaller fur around his waist, then draped it over his legs, but found Thea had her head turned to avoid having to look at the part of him she touched.

She placed a small tray on the chaise beside him and handed him a cup of some steaming brew. "Do you need my help?"

The tensing of his muscles as well as the growl that left his lips was involuntary. Galen accepted the mug from her hand and brought the hot liquid to his lips, not asking what the mug contained. The bitter brew scorched his mouth. He almost gagged as he controlled the impulse to spew the disgusting drink across the chamber.

71

"What is this?"

To his utter astonishment, she made a nasty face, then took a moment to compose herself before answering. "It's herb tea, Alec. Drink. It will make you feel much better."

Galen almost laughed. Instead, he tipped the mug to his lips again, braced himself for the bitter concoction, and drained the contents of the cup before he held it out in front of him.

"Good. I'd like some more."

Thea stared at him, mouth agape.

"I'm hungry, Thea. Did I not hear you say you had something for me to fill this emptiness?"

Her expression changed immediately. "I don't have to put up with your surliness, Alec. I'll send Nola in to help you with your meal." She turned away in a swirl of softness.

He couldn't let her leave. "I'm sorry. I'm not used to being so helpless." No truer words had he ever uttered.

Thea turned back to stare at him. A sweet smile crossed her face. She returned to his side, lifting a bowl of something that smelled delicious and caused a wild grumble from his empty stomach.

"I'll help you."

"You can help by answering a few of my questions. Things are very confused in my mind." Galen knew he'd touched a soft spot when Thea sat on the floor in front of him and stared up into his eyes.

"How much do you remember?"

Galen intentionally fumbled with the spoon she'd left in the bowl, then carefully brought it to his mouth. He took his time, savoring the delicious grain mixture. "Nothing beyond waking to find you hovering over me."

Thea reached forward to place her hand upon his knee. Her light touch scorched his skin through the fur. "Do you remember that our father is dead and you were traveling to become leader of Glacia when you had your accident?"

Galen digested the wealth of information her brief words offered. Glacia! Arlin DeLan was dead. Alec, apparently his heir, en route to assume leadership, had met with an accident. Alec was her brother! His innards churned. Her damn brother! Not a lover nor a mate. A brother! And as such had no right to—

"Are you all right, Alec? You seem awfully pale." Her fingers grazed his knee again, and Galen almost jumped off the chaise.

"I'm fine," he managed. He slid back farther on the chaise to avoid her touch.

She folded her hands in her lap and stared down at her entwined fingers. "There was an avalanche. In the frantic flight for safety that followed, you were thrown from your equox. Your men and animals were killed, your supplies lost. Only a miracle saved you. A messenger sent to greet your convoy found you unconscious and near frozen. He brought you here. Gustoff and I have treated your illness."

She never looked into his eyes as the lies fell apparently effortlessly from her lips. But why?

"Berezan has sent word he will come to Glacia," she whispered. "We have no idea why he intends to visit, unless he's heard news of Father's death. It is imperative you get well and regain your sight before he arrives. Gustoff will help you. If you'll let me, I'll do everything I can to see to your recovery. In your present condition, no matter how much you disagree, Berezan can present an ultimatum to Council that you are unfit to rule, and . . ." Tears wet her lashes as she turned away.

And what? Galen had no doubt Alec had somehow met a tragic death en route to Glacia. Thea and the old man Gustoff had then kidnapped *him*. Because they believed he had no memory of his past, they'd tried to make him believe he was Alec DeLan. He taxed his mind for anything that might explain this desperate act.

He stared at Thea's back. Was she Berezan's pawn? Some instrument of torture Berezan had devised to wrench the soul from unsuspecting males?

Galen decided to use whatever Thea plotted to his advantage. He could spend many moonrisings attempting to track down Berezan to extract his revenge. If he stayed, pretending to go along with whatever Thea planned, his prey would unknowingly come to him.

Years of mistrust for any people other than his own surfaced. Bone-chilling cries of terror echoed in his head. The images of children—beaten, struck down before they had the opportunity to enjoy life—swam before his mind's eye. Blood. So much blood. Burned, misshaped bodies, his father's lifeless face, his mother's mournful wail as she hugged her beloved mate to her breast until one of Berezan's mercenaries swung his sword.

Pain seized Galen's chest. Cold chills raced over his flesh. His people, the annihilation of his homeland, the torture he himself had suffered by Berezan's hand surged back full force. He'd sworn he would gain vengeance for the atrocities his people suffered. As *regis* of Borderland, it was his duty as well as his destiny to see those lives avenged.

"Where are my clothes?"

Thea looked up at him with a startled expression on her lovely face. When she reached out to him, he jerked away before she could press her hand against his flesh. "But, you're not—"

"I wish to clothe myself. Now!"

Thea whispered to one of the servants. The servant hurried from the chamber and returned moments later with Galen's leather leggings. "I've had the leggings you were found in cleaned," Thea said. "I'm afraid there wasn't much hope for the rest of your garments." The servant tried to assist him with his leggings, but Galen pushed him away and eased his legs into the soft leather.

He stood and intentionally stumbled across the chamber toward the bed. He bumped into the wooden sides, turned, and collapsed across its width.

Caught in the throes of memory, Galen did not hear Thea cross the floor. He suppressed a growl when the side of the mattress dipped and her warmth burned his side. He clenched his fists to still the desire to grab her and force her to tell him the truth, to explain why she persisted with such lies.

"Alec, don't be upset."

Galen attempted to ignore the tenderness in her voice, each soft word weaving in and around his tormented visions, threatening to shred what little control he had left. He held his breath and allowed bitter memories to enthrall him, to shield him from the delicate pursuit of a conniving female.

Guilt bore through him like a lance. Had he been in the Settlement when Berezan's men arrived, perhaps he could have done something to prevent the horrible massacre of his people.

Then, in his grief, he had foolishly gone after Berezan alone.

Which, in the end, had brought him into Thea's hands.

Galen kept reminding himself Thea wasn't important. Her needs, whatever they might be, were superficial compared to his. He had to keep her and her plight from his mind and concentrate on finding a way to destroy Berezan when they finally met face to face.

Thea turned her head to avoid the flash of fury that deepened the shade of the warrior's blue eyes to indigo. Even sightless, his eyes were like mirrors to his soul. She'd seen frustration crease his face, witnessed the anger of helplessness stiffen his body, known the anguish he must be experiencing to be unable to assist himself in the most minute tasks. Yet, there was something else. Something so shattering it gave her pause, for she couldn't quite place the emotion. Now that he was conscious, she couldn't probe his mind for answers without his consent.

Thea couldn't resist another look at his still form. His lashes were closed, shielding his eyes from view, his firm jaw set, lips rigid. A glance over his body revealed labored breathing, tension in his hands as he clenched his fists at his sides. What demons did he fight within his mind? Did he struggle to find some memory of his past or to forget whatever horrible thing left him in his present condition?

It pained her greatly to know, even with all of her skills, there was little she could do to help him. Tears burned her vision, but Thea stubbornly brushed them away and slipped from his side. The magnificent golden warrior was a pawn in a much larger scheme, as much so as she. No matter how many times she weakened, how many times she might wish it otherwise, the plight of her people, the devastation Gustoff had foreseen, must be foremost in her thoughts, her actions.

Drawing a deep breath to steady her faltering resolve, Thea turned away from the bed and stared into the fire pit. "Gustoff will be here soon to assist you with your needs, Alec. I have other matters that require my attention." She hurried out of the chamber and down the hallway, not pausing until she stepped out onto the balcony of her own chamber and leaned against the stone rail.

A shiver raced up her spine. Thea hugged her arms over her chest to ward off the chill. "I don't know what came over me. I have never . . ." Thea closed her eyes. Memories of the touch of him, the taste of him, the warmth of him washed over her. She trembled from head to toe. The same heat that had flushed her cheeks moments earlier now warmed her flesh.

She had had little experience with the male of the species. Though Gustoff had taught her all he believed she needed to know about life and the trials and triumphs she must face, he had never enlightened her about the strange, erotic sensations she might one day feel and not understand. Vivid, new emotions ran amok when she was in the presence of the warrior. In the last few days, he had captured more of her thoughts than she could afford to expend.

Clasping her hands, Thea squeezed them tightly in an attempt to stay her trembling. Guilt tightened her chest and churned in her stomach. She remembered the warrior as he was a few moments ago in Alec's chamber, confused, out of his element. Then she recalled the moment she'd awakened to find herself in his arms, atop his body, enjoying his kiss.

Warmth infused her veins, flushed her cheeks, and caused her heart to thrum rapidly. She used all of the powers she possessed to chase those forbidden feelings away. Other, more disturbing thoughts replaced them. Could she selfishly use the warrior in a game far more deadly than anything he may have faced before? Did she have any other choice?

A tear streaked down her cheek. Thea tried to rationalize the deceit she planned. Gustoff's words haunted her. All beings were pawns in the greater scheme of things. Good against evil. Right versus wrong. She, Gustoff, and hopefully the warrior and his people against Berezan's treachery. In the end, survival was their only goal, no matter how it had to be attained, no matter who was at risk.

She raised her hand and wiped another teardrop from her face. Long ago Gustoff had told her stories of how the people had lived when the Ancient Ones ruled the world. Since then, her dreams of uniting the world into one nation, one people, living in peace and harmony, had faded fast. Unless something was done to alter her mentor's dire warnings, her dreams would turn to nightmares. The world would become one under Berezan's evil rule. But peace and harmony would be no more than a memory.

A deep breath buoyed her weakening resolve. She needed to have a long talk with Gustoff. Before he began working with the warrior.

"Thea!" A sharp knock followed Nola's urgent summons. "Thea. Please! Open the door."

Thea stepped through the tapestries framing the archway to her balcony, and walked across the azure carpeting to the door. She slid back the bolt and turned the latch. Nola almost knocked her down when she pushed the wooden planks aside and hustled into the chamber.

"I *knew* bringing that beast here would cause trouble, but you wouldn't listen to me, Thea DeLan. You've never listened to me, no matter how smart my opinions might have been."

Thea stared at the agitated young woman, noting how her slight frame, a full head shorter and several stones lighter than Thea's own five and one half spans, seemed to vibrate with nervousness. She studied Nola's hands, frantically twisting and knotting the woolen fabric of her white apron, the chalky pallor of her face, the terrified glossiness of her blue eyes.

Alarm streaked through every nerve in Thea's body. "What's wrong, Nola? Is the warrior all right?"

Nola grabbed the hemline of her woolen apron and rolled it over and over in her hands until it hung near her waist like a muff. "They're here. I knew they'd come. I *knew* this scheme of yours wouldn't work. Now, we'll all be doomed."

"What *are* you talking about?"

"The Elders. They've sent two Messahs to meet with Alec. They're in the meeting chamber with Gustoff now. When the Messahs see that beast in Master Alec's chamber, in Master Alec's bed, they're going to know everything. Everything!"

Panic forced the breath from Thea's lungs. It was too soon! There hadn't been time to prepare the warrior to assume Alec's identity. No time to

79

guide him through what he must say, how he must act. Why now?

Inhaling deeply to calm her racing pulse, Thea counted slowly to ten, then exhaled. Thrice more she repeated this ritual, until she had mastered the panic that threatened to place her in a state similar to Nola's. Breathing evenly, Thea concentrated on Gustoff, desperate to seek his guidance. Chills peppered her flesh. Every cell tingled. She placed herself deeper and deeper into a trance. Her senses became acutely aware of every function within her body, each heartbeat magnified tenfold until she could feel and hear the swish of the blood through her veins.

Thea closed her eyes. She focused on Gustoff's presence, the space he occupied, the visual aspects of the room. She remembered the three tall arches that led to the enormous balcony, the vermillion draperies drawn back to welcome the warmth of the sun, the long table where her father had conducted many conferences. When she opened her eyes again her essence filled the meeting chamber, neither seen nor felt by the two men cloaked in gray who stood before Gustoff as he sat in her father's chair.

Gustoff's thoughts touched hers. *Thaddius and Jermaine are here to assure themselves of Alec's well-being, Thea. They are demanding an audience with him. I have explained his condition and the circumstances that have endangered his health, but they will not be dissuaded.*

Jermaine continued with his argument, unmindful of Gustoff's communication with another being in the chamber. "We will do nothing to endanger Master Alec further, Gustoff, I assure you. But you must understand the Elders' concerns. With Arlin's death, the populace of Glacia is in turmoil. Word of Berezan's intended arrival has reached Council and is rumored throughout the whole of Glacia. Master Alec's condition must be assessed so Thaddius and I may return with news that will appease the Elders so they might reassure the masses."

"We have been instructed to insist you abide by the Elders' wishes, Gustoff," the second Messah added. "We do not hesitate to remind you that, though DeLan inhabited the ruling house of Glacia, his heir must defer to the dictates of the Elders in all matters that affect world harmony. Should Master Alec be unfit to lead . . ." Thaddius shook his head.

Gustoff's thoughts once again touched hers. *Thaddius is delicately attempting to remind me that, under the* Articles, *without a male heir to rule the House of DeLan, Council must relinquish leadership of Glacia. Any individual powerful enough could seize control. In other words, Berezan's arrival could cause catastrophic repercussions.*

Thea felt the energy that sustained her weakening. She could not remain out of body for much longer without endangering reentry. The chamber around her began to waver and dim. Gustoff and the two Messahs appeared no more than shadows. Holding on with the last ounce of her strength, she probed Gustoff's mind one more time. *What can we do? How will we keep them from discovering the warrior is blind?*

Go to him. Do everything possible to prepare him for their visit. I will give you all the time I can, but I am afraid I cannot postpone the inevita—

"Thea! This is no time for you to slip away. Answer me!"

Thea was jolted. The firm pressure of Nola's fingers clinging to her shoulders captured her attention. She cast a hurried glance around to find herself in her own chamber, Nola doing everything in her power to make her answer some question.

"I must go, Nola." Thea shrugged off Nola's grasp and hurried toward the door. Casting a glance over her shoulder, Thea said, "Have refreshments prepared and bring them to Alec's chamber."

"But—"

"There is no time to explain. Go now, and please, be quick about it." Thea closed the door behind her.

In the hallway, Thea paused, drew another deep breath, then offered a silent prayer for assistance before walking down the luma-lit length toward Alec's chamber. Without knocking, she opened the chamber door and slipped inside.

Elijah, who had been left to tidy up, turned. Thea greeted him with a smile, then sought the warrior. She found the chamber empty. Elijah motioned to the tapestries shielding the balcony. She nodded and walked toward the open portal.

Chapter Seven

Oblivious to the cold, Galen stared out over the frozen countryside, studying a region foreign to his jungle home. Vegetation was sparse. Only a few *picea* trees clung to the mountainsides and lined the avenues below. He knew from his studies of Glacia that the climate remained as it was now year-round, the heavy snows never leaving the ground.

He had also been taught as a young boy to understand his mission fully before he began a quest, to discern all there was to know about his enemies, to carefully consider all tactics before he initiated any plan, and to have a firm path of retreat at his disposal once his mission had been completed.

But he knew nothing of the culture of the Glacians, how they earned their livelihoods, grew their food. Curiosity overcame him. He glanced once again over the countryside. No gardens or hothouses were present, yet he had eaten grain, drunk herbal tea.

Galen shook his head, adding yet another question to the many that needed answering. He counted the cottages that lined the cobbled, ice-covered roadway, traced the path of the cobblestones until they disappeared around a distant bend.

Several equox-drawn carts rolled by, appearing as toys from his vantage point more than a hundred spans above the surface. People, tiny as insects, darted to and fro, going about their daily routines, obviously unaware of the treachery taking place within the walls of their own ruling house.

Galen turned and rested his buttocks against the stone wall. He gazed up past the portal he had exited to examine the construction of the dwelling. Built from blocks of the light gray, silver-flecked granite that formed the numerous mountain ranges crossing Glacia and Borderland, the structure sparkled in the sunlight. Suspended perhaps 30 spans above his head was another balcony, yet another floor. Beyond that, stone walls reached higher still until they were capped by deep eves laced with immense icicles that sporadically broke loose to crash onto the walkway below.

Glancing down, he noted that the entire dwelling seemed to be located on a shelf carved out of the mountainside. He looked around. There didn't appear to be an outside entrance. Yet another question to add to his ever-growing list. A list that need to be answered before Berezan arrived.

Voices filtered out to him through the open portal. Galen turned away from the exit, spread his hands wide on the snowcapped balcony wall, and tensed every muscle in his body as he fought for control. He had managed to keep Thea out of his mind for almost an hour by occupying himself with thoughts of his upcoming revenge. When her soft words flowed over him, warming him to the core, every physical discomfort she caused came back to haunt him. His groin throbbed, his chest tightened, and his heart clamored so loudly beneath his ribs he could count every beat.

Closing his eyes didn't help. Visions appeared, reminding him of her glorious body melded against his, of all that beautiful hair. The taste, smell, and warmth of her lush curves tormented him, with no alleviation in sight.

Her damn brother! Would this torture ever end? He tightened his grip on the stone rail and stared out over the snow-covered countryside.

Sunlight played a delightful symphony with the warrior's golden hair, causing it to sparkle when the light breeze that stirred the powdery snow atop the balcony wall lifted several long strands to flutter around his broad shoulders and back. The urge to reach out and touch was almost irresistible. Thea curled her fingers into her palms to curb the impulse.

The warrior stood barefoot on the icy surface of granite that formed the balcony floor, his back toward her, clad only in the taut leather leggings and emerald robe. The muscles in his calves were extended, tense, as if he tried hard to hold the statuelike pose he had assumed. Large hands, spread wide on each side, gripped the edge of the balcony.

Thea wondered how long he had been standing in the cold. "Alec?"

He turned slowly, leaned against the stone wall, and crossed his powerful arms over his chest. He said not a word, merely stared at her, his light gaze penetrating deep into her being, though Thea knew he couldn't see her.

Heat suffused her body. She couldn't tear her gaze away from his sensuous lips. Memories of the feel of his mouth pressed close to hers, the marvelous sensations he had created with his tongue, stole all thoughts but one: the wish to experience and understand the strange things that happened to her body, her mind, when the warrior exercised his mysterious control over her being.

Mentally shaking herself, Thea took a step forward, lowered her head, and placed her hand upon his forearm. "We have work to do, Alec. Please come inside and warm yourself before the fire while I explain." She felt his muscles tense beneath her fingers, but she dared not look up into his eyes for fear of raising the confusing emotions she'd felt earlier. With a gentle tug, she tried to lead him inside. She had to be a bit more persuasive when he resisted.

"Please." Thea glanced up. The intensity of his stare unnerved her. Held hypnotized, she gazed into his warm blue eyes, feeling the stirrings of an emotion stronger than she'd ever experienced in her life. She was frightened by it. He shifted until he could place his large hand over hers, fusing flesh against flesh, making it very difficult for her to draw a steady breath. Thea had the unexplainable urge to transport to some quiet corner where she could be alone to savor the intensity of the emotions threatening to overpower her, understand the curious flood of warmth that seemed to migrate from her chest to her womanhood.

But his spell-casting eyes and the pressure of his hand held her more securely bound than any chain ever could. "Please," she whispered.

His grip loosened, but he did not release her. Using the powers of her mind to carefully school her thoughts and concentrate on the task ahead, rather than on the magnificent male within reach, Thea jerked her hand away. "The Elders have sent Messahs to meet with you. They are in the meeting chamber with Gustoff and have insisted upon seeing you immediately. Gustoff has tried to stall their interview, but they would not be dissuaded. Come with me. It is necessary to prepare you to receive them." Thea turned and walked inside, nodding absentmindedly to Elijah as he left the chamber. The warrior followed her in.

Thea paused before the fireplace, her back toward the balcony, and stared down into the glow of the banked fire. "I have no idea what questions the Messahs will ask. Perhaps they are here only to see to your well-being. Since you can't remember anything past waking to find yourself in this chamber, I would caution you to keep your audience as brief as possible."

"Will you remain in the chamber while they are present?"

Thea jumped. She had not heard him cross the room, had had no idea he was behind her. She turned around and found herself standing less than a hand's span from him, her forehead at equal height with his breastbone, the width of his golden flesh filling her vision as she stared into the deep V of the jade robe.

A quick step back caused her to come dangerously close to the fire burning in the hearth. The necessity of escape overwhelmed her. She thought about transporting to the other side of the chamber, but rejected the idea. Further use of her gifts in the presence of the warrior was something she could not risk. Nor would it be fair to place him at a disadvantage when he could not see or understand her actions. She stepped to the side in an attempt to walk around him.

His arms rose quickly; his hands lashed on to the wood of the mantel, blocking her exit, imprisoning her within the arch of his body. He took one step forward. The need to press her own body into the heat of his was powerful. She inched nearer. Lazy locks of long blond hair fell over his shoulders as he bent his head downward. Thea lifted her chin. The warrior edged closer still. Closer. She could feel the warmth of his breath brush her face, smell the maleness of him.

He touched her cheek. Every bone in her body melted. She watched his gaze drop from her eyes to her lips, to her breasts. Her mind cried out: He's blind! He has no idea how his gaze is affecting me! But logic evaporated, willpower fled, and she could no longer stand on her own. Thea buried her face against the corded muscles of his chest. His arms encircled her, one hand paused at the small of her back, and the other traced the length of her spine until it held the nape of her neck. Long fingers burrowed into her hair, only to disappear a moment later, then reappear to cup her chin and raise her face higher.

Her lips parted.

"Thea!"

Startled by Nola's shrill voice, Thea wrenched out of the warrior's embrace. Heat suffused her cheeks and caused her hands to tremble so hard she had to grasp folds of her satin gown at the hips to steady herself. She took a step back. The heat of the fire rose beneath her hemline and burned her buttocks. She risked a glance at the warrior, to find he stood in the same spot, but had dropped his fisted hands to his hips as he looked over his shoulder to follow the sound of Nola's voice.

The Elders! This mysterious, sensual power the warrior exerts over me obliterates all of my faculties!

Thea relinquished her hold on the fabric she used to balance herself, raised her arms to splay both hands against the warrior's muscular chest, and pushed. Hard. Caught off guard, he stumbled back several paces, allowing her enough room to scoot around him and hurry across the chamber.

She stared into Nola's face, wondering if the servant had seen her cradled in the warrior's arms, wanting, needing his touch, his kiss. Thea pushed those thoughts away. Nola could be dealt with later. "Please place the refreshments you've prepared on the table, Nola." She turned, not waiting for Nola's response, and walked to the warrior's side.

"We have to get you into bed and make you comfortable before the Messahs arrive, Alec," Thea said shakily as she raised her hand and placed it gently on his forearm. Glancing over her shoulder, she asked Nola, "Have they left the meeting chamber?"

Nola shook her head.

"Good. Please, Alec, it's best you not be found up and around the chamber." Thea tugged on his arm, wondering what she'd do if he resisted as he had on the balcony. Then she almost smiled when she allowed her to lead him to the bed.

While he slipped the jade robe from his shoulders, Thea busied herself with piling the fluffy pillows higher against the headboard instead of gawking at the magnificence of his muscular body. She made a mental note to have some more clothing prepared for him. Fast!

A faint buzzing entered her mind. Thea paused, raised her fingers to her temples, and waited.

We are leaving the meeting chamber now, Thea. Be prepared!

Gustoff's silent warning sent her pulse into a frenzy. She risked a glance toward the warrior, and found he had slipped into the bed. A quick tug at the fur coverlet and almost all of that hot male flesh disappeared.

"Thank you," Thea whispered before walking across the room to pause before the table Nola had prepared. She placed her hands upon the table edge to brace herself for the events to follow, lowered her head, and offered a swift prayer.

All secret planning would be for naught if the Messahs exposed the warrior as an impostor.

Though her hands shook, Thea managed to pour a goblet of sweet wine and carry it across the room to Alec's bed. She climbed the steps and sat carefully on the side of the mattress, then grabbed the warrior's hand and placed the wine goblet into it. "This is wine, Alec. Your favorite."

Tempted to continue holding his hand and help him raise the goblet to his lips, Thea shook her head and slowly slid her fingers away.

She raised her hand and brushed several locks of blond hair from his forehead, as she had done so many times while he lay unconscious. "The Messahs do not know you have lost your sight, Alec. It's best that they don't. If they did, they might . . ." Thea couldn't face what might happen if their ruse failed. "I'll try to remain by your side as long as possible. If I am forced to move away, I'll place myself between the Messahs. Direct your comments to the sound of my voice."

Galen stared into Thea's frightened eyes as he listened to her instructions. The quiver in her voice tugged at some deeply hidden cord within him, but he ignored it as the numerous lies she'd already told surged to the fore, reminding him of his own plans for revenge.

The Messahs offered him a chance to evade whatever devious plot Thea and Gustoff created for him, presented him with an opportunity to end the deception he had begun by confessing who he really was and how he'd come to be here in Glacia, posing as Thea's brother Alec.

A tiny voice of caution echoed in his mind. The Messahs might be just another of Thea's devices to bind him more firmly into her schemes. Could he afford to give up the footholds he'd created by pretending to be blind and weak in order to have the freedom he needed to explore Glacia? He glanced around the chamber. Comfort and warmth surrounded him. If he disclosed the truth, would Thea move him to a dungeon to await Berezan's arrival?

Trudy Thompson

He shifted until he could see Thea's face clearly. Tiny teeth chewed the fullness of her bottom lip. She wrung her hands in her lap and tapped her slippered toe nervously against the top step of the stool. Could she be so skilled in the art of deception she made a conscious effort to keep up her pretense of fear even when she thought he could not see her actions?

Nagging doubts assailed his conscience. Galen forced those doubts away, and decided to make his decision after he had fully assessed the Messahs and their questions.

A knock caused Thea to jump. Galen covertly watched her reactions as the servant Nola hurried to open the door. Thea breathed in shallow, quick gasps. Instead of wringing her hands, she spread her palms against her thighs, grasped handfuls of the silky fabric covering her limbs, and twisted it into knots. She drew a deep breath, held it, exhaled, repeated the ritual three times, then unclasped her hands and smoothed the fabric she'd crumpled. She glanced at him, smiled, and reached to touch his hand, almost as if she offered him reassurance.

"Thea, Messahs Thaddius and Jermaine wish a moment of Alec's time," Gustoff announced as the two men followed him into the chamber. Galen noted the lack of expression on the old man's face. The white hair that covered his head draped past his shoulders and blended with the snowy beard that touched his breastbone. He watched Gustoff's withered hands as he ushered the other gentlemen toward the chaise and motioned for them to have a seat, then, with a quick gesture, ordered Nola, waiting patiently by the door, to prepare refreshments for the Messahs.

"Thea, you are looking well, child," one of the men in gray on the chaise offered.

"Thank you most kindly, Messah Thaddius."

Galen observed in silence as Nola handed a goblet to each man before hurrying back to her station.

"Though your lovely presence always delights us, Thea, we are here to see Master Alec. Please remove yourself to another part of the chamber," the other man, obviously Jermaine, ordered.

Thea stiffened at the man's terse words, bowed her head in acquiescence, cast a nervous glance at Galen before she stood, descended the steps, and walked slowly across the room. As soon as she positioned herself behind the chaise, she said, "Alec tires easily, Messah Jermaine. I hope your visit will not tax him too much."

Galen knew Thea's words were for his benefit. He fought the anger that had flared inside him when the Messah spoke such demeaning words to Thea. Still, this event could be a part of her plans. To judge her reaction more clearly, he stared directly into her eyes. "Thea has been of great assistance to me, Messah Jermaine. Without her constant vigilance, I daresay my recovery might not have been so swift."

Fear, stark and vivid, glistened in Thea's eyes. Had he overstepped his privilege as ruler of Glacia by chastising the Messahs? Galen cast a quick glance at Gustoff. An expression of delight twinkled in his eyes, and Galen swore he saw the twitch of a smile raise the old man's beard.

"We did not mean to discount your sister's services, Master Alec. It is just that our visit is of grave importance, and we have been advised we cannot take up too much of your time." This from

Thaddius as he glanced toward Gustoff.

"You wish to see for yourselves that the avalanche didn't do me any permanent harm, isn't that what you mean, Thaddius?"

Thea's cheeks went from pink to deep red. Her teeth once again scored the tender flesh of her bottom lip.

The other man in gray stood abruptly and began to pace. "The Elders are very concerned over your health, Master Alec. When news of your accident arrived so soon upon the heels of Berezan's intentions to visit Glacia . . ." The old man shook his head, obviously taking time to choose his words more carefully. "Needless to say, several members of Council panicked."

Galen took advantage of the opportunity the old man presented. "Did Berezan give any indication why he plans to visit Glacia?" He studied Thea's face. She seemed as anxious as he to hear the Messahs' answer.

"Berezan never gives reasons for the things he does, Master Alec. He believes himself above the *Articles* and has forbidden the Council of Elders any voice in Solarus. No one can second-guess his evil, but you should know that well enough."

A maelstrom of confusing thoughts bounced around in Galen's head. Had Alec DeLan at one time encountered Berezan? Thea's stricken expression implied she had no idea. Were the Messahs suspicious of Alec DeLan for some reason? Could this be the impetus behind their interrogation? How well did Thea actually know her brother? Galen almost groaned aloud. He didn't need more questions without answers.

The silent pause stretched until tension crackled in the chamber air. The Messahs awaited his response, but Galen agonized over how he should answer. He took a moment longer to examine how he would react if he were collaborating with an evil power to overthrow another region. The first item on his agenda would be to gain the trust of a powerful individual in that region. Secondly, he would learn all he could about the inner workings of the hierarchy, then use that information to—

"You have been away from Glacia for many winters, Master Alec." Unnoticed as Galen considered his answer, the Messah Jermaine had stepped near the bed until he could get a good look at what the shadows created by the tapestries hid. "The winters have been kind to you, Alec. One would never think that the lanky, timid lad you were at fifteen would mature into such a magnificent specimen in only ten years."

More questions surfaced. Why had Alec left Glacia to live elsewhere? Thea had told him Alec's party was destroyed by an avalanche as he traveled from his mountain home to assume leadership, but she had given no hint that something had happened between Alec and Arlin DeLan to cause unrest. Ten years of Alec's life were unaccounted for. Ten years in which Alec DeLan might have sought revenge against his father by plotting with Berezan.

"It is a pity your mother could not journey to Glacia with you, Master Alec. Though I suppose it was a blessing that kept the dear woman at home and out of danger. Poor Thea could not have stood the death of her stepmother so close upon the tragic loss of her father."

Stepmother? Alec was Thea's stepbrother, not flesh of her flesh. The thought sent a jolt of anxiety through his groin. Galen shifted uneasily on the bed.

Jermaine turned and propped his cloaked buttocks on the side of the mattress. His view no longer blocked by the man's bulk, Galen glanced toward Thea, only to find she had removed herself from the spot she'd occupied behind the chaise.

A strange sense of caution streaked through his mind. Out of the corner of his eye, Galen noticed that the Messah Jermaine waved his hand slowly back and forth, almost as if he tested Alec's vision.

"Alec is tiring, Messah Jermaine. I fear he must rest now."

Thea's soft words came from the foot of the bed. Galen turned his head to stare into her eyes. Panic dilated her pupils. Knowing there was no way she could convey the Messahs' gesture to a blind man without describing his actions, Galen decided to alleviate her fears.

"Why is it that I get the impression you are testing me?" Galen almost laughed at the man's stricken expression.

The Messah stood abruptly. Guilt drew all color from his face as he struggled to explain his act. "A hundred pardons, Master Alec. It is just that—"

"Rumors reached the Elders that your sight was lost because of your accident, Master Alec. You must understand how such falsehoods fly around from one gossiping servant to another," Thaddius said, taking up the explanation when Jermaine appeared at a loss for words. "The Elders sent us to determine the truth of these rumors and to judge your ability to rule Glacia."

Nola cleared her throat loudly, reminding Galen she was in the room.

"The servants in the House of DeLan are trustworthy, Messah Thaddius. Not one would utter such lies," Thea exclaimed.

Jermaine directed his comment toward Galen, ignoring Thea's statement. "You know how things like this happen, Master. A whisper is overheard, then passed on."

Galen tightened his fists to keep from reaching out and strangling the disgusting man. "Have I satisfied your curiosity? Do you believe I'm capable of ruling Glacia and, if necessary, defending our homes against Berezan? Or is there some task you wish me to complete before you are convinced?"

Thaddius rose from the chaise and hurried to Jermaine's side. "We are convinced you are in good health, Master Alec. We shall report our findings to the Elders at once."

Galen realized the ambiguity of the Messahs' statement. He would be pronounced physically able to assume the position of leader of Glacia, but not trusted until he proved himself worthy.

"Good rising, gentlemen. I am tired and wish to rest. Gustoff, please see the Messahs on their way." Galen closed his eyes to the furious expressions on both men's faces.

He listened as Gustoff explained away his surliness, apologizing as he led the Messahs through the door and closed it softly behind them. Tinkling sounds rippled through the air. Nola cleaned up the mess. The door opened and closed again.

Galen opened his eyes slowly.

97

"Thea." He couldn't see her face in the shadows, but he heard her soft footsteps as she shuffled around the chamber, capping the lumas and causing darkness to fill the area until only the light of the fire remained.

He waited while she added another log to the grate and poked at the burning embers. A roaring fire belched smoke up the chimney. The crackling of the fire, the hissing of sap as it escaped the burning wood, the whisper of the light breeze dancing over the tapestries shielding the portal from the cold outside filled the room with soft, soothing sounds.

"Come *here*, Thea." Galen patted the side of the mattress and waited.

She did not turn to look at him, and he wondered about her gesture until he noticed her shoulders shaking softly.

A flash of bright light filled the chamber, burning his eyes with its intensity.

Galen blinked and found himself alone.

Chapter Eight

The wooden chair grumbled under Gustoff's weight as he shifted for a more comfortable position. To stretch the stiff muscles in his neck, he gazed up through the lone tower window into the heavy-laden gray sky. Less than two hours ago, warm sunshine had glistened over the hills and valleys. Now, unstable weather, normal in the mountains of Glacia, blew down from the higher peaks.

Studying the rapidly darkening sky, Gustoff sighed. How dismal the clouds appeared, much like the turmoil that rose and ebbed within his chest. The heaviness of the secret he had carried for so many cycles pressed hard upon him, threatening suffocation. Gustoff dropped his head into his hands.

With whispered incantations, he called upon the Ancient Ones to guide him through the next few mooncycles. "I have lied, Ancient Ones. Misused the gifts bestowed upon me to deceive the one person I should have been honest with from the beginning. Now, because of my duplicity, I must send my beloved prodigy into battle unequipped to meet the foe she must defeat."

A tear streaked slowly down Gustoff's cheek to wet the hair of his beard. "Thea. Lovely, Thea. Chosen to defend those who will never honor you. Too much rides on your ability to protect Glacia, the whole of our world, to confess my mistakes at this late date." Gustoff closed his eyes. The power of the Sphere of Light relied on Thea's strength of conviction, her sense of wrong and right, her distinction between good and evil. Were she somehow to discover her own brother was behind the malevolence she must meet and destroy, her faith in Gustoff and all that he had taught her would be obliterated.

"My weakness has doomed us all," he whispered.

Visions came unbidden once again to his mind. Through a haze he saw Thea, eager to please, hungry to understand the strange powers within her. The Creean warrior stood tall and powerful by Thea's side, not as a deterrent to her quest, but the strength she needed to see her mission through. Then, in a flash of yellow light, Gustoff witnessed his own passing. His body quaked as the breath of life slowly escaped from an open wound in his chest. His fingers grew cold. His blood, sluggish in his veins, appeared to harden.

The images vanished.

Gustoff opened his eyes and searched the chamber. Chills penetrated to the very marrow of his bone, yet a fine sheen of perspiration dotted his forehead and dripped into his eyes. He raised a shaky hand to wipe the moisture away.

Another chill streaked through his body. To warm his aged bones, Gustoff stood and walked slowly around the tower, pausing only to gaze through the window at the threatening sky, now charcoal and indigo. He would not be physically present to offer Thea support and advice when she faced Berezan, or to explain he had exiled her brother because the *Articles* would have made him the next heir to Glacia. Thea would never know he had done what he believed at the time was right, or that the capacity for evil within the young Berezan was another part of the prophecy he had passed to her.

Unless . . .

Since the beginning of the plot Thea had created to deceive Berezan with an impostor, and especially since his finding the Creean in the dungeons of Dekar, Gustoff had believed the warrior would ruin all they had worked so hard for. His vision proclaimed otherwise.

For decades, he had discounted the Creean race as uncivilized, warriors bred of Shakara, unable to understand the intricacies of peace between nations or the powers greater than those in their jungle world working to defeat all of mankind.

Perhaps, he had been wrong.

The warrior had displayed keen intuition and cunning when handling the Messahs. Whether by intent, or ignorance of the power wielded by the Messahs, he had outwitted them at their own game. He had understood their methods of interrogation, the riddles cloaked by carefully chosen words, and had held his own admirably. Gustoff remembered the stricken expressions on Thaddius's and Jermaine's faces when the warrior had all but ordered them out of the chamber so he could rest.

More importantly, why had the Messahs alluded to the fact that Alec DeLan might have had some contact with Berezan during his sojourn from Glacia? Though Gustoff never fully understood their ways, he knew the Messahs and Elders could discover anything they wished to know about events taking place throughout the world. He speculated their spy network reached far and wide, must even be active within the walls of the governing house of Glacia, for how else would they have suspected the warrior's blindness?

Gustoff thought about the past, and specifically, why Alec had been separated from his step-sister shortly after Thea's second and tenth winter. Any reason at all might shed light on the Messahs' suspicions.

Arlin DeLan had never fully recovered from what he believed to be his only son's demise. In order to relieve some of his grief, Dimetria, Berezan's mother, had tried for almost a decade to become pregnant and offer Arlin another child to love. By the time Arlin's seed finally grew firmly within her womb, Dimetria had grown weak from numerous miscarriages. The strain of Thea's difficult birth taxed her beyond her endurance, and she died shortly after. Years later, after much suffering, Arlin had wed the widowed Nadia of the Peaks and accepted her only son as his heir.

Marital bliss lasted but a few years. Nadia, furious at her inability to take the place of Arlin's beloved, grew shrewish and finally took her 15-year-old son back to his high mountain birthplace. Alec had visited Glacia numerous times over the years, and no hint of any animosity had ever been present in the coltish young boy. Arlin had treated Alec with the greatest respect, taken him under his wing, prepared him to one day take his awarded place as ruler of the House of DeLan.

During those visits, Gustoff had been too busy instructing his own pupil to pay much attention to the comings and goings of young Alec. A mistake, he now realized. By his neglect, Gustoff may have overlooked something hidden within the boy that could have forewarned him of any mischief the heir to Glacia might have been involved in while under his hostile mother's care.

Gustoff shook his head. Alec DeLan's death might have been a blessing. Unknowingly, Thea might have welcomed Berezan's own puppet with open arms.

Turning his thoughts from the past toward the mooncycles ahead, Gustoff reconsidered Thea's idea to offer rule of Glacia to the Creeans of Borderland in exchange for an alliance against Berezan's threat.

Thea believed the Creeans would join Glacia, not Solarus, in a quest for world domination. His own vision still fresh in his mind, Gustoff wondered if her surety had been caused by a prophecy from the Ancient Ones. Maybe she had experienced a glimpse of the future and thought the premonition her own.

She had always been adamant in her desire for one world, one people. The ways of the Elders did not sit well with her perception of how things should be. The dictate that climate alone should be the determining factor to separate the races was as absurd as the laws regarding females. All beings should be treated equally and permitted to experience the snows of Glacia, the warmth of the Solarus deserts, the lushness of Borderland. Cultures could be exchanged. Enemies could be turned to allies.

However, as a female, Thea was of little consequence in the Glacian structure, and her words had never been heard by anyone other than himself. Though he knew he would never live to see it, he prayed that one day Thea's world would exist.

Berezan would arrive in Glacia in 20 moonrisings. The time for Gustoff's journey into Borderland to meet with the Creean rulers could be delayed no longer. Thus decided, Gustoff began to prepare for his departure, planning to advise Thea before first light. He extinguished the lumalantern at the table's center, walked to the door, took one more look around the lonely tower, then disappeared, thoughts of his impending task occupying in his mind.

Galen closed his eyes and remembered another time when he saw someone disappear before his eyes. Berezan! After his capture, Berezan had come into the cave where he was being held, taunted him with unthinkable tortures meant to pull information from him, then vanished in a flash of light so intense it burned Galen's eyes.

Chills crawled over his flesh. He had underestimated Thea. Her actions reaffirmed his earlier convictions. She *was* Berezan's pawn. Whatever devious plans she had for him were obviously an extension of Berezan's control.

Galen shook with the intensity of the anger tearing him apart. He cursed Thea, Berezan, everything that had taken him from the serenity of his jungle home.

He grabbed a pillow from behind his head and threw it across the room. Another followed.

Finally, gaining some control, Galen shifted until he sat on the side of the mattress.

The game was over. There was no more time to waste playing invalid while he awaited answers to his questions. Berezan could arrive at any time, and he knew no more about Glacia than he had when he awoke to find himself a prisoner. He must explore the House of DeLan, to make plans to gain his revenge, then escape to Borderland, as far away from Thea DeLan as possible before he did something he would truly regret.

A light tap on the door drew his attention. Galen stiffened and watched in silence as the wooden panel opened slowly and a sliver of light from the lumalanterns in the hallway crept across the chamber floor.

"Master Alec?"

Galen recognized the voice of the servant Elijah who had sung merrily while he cleaned the chamber at yesterday's rising. Galen remained still. Elijah and another other servant walked to his bedside, the swish of their copper-colored woolen robes the only noise in the room.

"Master Alec?"

"Who is it?"

"Elijah, Master Alec. Mardus is with me. Gustoff has requested we accompany you to the lower chamber and assist with your bath. He wishes to speak with you and believes you will feel more relaxed if you meet him in the steam room."

Not wishing to pass up an opportunity to explore the interior of the keep, Galen threw the thick fur coverlet aside and dropped his legs over the edge of the mattress.

"Take my hand, Master Alec. I will assist you as you robe yourself. I will guide you to your destination," Elijah said.

Blindness did have its advantages. No one would attempt to alter their normal routines when he was about or hide whatever secrets the keep might hold. Escape plans could be easily formulated, vantage points mapped. The charade that had caused him so much discomfort finally became a valuable strategic asset.

Galen observed Elijah's silent partner, Mardus, shuffle around the chamber, emptying cold ashes from the grate. He paid little heed to Elijah's gentle ministrations as the man lifted Galen's arms and slid the cool fabric of the jade robe over his limbs, then belted it securely about his waist.

"It is a pity your possessions were lost in the avalanche. Glacia's seamstresses are constructing garments, but I'm afraid they are several risings from completion. We will arrange something more suitable for you to wear after your bath."

Galen wondered if he would be provided another, larger robe similar to the ones Gustoff and Thea wore, but shoved the thought away when Elijah's warm fingers wrapped around his wrist.

"Come, Master Alec. I will walk slowly and advise you of every turn and stair long before the need arises."

Elijah paused in the hallway. Mardus closed the door behind them, then shuffled ahead to clear any obstacle from their path. Galen gazed about in awe. He had thought his chamber comfortable and warm, but the cavernous hallway, created entirely of the same sparkling granite blocks that made up the outside walls of the keep, held him spellbound.

The keep was round. Numerous doors, all polished to reflect the lumalight and framed by intricate scrollwork carved into the rock, circumscribed the balcony.

Galen reached out to steady himself as he walked, traced the waist-high granite wall that formed a railing. His fingers skimmed along the smooth stone until he reached a support beam, then dropped to his side.

"We are about to reach the first step down, Master Alec. Thirty more before the next landing. Please step now."

Elijah's words caused him to miss a step. Galen recovered and paid little attention to Elijah's step-counting, contemplating instead the stone stairs. There were no windows in the granite spiral, no source of heat that he could see, yet the stone beneath his bare feet and the air around him were very warm.

An enormous chandelier, constructed of thousands of lumastones glittering in black iron sconces, hung from the ceiling two stories above, and dangled almost 30 spans down the center of the circular stairway. Galen studied the core of the building, and counted at least three more floors and 20 more doors from his vantage point.

"Next landing in two steps, Master Alec. Twenty more paces and we will reach the glide to the lower level."

Several slight women garbed in copper robes draped with white woolen aprons hurried past and disappeared into a door at his right. Galen didn't have time to contemplate what might be beyond the door.

"Careful, Master Alec. The glide is another of Gustoff's brilliant inventions, installed since your last visit, I believe. I wish I had the knowledge to explain how it works," Elijah said. "All I know is it operates with a series of pulleys and ropes, weights and balances. It is truly a shame you cannot see it for yourself, Master Alec. This is one of Gustoff's masterpieces.

"Hold on here."

Elijah grabbed his hand and guided it toward a rail protruding up from the floor. After wrapping his fingers securely about the iron bar, the servant reached in front of Galen, closed a mesh grate, then raised his hand to some sort of lever and pulled it.

The floor began to sink, silently, effortlessly, into what Galen judged to be a cylinder cut into the granite.

Swallowing hard to dislodge the lump in his throat, Galen battled the urge to reach out and touch the smooth granite walls as they slipped by. The feeling that he was being lowered into a well overcame him. Sweat beaded on his forehead. Chills raced along his flesh and raised the hair on his arms. He had never had any specific fear he knew of, but this experience was fast becoming something he had no desire to repeat.

He closed his eyes, then quickly reopened them when his stomach turned a somersault. He grabbed his abdomen with his free hand.

"The glide has unsettling effects on everyone the first time it's used, Master Alec. You will become accustomed to it."

Elijah's soft words were meant to reassure, but offered little comfort. Galen prayed silently for the torture to end. He gripped the iron handrail harder.

Movement ceased. Elijah reached around him to release the metal grate.

"Take two steps forward, please, Master Alec."

Galen stepped into a chamber approximately 300 arm spans in diameter. A series of granite walkways crisscrossed the interior, and were suspended over an enormous pool that appeared to be no more than two or three spans deep. The water frothed and bubbled, spewing clouds of steam upward. Beneath the surface, fluorescent rocks, apparently lumastones, lit the liquid. The chamber around him was bathed in bright light.

Looking up, Galen discovered a conveyor system that zigzagged the entire chamber ceiling. Thousands upon thousands of different plants were suspended from the conveyers by cords that lowered each until their root balls were only several spans above the frothing pits so the steam could give needed moisture.

Vegetables, grains, fruits, nuts, and every imaginable source of nutrition danced above the glowing water. Stunned, he glanced about slowly. Several dozen servants worked switches and levers that caused the conveyers to move so the plants could be brought to a center station. Each plant was carefully handled. Leaves pruned, roots checked, the plant was then sent to another station where the bounty could be removed and placed into baskets upon the stone floor. Another group of servants carried the full baskets through an archway and disappeared down what appeared to be another hallway.

Galen forced away a smile when Elijah tugged gently on his sleeve. The question of food was answered.

"Come, Master, Gustoff awaits you in the bathing chamber."

Elijah led Galen down the walkway, turned right at the center station, then through a granite archway to their left.

"We must not dally, Master Alec. To disturb your rest at this late hour, Gustoff must have something important to discuss with you."

Galen followed the servant in the flowing copper robe down another series of hallways, deeper and deeper into the bowels of the mountain, anxious to finally be able to speak with the old man alone. He had something important of his own to discuss.

Gustoff walked slowly around the pool in the bathing chamber. He ignored the steam that drenched his flesh and caused his purple robe to cling to his legs as he paused, then closed his eyes. In order to gain knowledge of Borderland and Omar Sar, leader of the Creeans, Gustoff had to break another of the Ancient Ones' sacred laws. He must touch another's mind against his will, steal information locked away in the recesses of his subconscious, and use the knowledge gained for his own purpose.

Footsteps echoed in the outside hallway. Gust-off opened his eyes and watched Elijah lead the warrior into the chamber. A suspicion he had nurtured proved to be true as the warrior's gaze devoured every inch of the room. Gustoff wondered if his sight had recently returned or if it was a ruse the Creean had used from the beginning. He decided to gain the answer to his question while the warrior was under mind probe.

Galen clenched his jaw tightly to stifle the instinct to gape as he stepped inside the bathing chamber. Like everything else he had encountered since leaving the bedchamber, this room was round. A short stone wall rimmed a deep pit hollowed out of the granite floor. Lush cushions of purple and red were piled upon the wall, forming benches wide enough to lie upon and soak up the warmth of the chamber.

The pool itself was similar to the one he'd encountered in the hydro chamber, though much smaller. The water, illuminated by lumastones, spumed and bubbled like the hot springs he was accustomed to in the Borderlands. Steam clouded the air. The light of the lumas reflected off the beads of moisture, glistened on the flecks of silver in the granite walls, and set the entire chamber aglow.

"Alec?"

Galen turned toward the voice. "Gustoff?"

"Lead him to this side of the pool, Elijah."

Galen allowed himself to be guided by the arm around the stone walkway that edged the pool. When they reached their destination, Elijah bowed, then backed away.

"Why have you summoned me here at this hour?"

"In due time, Alec," Gustoff said. "Elijah will remove your clothing. The steam baths are delightful and will ease the cramps and aches in your muscles that must have accumulated over so many days of dormancy."

Galen untied the sash at his waist. He shrugged his shoulders. The jade robe fell to the stone floor. "I'm not an invalid." He peeled the taut leggings from his body and stepped free.

"Nicely done, Alec. I appreciate the fact you feel angered by Thea's insistence that you are unable to handle even the most mundane tasks on your own. I know I would, were I in your place. Come, the stairway is here." Gustoff placed his hand on Galen's arm and led him to the steps.

Galen tentatively eased into the hot water, expecting the frothing liquid to burn his flesh, but found the temperature perfect. Jets buried within the lumastones sent tiny bursts of air up through the water to massage his aching muscles, shoulders to toes. Galen couldn't help but relax as the tension ebbed slowly away.

He closed his eyes.

A gentle presence touched his mind.

"Sleep, warrior. While the pool works its miracles upon your body, I will take what I need from your mind."

Gustoff knelt behind the warrior by the pool's edge. He leaned forward, pressed his fingertips to the warrior's temples, then closed his eyes. He felt muscles work to expand and deflate powerful lungs, heard blood pump sluggishly through the warrior's body, experienced every emotional or physical change that occurred within Galen's body as he delved deeply into the man's mind, weaving slowly through every thought, pausing to examine more deeply when something of interest caught his attention, then pushing on.

Moments ticked by. Perspiration dripped from Gustoff's forehead. His arms shook, protesting the position he held them in for so long, but neither his fingers nor his concentration wavered. Until he reached a mass of knotted emotions even his power could not breach.

Gustoff probed harder to ascertain and shift through thoughts the warrior, even in sleep, fought hard to hide. Bits and pieces surfaced. The warrior's homeland in devastation. People dead and dying all around. Blood. So much blood. Torture. Pain. Gustoff saw the warrior escaping the clutches of some unknown force.

Blood pumped furiously through the warrior's veins when the sensation of running hard came upon him.

Exhaustion. More running. Cold. So very cold . . .

Gustoff began to tremble. Chills crawled over his flesh. The turmoil in the warrior's mind caused his stomach to quiver. He drew a deep breath and continued. Drugs entered his system, slowing his heart rate, making it impossible to move his arms or close his fists. Raising his eyelids became a monumental task.

Exhaustion.

More running. This time internally as his mind attempted to flee whatever was being done to him.

Gustoff's breathing constricted.

Thea's face appeared, her expression full of concern and longing. Something within the warrior warmed, then blazed red-hot.

Lust. Blood pumping frantically to the warrior's loins.

Gustoff's old heart raced to accommodate the flow.

Perspiration dripped down Gustoff's cheeks, pooled against the flesh of the warrior's temples, wet his fingertips.

Gustoff's skin grew cold, clammy.

Something black and forbidding caused Gustoff to jerk spasmodically. Hatred. Deep. Consuming.

Berezan's face.

Blood. More blood. Then deep agony.

Gustoff opened his eyes. He released his fingers from the warrior's temples and sat back to steady his own frantic breathing.

With the assistance of Elijah, Gustoff slowly gained his feet. He stared down at the warrior's prone form. "You will sleep for several more moments, warrior."

He turned toward Elijah and whispered, "Leave the warrior alone. Allow him to depart the chamber unattended and explore to his heart's content. He cannot leave the keep."

Elijah nodded.

Gustoff walked around the pool, cast a last glance over his shoulder toward the warrior, then shook his head. If all he had discovered was true, he must begin his journey to Borderland immediately. Gustoff closed his eyes and prayed it was not already too late.

Chapter Nine

"Thea."

A cold hand touched her bare shoulder. Thea adjusted her gown, then grasped the coverlet and pulled it around her body. The sound of Gustoff's voice had not awakened her. Too many troubled thoughts had occupied her mind. Sleep, and the wondrous escape it offered, had eluded her for over an hour.

"Thea. Wake up." Gustoff's voice echoed through the darkness. "Now, child. There is much you should know, and time is of the essence."

Thea sat up in bed. "I'm awake."

"Good."

The mattress sagged under Gustoff's weight. His cold fingers entwined with hers, offering comfort. "I must leave for Borderland this night, Thea. I may already be too late."

Thea rose from the bed. She felt her way across the chamber until she located the lumalantern on the table near the hearth and slid the cap upward. Weak light spread over part of the chamber. "What's happened?"

"I cannot go into details now. We need to make plans for the moonrises ahead."

She returned to the bed, grasped Gustoff's hand. "I've been giving Glacia's destiny a lot of thought, Gus."

Gustoff squeezed her hand. "Have you drawn any conclusions?"

Thea met her mentor's kind gaze. "Should anything happen to you or me, the people of Glacia must be protected. Without the power of the Sphere of Light, we cannot expect our gentle subjects to take up arms against Berezan. Unless we have some alternative, I fear they will become victims of Berezan's evil."

"Go on."

"I cannot get Dekar out of my mind, Gus. The reconstruction will be completed within a few moonrises. After the people of the Settlement move to occupy the upper levels, the fortress will be partially empty."

Gustoff rose and walked to the hearth. He placed several dried *picea* boughs into the grate, poked at the smoldering embers until a bright blaze filled the pit, then returned to her side.

"I've been working on a plan to evacuate the people from Glacia."

"To Dekar?"

"Yes. I remembered the old tunnels—the ones the Ancient Ones created in the *picea* forests. With enough time, the people of Glacia could use these tunnels to flee to safety."

"What of the Elders?"

"The Elders will do nothing to alter the fate of the people, Gustoff. It is our duty, my destiny to protect all, whether or not the Elders consent."

Gustoff smiled. "I agree."

"I have also devised an alternative plan in the event the people do not have enough advance warning to flee Glacia." Thea sat beside Gustoff on the bed, grasped his hand. "I plan to solicit Nola's and Elijah's help, Gus. They are well known among the people of the village, and if evacuation fails, will be able to speak with the masses and caution them not to resist Berezan's takeover of Glacia, to acquiesce to his wishes, and do nothing to cause themselves harm."

"You will be committing the people of Glacia to slavery, Thea."

"Slavery is better than death. As long as the people of Glacia live, there is hope."

Gustoff stood. "While you initiate your plans, I will be in Borderland. I think you should take special care of the warrior. See that the Messahs do not meet with him again. And Thea . . ." Gustoff considered telling Thea all he knew of the warrior's past, that he was not, had never been blind. He weighed his discovery of the warrior's reaction to Thea against the response he had felt by holding Thea's hand when he mentioned the warrior, remembered his vision, and decided to let destiny take its course.

"What, Gus?"

"The warrior grows stronger by the day. He needs exercise. He should get out and about."

Thea nodded.

Gustoff released her hand. "I should return within six moonrisings."

"I pray your mission will be successful, Gus. Please, go with care. I love you," Thea whispered, but knew her words were uttered to an empty chamber. Gustoff had gone.

Thea walked to her dressing table, picked up the brush, and tried to work the tangles out of her hair. Frustrated by the futile attempt, she dropped the brush on the table, turned, and opened the door of her wardrobe to snatch a clean gown from the hanger. Without a backward glance, she left the chamber.

She paused briefly before the warrior's door. Fighting the palpitations of her heart and the strange ache in her belly, she hurried down the flight of stairs that led to the glide. A warm bath would soothe her distraught nerves, wash the warrior's scent from her body. Thea shook her head. Water might flush away the warrior's touch, but nothing would erase the want, the need, from her heart.

Thea closed her eyes as the glide slipped silently downward. She wished she had someone to talk with, someone to explain what was happening to her body. Nola's sweet face materialized in her mind, but Thea brushed it away. There were some secrets she couldn't reveal, even to her most trusted friend.

The word *lust* sprang into Thea's mind, and she realized exactly what she was doing. Lusting for the warrior, craving him with a hunger that went far deeper than anything she had ever experienced before.

Lust. She considered the word and its definition. Fire claimed her cheeks. She did feel a powerful need to be near the warrior, a craving for his touch, his . . . No. Her feelings were deeper, less easily defined. His welfare was foremost in her thoughts—most of the time. She cared that he recovered from his ordeal at Dekar, wanted him to regain his sight, his memory. More than anything, she desired to erase that haunted look from his eyes.

The glide stopped. Thea opened her eyes. She drew three deep breaths to control herself, exhaled, then hurried from the glide, across the granite walkways in the hydro garden, down the hallway toward the bathing chamber.

Thea skidded to a halt at the arched entrance of the chamber, and had to grab the granite wall beside her to steady her balance. The warrior stood in bubbling water. Thea exhaled slowly. Obviously he hadn't heard her approach. He was too intent upon scrubbing his chest and arms with a large bar of fragrant soap.

She had to bite her tongue to keep from gasping aloud when he raised his powerful arms to work a rich lather through his hair. The muscles in his broad back bunched and relaxed. A trail of bubbles snaked slowly past his shoulder blades, down the curve of his spine, paused momentarily in the small of his back, glided sensuously over his firm buttocks, his upper thighs, then disappeared into the pool.

Thea leaned hard against the wall, desperately needing the support her wobbly legs failed to give. Breathing was no longer a normal bodily function. Each gasp for air had to be forced into her collapsing lungs. Her heart felt as if it had stalled and now raced to catch up with the frenzied blood flow through her veins. She tried to close her eyes, to block out the vision of the warrior before her, but her brain had ceased to function and refused to respond.

The warrior dipped below the surface of the pool to rinse the soap from his hair. He surfaced, standing tall and proud once again in the center. He shook his mane of blond hair, and water flew from it. He turned.

Thea stood transfixed, unable to pull away from the supporting wall, incapable of retreating.

No! She had no idea she'd uttered the word aloud.

Under different circumstances, Thea might have been amused by the expression that crossed the warrior's face when he realized he was not alone in the bathing chamber. But these were in no way normal circumstances. She wasn't in the chamber staring at the warrior as he lay upon the bed, the fur coverlet hiding his muscular physique from view. Nor did her traitorous thoughts help the situation.

"Thea?"

She opened her mouth to respond, but her vocal cords were as helpless as the rest of her body. Her eyes seemed to have a will of their own, and they devoured the warrior's taut body visible above the water, beginning with the long locks of hair plastered to his chest, then dropping, inch by inch, over the ripples of muscle that coiled across his midsection. A sleek line of darker blond hair swirled around his navel and lower to form a mysterious shadow at his groin before being hidden by the bubbles and steam.

"Thea?"

She gasped. All muscle control dissolved. She slid slowly down the wall until she sat on the corridor floor.

Galen blinked the water from his eyes, cursing himself for the lack of control he had over his composure. He did not like being caught unawares, especially by Thea. If she were to witness one false move on his part, his ruse of blindness would be shattered, his newly found freedom lost.

As discomforting as it was to feel her beautiful brown eyes upon him, it was doubly distracting to realize that his groin failed to remember the way she'd left him last eve, exposing powers he had witnessed in only one other individual—his greatest enemy. Berezan.

A nagging voice warned him to be careful, to avoid the sensuous web she wove. But the voice was not powerful enough to override the rest of his senses, didn't stop his gaze from wandering over her lush curves as she sat upon the stone floor, or from caressing her fiery hair as it spilled over her slim shoulders like the lava of *Naro*. Its radiant glow emphasized the whiteness of her face, the erotic almond shape of her eyes framed by thick, lush lashes, the fine lines of her nose and chin, the kissable puffiness of her mouth.

Galen exhaled in a hard gush and took a step toward her. "Come into the pool, Thea," he ordered quietly. Several more paces and he stood before her seated form. "You obviously came for a bath. I have no desire to deny you that pleasure."

Thea could only look up at him, aghast. She swallowed hard. "No . . . I want . . . I came looking for you." The steamy air seemed to be filled with the scent of his closeness. She looked away, unable to think straight with him standing so near.

"Thea," he whispered. Long, tanned fingers worked through the thickness of her hair to cup her chin and turn her face toward him. "Do not be embarrassed. Take my hand."

The heat that had turned her muscles limp moments before was all but paralyzing her. She could only stare up at his proffered hand, wanting to accept it, accept him.

Thea's hand shook when she released her death grip on the fabric of her gown and lifted her fingers to meet the thicker, stronger ones awaiting her touch. She watched in awe as his fingers closed around hers. Thea could not stop the small sigh that escaped her lips.

"Your bath awaits." He bent and picked her up as if she weighed no more than a bundle of fleece.

Thea squeezed her eyes shut, willing away the waves of pleasure his touch evoked. This was not right. Not possible. She couldn't love him. It would be unthinkable! He was her prisoner, held to portray her stepbrother in a charade to save her home, and his.

Galen's steps were slow, careful, as he treaded toward the pool. He descended the pool stairs before releasing Thea from the cradle of his arms and allowing her body to glide down the front of his. The warmth of her flesh, the steam and bubbles from the pool, the sensuous slide of wet silk against his skin caused him to tremble. Galen knew his control was close to the end. He released her and took a step back.

Thea groped for the edge of the pool. She looked quickly about the chamber for a means of escape. She found only the wall of muscle, still as a statue, beautiful and godlike in his nudity, between her and the chamber exit. The mist and shadows and eerie pale light of the lumastones surrounded them in an ethereal glow.

Despite the moisture in the air, her throat felt dry, her mouth filled with cloth. Every breath she drew stretched the wet silk of her gown, sliding the fabric over her taut nipples, sending spirals of pleasure to the core of her womanhood.

Thoughts of leaving disappeared. Memories of who she was, who he was, dissolved. The broad expanse of his chest filled her gaze, lured her fingers like metal to a magnet. She reached forward timidly to lay her palms against the muscles of his chest. Of their own accord, her fingers climbed slowly upward, across the wide span of his shoulders, then to the broad base of his neck, and higher to the lush fullness of his long hair.

Thea's lips trembled. She had no idea how to proceed, what to say to make him kiss her again.

Galen had not moved; he did not move now as Thea stood before him, pleading with her eyes, begging with her touch. He had dreamed of her like this so many times. He was determined he would do nothing, *nothing*, to scare her away.

He reached forward slowly, closed his hands around her waist, and drew her to his chest. His lips smothered her whimper of protest when he tightened his embrace. His mouth moved forcefully, possessively, over hers. His tongue reclaimed her sweetness.

Thea cried out when his lips left hers, slipped over her chin, down her neck, and blazed a path of fire to the tautness of her silk-clad breast. She gasped as moist, suckling heat enclosed her nipple. She felt him lift her, recognized the hardness of the stone pool rim beneath her buttocks, realized his hands were tearing at the sash of her gown. She could not find the words to deny him as he pushed the silk from her shoulders and bent to lave her bare nipple with his tongue.

All coherent thought fled as pleasure rushed through her body from deep within her belly. She twisted her fingers in his hair.

He was touching her, causing tremors to race through her body. His fingers wove a magical spell, delving inside her, retreating, then moving more deeply. She matched the rhythm of his caress, unashamed of the wanton way she met each thrust. Something within her coiled tighter and tighter. The friction of his fingers increased—faster, faster. Spasm after spasm of ecstasy rocked her body, threatening to destroy all traces of sanity.

She gasped for breath, yet she did not give up her hold on his hair. Everything about her blurred. She felt as if she were floating, experiencing an out-of-body trance. When her world righted itself, she was lying on the pillows of purple and red that topped the wall around the pool.

The heaviness of the warrior's body was upon her. She cried out when something hot and hard pressed against her thigh, and she instinctively tried to resist the force that coaxed her legs open.

"Don't leave me, Thea," the warrior whispered against her ear. Thea released his hair and clutched the taut shoulders above her. She had no intention of leaving him, ever, if she had her way. She sighed when his weight bore down more fully on her, welcoming him, accepting him.

He breached her hard and fast, stretching her, filling her. The tiny pain she felt fled instantly. She met each wild thrust, moving with each surge—deeper and deeper—until he touched the very depths of her soul.

Galen had heard Thea's cries of awe, felt the tearing of the thin membrane that sheltered her innocence, recognized his own astonishment when her untutored body arched to meet his. He was cognizant of her tightness, of how miraculously her body stretched to accommodate his. He slid his hands beneath her buttocks, raised her higher, filled her as the quivers that mounted within the folds of her sweet flesh closed tightly around him.

Galen flipped over on his back, bringing Thea to lie upon his stomach. He clamped his rough, callosed hands over her buttocks and guided her movements until her climax ebbed and he found his own release.

As she lay exhausted above him, he closed his eyes and cursed himself for a fool. He had thought one taste of her would ease his lust and permit him to concentrate on his plans of revenge. Instead, as he clung to her as fiercely as she clung to him, he realized he would never have his fill of his enchanting keeper. She would permeate his every thought, the very essence of his being, until he drew his last breath.

Berezan slapped a leather riding crop against his satin-covered leg. He paced around the small table in the center of the tower, pausing at the window to shake his head, then continue. One final circle and he stopped before his commander. "Prepare my army to march immediately, Rhem."

The tall man bowed his head in acknowledgment. Berezan gazed to Elsbar. "Elsbar will tell you all he knows of Glacia."

Again, the soldier nodded. "All will be ready, Master."

Berezan grasped the other end of the crop and bent it until the brittle leather almost snapped. "Good. See to your men."

Rhem rapped his fist against his chest three times, turned, and left the tower.

Berezan threw the crop on the table. He walked across the tower to the window, clasped his fingers atop the sill, then lowered his forehead to rest against his hands.

"I remember Governing House as if I last saw it yesterday, Elsbar. I see each corridor, the meeting rooms, the hydro gardens beneath the main floor. In my dreams, my nightmares, I have counted each and every granite stone, doorway, and step. I've even envisioned myself sleeping in my father's chamber, snuggled before the warmth of the carved fireplace."

"Two and a half decades is a long time to hold a memory, my son. You cannot rely on the visions of your youth to guide an invasion. Much will have changed in your absence. You must have facts. Gustoff may be old, but he is in no way stupid, and though his powers may have weakened with age, he is still a very dangerous adversary. He will know you are coming to Glacia to search for the Sphere of Light. He will use every available weapon to protect it."

Berezan raised his head. He turned to face Elsbar. "The Glacians are not the Creeans, old man. They have no armies to fight my soldiers. Will Gustoff oppose me if all he knows and protects is threatened? I think not."

Elsbar folded his hands in front of him on the table, then shook his head. "You take Gustoff too lightly, Berezan. The power of the Sphere guides him. No armies, no weapons, no might of any type can defeat the ultimate Light. Warriors in armor, men cloaked by magic, even you, will be destroyed if the power is unleashed against you.

"The Ancient Ones were educators. In our quest for retribution, we have twisted their scriptures, nurtured the darkness until it has grown into a living, dangerous thing. We have destroyed all who were able to stand in our way to this point, but we have not truly been tested."

"I have no intention of failing when the end results will produce what I have desired my entire life," Berezan growled.

"You have grown insolent, Berezan. We cannot waste twenty-five years of hard work by allowing the hunger for victory to overshadow common sense. Caution is the key to success, not might. Do not forget my latest vision. I foresaw blood, death, and destruction so great it shook the world from axis to axis. I cannot say whose death the vision foretold. It could be yours or mine."

Berezan raised his hands, ran long fingers through his hair. He stared at Elsbar. Finally, after exercising what little control he had over his fierce temper, he traversed the tower floor, placed his hands upon the table where Elsbar worked, and leaned down until he was almost nose to nose with the old man.

"I will not fail, Elsbar. You have given me much, but I am strong on my own account. I have no doubts I will meet and destroy Gustoff. The Sphere of Light will be mine!"

Elsbar stared up into Berezan's brown eyes. He

studied the flush that turned the younger man's ruddy complexion a deeper hue of red, the disruption of his russet hair where his fingers had passed repeatedly in his frustration.

"You do not understand all that you will encounter in Glacia, my son. You refuse to comprehend the power of the Sphere. You glory only in the knowledge you possess, but do not fathom how anything could be greater.

"You are young, Berezan. Power and the ability to use it come with age. Do not allow the few petty victories you have gained thus far to inflate your ego further. These triumphs have been but small skirmishes in our overall scheme. The rulers of Solarus were weak. They believed themselves safe from any and all harm simply because of their numbers.

"Annihilation of the Creeans came about because your soldiers murdered old men, women, and innocent children. The warriors of Borderland did not arrive until your massacre had been completed and all but a few members of your army had begun the journey home to Solarus.

"Your capture and torture of Omar Sar's son confirmed the information you had already extracted from Omar's dying words. The Creeans have no knowledge of the Sphere of Light. The search you conducted proved this."

Elsbar reached across the table and touched Berezan's hand. "The warriors of Borderland have not been defeated. They are still out there and, I fear, waiting. When Galen Sar escaped your henchmen, I am sure he returned to his home to unite with his warriors and plan for your defeat.

"You did not heed my warnings when I tried to prohibit your invasion of Borderland. Instead of gaining aid in your quest, you have created more enemies, foes far more dangerous than those you will face in the gentle people of Glacia. The heirs of Shakara will seek to end your lifepath before you reach your destiny, my son."

"You cannot see my final destiny, Elsbar. You have told me this a hundred times. Should Galen of Borderland try to lead an army against mine, he will be exterminated as he should have been while I had him in my possession."

Elsbar ignored Berezan's threats against the Creeans. "Your lifepath is clouded. No definite course has been laid out for you to follow to the Ancient Ones. I believe Gustoff knew this. I also think he had not the knowledge to turn your path according to his wishes. The old servant woman knew you had been exiled because of the evil Gustoff sensed. His fear of castigation by the Ancient Ones must have kept him from ending your life."

"His weakness, you mean!"

Elsbar drummed his gnarled fingers against the wood of the table. Berezan's stubbornness tested his patience almost beyond control. "One more time. Gustoff is not weak; he's strong. The Sphere adds to his power and will destroy you if you do not proceed according to the plans we have made."

"If I destroy Gustoff before he is able to reclaim the Sphere from wherever he's hidden it, Glacia will be under my power. I'll be able to search Governing House at my leisure. Without Gustoff to lead a resistance, no Glacian would dare take a stand against me!"

"I will not be there to guide you when you attempt absorption."

129

Trudy Thompson

"I know the words, old man. I understand the ceremony. I can control the Sphere. Glacia and the Sphere will be mine if I have to destroy every other being upon this world. All *will* be mine!"

Chapter Ten

Thea opened her eyes slowly. Her head was pillowed against a fluffy purple surface, her spine arched to accommodate the powerful arm that lay beneath her. She tried to move her legs, only to find them entwined with longer, stronger ones.

She uttered a tiny gasp of dismay. Fear, uncertainty, a tardy conscience, and an awareness of where she was—lying naked in the warrior's arms—caused her to shudder. Three deep breaths did not calm the escalating pace of her heart, nor chase away the sense of panic that sent chills racing over every inch of her flesh.

She tried to wiggle her legs free, only to feel the warm pressure of the warrior's hand spread across her upper abdomen, his fingers touching the underside of her breast. She froze, fearing any motion would wake the warrior.

A strange warmth whorled in her belly. Memories, vivid, wild, streaked along each nerve. Self-recrimination followed. She should have heeded Gustoff's warning and never given in to the emotions the warrior created. It might have been possible to use the powers of her mind to overshadow the warrior's magical allure, but she had never truly tried to resist him. Even now, she longed only to lie in his arms, to forget the future and all of the evil it held, to allow the steamy air to caress their naked flesh, and to experience again and again the pleasure of his hard body fused with hers.

Thea inhaled in a gasp. Heat suffused her cheeks. Shame tightened around her heart like a vice. While she mentally relived her sins of the past hours, Gustoff was risking his life to travel to Borderland and seek help from the Creeans.

Tears wet her lashes. Thea blinked to force them away. All of the plans she and Gustoff had spent so many moonrisings devising seemed to melt like snowflakes upon a fire. She had failed Glacia, failed Gustoff.

In one moment of weakness, she had seduced the man she had kidnapped to portray her step-brother. She had enjoyed it. Immensely. Some Chosen One she was! She couldn't defeat her own weaknesses. How would she face Berezan?

Thea cast a cautious glance about the chamber. The robe she'd worn lay at poolside, soaked. Her other gown, hastily chosen from the wardrobe before she had left her chamber, lay on the floor in the center of the archway where she'd dropped it earlier.

Her fingers trembled as she reached forward slowly to lift the warrior's hand from her abdomen and position it on the pillows beside her. The urge to kiss his cheek was almost stronger than her will to resist.

To compensate for her weakness, she disappeared in a flash of light.

Thea stood in the middle of Gustoff's dark tower. She shivered when the cold air touched her bare flesh. Wrapping her arms around her waist for what little heat they offered, she hurried to the other side of the tower and pulled a gray robe from the peg where Gustoff had left it. The woolen cloak swallowed her up and brought renewed warmth to her body. She folded the cuffs over several times at her wrists, reached up, and covered her damp hair with the cowl, then turned toward the fire pit at the tower's center.

She bent and threw several small, brittle pieces of *picea* beneath the cauldron Gustoff kept suspended over the center hearth, struck the tinder she found in the pocket of the gray robe, and watched as the dried bough flared to life. After adding several more pieces of the *picea*, she walked to the chair beneath the window and watched the fire grow, felt it take the chill out of the air.

Thea closed her eyes. Many times during her life she had come to the tower with Gustoff. Each visit had been for another lesson in the strange powers she possessed. She thought about the words of caution that always preceded Gustoff's instruction, reminders of the danger she would be in if her abilities were discovered. Repeatedly, she had promised never to tell anyone what they did in the tower, never to reveal the secrets passed to her, and most of all, never to expose her talents to anyone.

Over the years, she had kept all but one of those promises. She shook away thoughts of her most recent transgression when she had transported away from the warrior last eve, and considered the summer of her fifteenth winter when Nola's younger brother had fallen and broken his leg. The keep healers were summoned, but in the panic that ensued, Thea had forgotten all of her sacred promises and touched the youngster's fractured limb.

Five servants had witnessed her action.

In order to keep tales of her deed from spreading over Glacia, she and Gustoff had taken the servants into their confidence, explained the talent Thea possessed, the danger to her life should the gifts be exposed, and the nearly unconscious sleep Thea required after using her powers to restore her strength. The servants swore never to reveal her secrets to anyone, and to this day, no one else within the keep knew of her special powers or her vulnerabilities.

Except the warrior.

Thea opened her eyes and stared up into the graying night sky. Memories of the warrior filled her. She had made another dreadful mistake this moonrise. She had allowed herself to weaken to the strange cravings of her emotions and body, accepting a moment's pleasure from the warrior's touch. The aftereffect of the warrior's lovemaking had left her confused and ashamed. She needed to work through what she felt for the warrior, be it love or lust. She needed to understand the wonderful things that had happened within her, the magical pinnacles she had achieved.

But there was no one to help her through the turmoil that grew in her mind.

She rose and walked to the table. She picked up the lone candle, touched it to the fire beneath the cauldron, then returned it to its position on the table. Closing her eyes, she spoke words taught to her many years ago, foreign words. The candle flickered and flared. White light filled the tower.

"Help me, Ancient Ones," she whispered. "I have taken a man into my body and have offered him my love, though I have not spoken the words. I have dreams. Strange fantasies. I suddenly want things I have never imagined before. I know my life has been predestined, Ancient Ones. I realize I am for a greater purpose. Is it selfish of me to want love and happiness?

"I am confused. Things are not so easily defined as they once were. Help me see into the future and know for certain what fate awaits me. Gustoff has taught me all he can, Ancient Ones, but I feel I am not prepared to undertake the quest you have set before me, nor do I feel worthy. I fear I will fail and all the world will suffer."

The light grew brighter.

"The Sphere of Light lies dormant within me. I have never felt its existence, but I do not doubt what Gustoff has taught me. I try to understand what is expected of me, but I do not know how I, one person, shall accomplish such a task without help."

The light dimmed until its luminescence filled no more than a hand's span of space. Thea concentrated hard on the light, watched it flicker, felt the warmth flood her face. She closed her eyes and spoke once again the ancient incantations.

Through a haze, a great army of men marched toward her wearing cloaks that matched the sand beneath their feet. More men riding equox followed. Hundreds. Thousands. An enormous cloud of dust choked the air, filled the sky with darkness.

More men came.

Thump! Thump! Thump! The noise from their march was deafening.

And still they came. Marching. Riding. Closer. Closer.

The terrain changed. Trees surrounded them. Great, mighty specters of green reached high into the sky, so thick they blocked out the heavens.

Still the men came.

Marching. Hacking with enormous swords. Cutting away the undergrowth that hampered their progress.

A huge black equox filled the light. Atop the beast, another, more menacing creature sat, emerald cape swirling in the air, gloved hand raised high. Lightning bolts sprang from his fingertips. Blood flowed profusely from the equox's nose. Thunder rumbled over the pounding of booted feet.

Marching. Marching.

A scream filled the tower. Another followed until the unearthly sound echoed off the stone walls.

Thea opened her eyes. She wiped at the tears that streaked her face, but the moisture flowed too freely, making her efforts futile. She stared into the flame of the candle, no more than a flicker now, and prayed what she saw was a dream, a nightmare.

"No!"

The beast in the emerald cape could be none other than Berezan. "He comes!"

But did the vision tell of the future, or of events currently taking place?

How could she have been so self-centered to consider her own wants and needs when all around her danger threatened everyone and everything?

"If only Gustoff were here." Thea rose and paced the tower. She forged beyond the panic that threatened to consume her and tried to consider what her father might have done if he were aware of an upcoming threat to the populace of Glacia. There was no way to fight a force of such strength, no way to thwart their attack.

Thea plopped into the chair beneath the window and wrung her hands in her lap. Thousands would die needlessly if something wasn't done immediately. Would the plans she had discussed with Gustoff work to protect the people of Glacia?

Thea stared through the tower window, offering a prayer for guidance. She could not meet and defeat alone a foe many thousands strong, one led by a force of evil no average man could even understand.

But what if her vision only predicted some future event? Could she risk alarming the populace of Glacia unnecessarily? Mass panic would follow information of an invasion.

Thea thought about all Gustoff had told her of Berezan, and realized they never should have trusted him to hold true to his arrival date.

Could Berezan have learned of Alec's demise?

Chills once more prickled Thea's body. Berezan's evil reached far and wide. It could be possible to have an informant within the walls of the keep. Hadn't the Messahs heard whispers of Alec's blindness?

The warrior's face, and everything Gustoff had told her of the Creean race, filled her mind. The Creeans were trained in combat, had been for centicycles since Shakara walked the Borderland, but the people of Glacia were like lambs being led to slaughter.

Thea closed her eyes, summoned Nola and Elijah to her chamber, then disappeared in a flash of light.

Galen opened his eyes to find himself alone atop a pile of pillows. He pushed himself up and studied the chamber. Nothing had been moved. He spread his hand over the pillow where Thea had fallen asleep and found it still warm. He inhaled the scent of her still clinging to the silky fabric. He had made love to her twice, but his need hadn't been sated. Plans to have her once more were thwarted when she fell asleep and he was too tired to wake her. Now she was gone.

Cursing the total exhaustion that overtook him at the most trying times, Galen threw his legs over the side of the pillow-lined wall and sat up.

He had known Thea would try to escape without waking him and had planned to pretend sleep so he could follow her back to their chambers, hoping she'd use another route than the glide he'd experienced earlier.

Galen stood, picked up his discarded leggings, and pulled them on. He turned and discovered Thea's wet robe at the edge of the pool, then looked toward the archway and found the garment she'd brought to change into lying upon the stone floor.

Galen smiled. Wherever she'd gone, she would arrive naked. Thoughts of all that beautiful flesh exposed stirred now-familiar longings in Galen's groin. He cursed himself again for being unable to control Thea's effect on his body, and walked through the archway, determined to find out where his enchanting little warden had taken herself off to, but not before he took time to explore the lower chamber of the keep.

Galen put his shoulder into the ancient door he'd discovered, hoping to use his strength to push it open. The brittle wood creaked beneath the blow, but did not give. He stepped back and studied the rusted hinges. He tried again, knocking the wind from his lungs with the force of his shove, but the door held firm.

He leaned against the opposite side of the hallway to catch his breath and looked around. For over an hour he'd explored every cavern and corridor he'd found in the lower chamber. He was about to give up when he pressed against the stone wall and felt cold air blow over his bare back. Upon investigation, he'd discovered what he believed to be a hidden passageway and had set about attempting to open it.

Running his fingers slowly over the smooth granite stones until he'd mapped out what appeared to be a doorway enclosed in the rock, he'd felt for a hidden switch to open it. After many moments and no success, he'd allowed his temper to get the better of him and had kicked the stone, receiving bruised toes and a crack in the stone large enough to place his fingers into as a reward.

It took all of his strength to shove the doorway open, but inside he found a dark passageway. He'd secured a lumalantern from one of the sconces in the outer hallway and, wiping years of accumulated cobwebs from his face, had followed the passage, twisting and turning for almost 300 spans until he came upon this ancient wooden door.

There was no handle to open the planks. Galen assumed the door was barred from the other side. Sure he had located the path of escape he needed to set his plans for revenge into action, he'd spent the last few moments attempting to open the door.

Very cold air entered through the tiny cracks near the hinges, and more through the inch-wide opening beneath the planks. Galen shivered and wished he'd thought to find something warmer to wear before he began his venture. His feet were numb. His toes, even the ones he'd bruised, tingled. The leggings from his jungle homeland did little to warm his legs.

Frustration grew. Galen pulled away from the cold wall and tried once more to break down the door. Again he failed. He shook his head in defeat, pledged silently to bring something to use as a wedge with him on his next sojourn, and bent, picked up the luma he'd left on the floor, and walked out of the passageway, following the path of disrupted cobwebs back to the secret entrance.

Sure he'd been on his own long enough to have been missed, Galen hurried back to the center station in the hydro garden and sat down, determined to put his ruse of blindness back into effect here where he could warm his frozen bones. He waited for someone to come and lead him back to his chamber.

"Thea?"

Thea turned her head. Nola and Elijah stood in the doorway. She smiled. "Come in."

"Did you wish our services?" Nola asked, and hurried across the chamber to pause by the chaise where Thea sat.

Thea slid from the chaise and made herself comfortable on the chamber floor. "Sit with me. I have much to tell you this eve." She waited while Nola and Elijah took a seat beside her. Thea looked into Nola's eyes.

A sadness tugged at Thea's heart. Nola. Sweet, nervous Nola—a curious little woman with pale blonde hair and expressive blue eyes, three years older than Thea's own 22 winters. Friend. Confidante. Companion. Thea smiled. Nola might fidget and fret, but in the end, she would handle the responsibilities about to be placed upon her shoulders like the most steadfast of warriors.

Thea looked at Elijah. At 55 winters, the slender, gray-haired man had been her most avid supporter. He had come to serve in the keep shortly after his lifemate of 20 years had passed away. His two sons were grown and had families of their own living among the people of the village. Elijah would need his sons' support to carry out the task she was about to assign him, but Thea had no doubt Elijah would do everything within his power to see his mission succeed.

"You two have been trusted friends my entire life. I don't know what I would have done without you."

Nola shifted uneasily.

Thea touched her hand. "I must ask you once again to hold a secret for me, one that must be revealed only if the people of Glacia are in danger."

Thea told Nola and Elijah of the vision she had seen in Gustoff's tower, of the threat Berezan was to the people of Glacia.

Though his voice trembled, Elijah asked, "What can we do?"

"Gustoff has gone to Borderland to seek an alliance against Berezan with the Creeans. Should his mission fail, the people of Glacia will be left to their own devices to resist Berezan's evil." Thea stood and paced the floor. She resisted looking into Nola's or Elijah's eyes, fearing the tears she fought so hard to dam would spill.

"But the Sphere of Light—"

"Is the object of Berezan's quest," Thea said, cutting Nola off in mid-sentence. She didn't want to hear the rest of Nola's question, couldn't yet face the answer. "The Ancient Ones have entrusted me with the destiny of protecting world peace. It is my duty to see that the people of Glacia are not placed into danger by Berezan's evil."

"Thea, you cannot hope to meet Berezan alone!"

She looked into Elijah's eyes. "I will do whatever I must, my friend."

"But . . ."

Thea waved away Nola's objection. "Several moonrises ago, Gustoff and I set plans into motion to radically change the circumstances at Dekar Facility. Acting in Alec's name, we ordered the fortress to be refurbished to house the people who live in the Settlement. Yet the majority of the structure is still unoccupied."

Thea walked across the chamber and stared down into the fire pit. "While I have never walked among the people of Glacia, nor spoken to anyone other than those employed in Governing House, you two are trusted by all outside of the keep walls. You have friends and families among the population."

Thea sat down between Nola and Elijah. She grasped each one's hand. "I must ask your help."

"Whatever we might do to assist you will be our honor, Thea," Elijah said.

Nola agreed.

"I have devised a plan to evacuate the people of Glacia to the safety of Dekar." Thea looked into Elijah's eyes. "Are you aware of the ancient tunnels hidden in the *picea* forests?"

Elijah nodded.

"Should something unforeseen happen, I want you to speak with the people, have them gather their belongings, follow you through the tunnels, down the mountain, and into the tundra. You will seek refuge at Dekar in Alec's name and remain there until it is safe to return to Glacia."

Nola pulled her fingers from Thea's grasp, wrung her hands. "What if there is no time?"

"If ample warning is not given to leave Glacia, then pass messages among the people, advise them not to resist Berezan in any way. I don't believe he would have a reason to hurt anyone if he meets no opposition."

143

Tears slipped down Nola's face. "I cannot leave you, Thea."

Thea hugged her dear friend. "I will be fine, and so will you."

"What of the warrior?" Elijah asked.

Thea sighed, memories of the last few hours swelling inside her heart. "I wish I knew."

Chapter Eleven

Gustoff brushed the heavy fur aside and stepped into yet another empty house. He looked around, noting that, like the others, nothing there had been disturbed for quite a while. He backed out. He walked to the center of the encampment and paused to study the heavy foliage surrounding the village. Giant *iferas* hid the sky above. Plants with leaves as wide across as a man's arm span hugged the jungle floor. Greens in hues from pale to almost black shadowed the clearing. Flowers of every imaginable size and color sprang from vines that wrapped around tree trunks, dangled from limbs, attached themselves to the houses, then descended to the ground to disburse in vibrant patches of life.

He studied the construction of the dwellings, each built from granite stones similar to the ones used in Glacia, but cut into smaller blocks and fitted with a strange mortar that looked almost black against the glittering stones. The houses were small, perhaps only three or four rooms. Strange, tanned animal furs hung at the windows and covered the doors.

Pens, built of logs cut from the numerous species of trees that thrived in the jungles, were scattered about. All empty. Neither human nor beast was about. No creatures chirped in the foliage; no birds sang from the trees. A deathlike silence crept along with the wind rippling through the leaves.

This was the third such village Gustoff had visited. He had taken time to study the tools the Creeans used, the weapons scattered about. He had believed the people of the Borderland to be primitive, had not expected their civilization to be so advanced in some ways, as indicated by the construction of their weapons, yet so backward in others, as evidenced in the tools they used to cultivate their foodstuffs.

He thought about Thea's wish for one world, one people, and how the advancements of the Glacians could benefit the people of Borderland.

A strange premonition crept over him. *If there are people of the Borderland.*

Gustoff closed his eyes. He tensed every muscle in his body and reached out, seeking a human presence. Nothing. He drew deeply for greater strength, and tried again. Still nothing. He opened his eyes.

There was one more village to search.

Gustoff concentrated on the place he understood to be the home of Omar Sar. A flash of light brightened the surrounding jungle momentarily. Then disappeared.

146

*   *   *

Gustoff found himself before an enormous dwelling three stories in height and at least 50 spans across. He stared at the bronze doors that barred entrance to the abode.

A wide stone stairway, guarded by a pair of bronzed beasts Gustoff did not recognize, beckoned. He stepped carefully, honing his senses to be cautious as he ascended, then paused before the bronzed doors. He sensed a place of great reverence, a temple of some sort, and dared not physically breach its walls. Instead, he closed his eyes, placed himself into a trance, and concentrated on the center of the dwelling.

His essence filled the chamber. He floated above the floor, not desecrating the holy place with his tracks. He paused at an enormous stone altar and studied the bronzed sun suspended above it. He concentrated on the sun, feeling a power foreign to anything he had ever encountered. It called to him, enticed him to hear its cries. He focused all of his energy to answer the plea.

Visions swam before him. Masses murdered. Villages beyond the city of Cree destroyed. The mount of *Naro* violated by hordes of warriors trespassing through its ancient tunnels. And then, more clearly, hundreds of faces came to him— young ones, old ones. Some strong, some weak. All begging for help.

Gustoff opened his eyes to find himself standing on the stairway between the two bronzed creatures that guarded the sanctuary. A voice spoke to him, telling him to trust his instincts and to go to those people he had sensed, to offer whatever he could to ease their suffering.

147

Without knowing where he traveled, he closed his eyes and transported.

"What are you about, old man?"

Gustoff turned to find himself surrounded by 12 huge warriors, all similar in appearance to the warrior at Glacia. He studied their clothing, the same as the warrior had worn in Dekar, and noted the same length of hair, ranging in color from deep brown to near white.

"I mean you no harm, warriors of Borderland. I come in peace to offer whatever assistance I can to your people."

A warrior stepped forward. "We trust no one, old man."

"I can understand your hesitation, warrior. But I am old. What possible harm could I do against mighty men such as you?"

The warrior turned to look at those around him. All seemed to silently communicate agreement with Gustoff's statement.

"Who are you?" the warrior before him asked.

Gustoff bowed his head, then raised it to look the warrior in the eye. "I am Gustoff of Glacia. I have traveled far to meet with your leader, Omar Sar. The business I have will be for his ears only."

A series of whispered conversations erupted around him. Gustoff tried to concentrate on the words, but was distracted when a small girl child pushed between the ring of warriors and ran forward to touch his shiny purple robe.

"Pretty."

Gustoff looked into sad eyes, eyes that had witnessed too much tragedy at a young age. He raised his hand to place it upon the girl's blond head. "What is your name, child?"

The little girl smiled up at him. "I am called Deana, *regis*."

Gustoff shook his head. "I am no one's *regis*, child. Do not address me so."

The warrior who had assumed leadership of the small band stepped closer and placed his hand upon the child's shoulder. "Find your mother, little one. Go now."

The girl bowed her head and hurried away.

"I am Kajar, old man. Omar Sar has been murdered. His son taken, we fear also killed, by those who came to destroy the Borderland. I have been placed in charge of the people who remain and look after their welfare. Any business you might have had with Sar will be told to me."

Gustoff tried hard to regain his composure after hearing the warrior's tale, but his heart refused to answer his commands and beat furiously in his chest. He recalled the memories he had stolen from the warrior's mind at the keep and wondered if the warrior might have witnessed the annihilation of his people.

"State your business, Gustoff of Glacia. We prepare to go to battle again and have no time to waste."

Gustoff's thoughts were disrupted. "Battle again?"

"I have placed lookouts high in the peaks of *Naro*, old man. We have seen the advancing armies that come from Solarus. We make ready to defeat them."

"How many warriors do you have?"

"Twenty here, old man. One hundred or so more will come in from the jungles."

"So few men against thousands. Do not be foolish. Hide. Berezan must believe he has already destroyed Borderland. He will not expect resistance. Do not risk yourselves needlessly. Protect your people, Kajar. Do not waste the few lives left."

"You speak strangely, Gustoff of Glacia. Warriors of Shakara must fight. Honor demands it."

Gustoff touched the warrior's arm. "Does your honor call for you to risk the eradication of your entire people, Kajar? Berezan's army will wipe the people of Borderland from the face of the world. He does not care about anyone or anything but his quest. And that lies in Glacia. Hide yourselves, Kajar. Protect your people by saving them from pointless slaughter. Allow Deana to grow into an old woman to hold her own grandchildren to her breasts."

The warrior closed his eyes. "Omar Sar would have been honored to have met you, Gustoff of Glacia. Your words are of wisdom. We will protect our loved ones."

Kajar placed his hand upon Gustoff's shoulder. "Tell me of your troubles. For what reason did you seek Sar?"

"I sought the might of the Creeans to form an alliance against the very one who has almost destroyed Borderland, Kajar. Now, I realize that only one can face and defeat the evil Berezan has created, and I must go to aid her before it is too late."

"Were it in our power to assist you, we would be honored to form such an alliance, Gustoff of Glacia."

"Protect your people, Kajar. Keep them safe, and one day, when the evil is no more, our people may be as one."

Gustoff shook hands with the mighty Creean

warrior and, in order not to create any more unrest within the people of Borderland, walked into the jungle surrounding the City of Cree, then disappeared.

The warrior was not in the bathing chamber. Someone, perhaps Elijah, must have come and led him back to his bedchamber. It was probably for the best, Thea decided. Thoughts of facing the warrior so soon did little to still the emotions raging within her.

Thea picked up her wet robe from the rim of the pool and folded it carefully over her arm. She walked across the floor toward the archway and bent to retrieve the gown she'd dropped earlier. She cast a final glance over her shoulder toward the pool, pushed away her forbidden memories, and turned to walk back down the corridor toward the center station.

A flash of bright light burned her eyes.

"Gustoff?"

"Hurry, child. We do not have much time." Gustoff held out his hand.

Thea placed her hand into his. "What are you doing here, Gus? I thought you were to be gone six risings."

"Come, child. We cannot speak here."

Another flash of light appeared.

Thea looked around the tower and wondered why Gustoff had brought her here. "Gus?"

"I could ask why you are wearing my robe. I am sure the answer would be interesting, but I fear it will have to wait. Sit." He pointed toward the chair beneath the tower window. Thea immediately did his bidding.

"I have been to Borderland, Thea. I found

destruction beyond your imagination. Berezan attacked the Borderland mooncycles ago. He killed hundreds of men, women, and children as he searched for the Sphere of Light."

"No!"

"I located a small group of survivors. I met warriors similar to the one we rescued from Dekar. Kajar, the warrior left in charge, told me that Omar Sar had been murdered, his son taken hostage and presumed dead. There are only one hundred and twenty warriors left, Thea."

"Please, Gus. The warrior we—"

"Must have witnessed the massacre of his people. I believe he may be blocking the memories from his mind."

Memories of her own stampeded through her brain. The pain she had witnessed many times in the warrior's blue eyes haunted her. The strange emotion she'd seen and could not identify became clear. Hatred. Her own scheme to use the warrior to serve her purpose now sickened her. He had been through so much, and she had plotted to place him in even more danger.

Agony ate away at her heart. The need to be with the warrior, to touch him, to comfort him in some way, became foremost in her thoughts.

"Berezan's armies are coming, Thea."

Thea shook her head at Gustoff's words.

"I visited the tower a while ago, Gus. I felt lost. I needed to be alone to gather my thoughts." She turned away, unable to look into Gustoff's eyes. She thought about telling him of her intimacy with the warrior, but decided against it. "I called upon the Ancient Ones to show me the future. I asked them to enlighten me as to what I could expect."

She drew a deep breath. "I saw an army, thousands strong, garbed in cloaks the color of the desert. I also saw men riding equox, carrying weapons. In the center of all these forces, a horrible man rode a huge black beast spewing blood from his nostrils. Lightning cracked from his fingertips. Thunder, louder than the army's marching boots, shook the ground."

Gustoff placed his hand upon her shoulder. "Thea."

She shook her head. "Berezan comes, Gustoff. I saw him. Felt him. Feared him."

"He seeks the Sphere, my child. We must protect it at all costs."

"I don't know if I can, Gus. I don't know if I'm strong enough."

Gustoff remembered the vision of his death. He would not be by Thea's side when she faced her brother. Would not be near to help her wield the talisman that would destroy the evil. A tear slipped slowly down his cheek.

"Thea, you *are* strong enough to fulfill your destiny, child. Only believe in yourself and your sense of good."

"I'll try, but somehow, I don't think—"

Gustoff touched her hand. "The strength of our own will is all we are given, Thea. Although we are all Guardians of the Sphere, the power reacts differently on each of us. The blessing, and curse, of the Sphere is blind faith. I cannot tell you what will happen when you finally meet your destiny. I have no way to describe how the Sphere will extend its powers through you. You must believe in your own capabilities, rely on the powers nurtured your whole life, and your distinction between good and evil.

"We all have misgivings, anxieties, that must be faced. The responsibility we bear is great. It takes courage to face those self-doubts and fears, my child. Courage you will find when you look deep within your heart."

"But, Gus . . ."

Gustoff touched her cheek. "Go to your bed, Thea. Place yourself into a trance and sleep. Forget all of your troubles until the morrow. Sunrise may bring hope."

Thea turned, kissed Gustoff on the cheek, then left the tower.

Gustoff walked to the window, raised his head, and looked heavenward. Visions of what he had seen haunted him. Guilt ate at his heart like a cancer. All of these senseless tragedies could have been prevented if he had only been strong enough to end Berezan's life years ago.

"Forgive me," he whispered.

Thea bent her head to stare down into the fire. Purple, blue, white, brilliant orange, and red blurred before her eyes into wavering lines of heat. She turned from the hearth and made several more sweeps of the chamber, then glanced toward the bed at room's center and shook her head. She had not heeded Gustoff's directive. Placing herself into a trance to sleep away the hours until sunrise would have accomplished little but wasted time. Time she could not afford to lose with destiny so close at hand.

She walked to the thick tapestries that shielded the chamber from the cold, parted the fabric, and stepped outside. Several inches of new snow from last eve's storm coated the balcony floor. Thea ignored the cold that seeped through her thin slippers. She placed her hands upon the balcony wall, lowered her head, and prayed.

"Give me strength. Bless me as I walk the path chosen for me by the Ancient Ones. Help me to be steady in my beliefs, to hold fast to everything Gustoff has taught me."

Thea opened her eyes and studied the sky. Streaks of silver rose like an aura beyond the cliffs, reaching higher, then higher still, to crown the mountains of Glacia with an ethereal glow. The sun, a brilliant yellow sphere, parted the shadow of the peaks and slipped silently into the blueing of dawn.

Yet sunrise offered no new hope, no apocalypse that would free Glacia and the whole of their world from the evil that threatened to destroy it. Thea drew an unsteady breath. She placed her hand over her breast, felt the steady beat within. She made a decision. Time for deception had passed.

She closed her eyes and mentally reached out to touch Elijah's mind, instilling the need to have the warrior brought to her chamber immediately. Then she opened her eyes, turned, and entered the chamber. She closed the tapestries tightly against the new day, then walked to the chaise to await the warrior, determined to set right the one wrong she could control.

Voices woke him. Galen stretched and turned to his side, sinking deep into the mound of purple and red pillows that cushioned his weight. He opened his eyes, wondering what time it was, how long he'd been sleeping. He glanced around expecting to find several people in the bathing chamber, but found himself alone.

A frown creased his brow when he turned toward the arched chamber door. Strange voices, curious humming noises, and a mysterious whining filled his ears. Galen sat up, eased his legs over the side of the wall, and dropped his feet to the stone floor. He looked at the luma-lit pool, struggled to commit to memory the wondrous experiences he and Thea had shared hours before, then stood, reaching high over his head with fisted hands to stretch his stiff back.

He grabbed the jade robe from the peg where Elijah had left it, slipped it over his shoulders, then walked from the bathing chamber. Pausing in the corridor beyond the hydro garden, Galen watched numerous servants hustle about, working to gather the fruit of their labors. He looked up. The whining sound he'd heard came from the conveyors moving effortlessly along their given paths to deliver each potted plant to the center station.

Galen considered the drudgery each Creean suffered to provide nourishment for his family. The hours of backbreaking work put into tilling the soil, planting seedlings, nurturing each tiny sprout until it bore its crops—*if* it survived the hordes of insects that thrived in the jungles, the torrential rains that flooded the streams and valleys, the stampedes of wild animals.

Anger flushed through him. The Glacians faced none of these hardships. Their crops were protected by walls of solid granite. A constant source of light and moisture insured healthy growth.

Galen glanced around the hydro garden. Hours ago he'd sat at the center station, waiting for someone to come and lead him back to his chamber. Cold, tired, and hungry, he had given up on an escort and, after deciding he didn't want to risk another ride on the glide, had returned to the bathing chamber and fallen asleep on the pillowed wall.

The center station now bustled with activity, yet no one seemed to be aware of his presence. Galen stepped out onto the stone walkway suspended above the luma-lit water and walked the path to his left, retracing the journey he'd made earlier that had ended at the hidden door. His mission was twofold. He needed to be certain he could remember the way back once he'd secured warmer clothing and tools to open the portal. He also wanted to judge the servants' reactions when he walked among them to ascertain if they believed him to be Alec.

Galen paused in the hallway. Two copper-robed men walked in his direction. Noting how they bowed their heads when they stopped before him, he suspected word of his recovery had reached far and wide.

"May we serve you?" one of the men asked.

Galen inhaled and exhaled quickly. The last thing he needed was two humble servants tagging along while he explored the corridors. "I require nothing except to exercise my stiff muscles. Go on about your tasks."

The two men hurried off, and Galen continued down the corridor.

"Thea!"

A gentle knock followed the summons.

Thea turned to stare at the door, breathing deeply to gather her courage. Elijah's voice announced the arrival of the warrior. Her time for confession was upon her. She stood, turned, and walked toward the chamber door. Her fingers shook as she raised her hand to touch the handle. Pulling the planks open slowly, she nodded to Elijah, then glanced behind him, expecting to find the warrior's tall form.

"Where is he, Elijah?"

"I do not know. I entered his chamber to discover it had not been slept in. Thinking perhaps he'd remained in the bathing chamber, I hurried there and found it also empty. I don't know where he might be." Elijah gestured nervously with his hands to emphasize his words.

"Perhaps he is with Gustoff," she said, knowing deep in her heart her words were untrue. Gustoff would have had no need to seek the warrior out. "Go to your bed, Elijah. I am sorry I disturbed your rest."

Elijah nodded and backed from the doorway. Thea closed the panel and turned to lean against it. Where could the warrior be? How would a blind man find his way around the keep without assistance? Maybe one of the other servants had found him in the bathing chamber alone and . . . And what?

Thea concentrated hard on the warrior, seeking his presence wherever he might be within the keep. The warrior's image filled her mind. She studied his movements about a darkened hallway. He appeared lost, confused.

She disappeared in a flash of light.

Chapter Twelve

Thea kept to the shadows and watched the warrior feel his way along an ancient hallway, one she'd never found the need to explore. His footsteps were cautious, one forward, one back, as if he searched for something on the wall. He splayed his large hands against the stone, felt each crevice between the blocks.

Thea wondered what he could be up to, but pushed that thought aside when the warrior stepped back into the center of the hallway and placed his fists upon his hips. A heated curse spilled from his lips.

Thea had to bite her lip to keep from calling out his name when he took a step closer to the wall and banged his fist against the stone. She wondered at his strange action, then leaned against the wall to try to understand what the warrior was attempting.

Galen cursed the stones of granite for the hundredth time in a few moments. The secret doorway was here. It had to be. He'd traced every inch of the corridor with his fingertips and this was the only area that felt cold to his touch. Frustration grew. He slammed his fist into the wall again, scraping his knuckles.

He turned, grabbed the lumalantern from the sconce behind him, and brought it closer to the wall to examine the seams of rock. One spot caught his attention. He splayed his hand over the separation. Cold air tickled his fingers.

He stepped back and raised the light higher, following the seam until the faint image of the doorway appeared. Satisfied he'd located the exit he sought, Galen turned and placed the luma back into its holder. He strode down the hallway, intending to find a servant and request an escort back to his bedchamber.

Thea held her breath as the warrior stepped nearer to her hiding place in the shadows. Fury chased away the feeling of betrayal that clamped around her heart. The warrior wasn't blind. He probably never had been. All of those moments she had spent tending him, dressing him, feeding him, he had watched her every move.

What if he had recovered his memory? If he knew from the beginning that she had . . . had—

Anger overshadowed her sense of caution. Thea stepped out into the middle of the corridor, blocking the warrior's path. She placed her hands upon her hips and waited.

He moved with a lithe grace, muscles bunching and relaxing just as she had imagined they would moonrises ago. His hair, that glorious mass of gold and platinum, swung about his broad shoulders and tickled his collarbone.

Thea felt her heart rate quicken; her mouth once again fill with fleece. A strong feeling of want, need, flashed along every nerve ending in her body, pooled at the junction of her thighs, and caused her womanhood to quiver.

"Thea?"

He was intimidating, staring down at her from his imposing height.

"Thea, is that you?" He reached out, his fingers pausing less than a hand's span from her cheek.

Thea shuddered and stepped back. Outrage choked her. Ire, unlike anything she'd ever felt, consumed her. She had trusted him. Wanted him. Given him her most precious gift, and he had betrayed her.

Just like you intended to betray him, a voice from within in cried. Thea ignored it.

She met his intense stare. "You can see me, can't you? You have pretended to be blind from the beginning."

He broke their eye contact, turned his head. "Thea, I—"

"Don't lie to me! There are enough lies between us. I brought you to the keep, helped to restore your strength after your stay at Dekar, and you betray me by pretending to be blind so you could spy on—"

"Enough!" He grabbed her arm and pulled her so close she could feel the heat of him rush over her. "Who betrayed whom, Thea DeLan? Do the gentle subjects of Glacia know you brought a stranger into their midst to impersonate your stepbrother? Who are you to find fault? You are the one who connived in this scheme to defraud

161

the Elders, the citizens of Glacia, and who knows who else with your wickedness?"

Thea gasped. "W-wickedness?"

He released her and pushed her away as if the touch of her flesh burned him. Thea steadied her balance by placing her hand on the stone wall. She gulped several deep breaths, tried in vain to count to ten, then exhaled.

Thea finally looked up into his eyes, meeting him stare for stare. "Is it wickedness to try to save my people from an evil they cannot fight? To save an imprisoned warrior from his own death by bringing him into my home, offering him nourishment and warmth, healing his broken body?" She pulled away from the wall and paced.

"Or could it possibly be more wicked to take the comfort offered, eat the food supplied, bask in the warmth created by a welcoming hearth instead of a damp, cold cell, and play those who offer this abundance for fools?"

Galen watched the faint light of the luma strike the streaks of gold in her hair. Fury burned brightly in her eyes, shadowed her cheeks with a flush, and caused her breasts to rise and fall rapidly with each gasp of air she drew. He clenched his fists tightly at his sides to restrain the need to reach out to her, to bring her into his arms, to smother her fury with another type of passion. His loins screamed for relief. His heartbeat clamored against his ribs, echoed through his body, slammed into his ears.

He silently recited the reasons for perpetrating the ruse he had begun moonrises ago. Berezan. Vengeance. Fury smoldered within him and blocked all other thoughts. He stared into Thea's eyes, willing his temper to calm enough so he could demand answers to the numerous questions he had struggled with during his stay in Glacia.

"If not for wickedness, what other reason would you have to bring me to your keep and present me to the Messahs as Alec DeLan?" he demanded.

Thea glared at him.

Galen cursed. Even faced with her betrayal, he wanted her still.

Her lip trembled. "Why should I tell you anything?"

He grabbed her wrist and pulled her close, bending until they were almost nose to nose. "Because I'm not weak, Thea. I have never been. Many times I've had the opportunity to hurt you, but I've restrained myself. I've played your game, kept your secrets. Now, I demand answers."

Thea swallowed hard and tried to wiggle free from his grasp. A dark flush suffused his handsome features. Fire burned in his blue eyes. For the first time since she'd seen the warrior in the dark cells of Dekar, she was frightened of him.

"Let me go!" Thea demanded, attempting to pry his fingers from her arm.

"Not until you answer my questions." His voice, deep with anger, chilled her spine.

Thea closed her eyes to the fury distorting the warrior's face. She could transport to safety or use any of her hidden powers to escape the warrior's grasp. But she had sent Elijah searching for the warrior in order to confess the sins she had committed against him, to tell him the truth, and to beg his assistance in her upcoming confrontation with Berezan.

"Release me. Please," she said softly. "I will answer all of your questions." She opened her eyes and looked up into his face.

Thea knew he was deciding whether or not to trust her. She didn't attempt to defend her statement. Her actions over the past few moonrises spoke volumes. Deceit and betrayal offered little assurance of trustworthiness.

"How would I know if you spoke the truth or not?"

"I swear on my life I will not lie to you, warrior." Thea tried to will the truth of her statement to shine in her eyes.

Galen nodded. He watched the expression on her face, noting she looked as upset as she had when the Messahs visited Alec's chamber. He considered her actions carefully.

He had been taught from a young boy never to trust anyone other than his own people. Over the past risings, he had allowed another being to wiggle under his hide, to touch him more deeply than any Creean female ever had. They had come together twice as male and female, not as Glacian and Creean, nor as enemy against enemy. What they shared had been good. Very good.

Yet were the truth to be fully out, he had used Thea DeLan in much the same way she had planned to use him. He'd pretended to be weak, mindless, and blind in order to gain knowledge of the people of Glacia, their habitat, and defenses, all the while planning to forgo the welfare of these people in order to await and destroy Berezan.

If the reasons Thea gave for her actions proved to be truthful, perhaps he should consider answering the questions she must have about him.

"Could we go someplace warmer?" Thea rubbed her forearms briskly to stave off the chill of the hallway.

"No."

Thea nodded. The sooner she got her confession over with, the sooner she could return to Gustoff's side and plan for her meeting with Berezan. "All right. By what name are you called, warrior?"

"Galen."

"Galen." Thea tested the sound of his name upon her lips.

"Why did you bring me here?"

Thea swallowed. "What I told you about Alec is mostly true, Galen. He was killed in an avalanche as he traveled to take his rightful place as heir to the House of DeLan. I don't know how familiar you might be with the *Articles*, but with my father and his heir dead, and me the only survivor of the House of DeLan—a female who is forbidden to take power—Glacia would have been vulnerable."

His fingers loosened, and Thea slipped free. She paced three steps and leaned against the wall. She looked at the stone floor rather than gaze into his eyes as she spoke. "After news reached us of Alec's death, Gustoff and I searched for many moonrisings for an individual to impersonate my stepbrother. When you were found in the dungeons of Dekar, I believed my prayers had been answered."

She paused, unsure how to proceed with her story.

"Go on."

"Gustoff bribed a guard to allow us to visit your cell." She closed her eyes. Memories surfaced. "You were very ill, Galen. They had drugged you and had offered very little by way of nourishment to keep you alive. I feared the trip to Glacia through the extreme cold of the tundra would kill you."

The warrior moved. Thea glanced up to find he had leaned against the opposite wall, crossed his arms over his chest. He stared at her with cold, calculating eyes. Thea lowered her gaze again. "We brought you here, placed you in Alec's bed, and I nursed you back to health."

"Why?"

Thea met his heated gaze. "I was told you had no memory of your past. I believed I could convince you that you were my stepbrother long enough to accomplish my goals. When I discovered you could not see, I wanted to help you regain your memory, your sight. I—I—"

"When did you decide I was blind?"

Thea blinked at the hostile tone of his voice. "On the third rising after you arrived you finally awoke from your drug-induced slumber. I watched you for several moments, and even though I stood in full view, you gave no sign you saw me. I touched you. You . . . you . . ."

"I *what?*"

Another tremor raced along her backbone. "You grabbed me. You tried to hurt me. I told you I meant you no harm, but you wouldn't listen to me. You ranted and raved about me stealing your memory, your sight. You couldn't see me."

Tears clouded her vision. Thea blinked them away. She looked up to judge the warrior's reaction. He hadn't moved. "I had to restrain you before you killed me." Memories of just how she had restricted him caused heat to flood to her cheeks. Thea tilted her head so the warrior could not see her reaction.

"I stunned you. Then I fell asleep. When I woke, I found Gustoff had restrained you with ropes to the posts of the bed. I tried to tell him to remove the binds, but he refused."

"By stunned do you mean you somehow knocked me out?"

She bit her bottom lip. "Not exactly. I merely touched you and . . . and . . ."

"Like you healed my wrists?"

Thea snapped her head up to look into his eyes. "You saw that? Of course you did. You weren't blind then, were you? How could I have been so foolish? Why didn't I realize your loss of sight might have only been a temporary effect of the drugs?"

Galen closed his eyes. He tried hard to remember the events Thea spoke of, but nothing surfaced beyond waking to find her in bed with him. He wondered what other strange powers Thea might possess besides the ability to stun someone, heal wounds, and vanish without a trace.

Her slow movement captured his attention. The last thing Galen expected Thea to do was touch his arm. "Why were you in the tundra, Galen? Do you remember how you were captured and taken to Dekar?"

He remembered. Vividly. But he had no intention of telling her anything. He dropped his arm to his side, avoiding her touch. He closed his mind and heart to the look of rejection on her lovely face. "Why is Berezan coming to Glacia?"

Thea cringed. Could she possibly tell him the truth about Berezan? Should she bring up what Gustoff had discovered in Borderland?

"Everything I've told you about Berezan's arrival is true. I don't know what reason he would have to visit Glacia unless he has heard news of my father's death, perhaps of Alec's, and comes to assume control of Glacia like he took over Solarus."

Liar! Galen clamped his teeth together to keep from uttering the word aloud. Thea knew more about Berezan than she had disclosed. If what he'd suspected from the beginning was true, she was in alliance with Berezan. He must not forget it.

Galen pulled away from the wall and took a step closer to Thea. "You mentioned my impersonating Alec until you accomplished your goals. What goals?"

Thea offered a silent prayer for guidance. In order to confess everything to the warrior, she had to tell him of Gustoff's trip to Borderland.

"What goals, Thea?"

"The Glacians are a docile people. We have no armies, no militia of any kind. Many hundreds of decades ago, we gave up the need to defend ourselves, believing instead in the *Articles,* and before that the Ancient Ones, to protect us.

"When news arrived of Berezan's intended visit so soon upon word of Alec's death, Gustoff and I believed we needed help to withstand Berezan's evil. Your impersonation was only to buy time while Gustoff traveled to Borderland to seek an alliance with the Creean people against the threat Berezan posed to both of our worlds.

"We believed the people of Borderland were as vulnerable as the Glacians to Berezan's wrath, that a joint effort to defeat him would protect all of our people."

Memories, stark and graphic, swamped Galen's mind. Visions of his homeland destroyed, his people murdered, caused his hands to tremble. Galen clenched his eyelids together and drew a deep breath in an effort to hide the effect of Thea's words. "What would the *docile* people of Glacia have offered in a joint defense, Thea? Would you have expected the warriors of Borderland to do all of your fighting while you remained here in your safe ice world?"

Thea slid slowly along the stone wall, farther and farther away from the rage she sensed building within the warrior. "The people of Borderland would have been well compensated, Galen."

Galen lost control. He sprang from his position against the wall and grabbed Thea. Her futile struggles fueled his anger as he pulled her to his chest and crushed her lush breasts against his body. "Like you compensated me last eve, Thea?"

Pain, sharp and intense, rushed through her chest. His hateful words took the wonderful things they had shared and twisted them into something dark, something evil. She felt defiled, unclean. She had given him her heart, her love. He crushed it beneath his feet, threw it back at her like a cheap trinket.

"Release me!" The command was followed by a sharp mind probe that made it impossible for him to refuse. He dropped his hands to his sides and stood motionless while Thea backed away.

Thea shook with rage and hurt. She stared into the warrior's eyes, full of disbelief that given all of his physical strength, she could hold him powerless with only a look. "You cannot move, warrior. I will not allow it. Even with all of your muscle and size, your body cannot function unless your

169

mind commands it. I control your mind."

She stepped closer. "I don't know why I do this, warrior, except I made a vow to confess all of my transgressions. I believed what we shared to be special. I felt something deep for you, warrior, something very different than I've ever felt for another human being. You trample my feelings beneath your feet as if I were nothing but dust." She spun away and paced the corridor.

"No male lives to assume leadership of Glacia, warrior. Because of this, I would have offered rule to Omar Sar if he would have agreed to an allegiance with Gustoff. But Gustoff has traveled to Borderland to make this offer and found Borderland to be devastated by Berezan's evil.

"Omar Sar has been murdered, his heir captured and believed dead. There are only one hundred and twenty warriors left to defend the hundreds of survivors of Berezan's invasion."

She stopped pacing and turned to stare into the warrior's eyes. "Even as we stand here wasting precious time, Berezan's armies are coming to overthrow Glacia. He is destroying everything in his path, warrior. Everything!" Tears streaked her cheeks.

Galen struggled to break the hold Thea had over him. He closed his eyes, echoed every word she had said in his mind. How could he believe her? She possessed strange powers, much like the magic he had experienced under Berezan's hand. Did she believe him to be fool enough to think Glacia would be offered to the Sar family in payment for an alliance?

Why should he? He had witnessed firsthand how far this female would go to manipulate those around her.

Nagging doubts assailed him. Only 120 warriors. Hundreds of survivors. Were her words truth, or more fiction to sway him toward her cause?

Thea looked at the warrior. The strain of fighting her control caused the tendons to protrude in his neck, sweat to bead his forehead, his lips to tremble. She closed her eyes and released control.

The warrior pulled away from the wall, shook his arms, took a step toward her, hesitated, then crossed to the opposite side of the hallway. "Why should I believe anything you tell me, Thea DeLan?"

She turned away from his intense stare. The pain of knowing how poorly he valued the love she'd offered him burned too deeply to continue looking into his eyes. Hurt tinged her voice with defiance when she said, "I don't care what you believe, warrior. Nor do I have any more time to waste trying to convince you of my needs. I had thought to request your help in planning strategy against Berezan, but . . ." She shrugged her shoulders.

"You have wasted more time than you know. While you sent your man Gustoff on a fruitless search for the leader of Borderland to offer your so-called allegiance, you had the *regis* of Borderland in your possession. My name, Thea, is Galen *Sar*."

Thea's gasp echoed off the corridor walls.

Galen stood in the middle of the corridor, arms crossed over his chest, feet spread to aid his balance. "Yes, Thea. The warrior you captured to portray Alec is the very one you needed to convince of your willingness to join in a battle

171

against our mutual enemy. Too bad I've seen you in action, little one. I know not to trust one word that falls from your beautiful lying lips."

Thea spun to face the warrior. Her temper flared beyond her control. She raised her hand and slapped his handsome, arrogant face.

Chapter Thirteen

Borderland . . .

The encampment was less than a mile away. The Creean people, the survivors of Berezan's attack, had to be warned. The runner's gaze darted to and fro, searching deep into the thick foliage that covered the jungle floor to avoid detection. He continued to run.

A half mile, another quarter. The lush greens of the jungle parted slowly to expose a wide, natural path in the vegetation. Only the towering *iferas* blocked out the sunlight and darkened the mossy ground. Another quarter mile. Suddenly, the hiding place of the people of Cree was within view. Renewed energy supported his strained muscles, increased the blood flow from his thundering heart. His fingers shook as he climbed the rock embankment surrounding the caves within which the Creeans hid.

Stumbling into the secluded entrance, he fell to his knees, raised his chin high into the cool cave air, and drew deep gulps of air into his chest.

"K-Kajar!"

Several warriors rushed toward him, all speaking at once as they attempted to discover his message. He shook his head to clear the fuzziness that engulfed his brain, swallowed hard, fighting the allure of unconsciousness beckoning his exhausted body.

"Kajar!"

A tall warrior dropped to his knees on the ground beside him. He placed his hand upon his shoulder, shook him gently. "I am here, Donel. What news has brought you from your station high in the peaks of *Naro?*"

The fatigued warrior turned his head to stare into eyes of deep blue. He drew another steadying breath and exhaled. "The armies from Solarus have crossed into Borderland, Kajar. Even now they forage the jungles in search of a place to camp." Donel slumped forward, giving in to the hours of exertion he'd expended to bring his warning to Kajar.

Kajar stood and gazed into the worried eyes of the six other warriors standing about the cave entrance. "Take him into the caves and make him comfortable. See that the women give him drink and nourishment. Allow him to recuperate as long as he feels the need. He has served us well."

Three men stepped forward to do Kajar's bidding. They bent, picked up the exhausted warrior, and carried him deep into the shadows of the cave.

"What are we going to do, Kajar?"

Thorn, Kajar's friend, stepped closer. Kajar looked down at Thorn's chest, noted the bloody seepage that spilled through the bandages about his midsection. Only 30 summers, Thorn had the look of an old man. His shoulder-length brown hair was caked with mud and debris from his flight through the jungle. His shoulders, wide and strong, slumped from the pain that remained constant, not only from his injuries, but from the warrior's heart, hurt by what he had seen and could not avenge.

The mighty warriors of Borderland had been seriously depleted by Berezan's first attack. Of those still within the encampment, most were wounded, some grievously. Kajar had sent the ones healthy enough to travel into the jungles to gather the warrior force patrolling the boundaries of Borderland, to bring them back to fortify the last hiding place of the Creean race.

No matter how much it went against everything he believed, all he'd been taught, the only thing left to do so the mighty people of Borderland could survive was to hide.

"The old man from Glacia spoke wisely, Thorn. We are too few to meet a force of so many. We must protect our people as Galen or Omar would have done were they here to lead. We will send every one able into the surrounding jungle, and have them gather any evidence of our presence and bring it back to the caves.

"We will hide the sick, the old, the young, and the injured deep within the underground passageways of *Naro*. Our women will tend them to the best of their abilities while we disburse ourselves at strategic locations in and around the mountain to protect what is left of our people."

Thorn nodded. "The foodstuffs stored in the hollows of *Naro* will last no longer than a few sunrisings, Kajar. I can send a few warriors deeper into the jungles to forage. There are fruits and nuts aplenty on the western slopes. It would take only a sunrise for a small force to go there and return."

"Go quickly, my friend. See our plans placed into motion. By what Donel has told us, we have less than two sunrises to bring all of our people together."

Thorn grabbed Kajar's shoulder. He squeezed tightly, then dropped his hand. Taking the two warriors who guarded the cave entrance with him, Thorn set out to see Kajar's orders done.

Berezan reined in his equox and surveyed the humble village around him. The crude, empty houses beckoned his weary bones as if they were luxurious castles. He threw his leg over the horn of his saddle and dismounted, taking time only to pull the black gloves from his hands and release the golden clasp of his cloak before he threw his discarded garments over the saddle, then turned to locate Rhem.

His commander, clad in robes of beige to match the desert, stood out glaringly against the lush greens of the tropic region.

"Rhem!"

The commander hurried to his side.

"Discard those robes immediately! Have the rest of my army follow suit. I don't care what you do with them. Burn them, bury them. Just get them gone before I next see your face!"

Berezan spun away, slapped at the fur hanging over the doorway of the house closest to him, and entered. His long strides took him across the tiny room in three paces. He kicked aside a three-legged stool before the fire pit, propped his booted foot against the hearth, then leaned down to place his head upon the bent arm he rested on the mantel.

Visions clouded his tired mind. Through a fog he climbed the circular stairway of Governing House, passed by scores of elaborate doorways, carved centicycles before by craftsmen of the Ancient Ones. He paused at the rim of granite railing each floor, looked up at the chandelier of lumastones that gave light.

The vision faded.

A strange sense of melancholy grew in his chest. The years he had missed, the hardships of his youth as he struggled to survive in the harsh desert clime, haunted him. Berezan remembered the thirst that never seemed to be quenched, the feel of flesh that never came clean. He thought about the abrasions on his young skin as the hot desert wind constantly blew sand particles to strip away the resiliency of his flesh.

Gustoff had cheated him out of a life of abundance and comfort. He had taken it upon himself to deprive a young heir of the heritage he had been born to and he had cast a helpless six year old aside to die as heartlessly as one would destroy an ailing animal. For this, the old man would die a slow and agonizing death, but not before Berezan took possession of the Sphere of Light.

The muscles in Berezan's arm tensed and bunched. Berezan's fingernails burrowed into the flesh of his palms. He raised his head and stared unseeingly at the stone wall above the mantel.

177

Moments passed. His body trembled. Perspiration broke on his forehead and dripped into his eyes. Berezan did not blink, nor did his concentration waver.

Incantations—strange, foreign—spilled from his lips.

Suddenly he was soaring high above the jungle, a big black bird of prey. He drew a deep breath, expanding his lungs far beyond their normal capacity to accommodate the heady sense of freedom that rushed over him as he swooped nearer to the lush foliage of the dense trees below, coming dangerously close to the treetops before he spiraled upward again, past clouds that threatened rain, until he drew in deep, clear breaths of untainted air.

He dove again, spreading his mighty wings to soar through the air, farther and farther away from the village where his body remained entranced, where his army made camp. Beneath him, the landscape sped by at a harrowing pace. Trees and foliage blended together until they appeared no more than a solid blanket of green.

He ascended. Higher. Higher still.

The peaks of *Naro* jutted up before him. Volcanic smoke and ash sputtered into the air from the crest. Steam blurred his vision momentarily. He circled the mountain like a vulture, around and around. Each pass took him lower and lower, until once again the foliage of the jungle threatened.

Something glittered through the trees and caught his attention. A predator's heart clamored within his breast. He extended his legs, sharp talons exposed, collapsed his wings tight to his body, and dove. The shiny object grew larger.

Trees, each leaf and branch, became visible as he neared the ground. He salivated, tasting the thrill of capture, experiencing the glory of the kill.

"Master!"

Berezan jumped. He shook his head and turned to find his commander standing in the doorway, beige robes discarded in favor of taut dark leggings and a matching tunic constructed of leather from the hide of the oxum that roamed wild in the hot desert sun.

He drew a deep breath, willing his thundering heart to slow.

"Master?"

Gritting his teeth against the instinct to kill that bore down upon him, Berezan met his commander's questioning gaze. "What do you want?!"

Rhem bowed his head. "All robes have been destroyed as ordered, Master. Camp has been established. Your army awaits further orders."

Berezan stepped away from the hearth. He glanced about the small room, noting for the first time the shabbiness of the interior. Several hand-hewed chairs were placed before a table constructed of a wood foreign to him. A coarse mat of braided straw formed a rug for the stone floor. Several lanterns were scattered about. A cupboard, several other chairs, and a barrel filled the rest of the space.

Berezan thought about his entranced flight, about the glittering object he'd seen and had not been able to explore. Elsbar's words came back to plague him. Was it possible the warriors of Borderland planned an assault?

"Place guards at the perimeter of camp. Elsbar believes the Creean warriors have not been destroyed and will do all within their power to stop our assault. Any warriors found are to be executed on sight. Have my stallion tended, my belongings placed into this shack, the men fed and bedded down for the moonrise. See that I am not disturbed again until sunrise."

Rhem shuffled his booted feet and finally gained the courage to look up and meet Berezan eye to eye. "But, Master, you have not eaten."

"The hunger that festers within me, Rhem, will be assuaged only when I reach Glacia." Berezan turned his back.

"By your wishes," Rhem said. He slapped his fist to his chest three times, then turned to leave the chamber.

"Have more scouts sent out just before dawn. Make sure they scour every inch of the surrounding jungle for any survivors from our last venture into Borderland. Again, anyone from Borderland discovered is to be killed immediately."

"Yes, Master." Rhem stepped into the doorway.

"Have my army ready to march at sunrise. I will tolerate no other diversions from our route to Glacia. Is that understood, Rhem?"

"Yes, Master." Rhem left the room.

Berezan glanced down into the grate and found several logs suitable for burning. He bent, suspended his open hand in the air, then uttered yet another incantation. Arcs of fire sprang from his fingertips to ignite the wood.

He sat down on the floor before the blazing warmth he had created, crossed his booted feet, then pulled his ankles closer to his body. Resting his hands palms up on his knees, he closed his eyes and slept.

Chapter Fourteen

"Galen of Borderland!"

Galen paused in his furious stride. Chills rippled along his spine as Gustoff's voice permeated every nerve in his body. He gulped for oxygen, forced away the need to strike out in anger, then turned slowly to face the old man clad in purple who stood in the corridor behind him.

"You know my name, old man?"

Gustoff stroked his long white beard. Galen could feel the path of the old man's gaze as it slipped slowly over his body, head to toe. A strange sense of foreboding tingled in his mind as he wondered if the old man had witnessed his encounter with Thea.

Purple robes swished in the silence of the corridor as Gustoff took a step closer. "I overheard your argument with Thea, Galen of Borderland."

Gustoff's words renewed the frenzied cadence

of Galen's heartbeat. Galen clenched his fists, fighting the tremors that flowed through his body. Bitterness welled within him. For sunrise after sunrise he'd been kept from his people. A prisoner within walls of stone, held captive because he had tried to avenge the deaths of his mother and father and the countless other murders committed by the very one who now threatened Glacia.

Revenge was at hand. He could feel it to the marrow of his bones. He had no more time to waste with the old man. "My identity has been established, Gustoff. I see no need to remain here. By Thea's words, the people of Borderland are in danger. I must go to them."

"You cannot."

The old man's words were soft, but the finality in his statement gave Galen pause. "Are you going to stop me, old man?"

Gustoff took another step, bowed his head. "If I must."

Galen smiled. His stay in Glacia's keep had replenished the strength he had lost during his incarceration at Dekar Facility. Gustoff's bones were old and brittle. One well-positioned blow and the man in purple would crumple to the floor, helpless. He drew a deep breath, took a step forward.

Gustoff raised his withered hand, uttered several strange words, and Galen froze, unable to do more than breathe and stare in disbelief at the man before him. He strained against a mysterious force holding him immobile. His arms ached at the force he exerted to reach forward.

"I have many powers to hold you, warrior of Borderland. To struggle against my will is useless. Until I wish to release you, you will remain as you are. Paralyzed." Gustoff stepped closer. Galen could only follow his steps with his eyes.

Gustoff continued to stroke his beard as he spoke. "I wish you no harm. Nor does Thea. You were brought here to delay the discovery of Alec's death long enough for me to go to Borderland and seek your father's aid against the evil that threatens us all."

Galen closed his eyes and strained once more against the invisible bonds the old man used to hold him.

"I will release you if you pledge to hear me out as I tell you all Thea has been forbidden to disclose."

Galen swallowed in an attempt to release Gustoff's grasp on his throat muscles. He opened his eyes and stared intently into the old man's gray gaze.

Gustoff waved his hand.

Galen collapsed against the stone wall.

"I have no wish to use my powers against you, warrior. I think it would be wise if you listened to the words I have to say. I have been to Cree, witnessed the plight of your people firsthand. I can tell you how they fare. But before I do, you must agree to hear all I will tell you."

Galen stared into Gustoff's eyes, searching for the deceit he expected to find. There was none. He considered what other powers the old man might use to restrain him if he refused, then nodded.

"I must tell you first of Thea's heritage, warrior. To understand her destiny will enable you to comprehend why such drastic measures as the ones we undertook were necessary." Gustoff waited while the warrior digested his words. He studied the blond giant's eyes, read the hatred that flowed freely, and understood how such might be so.

"I must ask for your trust, Galen of Borderland. The words I speak will be strange to your limited knowledge of the Ancient Ones, but you must believe each thing I say is truthful."

Galen nodded.

Gustoff explained in detail the history of the Ancient Ones. He told of the formation of the Elders, the *Articles* they devised, and the bloody wars that forced the separation of their world into three regions. He touched on the part Galen's ancestor Shakara had played in the development of the *Articles*, then told Galen of the evil that once again threatened their world, and spoke briefly about the Sphere of Light.

A thousand questions bounced around inside Galen's head. "Berezan killed my people to possess this Sphere of Light, Gustoff. What is this Sphere you speak of, and why would he believe the people of Borderland might possess it?"

"The Sphere of Light is the last talisman of the Ancient Ones that protects our world from destruction, Galen. I have no idea why Berezan would think the Sphere was in Borderland, unless he believes I would not be foolish enough to hide it within Glacia."

"You?"

"I am one of the remaining descendants of the Ancient Ones, Galen of Borderland. Berezan also carries their blood within him."

"Who else?"

"Thea."

"Thea?"

Gustoff ceased stroking his beard and crossed his arms over his chest. "Yes, warrior, Thea. Long before Thea was old enough to understand the strange powers she carries within her, I foresaw her destiny. Throughout the years of her life, I have tutored her, helped her understand the powers she holds. The gifts she possesses are numerous. Some of them you have experienced firsthand."

Galen thought about Thea's power to heal, then recalled the strange magic she'd used earlier to restrain him, much like the force Gustoff had exerted. He pulled away from the stone wall and paced, trying to understand what Thea and her curious powers had to do with him.

"Thea and the Sphere she must wield are all there is left to protect our world from Berezan's evil, Galen of Borderland."

Galen turned abruptly to stare into the old man's eyes. A quick vision of Thea flashed before his mind's eye. Thea, beautiful and seductive. The way she touched his body, his heart, his soul. Auburn hair and sensual brown eyes. The pout of her lips, the softness of her body.

A fierce sense of protectiveness welled within him. "The warriors of Borderland are mighty and fierce, Gustoff. We were not powerful enough to destroy Berezan. How could you expect a lone woman to accomplish what we were unable to do?!"

Gustoff raised his hand and pointed a crooked finger at Galen. "As long as Thea does not doubt the powers within her, she will be successful."

"Doubt? Within her? Old man, what foolishness have you filled her head with?" Galen charged forward, only to stumble when the old man raised his hand in a fashion that threatened to immobilize him again. "I will not allow you to use Thea in your schemes to destroy Berezan, old man. I will not allow it!"

"I have seen the future, warrior. I know what trials and triumphs lie ahead for Thea. To face Berezan is her destiny. Neither you nor I can change that. All things in life have a purpose, my son. Thea's objective has been foretold. Yours also."

"My purpose is to save my people," Galen gritted out.

"Your function is to stand by Thea's side, to help her see her destiny through."

Galen shook his head. "No, old man. I have to avenge the lives of my parents, to protect those entrusted to me when I became *regis* of Borderland. Many lives already depend upon me. You cannot expect me to stand by Thea's side and watch her be killed because of some foolishness you believe in.

"I will take Thea away, hide her in the caves of my homeland. She will be safe from Berezan— and from you!"

Gustoff studied the warrior carefully. He noted the massive muscles that bunched and coiled across the warrior's chest, the confidence in his stance, the proud cock of his blond head. Galen Sar of Borderland was well trained in the arts of combat. He believed wholeheartedly in his ability to protect Thea and his people from all evil. But the warrior knew only of such skills as one acquires by practice with swords, knives, and clubs. Physical stamina and prowess honed by many cycles of physical exertion. He had never understood, nor would he ever understand until he came face to face with such powers, that evil and the power to wield it did not need any of the skills the warrior had so laboriously acquired.

"What say you when I tell you all the physical prowess you possess will be useless when faced by Berezan, warrior? Will you throw spears against arcs of flame? Use swords to cut flesh, when the power Berezan possesses can melt the flesh from your bones?"

Gustoff placed his hand upon the warrior's arm. "I sense a deep affection within you for Thea, warrior. In your need to protect the one you care for, you will make serious mistakes and place Thea into even more danger."

"Stand aside, old man. Let me pass. I will take Thea to safety!"

"There are but one hundred and twenty or so warriors of Borderland left, Galen. Many of those warriors are seriously wounded. Hundreds of the survivors of Berezan's attack are in need of medical attention. As each day passes, more may die from lack of care. Your crops and livestock have been destroyed. The rivers that run through Borderland are polluted. With Berezan's army encamped in the Borderland, there is no way for your men to forage for food. Your people will starve if you interfere in something you cannot control."

Galen's stomach churned at Gustoff's words, but he could do little more than clench his fists.

"Food grows aplenty here in Glacia, Galen. Enough to feed your people and ours. But if you take Thea away from her destiny, Glacia will fall into Berezan's hands and there will be no hope for any of us. You must believe me. Thea has the power to destroy Berezan. She must be in Glacia to wield that power."

Galen stared furiously into Gustoff's eyes. "And

what of you, old man? What will you be doing
while you send Thea to meet Berezan? What part
do you play in the massacre you plan?"

"My lifepath is now short, Galen. I cannot fore-
see how much longer I will be alive to guide
Thea on her chosen path. For this, I need your
strength, your sense of right and wrong. Thea
needs you, warrior. She requires your support
to see her destiny through. But she loves you. If
you attempt to convince her to leave Glacia and
escape into the jungles with you, she will go and
forsake her destiny. Then all will be lost."

A hard knot twisted in Galen's chest. Warmth
flowed to every nerve in his body. Anger followed
it. He clenched his fists tighter, longing to strike
out at something, anything.

Closing his eyes, he tried to still the rage churning within him. The memory of Thea's hands gliding slowly over his flesh, the sweet smell of her
permeating his every pore, the feel of her woman's heat engulfing him, cradling him . . .

"No!"

"You cannot defy destiny, Galen of Borderland.
What has been foreseen cannot be changed.
Berezan's armies are within six moonrises of
Glacia. The threat is real and very near. Thea
must wield the Sphere of Light against Berezan
and destroy the evil that threatens to overtake
us all!"

"Where is Thea now, old man? I must go to
her, convince her to hear my words and disre-
gard yours." Galen attempted to push his way
past Gustoff. A light pressure on his shoulder by
Gustoff's hand ceased all motion.

"Thea will not listen to you now, warrior. Your
last encounter here in the hallway still weighs

heavily on her mind. She needs time alone to sort through her thoughts and feelings, to come to grips with that which must be done.

"Leave her alone. Do not make me restrain you again, warrior. It does neither of us any good."

"How far will you go to keep me from her, Gustoff? You are old and soon you will weaken from your exertions. I can wait until you have tired, but as we battle to determine which of us is the stronger, we waste time you claim we do not have."

Galen crossed his arms over his chest and stared into Gustoff's eyes. "Kill me, Gustoff. It is the only way you will keep me from going to Thea."

Chapter Fifteen

Thea woke to find herself sprawled across the bed in her own chamber. She sat up slowly, blinking at the bright sunshine that poured in through the open tapestries at the balcony. She wondered about the time, swiped her palms against her eyes to wipe away the gritty residue of her tears, then dropped her feet to the floor.

The feeling she was not alone crept over her. She cast a cautious glance over her shoulder to find Galen standing in a stream of sunlight, the golden glow emphasizing every muscle and hardened plane of his tall body. He wore the leggings he'd arrived in, and someone had given him one of the bronze wool tunics the seamstresses of Glacia had been working so hard to complete.

The tunic was long, hanging to mid-thigh, but it did little to hide his magnificent torso. The neckline plunged to a deep V and exposed more than an abundant amount of golden chest. The long sleeves fit tightly to his wrists, outlined each hard bulge and valley in his massive arms as he stood before her, tense, waiting.

"Thea," he whispered.

She stared at him. Pain knifed its way to the middle of her chest. She had given this man more of herself than she'd ever afforded another being, even Gustoff, and he'd hurt her. Deeply.

Thea studied the warrior's face, the tensed muscles in his firm jaw. She had used him, would go on using him as long as he permitted. He had also used her. His sensuous lessons of a love that could never be were his method of extracting payment for the schemes and plots she connived for him.

A warrior's revenge. Bittersweet, but unforgettable.

"Thea." The tone of his voice was louder, harsher, as if he grew impatient with her silence.

Instead of answering, Thea turned away and walked to the open tapestries to stare out over the snow-covered mountainside. She listened to his footsteps as he crossed the chamber, felt his breath on her neck when he paused behind her.

Thea closed her eyes. "Berezan will arrive within a few moonrisings, Galen of Borderland." She shivered when the pressure of his hand warmed her shoulder. Drawing a deep breath, Thea continued, "I understand your need to be with the people of Cree and will have Elijah gather the supplies needed for your journey."

Heat seeped from the point of his contact with her shoulder to penetrate her entire body. Thea inhaled and exhaled three times, cautioning herself to fight the mysterious magic the warrior cast over her being. She shrugged away from his touch and stepped out onto the balcony. Cold air prickled her body with gooseflesh, erasing the effect of his touch.

"I have spoken with Gustoff, Thea. He verified the words you spoke in the corridor."

Anger chased away her chills. Thea turned to stare up into the warrior's intense gaze. He believe Gustoff's word over hers, even when she'd pledged with her life. Curse him!

The warrior could believe, or not believe, anything he wished. There was no time to waste trying to sway the Creenan to her cause, no time to squander when there was much to do before Berezan's arrival. Narrowing her gaze until her attention was fully focused on his chilling eyes, Thea said, "Gustoff must have also told you of my destiny. Knowing this, you should realize I have to prepare." She tried to step around him and enter her chamber, but a strong hand to her forearm halted her progress.

"Gustoff told me he has spent years filling your head with foolish ideas that you alone can defeat Berezan."

His words washed over her. "Foolish?" Thea shook her arm free of his grasp and continued across the chamber. She paused before the fire pit, her back toward the warrior, and stared down into the flames. "I know not what convictions you honor, warrior, nor do I denounce those beliefs. Yet you are quick to say nay to what I hold as truth without understanding all there is to know."

"Gustoff informed me of the powers of the Ancient Ones. He also explained the part my ancestor, Shakara, played in the shaping of history. Much of this I was also told by my own father."

Thea heard his footsteps approach, and tensed every muscle in her body to withstand him and the consuming emotions he created. Though she knew he neared her position, she still jumped when his breath whispered over her ear.

"Even I, fool that I have been, cannot deny the strange powers you possess. But will these powers protect you from Berezan while you are attempting to defeat him?"

Thea turned slowly and lifted her head to stare into his eyes, seeking the anger she heard reflected in his words. Shafts of sunlight glistened off his golden hair. A spark of energy streaked down Thea's arm to settle in her fingertips. She curled her fingers into her palms to resist the impulse to raise her hand and tangle her fingers in his hair. She swallowed softly and exhaled. "Yes."

Galen trembled from the intensity of the emotions running rampant through him. He took a deep, steadying breath, then wrapped his hands across her shoulders, fighting hard the instinct to shake some sense into her. He released her shoulders slowly, and his hands slid down her arms to grasp her elbows before he dropped his hands to his sides and stepped away.

She was so small, yet so desirable. She fit perfectly into his arms, folded naturally against the planes and valleys of his body as if she were created specifically for him. Her hair, those glorious flaming tresses he so liked to wrap around his hands, sparkled in the sunlight filtering in through the open tapestries. Her body—the lush swell of her breasts, the narrowness of her waist, the length of her legs—was highlighted in tones of sunlight and shadow.

His hands burned with the memory of touching her, exploring every inch of her tender flesh. His heart ached with the knowledge of what she believed she had to do, what he knew his own responsibilities were. Images, vivid and devastating, streaked through his mind. Galen fought hard to resist the memories that caused his heart to race, his body to quake.

Blood. So much blood. So much death and destruction.

Berezan's arrival in Glacia would turn the icy wonderland into a battlefield of bloody carnage like the one he had witnessed in Cree. The gentle people of Glacia could do nothing to halt their demise, just as the Creeans were helpless against a force of so many, guided by such evil.

The chill of impotency rushed over him. Intense anger followed. He silently cursed Berezan, his own weakness, and Gustoff for instilling such foolish ideas into Thea's beautiful head, making her believe she could succeed where all else had failed.

Thea watched, mesmerized, as the color of Galen's eyes changed from light blue to the darker shade of midnight. She had an inexplicable urge to touch his mind, read his thoughts, until she realized she had seen that same expression days ago and had named it hatred. For an instant, fear surged through her. She drew a deep breath, forced her fear away, and dropped her gaze to the floor.

She knew and understood the memories that haunted him. She longed to wrap her arms around him, to kiss away the nightmare that made him tremble. But Galen had his own battles to fight, his own responsibilities. As leader of Borderland, Galen Sar was needed by his people.

The protection of Glacia was her fate.

"Galen . . ." Thea paused, uncertain. She glanced up at Galen to find his gaze firmly fixed on her face. Her breath caught in her throat. "I must go," she said, almost whispering. "There is much to do. Elijah will have your supplies readied and provide an equox for your transportation." Thea lowered her head so the warrior could not see the moisture that built in her eyes. She stepped around his tall form and walked away.

Thea paused. Without looking back, she whispered, "Good journey, Galen of Borderland. I'm sorry."

She hadn't heard him approach, and when his warm hand touched her shoulder, Thea almost collapsed to the floor.

"What of my needs, Thea?"

Thea turned to look up into his eyes. "What *of* your needs, Galen? You are free to leave Glacia. I have promised adequate supplies and transportation." Thea lowered her gaze to hide the moisture in her eyes. "Go to your people, Galen. See to their safety."

Galen grasped her shoulders and applied enough pressure to pull her toward him, and she went, unresisting, into his arms.

Thea sighed, melting into the safety of his embrace, casting aside all doubts, fears, hurts. Her lips quivered; her body arched closer to his muscular length. He bent his head. Her lips parted in eager anticipation of the magic spell his kiss would cast.

They stumbled toward the bed in a wild tangle of arms and legs. Thea groped for Galen's tunic, struggled to remove the wool from his body and still not break contact with his lips.

Galen ripped at the sash on Thea's silken robe, knotting it in his haste. He released his grasp on the back of her head, slid both hands around her back, and tore the sash in two. He shoved the slippery material from her shoulders more roughly than he intended, took a moment to thoroughly apologize with his lips, then lifted her high into his arms, leaving her garment to flutter to the floor in a pool of lavender.

He laid her gently upon the heavy fur coverlet on the bed and stepped back to remove his own clothing. Urgency threatened to destroy his control, but he stood paralyzed, mesmerized by the sight of Thea's loveliness as the sunlight poured in and enveloped her in a golden blanket. Her fiery hair was in disarray, long strands flowing out to cover the fur and form a burning halo around her body. One strand fell haphazardly across her shoulder, kissed her taut pink nipple, then cascaded over the soft white indention of her stomach to tangle with the matching nest that shielded her woman's mound.

Galen's heart thundered in his chest. His groin screamed in agony, but he couldn't move, couldn't take his eyes from the perfection before him. A radiant pink glow covered her cheeks, flushed her breasts. The lushness of her lashes almost hid the soft brown of her eyes. Each breath was drawn over quivering, moist lips.

The hypnotic spell was broken when she lifted her hand, beckoning him. Galen shook his head and tugged at the wool, jerked it over his head, and dropped it to the floor in one movement. He bent, peeled the tight leather leggings from his legs, and stepped free.

Thea gazed over every inch of the warrior she

could see from her prone position, from the long locks of his gorgeous hair that fell forward over his shoulders to graze the flatness of his manly chest, to each individual ripple of muscle creasing his abdomen. She studied the dark whorl of hair which grew about his naval, then dipped into a thick thatch that silhouetted the engorged evidence of his desire.

He raised his knee to the high side of the bed, then climbed in. There was no hesitation in her touch as she reached out to him, placing her palm firmly against the warmth of his stomach, then sliding it upward slowly across his breastbone to tangle her fingers in his hair and tug his head close enough to join with his lips.

He opened for her, devoured her, possessed her. She moaned, demanded, and received.

Thea ignored Galen's grunt of displeasure when she tore her lips free. She smiled at his sigh of contentment when she kissed his brow, his cheek, the tiny cleft in his chin. The warmth of his skin, the scent of him tempted her beyond her limited knowledge of sexual pleasure toward new horizons. She needed to feel, experience, all the marvelous adventures he offered, for there would never be another time.

Before sadness could overtake her, Thea wiggled out of Galen's strong embrace and planted soft kisses on his throat, his collarbone, the hardened planes of his upper chest. She teased his nipples to tautness with the tip of her tongue before continuing her exploration.

Thea sensed Galen's tenseness, heard his ragged breath echo in the silence, felt his hands about her waist tremble, and understood his hunger. Each touch, each caress she managed brought the fever burning in her body to a higher and higher peak. When his nipple hardened, hers responded likewise, each flutter of her tongue against his flesh bringing a strange and exciting quiver to her woman's heat.

But no matter the pain of denial, she continued, determined to etch forever into her mind the very essence of Galen Sar, warrior of Borderland. She trailed her fingers lightly over his navel, around and around in the swirl of dark blond hair that arrowed downward, following the growth, fascinated and in awe of his maleness. She brushed her fingers lightly up and down the length of his engorged shaft, gasping when it shuddered beneath her touch.

Galen's movements were too quick for her to anticipate. She offered little more than a startled cry when she found herself rolled over, then pinned to the mattress. For each swipe she had made with her tongue, the gesture was repeated threefold. Each kiss, each soft bite, turned into a profusion of exquisite little moments in kind, until she writhed beneath his onslaught.

She cried out in relief when he poised between her legs and thrust forward. Thea arched to meet his every thrust, straining to match his rhythm, grasping, clutching, holding, kissing every inch of his accessible flesh. She fought to prolong the rapture, to stave off the inevitable peak that would break the epitome they had achieved. Then all sense of reality evaporated, all awareness of time and space vanished. Nothing but bright, blissful light filled her universe. Galen reached the same pinnacle seconds later.

Thea had no idea how long they lay entwined, limp, replete. It seemed an eternity later when

Galen shifted to lie beside her. Thea turned her head slightly until she could see his face. She noted his uneven breathing, that his eyes were closed, his jaw set. She touched his cheek. A smile split his lips. He turned slowly and planted a soft kiss on her palm, then drew her more tightly against his side.

They lay together in silence for many more minutes. Thea wanted to say something, needed to say something, but no words formed that could adequately relate her feelings. In truth, she couldn't actually discern them herself. She couldn't ask him to forsake his duty, his people, any more than she could abandon her own destiny. Yet, were they both to undertake their chosen paths, she would never see him again, never experience the wonderful way she felt in his presence.

She loved him. No matter how confused her emotions or how deep her commitments, she loved Galen Sar and would go on loving him for the rest of her life.

She closed her eyes to the tumultuous thoughts and succumbed to her exhaustion.

Galen forced himself to lie still for longer than his protesting muscles would have allowed, waiting for Thea's even breathing to signal she slept. He sat up slowly and eased from the bed. For a moment, he stood beside the bed, watching her sleep, wondering how in such a few short sunrises he had gone from planning to use this lovely woman to aid in his revenge against Berezan to needing her as he needed air.

He wondered what it was about this tiny woman that drew him to her like none other. Numerous times over the last few summers his father had urged him to take a mate, to beget his own heir. Yet none of the females among his people had been able to reach into that sheltered part he kept closely guarded. None had stirred his lust so quickly, so hotly, then equaled his appetite, urgency, and passion.

Perhaps it was her confidence, stolid and unwavering at times, easily destroyed at others. Or the way she bravely prepared to meet a foe she knew she had no means of defeating.

Galen's heart skipped a beat. Thea DeLan would give her life for what she believed in, but because she was a female in the male-dominated world of Glacia, no one would appreciate her sacrifice or laud her accomplishments.

In the moments after their mating, he had decided to place Thea before his hunger for Berezan. To postpone his own destiny and take her away from Glacia to the safety of *Naro*.

But how? He couldn't force her to accompany him. With her mysterious gifts she would simply escape, and, as evidenced by the other times he'd come in contact with her abilities, he would be powerless to stop her. He couldn't appeal to her conscience as a healer, plead for her help to ease his people's suffering. The people of Glacia were facing catastrophic destruction that paralleled that of Borderland.

He had to think of something—fast.

Chapter Sixteen

Gustoff closed his eyes and ran the tips of his fingers slowly over the outline of the ancient doorway the warrior had found. Cold air penetrated the sleeve of his tunic and raised the hair on his arm. He fought past his discomfort and concentrated hard on the task ahead. A faint line of light glowed along the path he traced, then grew brighter as the old wood began to creak and moan. Moments later he stepped back to appraise his work. The door had seemingly disappeared. In its place was a solid stone wall.

Praying his illusion would hold, Gustoff shook his head and disappeared. Seconds later he stood in his tower reassessing all the plans he'd made since Galen had left him alone hours before.

Berezan's army had to cross the tundra before they reached Glacia, leaving less than five moonrises for strategies to be drawn. Had Gustoff an army to command, he would send his forces to meet their foe in the center of the frozen wasteland, because the soldiers of the desert would be ill-equipped to withstand the subzero temperatures.

But a withered old man, an untried female, and a reluctant Creean warrior did not make an army, no matter how powerful the magic they might create.

Gustoff wondered at the conviction of the Solarus army. Were the soldiers' beliefs stronger than Berezan's will could command? Or did they fear the evil that might befall them if they exercised their own free will?

Walking slowly to the tower window, Gustoff paused and stroked his beard. If Berezan met his demise, would his followers carry on a siege of Glacia or retreat to Solarus with the promise of everlasting peace?

More troubled thoughts invaded Gustoff's mind—questions that he had been unable to answer for a number of years. What force drove Berezan? Someone, for some reason, had to have instructed the young heir in the ways of the Ancient Ones. He could never have learned the evil magic he possessed on his own. But who? And why?

Gustoff thought back over the many years of his life, of the persons he had encountered as he rose through the ranks of the Ancient Ones. Because their numbers were so few, the competition had been great between the younger members to prove themselves worthy of being selected as Guardian to the Sphere of Light. Many equally worthy as he had been passed over when the Sphere was transferred into his keeping at his second and tenth winter and he began the training necessary to protect the Sphere.

Of those not selected, Gustoff remembered two who had turned their disappointment into hostility and had challenged his nomination with physical force: Meredian of the Peaks and Elsbar of Solarus. The Ancient Ones had dealt severely with their behavior and dishonored each with banishment from their studies, sending them home in shame, never to be seen or heard from again.

Gustoff gazed down at his withered hands and considered the 68 winters that had passed since he became Guardian of the Sphere. Had he made another mistake? Could he have neglected to consider the animosity that might have grown over the decades into a need for revenge so great it might have fueled Berezan's evil?

The answers could be found only in Solarus.

Gustoff closed his eyes and drew several deep breaths. The hour of reckoning fast approached. With a resolute shake of his head, he disappeared.

Bright light filled the chamber. Elsbar raised his crippled hand to wipe at his eyes. "Berezan?"

"No, not Berezan!"

The old man squinted, attempting to focus his cataractous eyes on the purple blur before him. "Who are you?"

"I am surprised you do not recognize me, Elsbar."

"Gustoff!"

Gustoff glanced around the tower to discover a structure similar to his own in Glacia. He noted the lone window, the hot sunlight that poured in through the opening, the swirls of dust floating in the furrows of light. He then studied the old man hunched over behind the center table, the parchment beneath his ink-stained hands.

"I thought you dead many decades ago, Elsbar."

The old man tapped his fingers upon the table. "Not dead, Gustoff, only banished from the Ancient Ones, and finally exiled by the devout Solarians because I refused to give up my practice of the ancient arts."

Gustoff stroked his bearded chin. "I have made many mistakes since I removed Berezan from Glacia. My most serious is never taking time to discover who was behind the evil that Berezan embraced."

Gustoff stepped closer to the table and studied the parchment Elsbar was working on. "Sixty-eight winters have passed since our last meeting, Elsbar, but I remember it well. You believed you should have been selected by the last of the Ancient Ones to guard the Sphere of Light. Instead, when you were rejected, you attempted to end my life, then fled Glacia in bitter defeat, never to be heard from again. Now, I find you have turned Berezan into an instrument to gain revenge."

"You have always been too softhearted, Gustoff. You could not destroy me when you had the opportunity, and you could not kill Berezan. You exiled a young boy because you did not believe you had the strength or the wisdom to alter his destiny."

Elsbar dropped his quill to the table and pointed a crooked finger at Gustoff. "The woman you paid to leave the young child in the desert was useful, old friend. When touched by my probe, she revealed the truth about young Berezan before she died.

"Berezan knows of his heritage. He will claim Glacia, and the Sphere."

"I have suffered much because of my weaknesses, Elsbar. Our world has suffered, too."

"Where is the Sphere?"

Gustoff stared into Elsbar's eyes and saw the greed, the hatred that had had too many years to fester and grow. "Do you believe I would be fool enough to bring it with me?"

The old man shrugged his bony shoulders. "One could only hope. Why did you come? Could you not sense that Berezan was not here?"

"I did not come for Berezan."

"Certainly you have not—"

"I have come to right one of the many great wrongs I have committed in my lifetime, old man." Gustoff raised his hands, spread his fingers wide. Incantations recognized by the old man before him spilled from his lips. Blue fire erupted on Gustoff's fingertips, growing in intensity until the glow filled the chamber.

Gustoff pointed to Elsbar. A shimmering aura of blue surrounded the old man, freezing the look of horror forever on his face seconds before he drew his last breath and crumpled to the tower floor.

Gustoff curled his fingers into his palms, extinguishing his blue fire, then walked to the table. He picked up the quill his old enemy had dropped, dipped it into the ink, scribed a message across the face of the parchment Elsbar had been working on, then stepped around the table and placed the quill in the old man's gnarled fingers.

Another flash of light brightened the tower. Gustoff disappeared.

Every nerve in Berezan's body quaked, jarring him awake. He gazed quickly around the shabby room, momentarily unsure where he was. Deep shadows created by the sunlight pouring in past the hides partially covering the hut windows cast most of the room in darkness.

Berezan uncrossed his legs and drew himself slowly to his feet. He filled his lungs with smoky air, then shook his head in an attempt to ward off the annoying ringing in his ears. He scanned the room again, looking for a reason for his abrupt awakening, but found nothing disturbed. He paid close attention to the sounds outside the hut. Again, nothing explained his odd behavior.

He focused within, concentrating on the noise that appeared to reverberate inside his head. Berezan closed his eyes.

Berezan. The hour has finally come for our meeting, but I will set the time and choose the place. For more than two decades I have regretted I did not destroy you when I had the opportunity. Because of my weakness, many people have suffered. But no more. No one else will feel the burden of my error. I alone will right the great wrong I have wrought upon mankind.

The object you seek is in my possession. To obtain it, you must meet me at the appearance of the second sunrise in the great valley of the tundra.

Fire shot through Berezan's body. Perspiration beaded his forehead and dripped into his eyes. The cadence of his heart echoed in the silence the absence of Gustoff's words left within his head.

He gulped for air, needing oxygen to steady his pulse, recover his equilibrium.

"Fool!" he barked, then realized his own good fortune and restructured his opinion. "Perhaps not." Berezan carefully considered Gustoff's words. He then remembered Elsbar's warnings that Gustoff was a cunning and evasive advisor who would use any ploy to outmaneuver his opponent. Berezan brushed aside his old mentor's words. Still, should Gustoff really be foolish enough to carry the Sphere of Light into battle, would the power of the Sphere enhance the old man's will and enable Gustoff to defeat all he'd worked for over the last 25 summers?

Self-doubt tugged at Berezan's mind for just an instant until he remembered how far he had come and what he had accomplished. Figuring Gustoff had concocted some carefully devised scheme to stall the inevitable, Berezan felt his confidence soar. Certainly the old man could not hope to defeat *him*. Not the son of Arlin DeLan's own loins and rightful heir to all Gustoff tried so hard to keep for himself.

Time would tell. For at the rising of the sun two days hence, he would be waiting to defeat his only foe.

Chapter Seventeen

Thea opened her eyes abruptly and drew several deep breaths to still the rapid pounding of her heart. Chills raced over the length of her body, forcing her limbs to tremble even though they were still firmly encased within the warrior's embrace. Strange emotions whirled around in her mind, all fighting to gain supremacy. The feeling was unlike anything she'd ever felt in her life.

Something was wrong—very wrong.

Wiggling from the confines of Galen's arms, Thea sat up slowly and looked around her chamber. Everything was as it should be. Nothing had changed, except sunlight no longer poured in through the tapestries and the air in the chamber had grown very cold. She guessed she had slept for several hours and the sun had long ago set behind the mountains of Glacia.

All seemed quiet and still, yet she couldn't shake the feeling that something important had taken place while she and Galen slept.

In order to sort through the jumble inside her head, Thea closed her eyes. She concentrated on the keep, seeking a disturbance in the natural order. Again, nothing appeared out of the ordinary. She then mentally searched for Gustoff. She needed to discuss her strange feelings and seek his guidance.

She probed Gustoff's tower room, the steam baths, the meeting chambers, then broadened her sweep when she could detect no trace of his essence.

Alarm raced through every nerve in her body. She quickly threw back the thick fur covering and slid to the side of the bed.

"Thea?"

Galen's husky voice reached out to halt her flight. She turned to meet his sleepy smile with a forced one of her own. Warmth infused her being when he pushed himself up on his elbows, causing the covering to fall away and the golden expanse of his chest to be exposed. Memories, vivid and wonderful, of the hours she'd recently spent in his arms flushed her cheeks and warmed the very core of her being. Familiar tinglings rushed to every nerve ending in her body.

Guilt for the time she'd spent lying peacefully enjoying Galen's company ate those memories away and dissolved the strong want that threatened to override her determination. There was too much to be done. No matter how much it meant to spend these last few hours with the only man she'd ever love, her attention should have been focused elsewhere.

Galen sensed Thea's anxiety as she slipped from his side. Shadows clouded her beautiful eyes. Something had happened to upset her. He quickly searched memories of the last few hours and felt his body harden in response. Thea had enjoyed their lovemaking as much as he, and Galen couldn't guess what had put the strange apprehension in her eyes.

"What's wrong, Thea?" He twisted until he could free his left elbow, and reached across the bed to touch her cheek. Her flesh was cold to his touch.

"Something's not as it should be, Galen. I have the strangest premonition that things have gone dreadfully wrong. I have searched the keep for Gustoff, but he is nowhere to be found. I can't imagine why he would leave when the time for Berezan's arrival is so near."

Galen could. He remembered the old man's face when he had challenged his reasons for sending Thea to do his own work. A sadness had been present Galen had never witnessed before. Galen wondered if the words he'd hurled at Gustoff in anger had struck some hidden chord within the old man. Could it be Gustoff had left Glacia to meet Berezan himself?

"I must find him." Thea scrambled down from the high bed and grabbed her lavender robe from the floor where Galen had dropped it. She wrapped the silky material around her and groped for the sash, only to find it severed in two. She threw the cord back to the floor. Placing her fingers alongside her temples, she concentrated hard on Elijah, summoning him immediately to her chamber.

While she awaited the servant's arrival, she hurried around the chamber, picking up Galen's discarded clothing and placing it on the foot of the bed. "You'd better dress. I don't think it would be wise for Elijah to find you in my bed."

Galen bit his lip to keep from saying he didn't give a damn what the servant thought, but reconsidered when he realized Thea's nervous state was worsening by the moment. He threw the coverlet back, dropped his feet to the floor, grabbed his leggings, and drew them on.

"Galen, I'm so—"

Whatever Thea was about to say was lost when a soft knock came at the chamber door. She shook her head, hurried across the floor, and threw back the bolt. Elijah walked into the chamber.

Galen noted the servant never looked into Thea's eyes, but kept his gaze downcast, almost as if he were hiding something.

"Elijah, I need Gustoff. Do you know where he might be?"

The older man reached into the pocket of his bronze robe and withdrew a piece of parchment. "I have no idea where he has gone, Thea, but he bade me to give you this." Elijah's hand shook as he handed the paper to Thea.

Thea's gasp drew Galen quickly to her side. She crumpled the paper into a tight ball and held it close to her chest. Tears streamed down her cheeks. Galen reached to wipe one away before prying the missive from her trembling fingers.

I have left Glacia to correct a great wrong I committed many years ago. Should I not return, know that I have always loved you and believe completely in your abilities. Be strong in your convictions, Thea DeLan, Last of the Ancient Ones. Hold true to your feelings and see your destiny through.

Convinced his assumptions were correct, Galen placed the missive back in Thea's hands and steadied her shoulders as he drew her toward the chaise. He turned back to the servant, who stood numbly by the chamber door. Elijah shook his head slowly, revealing he knew no more than what the letter said. Galen nodded and dismissed the servant, watching him leave the chamber and close the door softly behind him.

"Where could he have gone?" Thea cried. "Why would he leave Glacia at a time like this?"

Galen took Thea into his arms. He felt the tremors that shook her body, the tension that accompanied them, and wondered if he should make his suspicions known. Should he tell her he suspected Gustoff had gone to do battle with Berezan in her place? Undecided on the course of action he should take, he simply held her for many moments, waiting for Thea to regain the composure he suspected she rarely lost.

"This is not like Gustoff, Galen. He has never abandoned me. Now, in my hour of greatest need, he is not by my side to guide me. I don't know how to proceed from this point."

Galen placed his hand under Thea's chin and raised her face. He looked deeply into her brown eyes, trying to determine what her reaction to his theory would be. The temptation to kiss her trembling lips, to chase away her fears and doubts, if only for a moment, ate at him, but Galen resisted. He sensed Thea needed his support more than ever to see her through the next few hours.

212

He pulled her to his chest, stroked the length of her auburn hair, and placed his chin upon the top of her head.

"This is unlike him, Galen. He's never gone off without giving me some sort of an explanation."

Galen felt the stiffening of her body, and did not try to restrain her as she pulled from his arms and rose to pace the floor.

"Tell me you don't believe Gustoff would be foolish enough to go to Berezan's camp, Galen. Make me see how silly I am to even give credence to such thoughts."

She stood before him, looking him in straight in the eye. The temptation was there for him to turn from her gaze, but Galen resisted. Her untied robe hung open down the front, giving him a full view of all of her abundant charms. Galen felt himself harden at the way she strode around before him, giving no consideration to her state of undress. He cursed himself for the weakness in his loins where this female was concerned. She turned, advanced upon him. He almost put his hand out to restrain her as she paused before him and poked her finger into his chest.

"Do *you* know something of Gustoff's disappearance, Galen of Borderland? Did you come to my chamber to detain me while Gus slipped silently away? Did Gustoff solicit your aid, knowing I would do everything humanly possible to stop him from leaving Glacia?"

Each question brought another sharp poke to his chest. Galen reached up to grab her wrist. "Is that what you believe, Thea? Do you think the time we spent over the last few hours was nothing more than a diversionary tactic?" He pulled her closer, closer still, until he could feel every

breath she drew whisk across his face. He stared
into her eyes, challenging her to take what they
had shared and turn it into nothing more than a
ploy to detain her.

She stared back, meeting his gaze in a stubborn battle of wills.

He still held her wrist in one hand, but slipped
the other inside her robe, slid it slowly up her
side, and settled it over the fullness of her breast.
At her expression of shock, he caressed the heaviness of her, then rolled the nipple that had gone
pebble-hard between his fingers. "What do you
think, Thea?" he asked softly.

Thea fell forward and buried her head into the
side of his neck. "I don't have any idea what to
think anymore," she whispered.

Galen took a moment to thoroughly convince
her that their lovemaking was exactly what it had
seemed, wonderful and deeply binding.

As Galen's hand slipped downward to touch
the wetness of her being, Thea arched to meet
him. She opened her lips for him, tasting fully
the man she loved with all of her heart, drinking
in every ounce he would allow.

Reality threatened to give way to ecstasy when
Galen broke the kiss and pulled away. Thea looked
into his eyes, confused.

"I have not spoken to Gustoff since meeting
him in the corridor last eve. At that time he told
me nothing of his plans, but I suspect I know
where he has gone and why."

"He—"

Galen placed his finger over her lips. "Listen to
me, Thea. Promise me you won't interrupt until
I've finished explaining." She nodded. "I believe
as you do. Gustoff may have left Glacia to meet

Berezan in an attempt to thwart his invasion.

"I think Gustoff is trying to protect you in the only way he knows how, Thea. If he can meet and destroy Berezan before he ever reaches Glacia, there will be no need for you to—"

"I won't let him do this!" Thea jerked away and hurried across the chamber to her wardrobe. She threw open the doors and dug through the contents, scattering discarded items all over the floor in her haste.

Galen realized Thea was looking for warm clothing so she could follow Gustoff into the tundra. He rose from the chaise and walked across the room to stop her.

"You cannot go to him, Thea. If you should be discovered, all you have worked for over the past number of years will be destroyed. Gustoff obviously doesn't want Berezan to know you exist. Why else would he have gone off alone?"

"I *must* go to him. I have to. You cannot stop me."

Galen understood her threat well. There was really no way he could prevent her from leaving Glacia, but he could make sure she did not go unprotected.

"If you insist in going to Gustoff, I intend to go with you."

"No!"

"You cannot stop me either, Thea."

"You have your own responsibilities, Galen of Borderland. Your people need you. You cannot risk your life needlessly."

Galen folded his arms over his chest. He refused to debate the wisdom of his choice to accompany her. His heart had spoken for his mind, and there was no turning back.

215

"I'm going, Thea. If you choose to leave me, I'll find my way somehow. Berezan is also my enemy. You cannot deny me the opportunity to avenge my people and to protect you."

Warmth flowed freely from Thea's heart to her entire body. Her love for Galen grew tenfold when she realized even though he had never said the words that would confirm his returned love, he had just pledged himself to her safety.

It was her duty to protect him.

She reached forward and touched his cheek. "You cannot go with me, Galen. I intend to concentrate on Gustoff's essence and transport to his position. I have never tested the strength of the powers within me and have no way of knowing if it is possible to transport two beings. I cannot take a chance that you will be harmed in some way."

"Call Elijah."

Thea looked confused at his statement, but Galen decided to let her wait. He took over the work she'd begun, pulling through the ancient wardrobe for warm garments big enough for him to wear. He secured the heavy fur cape and gloves Gustoff had used in his disguise many sunrises ago at Dekar, then walked across the room and pulled the woolen tunic the seamstresses had constructed over his head. He had finished yanking on his last boot when a soft knock appeared at the door.

Thea had watched in fascination as Galen went about the chamber, taking charge of dressing himself in clothing suitable to withstand the cold beyond the keep walls. She wondered how he had known there were warm men's clothes in the wardrobe, and guessed he had done some nocturnal snooping.

Now she hurried across the room to shove the bolt aside so Elijah could enter again. She turned to find Galen standing in the center of the floor, looking much the same as he had several hours ago.

"Have two equox prepared for a long journey, Elijah," he said. "Make sure to pack plenty of blankets and food. Thea and I might be away from the keep for a lengthy period."

Thea pivoted her head quickly from Galen to Elijah to witness the servant's acquiescence to the warrior's orders. Elijah never questioned Galen, nor did he look to her for confirmation. He simply turned and set about handling his task, not bothering to shut the chamber door behind him.

Thea turned back to Galen. She had time to thrust her arms out in front of her as he shoved several items of heavy clothing in her direction.

"Put these on. We leave as soon as Elijah has readied our supplies."

Indignation rose at his assumption of command. Thea opened her mouth to protest his conduct, but shut it quickly at the determination burning deeply in his blue eyes.

"The choice is yours, Thea of Glacia. Either we ride together, or I follow you."

Knowing the decision had been taken out of her hands, she walked across the room and dropped the bundle of clothing on the bed. She could feel Galen's eyes upon her as she slowly peeled the lavender silk from her shoulders and allowed it to slip to the floor. She had to bite her lip to keep from chuckling when he swore silently, stalked across the floor toward the archway, flung the

217

tapestries aside, and stepped outside into the cold winter night.

Thea hurried to dress, wondering what the warrior thought about as he stood outside in the cold. Did he regret his decision to accompany her when he should have been traveling to Borderland to see to the welfare of his own? Or was his aid only an avenue to gain the need for revenge she'd sensed in him time and time again?

Answers to her silent questions had to be postponed. Elijah appeared in the doorway to announce all was ready for their journey. Nola stood at his side.

Thea glanced toward the tapestries, then walked to the door. She grasped Nola's hand and looked into Elijah's eyes. "Watch over Glacia in my absence, my friends. Should I not . . ." Thea bit her lip and turned away. Tears burned her eyes.

"Thea." Nola's soft fingers touched her cheek.

Thea brushed at the moisture on her lashes, then met Nola's gaze.

"Elijah and I remember all you have instructed. We will do our best to protect the people of Glacia until you return."

Another tear slipped down Thea's cheek. "I know you will."

"Protect yourself," Elijah whispered.

Thea squeezed Nola's hand and kissed Elijah's cheek. "I love you both."

"May the Ancient Ones watch over you," Elijah said.

Galen apparently heard the servant's comments from the balcony, and he entered the chamber. Without a word he followed Elijah and Nola out of the chamber. Thea hurried after them.

Within moments after exiting from the keep, Galen and Thea rode down the frozen cobblestoned roadway that led through the mountain pass and down into the tundra.

Chapter Eighteen

The equox of the north were magnificent creatures. Bred to withstand the frigid weather, they stood more than 17 spans high and weighed over a ton each. Their backs were several spans wide, capable of carrying great weights. The massive muscles in their legs enabled them to tread with little effort through deep snow, their cloven hooves picking their way carefully over slick ice, and their long shaggy coats protecting them from the elements.

Thea gazed down at the beast beneath her. Though they had traveled throughout the night and the sun now rode high overhead, the beast showed little sign of tiring. She wished she felt as little discomfort as the equox appeared to feel. Her hands, even gloved in thick fur, were frozen to the point that she could no longer feel her fingers. Her toes long ago had simply ceased to exist. And only the chattering of her teeth kept her from falling asleep.

Pushing aside the fur mask that covered her face, leaving only her eyes exposed to the elements, she glanced to her side at Galen. She wished there was something she could do to ease his discomfort. She had lived in the north all of her life, and her tolerance for cold was above normal. A product of the humid jungles, Galen was on the verge of freezing to death.

When they began their journey he'd sat erect on the back of the beast, shoulders squared, head constantly turning in all directions searching for any sign of danger. Now, many hours later, he slumped over the beast, fighting exhaustion and the bitter effects of the cold wind and subzero temperatures.

Thea wished he had allowed her to come alone. She could have transported directly to Gustoff, avoiding all of this unnecessary travel. Instead, in trying to protect her, he had subjected himself to this torture. She felt deeply sorry for his condition. But she could not change what had been started, could not forget her journey to assist Gustoff in whatever undertaking he had initiated.

Neither would she leave Galen alone to fend for himself in the frozen wasteland.

To fight the cold, she concentrated on Gustoff's essence, pleased to find it stronger and stronger with each step the equox took. She also sensed a great peace, a cleansing calm, and knew he was in no immediate danger.

Thea closed her eyes and wondered again why Gustoff had left without discussing his plans with her. He had to know she would not remain in Glacia if she believed he might face danger. Was

221

this another part of her training? She shook her head. Whatever it was, it didn't make any sense.

Looking up into the bright sky, she estimated they would have to travel at least four more hours before they could rest in the cover of darkness. She sighed when she realized how much she looked forward to the warm tent Elijah had packed in their supplies. A break from the constant wind that blew over the tundra would allow a few hours of rest.

Night fell quickly in the vast emptiness. Since there were no trees or rocks to produce shadows, the full moon created a wondrous white sheen over the ice and set aglow the particles of loose snow whipped high by the wind.

Thea glanced over her shoulder when she realized Galen's equox had stopped moving. Galen pointed to what appeared to be a huge snowdrift that would offer them some shelter. Turning her beast, she followed Galen and waited patiently while he dismounted, then walked to her side to assist her down.

They worked quickly, without a word, to erect the small tent and bed down the equox for a few hours' rest. Thea watched Galen feed the beasts from his saddle pouch, then scrape up small piles of snow for the animals to consume for moisture. Remembering her own duties, Thea filled a kettle with clean snow and carried it into the tent. By the light of several small lumastones, she built a fire with the dried *picea* boughs they carried and heated the kettle of snow, mixing in portions of special herbs and spices to form a strong tea.

Thea shielded the fire from the blast of wind that flooded the tent when Galen pushed the flap aside and entered. He thrust a small pouch into her hands before removing his heavy gloves. Thea opened the pouch, took out two large chunks of bread, some cheese, and several *domini* pears, then placed them on the plate she'd set over the fire to warm.

The thick fabric of the tent not only kept the cold air out, but after a while held the heat of the fire in. Thea slipped the fur from her shoulders and turned it inside out to use for a bed, allowing what little warmth remained from her body to be augmented by the heat inside the tent. She watched as Galen did likewise, and noted that he positioned his bed on the side of the fire near hers.

When he finally looked at her she noticed the redness around his eyes where skin had been left exposed by the fur mask, the strange pallor of his flesh, the purple stiffness of his fingers.

"Give me your hands, Galen." He looked at her strangely, then complied. Thea called forth a warmth from deep inside of her, felt it slip slowly down her arms to the tips of her fingers. She took one of Galen's large hands into the protection of hers and, as the heat flowed from her fingers to his, felt something inside her quiver, almost as if part of her being joined with him. She reluctantly broke the bond and captured his other hand. Again the strange closeness enveloped her. She didn't resist the urge she had. She raised his hand to her lips, kissing each finger warmed by her touch. He repaid her homage with a like gesture.

Galen released her fingers. Thea raised her hands to touch his face. Within seconds, the flesh around his eyes was healed and his skin glowed healthily in the light of the fire. She handed him a cup of the herb tea she'd prepared, and almost laughed when he took a moment to sniff if before he brought it to his lips.

"You have had this tea before, Galen." She chuckled, remembering that day that seemed so long ago now.

He met her gaze, winked at her, then drained the cup and held it out for more.

Thea ate the remainder of her meal in silence. After packing up their supplies, she turned in for a few hours' sleep, cuddling close to Galen to share the warmth of his body, too exhausted to think about more than the comfort of his arms.

Galen shifted his buttocks against the thick fur. He arched away from Thea's side long enough to stretch his back and relieve a cramp in his side. His actions did little to appease the discomfort caused by a long, sleepless night.

He'd spend hours listening to the wind howl beyond the tent, watching the fire dim and almost die. He'd gone over and over each thing he had experienced since waking to find himself bound to the bed a few sunrises ago.

Galen shifted until he could look down at the woman in his arms. What he had first believed to be deceit was the desperate act of a woman, a leader, attempting to protect her people. He suspected even without her strange powers or the Sphere of Light, Thea would do everything humanly possible to protect the subjects of Glacia if she knew they were in danger.

He remembered Gustoff's words from the corridor. Though the teachings of the Elders were not revered in the Borderland, Galen understood the *Articles* devised centicycles past. Shakara had created an assumed need for such scriptures because of the bloody wars she had led against Glacia and Solarus. Never again could a female rule any region of the world.

Alec's demise placed the House of DeLan, and Glacia, in the vulnerable position of having no male heir to rule, thereby making it accessible to Berezan.

The inequities of the *Articles* plagued him. Thea was as capable as any male to lead the people of Glacia, but she was being judged unfairly by his ancestor's deed. Thankfully, the Creean race had chosen their own disciplined lifestyle, separate and apart from the rest of the world. Words, no matter how honorable, were useless if they could not be enforced.

The time had come for great changes in their world. The Council of Elders' and the Messahs' effectiveness had passed, and along with them that of the *Articles*. In order to lead a people, you had to be able to protect those in your charge, not stand idly by preaching peace and harmony, then bow out sheepishly at the first threat of rebellion.

Galen thought about Gustoff. The people of Borderland lived a great number of years. His own grandsire had been 110 summers when he passed. But Galen could not guess Gustoff's age. The old man appeared to float rather than walk, his every movement slow and smooth, as if he calculated each action before it was taken. His eyes were almost colorless, yet in his gaze, Galen detected great wisdom and power. A sample of which he had also encountered in the corridor.

During the Messahs' visit, the hint had been dropped that Alec DeLan was associated with Berezan. Could the heir to Glacia have been Berezan's accomplice in a quest to rule the world?

Galen rubbed his temples to ease the ache in his head caused by more questions and no answers. He pulled Thea tighter into his embrace, determined to do all he could to keep her safe from whatever they might face on the morrow, and beyond.

At the first noise from the equox outside the cozy boundaries of their tent signaling the coming of dawn, Thea helped Galen break camp.

Several hours later they crested a hill just as the sun broke above the horizon, and Thea stared down at a horrifying, yet unbelievable sight.

Gustoff, clad only in his purple robe, stood at the bottom of a deep valley. Perhaps 100 spans away, another tall, imposing figure cloaked in emerald stood facing him. Thea could not hear what was being said from her vantage point, but it was apparent from the angry waving of each man's arms that they were in the middle of a heated confrontation.

"Berezan!" The word slipped from Galen's lips like a curse. Thea shivered in response. Thea could not see Berezan's face, but she could tell from his stance, his posture, he was a much younger man. He also projected a confidence that caused Thea's heart to flutter.

Unfair! The word echoed around inside Thea's brain. Gustoff was no match for Berezan. Age alone would be his downfall. They had always known Berezan was a much younger man, but it had never been their purpose for Gustoff to meet him. She was to have pitted her strengths against Berezan's, defeating him with the same advantage his youth gave over Gustoff's age. She could not allow this travesty to continue. She had to assist Gustoff in some way.

Thea jumped down from her equox and ran to the edge of the precipice that dipped into the deep valley. She threw her heavy gloves to the ground, and had just begun to scramble over the edge when a strong hand pulled her back.

"Don't be foolish, Thea," Galen hissed in her ear. "Gustoff needs all of his concentration to defeat that bastard. He can't commit himself fully to combat if he has you to worry about."

Thea turned and stared into Galen's concerned gaze. The need to be at Gustoff's side clawed at her heart, but Galen was right. She would do nothing to aid Berezan, even unintentionally. She had never felt so helpless.

"There must be something I can do." Thea looked around. "Berezan is alone, Galen. This is an opportunity to meet my destiny and face Berezan without endangering the people of Glacia."

Galen glanced around the tundra. A strange sense of foreboding flooded his mind. Something wasn't right. Berezan did not seem the type of man to come unprotected into combat. Nor did Gustoff, for that matter.

"Do not act hastily, Thea. Something is wrong here. I don't believe—"

The frozen ground beneath their feet began to shake. Ominous black clouds suddenly appeared in the sky above. Darkness covered the tundra. Great claps of thunder filled the morning air.

The tremors of the earth grew harder, almost throwing Galen and Thea to their knees. Thunder continued to boom directly over head, each blast louder than the one before.

Thea resisted the urge to cover her ears. Galen pulled her against his chest to protect her, attempting to shield her ears with his hands, but Thea scrambled away. Another strong quake caused her to fall to the ground, but something drew her to the edge, called to her as if it was necessary that she see what was happening in the valley below. Unable to regain her feet, she crawled to the edge and gasped loudly at what she saw.

Gustoff and Berezan had finished their argument. Apparently, nothing had been settled. Now, instead of hurling angry words across the space that separated them, arcs of fire similar to lightning, blue from Gustoff, red from Berezan, flashed back and forth over the valley floor.

Thea attempted to scramble to Gustoff's aid again, but Galen's arms tightened around her, holding her away from the edge. Another blast of thunder echoed off the valley walls. Thea watched in horror as Berezan pointed to the heavens and a bolt of lightning streaked down from the sky toward Gustoff.

Gustoff raised his arm, hand spread, and issued a bolt of fire of his own that deflected Berezan's and sent it ricocheting to the ground, where it melted a black hole approximately ten spans wide in the ice. Another bolt. Another deflection. The frozen ground around the combatants became pockmarked with deep black craters.

Smoke filled the valley. Arcs of blue and red light flashed back and forth. The thunder grew even louder. The earth began to shake violently. A huge ridge of snow broke free from the peak behind Berezan's back, sending an avalanche plummeting toward the valley floor.

Thea clung to Galen, unable to draw her gaze from the confrontation beneath them.

Gustoff was weakening. His return volleys were slowing.

Thea twisted in Galen's stubborn hold, fighting his restraint, but mysteriously not wanting him to let her go. She could transport into the heat of battle at any time, but she acknowledged a tiny voice inside of her that said to stay away.

A bolt of red fire struck the ground near Gustoff's feet. He stumbled. Something inside Thea snapped. "Let me go, Galen. I can't watch this any longer. I *must* do something." He shook his head. "Can't you see Gustoff is tiring?" she shrieked.

Galen placed his lips near her ear. "You will destroy all Gustoff has given if you make your presence known, Thea. Don't you see? Gustoff gave Glacia two barriers of defense by meeting Berezan here in the open. If he succeeds in destroying Berezan, Glacia will never know what danger it faced."

And if he doesn't? Thea refused to answer her silent question. "He needs my help."

Galen pushed Thea over until she was flat on her back in the snow. He straddled her, holding one hand in each of his and bent until they were almost nose to nose. "What will you do, Thea? Use those tiny sparks of light that warmed my fingers when we rested to destroy Berezan? Have

229

you ever tried to create those arcs of fire? Do you believe you can?"

Thea closed her eyes to shield her tears from Galen. She had no idea what she might do if pushed.

A loud, evil, spine-tingling laugh echoed over the tundra, drawing every nerve in Thea's body tighter and tighter. Then all was silent. Deadly silent.

Thea opened her eyes and gazed up at Galen. He looked not at her but out over the horizon in the direction of the battle they had witnessed. She raised her hands, pushed at his chest to free herself. He rose and helped her to her feet. They walked slowly to the edge and looked down at the carnage below.

Hundreds of craters blackened the snow, still steaming in the aftermath of battle. But no trace of Berezan. A tiny spark of hope sprang forth in Thea's breast until her mind cried out that Gustoff would never have voiced such a dreadful cry of victory. Uneasiness filled her. She searched frantically over the valley floor for Gustoff.

A scrap of purple flapping over the rim of one of the craters caught her attention. Thea closed her eyes and transported to the spot where her mentor lay.

Galen, stunned by the destruction below, did not realize Thea had left his side until he saw her at the valley floor, picking her way carefully around the deep craters. He scrambled over the edge and slipped carefully to the bottom.

Galen heard Thea's mournful cries long before he reached her position. When he neared the crater he saw Thea sitting in the charred, wet snow, holding Gustoff's body to her chest. She gazed up at him, and Galen knew he'd never forget the look of anguish on her beautiful face. She scrambled to the side, positioning Gustoff's body on the crater floor, then closed her eyes and touched him, willing all of her strength to heal the old man.

"Thea!"

She ignored him.

Several more times Galen called out to her, but she shook her head and continued to work over Gustoff. Galen hurt inside. Thea was irrational in her grief, and did not see what he saw when she looked at the old man. Where she saw a soul in need of healing, he stared into the empty eyes of the dead, saw the wound that mutilated his entire torso, leaving nothing but shreds of bone and flesh.

Still Thea would not give up.

Galen watched helplessly as Thea poured every ounce of herself into attempting to revive the old man. Finally, her wails of anguish echoed across the valley until she collapsed unconscious beside her dead mentor.

Galen sat for a moment to catch his breath. The climb up the frozen valley wall with Thea in his arms had been harrowing. He continued to sit, watching her sleep, feeling every ounce of protectiveness inside of him become fully charged.

Berezan would now believe nothing stood in his way as he marched to conquer Glacia. Galen remembered the battle he'd witnessed, and guessed Berezan would be correct in his assumption. Swords, knives, and clubs would be no match for Berezan's magic. No warrior he'd ever known could compare to one who spit lightning from his fingertips.

How could Thea DeLan expect to be such a warrior? Galen did not believe the gentle female he knew and loved would take a life instead of attempting to heal it. But if she continued to persist in the same foolishness that had cost Gustoff his life, she would eventually meet a similar fate. One he would not, could not allow.

Well aware he was powerless to prevent Thea from doing what she wanted, Galen prayed she would remain asleep until his own plans reached fruition.

Galen made sure Thea was completely covered in her fur cloak as he settled her more securely into his lap. He used the fullness of his own cloak to wrap them both in a cocoon of warmth and kicked the equox firmly to spur him into motion. He looked up, checked the position of the moon, and headed toward it.

Galen remembered nothing of his flight from Borderland mooncycles ago, yet he knew from Thea's earlier directions, that by traveling due south until he neared the melting snow, then turning west, he should arrive in Borderland before the sun rose twice. He looked over his shoulder to the place they had left. New snows would eventually create the grave for Gustoff he had not had time to make.

Galen grieved for the old man. He grieved for Thea. He knew the deep anguish that ate away at one's soul when a loved one was lost. Galen pulled Thea tighter into his embrace, wanting to do anything in his power to shelter her from such agony.

Chapter Nineteen

Just before the second sunrise, Galen rode into the foothills of *Naro*. He purposely bypassed villages in order to avoid the devastation he couldn't yet face. He studied the foliage they passed, the deep greens, the multicolored flowers that grew in no particular pattern.

Many hours before he had shed his heavy cloak and tunic. The warm sun felt marvelous against the bare flesh of his back. He had also removed Thea's thick cloak and gloves. He looked down, staring into her sleeping face for the hundredth time since beginning their escape to Borderland. He wondered how much longer she would lie in the throes of exhaustion.

At first, he had been relieved that she showed no signs of waking, but after many hours and no evidence of life, he had begun to worry. Such a lengthy sleep was unnatural. Still, the energy she had depleted in her attempt to resurrect Gustoff had cost her dearly. He had examined her as thoroughly as their position on the back of an equox would allow, determining that no fever burned her body, that her breathing was normal, and that she appeared in no danger. He almost dreaded the consequences when she finally did wake.

A rustling sound drew his attention. Galen pulled back on the reins, bringing the equox to a halt. With all senses of preservation fully charged, he stared into the foliage, listened for any abnormal sounds, and waited. He had no weapons to defend the woman cradled in his arms, no skills other than his own abilities to fight whatever threatened their passage.

"Who trespasses in the land of the Cree?" a gruff voice shouted.

Every muscle in Galen's body relaxed. "Who would ask such a question of a weary traveler?" Galen responded. "Come forth and show yourself."

Three Creean warriors, swords poised for a fight, stepped out of the foliage to block his path. Galen knew he had been away many sunrises and was presumed dead by his people. But these young warriors were known to him. He'd seen them many times before, yet could not recall their names.

"Stand down, warriors. I have business with your leader, Kajar. I wish to speak with him immediately."

"What have you in your arms, stranger?" one of the warriors asked.

Galen glanced down at Thea's sleeping form, then returned the warrior's stare. "My woman is ill. She requires rest from our journey. Take us to Kajar."

The three young warriors huddled for a moment of frantic whispering. One warrior, the tallest of the three, came forward. Galen watched his eyes and guessed the man to be in his eighteenth summer. A streak of pain flashed through Galen's chest. Before Berezan's raid, warriors such as these would be in training, not yet expected to defend their homeland. He considered the circumstances these young warriors were faced with, and knew they presented themselves well.

"We will take you to Kajar."

Galen nodded. The warriors positioned themselves around his steed and Thea's mount, one before, two behind. They lead him into the hidden passageways of *Naro*.

As they rounded a camouflaged bend in the rock, three large warriors stepped out from cover. The older warriors recognized Galen immediately, but he issued a silent command for them not to give his identity away. Each warrior nodded in turn.

"This stranger wishes to see Kajar," the young warrior who led them said. One of the older warriors nodded, turned, and entered the cave.

Moments later Galen's old friend ran to his side. "Galen! We believed you were dead!"

Galen shifted his gaze from his friend's face to those of the younger warriors before him. He noted the flushness of their cheeks and understood their mortification. "You have served Borderland well, warriors. I commend your actions, and I would speak to each of you on the morrow."

The young warriors bowed in unison and backed quickly away.

Galen leaned to place his precious burden into Kajar's outstretched arms.

"Who is she?" Kajar whispered, almost as if he were afraid to wake the beauty in his arms.

"Mine," was Galen's only answer.

Kajar gave him a curious look, which Galen ignored. "I will explain everything later. Right now, I require rest, nourishment, and a soft place for my female to sleep. We have traveled for five suns across the tundra."

Galen dismounted and quickly relieved Kajar of his burden. Kajar nodded, sending the two warriors standing near the cave entrance inside to carry out Galen's command.

"These are curious beasts, Galen."

"They are creatures of the north as you can see by their thick coats. See if you can find them a cool place to rest. They have served me well."

One of the warriors who had gone to prepare for Galen's arrival stepped from the cave and paused beside him. "Your bed and food have been prepared, *regis*. Please follow me."

Galen followed Kajar and the warrior inside the cave. He carried Thea to a secluded alcove jutting deep into the rock and laid her to rest comfortably on a thick pallet of fur.

"Where have you been for the past five mooncycles, Galen?"

Galen took a chunk of meat from the platter before him. He savored the flavor of a staple in his diet he had been too long without. After washing it down with *alsa* wine, he wiped his mouth on his hand and met his friend's gaze.

"I followed Berezan's mercenaries for several sunrises through the jungle. On my third waking,

I discovered they had changed the direction of their flight and, instead of heading south, turned north. I didn't expect their trap." Galen closed his eyes and struggled to remember what had happened after he was captured.

"Why would Berezan's army turn north?"

"They must have thought the warriors of Cree would follow them once they left the city. I believe they were disappointed when their ambush netted only me—until they learned who I was."

"You told them?"

"No. They took me to a cave deep in the northernmost section of Borderland, one I never knew existed. I don't recall how long I was shackled, but I remember thinking about my need to escape."

Galen closed his eyes. "Berezan came to me when my strength was almost at an end. He did little more than touch my flesh, but he learned everything he wanted to know."

"How?"

"All I remember is excruciating pain."

Kajar paled.

"I escaped and, knowing I could not lead Berezan's army back to our hiding place in *Naro*, I headed north towards the tundra. I don't remember anything else until I awoke in a strange chamber with a beautiful woman hovering over me." Galen glanced at Thea's sleeping form.

Kajar grasped Galen's arm. "You are home now, my friend. But I can see you are exhausted. Rest. We will talk more on the morrow." Kajar rose and left the alcove.

Galen finished his wine, then climbed into the furs beside Thea and fell promptly to sleep.

237

*   *   *

Raising her eyelids seemed to be a monumental task, but after several tries, Thea succeeded. She blinked at the strange light that danced on walls of rough granite and sparkled in the silver flecks. She wondered about the walls. They were similar to those in Glacia, yet somehow different, almost as if they were unpolished.

Thea fought against the weakness that threatened to place her back into a state of dormancy, and struggled into a sitting position. She studied her surroundings. She was in some type of a cave. The walls were high, almost 30 spans above her head, and the floor appeared to be cut into solid rock. There was only one entrance, and no hole in the ceiling for the smoke from the fire that burned at room's center to escape, yet the air was not tainted.

The cave was not furnished. Several mats made of some type of animal fur covered areas of the floor. She looked down. Similar furs were piled several spans deep beneath her to form a bed.

Something moved on her other side. Thea glanced over her shoulder to find Galen sleeping peacefully on the mat beside her. She watched the firelight flicker on his bare shoulders for a moment; then horrible memories flooded back, filling her mind and tearing at her heart.

Tears roll down her cheek as she relived the battle between Gustoff and Berezan. She saw herself standing on the sidelines, incapable of lending assistance. In the end, her lack of help had cost the life of her dearest, most trusted friend.

Thea drew a quick breath and reached deep inside for something she felt missing. A strange emptiness in the area of her heart felt as if a piece of the organ had been torn away. She glanced back at Galen. He'd turned over on his back. The fur had slipped until it exposed his entire chest to her sight. Warm stirrings fluttered to life in the pit of her stomach.

Thea reached out, gliding her fingers along the line of his cheek, but this gentle touch, this simple embrace cost a tremendous amount of her strength.

Thea had given everything she had to revive Gus, but in the end she had failed. From somewhere deep inside a tiny voice said naggingly that her efforts were doomed from the beginning, but she brushed the thought away and remembered holding Gustoff in her arms, seeing the lifelessness in his kind eyes, knowing he had died in her place.

Berezan had won. Her entire life had been torn asunder and nothing had changed. Berezan's armies still threatened Borderland and Glacia. Even now he probably entered the unprotected city of her birth, and she was not there to oppose him—not there to fulfill her destiny.

She cast another glance toward Galen. Pain welled in her heart. He knew as well as she that Berezan would stop at nothing to gain Glacia. Yet Galen had taken advantage of her inability and stolen her away.

Several times over the last few mooncycles she had given this man all of herself, only to have her gifts returned by treachery. She had believed he loved her as much as she loved him, but his deeds spoke of things his words did not.

One did not love one moment and betray the next. And no matter how much it hurt, from this moment forward, she would never forget that lesson.

It took almost more strength than she could muster to throw back the fur coverlet from her legs to discover her clothing had been removed and she lay naked in Galen's bed. Furious at her own inability, Thea cursed the fates that had brought her to this. She tried to rise. Dizziness assaulted her. She swayed to and fro for several seconds before gaining her balance. She pushed slowly to her feet. Her knees give way and dropped her right back to the bed.

Frustrated, Thea closed her eyes and concentrated on her own bedchamber in Glacia. She imagined every wardrobe, the poster bed, the lavender-covered chaise where she'd spent many hours relaxing, even the heavy tapestries that shielded her balcony. She drew a deep breath and wished herself there.

She cried out when pain streaked through every nerve in her body, almost as if she had tapped into resources no longer available. She shivered until the discomfort eased, hugging her arms around her midsection to ward off the prickly bites of pain that remained long after the initial bout subsided.

Tears wet her lashes, flooded her cheeks. Many moonrises from home, her energy drained, and the restorative sleep needed to replenish her body and mind incomplete, she could only pray Nola and Elijah would be successful in evacuating the people of Glacia to safety.

Thea hardly had the strength to sob as she collapsed back onto the thick pallet and allowed exhaustion to overcome her.

*   *   *

The fire in the pit at the alcove's center had dimmed until all that remained were hot red coals and ash. Shadows climbed high on the stone walls, darkening every imperfection in the granite and causing the silver flecks to peer back at him like tiny red eyes.

Galen arched his shoulders, shifting Thea's weight until the pinpricks that raced up and down his arms subsided. He rolled his buttocks, easing the cramp that tightened his left thigh, then looked down for the hundredth time in a few short hours at the woman asleep in his arms.

He tried to close his mind to memories of the hurt he had seen reflected in the tears that had poured so freely from her beautiful eyes. He wasn't strong enough. Each moment had replayed itself over and over, bringing another twist to the knife of pain that tore through his heart.

Almost as if he had read her thoughts, Galen had understood as each new expression had crossed Thea's face. As each horrible memory had repeated itself in her mind, he had witnessed her anguish, her grief. There had been nothing he could have done to ease her pain. Nothing to relieve the sense of failure or guilt he knew she felt.

What had hurt most, however, was the look of disbelief she had given him shortly before she closed her eyes the last time.

She thought he had betrayed her.

Perhaps he had.

Galen closed his eyes and leaned back until his head rested against the stone wall. He drew a deep breath. For well over an hour he had sat, holding her. Thinking. Planning. Hoping for a

241

miracle, when all around them seemed doomed.

Much, and little, had changed over the past five sunrises. Gustoff was gone, Thea weakened to the point of total exhaustion in her attempt to help her mentor. Galen had finally returned to his people. But Berezan represented the same threat he had before they began their journey away from Glacia.

Galen opened his eyes and glanced once again at Thea. No words of love or commitment had ever been spoken between them. Now it might be too late. Thea's belief he had betrayed her would turn quickly into hatred.

Sighing, he tightened his arms, drawing her even closer to his chest. Her hatred he could live with. Her death—

"Galen."

Galen turned to find Kajar standing in the opening of the alcove. He studied his friend for several moments, remembering the times they had shared as children. Love and laughter had filled their days. He recalled how confident they each had been in their training, invincible warriors, the strongest and the best of the best. Neither would have ever believed their future might be filled with bitterness and defeat.

"Is she still sleeping?" Not giving Galen time to answer his question, Kajar walked to the center of the cave, then stirred the embers of the fire until a bright glow lit the darkness. He added several small branches from the pile against the cave wall, and took a seat on the fur mat directly across from Galen's.

"I never thought I would see you again. After so much time had passed, I had all but given up." Kajar shook his head. "The people are asking for you. News of your return has spread fast. So, too, are rumors of the woman you carried into the cave."

Galen chuckled. "Rumors?"

"Our society has always encouraged our people to speak their minds. Young warriors—old warriors for that matter—converse freely when their leader brings a stranger into our midst, Galen. Especially a female."

"I didn't think you'd be satisfied with my earlier answers to your questions, old friend."

"Much has happened since you left our village to seek revenge against Berezan, Galen. I gathered all of the survivors together as ordered and brought them to hide in the caves. But we are a crippled people. Our numbers are few. Sickness is rampant. Hiding here like animals, we have been unable to forage herbs for medicines or nourishing food to make our people well. Our warriors have wounds that fester and steal their strength." Kajar dropped his forehead into his hands.

"Now, with rumors Berezan has once again traveled in our land . . ." Again, Kajar shook his head. "Several sunrises ago, the sense of helplessness began to eat away at me to the point I felt I had to do something. In frustration, I led a small band of warriors through the jungle to search for any evidence of a new invasion and stumbled upon a mysterious old man in the clearing of Cree."

"Gustoff," Galen whispered.

"You know of this man?"

"Yes."

"Then you can tell me if he spoke the truth when he said he was from Glacia."

Several seconds passed. Galen closed his eyes and remembered Gustoff's tale of what he had discovered when he visited Cree to seek Galen's father's aid. He opened his eyes and met Kajar's gaze. "The old man spoke the truth."

Kajar nodded toward Thea's sleeping form. "And this female?"

Galen gently lifted Thea from his lap and laid her down on the bedding. He covered her carefully with furs, then rose stiffly to his feet.

"Come, old friend. Walk with me through the caves of *Naro*. There is much for you to know and even more to be done."

Rhem raised his hand to shield his eyes from the brilliant flare of light that appeared before him. After several seconds he blinked, then lowered his hand to find Berezan, emerald cloak covered with ash, pacing before him.

All had been ready to begin their invasion of Glacia at sunrise. When he'd come to advise Berezan of their readiness and found the hut he occupied empty, Rhem had ordered the army of Solarus to stand down. Now, still confused by his Master's strange disappearance of hours ago, Rhem stood silently and watched Berezan, not daring to speak until spoken to.

Berezan stalked before him like a madman, taking three strides, pausing, turning, then stomping back to his original spot, where he would laugh that evil laugh that always brought the hair at Rhem's nape to attention and caused chills to ripple over every inch of his flesh.

Rhem wondered how fate had taken the turn that placed him into the service of this evil man. His life had once been peaceful, but he now lived in constant fear. That same fear caused him to carry out every order Berezan gave to the most minute detail.

Rhem now wondered if whatever horrible torture Berezan could manufacture to cause his death might not be better than waking each sunrise and wondering if some of the evil that drove Berezan might not be invading his soul.

Meanwhile, Berezan reveled in the accelerated beat of his heart that pumped blood through his veins like raging flood waters. Every cell in his body tingled with the thrill of victory.

"Fool!"

Shedding anything that encumbered his movement, Berezan ripped his cloak free and tossed it on the ground. He raised his fingertips to touch his temples and closed his eyes, seeking a vision of his mentor hundreds of miles away in Solarus. His sense of self-power grew twofold when the old man's conjured image appeared in his mind's eye.

"Arrogant, old fool. All of these years you have cautioned me that Gustoff would prove a worthy adversary. Well, you were wrong, Elsbar. Wrong!" Berezan shouted. "You should have been in the valley with me, old man. You would have seen for yourself how useless your teachings of the past twenty-five years have been.

"I have conquered the last obstacle that stands in my path. Nothing can stop me now. Nothing! The Sphere of Light will be mine. Glacia, and the whole of our world will answer to my call. Nothing, no one, can ever take away what rightfully belongs to me again!"

Dismissing Elsbar's effigy, Berezan opened his eyes, spun, and stalked in the opposite direction.

He noticed Rhem and halted. "Why are you standing there, gaping at me?"

"I thought we were to have marched at sunrise, Master. All has been ready, but—"

"Cease. The enemy has been conquered. Have someone fetch my clean cloak. I wish to be presented as befits my station when I arrive in Glacia."

"Yes, Master."

"I shall precede my army into Glacia, Rhem. Have my men ready to move immediately. I will await you . . ." Berezan passed his fingers through his hair. "No. I shall ride at the front of my army in the fashion I have earned. Send a messenger ahead to advise the Elders their time has passed and I expect to find all assembled when I assume the position denied me for so long."

Rhem nodded and hurried away.

Berezan raised his hands to the afternoon skies. Spreading his fingers wide, he uttered words that sent streaks of red fire from his fingertips to soar high into the heavens until they brought thunder down from the clouds.

Chapter Twenty

The aroma was delightful and unlike anything Thea had ever smelled in her life. Inhaling deeply to capture the heavenly fragrance, Thea willed her eyes to remain shut and allowed her senses to fully appreciate the softness and warmth surrounding her.

A rumble deep in her stomach destroyed her pretense.

Thea wiggled her arms free from the mound of fur that provided such warmth and stretched them over her head, tested her muscles for the strength she found missing upon her last waking. Still feeling somewhat weak, but refreshed, she opened her eyes and sat up slowly to find herself alone in the cave.

Searching for the source of the aroma that had awakened her, she discovered someone had left a pot full of something warming on a spit above the fire. The escaping steam hovered in the still air.

Thea remained sitting, afraid to put too much faith in her renewed vitality. When none of the dizziness returned, she climbed to her knees in the middle of the stack of furs and, unable to locate her missing clothing, wrapped the fur coverlet around her body, then scrambled to her feet.

Fur dragging behind her on the cave floor, Thea made her way to the entrance and peeked out. Another stone cavern the same height as the previous one filled her vision. To her left a tunnel ran for about 100 spans before bearing off to the right.

All was quiet. No one appeared to be about.

Thea considered following the tunnel to discover where it led, but discarded the idea in favor of the pleasant aroma that tantalized taste buds that hadn't tasted nourishment for more hours than she cared to remember. She turned and made her way back to the fire.

The mysterious someone who had left the food had also provided a wooden bowl filled with fruit of strange shapes and colors beside the fire pit. Thea couldn't resist plucking a palm-sized orange object from the bowl, bringing it to her nose. Another pleasant aroma filled her senses.

Unsure how to eat the unusual fruit, she pried it open with her fingernails and devoured the juicy pulp within. After wiping her mouth with the back of her hand, she tried another. Then the pot on the spit drew her attention. She discovered a wooden spoon on the floor, picked it up, and dipped it into the pot to sample whatever awaited to appease her hunger.

The tasty vegetables that made up the body of the stew were foreign but filling. Each bite renewed a little bit more of her strength. Finally, Thea sat back on her calves and surveyed the cave once more.

Anger sparked anew. It wasn't hard to discern that Galen had brought her to Borderland instead of taking her home to Glacia, where her abilities were desperately needed, or that he had obviously placed his people before her own.

The immediate danger to the people of Borderland had passed. Berezan's army would now concentrate on Glacia. With Gustoff gone, she alone could stop the inevitable destruction Berezan would bring.

Rising to her feet, Thea tried desperately to shake the feelings of incompetency overwhelming her. She closed her eyes and remembered all Gustoff had taught her, all she'd learned on her own through mind-links with the Ancient Ones. She turned her mind inward, probing for some evidence of the Sphere of Light that lived within her, hoping for some sign, some reassurance.

None came.

Doubts persisted. If some power were thriving within her, she should be able to feel evidence of its existence. Should be able to tap into the wealth of that power and gain insight into her abilities. But she didn't know how. Gustoff had never told her how to summon the power of the Sphere. He had never had time to enlighten her on the full scope of her abilities.

What she had witnessed in the tundra left her confused. She felt great inadequacy, creating uncertainty where at one time blind faith had been.

Just as she did now, Galen had questioned her ability to create the arcs of fire Gustoff and

Berezan had used as weapons in the valley of the tundra.

She raised her hands, palms up, and studied the tips of her fingers. Concentrating hard, she was able to summon no more than the tiny prickles of heat that had warmed Galen's fingers moonrises past.

Tears slid down her cheeks. Thea closed her eyes to stifle the flow. Prickles of heat offered no defense against the horrible lightning that had killed Gustoff. Nor would the abilities she'd mastered to date succeed where all else had failed. She opened her eyes and rose slowly to her feet.

Whether she understood the powers she possessed or not, the protection of Glacia was still her responsibility—her destiny. Nola and Elijah could do no more than pass her words to the people. It was her duty to eradicate the need for such precautions. Her obligation to rid the world of Berezan's evil.

But she couldn't do it from Borderland.

Thea cast another quick glance around the cavern. She had no idea where Galen had gone, or when he would return. Clothing or no clothing, the time for her escape was now, while she still had ability to stand on her own.

Ignoring the drain her activities of the past few moments had on her body, Thea reached deep for whatever was left of her willpower, inhaled, and counted to ten. Three more times she repeated this ritual, each time attempting to place herself deeper and deeper into a trance. Images of her home became clearer, fine details materialized through the fog. Her chamber stood before her, warm fire in the hearth, a soft bed to renew the remainder of her strength.

A startled cry destroyed her concentration.

"Reina?"

A soft voice reached out to her. Another cry, weaker this time, caused a strange tingle to crawl up Thea's spine. She opened her eyes, turned toward the opening of the cave.

Shadows partially hid the tall, thin form of a woman holding a bundle against her hip.

"I am sorry to disturb you, but Galen bade me to return your garments."

The woman stepped forward into the light of the fire. Thea stared in awe at a being almost two hand spans taller than she. She studied the woman's strange clothing, or lack thereof. For her entire life Thea had clothed herself in layer upon layer of fabric for warmth. This woman wore a whisper-thin garment of light blue that hung from her bare shoulders, clung to her abundant breasts, then was belted in at her tiny waist by a braided cord of the same fabric. It fell in a swirl to her knees.

Thea knew she stared rudely at the woman, but she couldn't help herself. All this woman had recently been through was depicted in the condition of her gown. At one time the soft creation must have been lovely. It now hung in tatters from the woman's frame. A great number of holes had been burned into the fabric, exposing bare skin. Dirt had accumulated on the skirt until the light blue appeared gray in several places. A dark stain ended in a long tear that capped the woman's left knee. Glancing down, Thea saw a partially healed wound on her leg, and assumed the stain must have been created by the woman's own blood.

A chill passed over Thea's body.

"I'm sorry. I don't mean to stare at you so, but I didn't expect anyone." Thea stepped forward to greet the woman and held out her hand. The woman draped Thea's heavy woolen robe over her fingers.

"You will need something lighter to wear in our climate, *reina*. The other women are searching their belongings for something small enough to fit you."

The sadness in the woman's voice spoke volumes. Everything the people of Cree had once possessed had been destroyed in Berezan's raid. Thea had a quick mental flash of all Gustoff had told her of the condition of the Borderland villages he had visited. Tears burned her eyes. With so little of their own, the women of Borderland would share their belongings with her.

Thea felt humbled.

"I'm sorry I have disturbed you for so long." The woman turned to walk away.

"Please wait." Thea held her hand out to the woman. "Are you responsible for the fine meal prepared for me?"

The woman glanced toward the pot on the spit and nodded.

"Thank you. It was delicious. I appreciate your kindness."

The woman smiled and attempted to leave the chamber again.

"I have eaten my fill. I hate to think such food would spoil. Won't you please share it with me?"

The woman cast a long gaze over her shoulder toward the pot, then shook her head. "My son is restless, *reina*. I would not have him disturb you."

"Your son? You have a baby in that bundle?" Thea stared in amazement at the bundle the woman held against her hip. It was small, but as she studied it more carefully, she could see the definition of tiny legs and a back outlined under the cloth that covered it head to toe.

A strange emptiness welled within her. Her sheltered life had not afforded her the opportunity to hold a baby in her arms, to touch its tiny body, to see its chubby little fingers and toes. With the exception of the keep staff, the people of Glacia were always glimpsed from afar, their laughter and sorrows diluted by distance.

The woman suddenly reminded Thea of Nola, of times when they were younger and sat outside the keep on sunny days to watch Nola's younger brother play on the ice. But even at that time, Nola's sibling had seen eight winters.

"Please, stay," Thea whispered. She pointed toward the fur pallet near the fire. "Make yourself comfortable. Your son will not disturb me." Thea watched as the woman looked cautiously around the alcove, then made her way toward the pallet. She placed the child down beside her and waited while Thea seated herself. "My name is Thea. Will you tell me yours?"

The woman finally met her gaze. Thea was taken back by the striking resemblance the female had to Galen. Blue eyes, blond hair. Was this a trait of the Creean people? A coincidence?

A strange feeling crawled over Thea's flesh. Who was this woman? Why had Galen sent her to the cave? Galen had never discussed his family. Other than the fact his father and mother had been murdered by Berezan, she knew little about him. Could this woman be . . . Her chest grew tight. Her heart skipped a beat. Was this woman Galen's sister? His mate? Could this little child be—

"Mya."

"Mya," Thea repeated.

"Yes." Tears glossed the woman's blue eyes, spilled over her lashes, and dripped down her cheeks. "The women of Cree gave me the task of tending you, *reina*. They think to take my mind away from the sorrow." Mya wiped her face with the back of her hand, then turned to retrieve her baby from the furs. "I cannot bring my troubles down around you. Deja and I will leave you to your rest."

Thea felt a desperate need to touch this woman's mind, to offer whatever comfort she could to ease the woman's way. "Please, do not leave me, Mya." She reached across the space separating them, touched the woman's hand. "I am a stranger in a strange place. I need a friend."

Mya cuddled her son against her chest, sniffed, then met Thea's gaze. "You are a beautiful woman inside and out. Galen has chosen well."

Thea tried hard to ignore the woman's words. She had to fight down the urge to scream out that Galen had chosen nothing. He had taken her love, betrayed her, left her with a pain inside nothing would ever take away. But this woman had enough problems of her own.

"Call me Thea, Mya." Thea squeezed Mya's hand. "I come from a place far different from Borderland. I have never seen caves such as this one, nor have I ever felt strong sunshine on my face. My home is covered with ice and snow for all the seasons. Other than the granite boulders that protrude above the snow line, I have never seen the earth, nor have I been able to walk around barefoot."

Mya looked down at her feet. A bewildered expression crossed her face.

Thea smiled. To take this woman's mind off of her troubles for a few minutes was worth the time she would lose in returning to her own home, her own problems. "Help yourself to what is left of my meal, Mya."

Mya placed her tiny burden back down on the fur beside her, then reached for the fruit bowl. She devoured several pieces before pausing to look back at Thea.

Thea's heart ached as she remembered the abundance of good, nourishing food grown in the hydro gardens of Glacia. Gustoff had told her the Creeans gardens and livestock had been destroyed. "Do all of your people live in these caves?"

Mya swallowed. "We were forced to flee here after . . . after . . ." Tears sprang to the woman's eyes again. She looked away.

Thea leaned forward. She placed her fingers alongside Mya's temple. "Mya, look at me," she whispered. Mya turned her head slowly, but Thea did not release her touch. "Close your eyes, my new friend. Relax and allow me to ease some of your burdens."

Mya's lashes dipped slowly to her cheeks.

Thea watched for signs of even, shallow breathing. She shoved aside the tiny flare of guilt she felt for touching this woman's mind without permission, then closed her own eyes.

"Tell me what has happened to you, Mya. Let me share your pain."

Mya nodded slowly. "Deja is crying. A loud noise has disturbed his rest."

"Go on."

"People are running, screaming. Smoke is so thick I can hardly find my way across the hut." Mya swayed gently back and forth.

"I cannot breathe!" Mya gasped for air, choking.

"Relax, Mya. You can breathe. Inhale slowly. Draw the air deeply into your lungs, then allow it to escape."

"My eyes burn. I cannot find my son. He's crying louder. I cannot get to him. I cannot see him!"

Mya rubbed her hands against her closed eyes. "Deja! Deja!"

Thea could feel the blood rushing through Mya's veins, the thundering of her heart.

"Fire! There's fire everywhere. I cannot get through. It's hot. My son!"

Mya began to sob. "My knees . . . My hands burn so badly I can hardly place them to the floor. I must get to my son. I must. Oh, Deja!"

Thea probed further into Mya's memory. The baby's cries are louder. He's terrified. He's in pain. Bits of burning wood are falling from the ceiling, charring Mya's back, burning her hair.

She's coughing. Crying. Crawling.

Great booming sounds erupt beyond the hut walls. People are still running. More and more pass the hut. The stone walls begin to pop and hiss with the heat. A great timber rafter engulfed in flames falls to the floor with a loud thump and an eerie hiss.

The baby is silent.

Mya reaches his pallet. She uses his blanket to wrap him up, not knowing the blanket is full of burning bits of wood. She crawls to the doorway, stumbles to her feet, and joins the fleeing multitudes.

Thea wiped at the tears streaming down her own cheeks. Every detail of this woman's anguish washed over her, but she forged on, past the gory details of the invasion to the aftermath.

She sees through Mya's eyes as the woman, babe in arms, stumbles numbly over what is left of her village.

Blood. So much blood. Dismembered bodies with the horror of what they have experienced etched into their faces.

Her mother. Her father. Her sister and her three small children.

Blood. So much blood.

So little hope.

Warriors' bodies. Strange. Garbed in cloaks the color of sand.

She passes people with grief-stricken faces so much like her own shifting through the ashes of their lives.

Searching.

Desperately searching for her mate, Nortu. Praying he did not return from the hunt with the other warriors of Cree.

Thea gently withdrew her touch. She did not need to experience any more of Mya's memories to know Nortu had not survived Berezan's attack of the Borderland.

Thea considered her own grief at Gustoff's passing. She realized such misery was the way of coping with things they could not change, accepting the hurt, and in time, allowing the fond memories to surface.

"Mya, there are things you have experienced you should remember, for those memories will make you wiser as you pass through your life. The pain you have suffered and recall so clearly will lessen in time. I cannot make that go away. But I promise you, I will do what I can for those who remain."

Thea touched Mya's forehead. "Wake up now, Mya."

Mya's lashes fluttered open. She stared blankly at Thea for several seconds.

"May I?"

Mya shook her head. "I'm sorry. I—"

"May I hold your son?"

Mya looked down at the infant at her side. "He is so sick. Trapped here in the caves as we are, there is no way to forage the jungles for the necessary herbs and roots for medicinal purposes. We are very lucky to have sufficient food." Mya reached down and brought the baby into her arms.

Thea studied the child's blanket. No evidence of fabric burns remained. She supposed Mya had disposed of the infant's charred wrapping in order to help her forget. "Please."

Mya looked cautiously at Thea, then slowly handed her precious bundle into Thea's open arms.

The child was so light, so tiny. But it was so hot, almost as if she'd been handed a burning log. Thea cast a questioning gaze at Mya.

"His fever is much worse. He has taken no nourishment in two days," Mya sobbed. "He's all I have left. Now he's being taken away."

The tiny infant squirmed in Thea's arms. "There is life left in his body, Mya, so there is hope," she whispered.

Very carefully, Thea placed the infant on the pallet beside her, praying she wouldn't find what she expected when she pulled the blanket away and exposed the tiny body within. She could not hold back the cry of anguish she made when she folded the fabric back to look at the babe.

Its tiny little arms were so weak the babe could hardly move them. Burns that had partially healed, then festered, covered his legs, his chest, his neck, and completely engulfed one side of the baby's face.

"He was burned in the fire that destroyed our home. I tried to get to him. I tried to save him such a horrible—"

"Shhhh, Mya. Your child senses your anxiety. He's very sick, and your grief is only making him worse."

Mya scrambled to her knees and crawled to the pallet beside Thea. She lovingly touched her infant's face, cooed soft words to him, and leaned to gently kiss his unburned cheek. "Deja, my sweet. Why couldn't it have been me? Why do you have to suffer so?"

Thea touched Mya's shoulder.

"My people have done all they can for him," Mya said. "I know it's only a matter of time before he joins my mate in the hereafter, but I cling desperately to him, Thea. I don't know what will happen to me when there is nothing left, no one to care for, no one to need me. I feel so helpless watching him pass slowly away from me. There are times I wish I could . . . could . . ."

"Your son will not die, Mya."Thea reached down and wrapped her hands around the child's naked body. She lifted him carefully to her chest, cuddled him in her arms. Should her powers ever fail her, she prayed it would not be at this moment, not when this tiny creature needed her so.

She bent her cheek to the top of the infant's head, closed her eyes, and rocked him back and forth. She drew three long breaths, holding each until her lungs burned, then exhaled, each time reaching deeper to touch the part of herself that had the power to heal.

The baby cried out. Thea's skin suddenly seemed to be burning, melting away from her bones, exposing all her nerve endings to the air, and causing excruciating pain. She held on, forged past her own discomfort, absorbed the child's agony.

From a distance Thea could hear Mya crying, but Thea's entire being was caught in a blinding white light, a light that nurtured her, healed her. The light began to fade, leaving in its place a sense of peace, calm.

Thea opened her eyes slowly to discover Mya had fainted and lay on the cave floor before her. She looked down to find a tiny pink infant, free from all blemish, gurgling softly and tugging on a strand of auburn hair.

Thea cried.

Chapter Twenty-One

"Mya."

Thea shook the woman gently. The infant in her arms regained strength rapidly, exercising its lungs to display his need as he fretted against her breast, hungry for the nourishment he had refused for the past two sunrises.

"Mya. *Please*, wake up." The sensation the tiny creature created when he clutched handfuls of her woolen robe, and rubbed his mouth against the heaviness of her breast, caused a strange warmth to flare in Thea's stomach, a deep yearning for something missing from her life. The acknowledgment that this was another of those emotional experiences Gustoff had never explained pulled hard on her heart.

The nagging feeling that she was never meant to experience the same emotions other females felt twisted deep, reminding her of the course of her life decided many moonrises ago.

Tears welled again in her eyes. She was the daughter of destiny, fated for a purpose far beyond that of other mortals, and Gustoff and the Ancient Ones must have deemed the joys of love and motherhood would interfere with her lifepath.

Thea closed her eyes and tried to distance herself from feelings rapidly crumbling her composure. She remembered everything Mya's memories had disclosed, the horror the people of Borderland had witnessed, the grief they must still carry.

Images of Nola, Elijah, and the numerous other servants of Glacia sharpened in her mind. If Berezan succeeded in his evil, each man, woman, and child of Glacia would experience a fate similar to that of the people of Borderland.

Time closed in around her.

Thea opened her eyes and glanced about the cave, at the woman waking on the mat across from her, then down to the babe in her arms. There was much she could do here to assist the people of Borderland in their struggle for survival.

But the Glacians were in imminent danger.

She had no idea how much time had passed since she'd witnessed Gustoff's death in the valley of the tundra. Berezan must have already entered Glacia. Even as she sat contemplating what her next step should be, her people could have suffered a fate very similar to that of Galen's subjects.

She had to leave Borderland. Now.

"Thea!"

The soft whisper was filled with awe. Thea met Mya's astonished gaze, then once again looked down at the babe nestled against her breasts. "Your son will live, Mya."

Mya sobbed great tears of joy as she scrambled across the cave floor and took her son into her arms. "A miracle! It's a miracle."

Thea hadn't expected Mya to bend before her and kiss the helm of her woolen gown, but she did.

"Thank you, *reina*. Thank you."

Thea reached forward and placed her hand upon the woman's shoulder. "Your son is very hungry, Mya. Go now. Give him the nourishment that will replenish his strength."

Mya rose slowly to her feet. "Bless you." She backed quickly out of the cave, cuddling her infant close to her breast, constantly kissing his tiny head.

Thea sat for a moment without moving, thinking about the look of torment on the lovely woman's face when she'd believed her son would soon die. How many other mothers were mourning children like little Deja?

Tormented by her need to return to Glacia, Thea drew a deep breath and closed her eyes. A few hours. How much difference would a few hours make in the overall scheme? Her strength was already depleted to the point she wasn't certain she could transport home. Each time she used her *gifts*, she siphoned even more. Could she risk taking the time it would require to place herself into a rejuvenating trance?

An ache blossomed in her chest, and grew in intensity until Thea knew that no matter what the cost, she could not leave these people there to suffer, could not withhold the powers she'd been born with.

She rose to her feet and took determined strides toward the cave opening. She did not pause when she stepped out into the tunnel she'd thought of investigating earlier, but turned left and continued to walk along the stone corridor, then right for another hundred spans until she stumbled into a large, open space about 200 spans across.

A hundred or so men, women, and children milled quietly around inside of the opening. None noticed her presence. Thea took a moment to study the interior of the huge cave.

A deep crevice split the open area into two sections. Upon closer observation, Thea realized that a clear stream ran through the crevice, giving the survivors of Borderland ample fresh water for their needs. Several large fires burned on each side of the crevice, but the air was not tainted. Thea looked up to discover an opening in the ceiling about ten spans across. Bright sunlight filtered in through the opening, casting a circle of warmth and light at the cave's center and setting the water in the crevice to sparkle.

Hundreds of lumastones brightened the walls, illuminated vast murals depicting strange animals and strong warriors, all in brilliant colors. Thea guessed that if she had time to study the paintings, she would find the history of the Creean people illustrated in the drawings.

Dragging her attention reluctantly from the walls, Thea searched for Galen among the people, expecting to find his tall, golden head towering above the rest. Disappointment tugged for a moment when she could not find him, but Thea decided it was for the best. Her emotions were still too raw to face him and his betrayal.

She stepped through the entrance and walked

toward the throng of people. All eyes turned toward her. Thea had never experienced the feeling of self-consciousness in her life, but when the people began whispering amongst themselves, she knew they were discussing her and she could feel the heat rise to her cheeks.

To overcome the unpleasantness of her feelings, Thea stared into the faces of the people she passed as she made her way toward the center of the cave. She couldn't help notice they all carried the same expression of hopeless despair.

A number of men, obviously warriors, were among the people. Thea compared these men to Galen. They were all tall, their flesh golden bronze from the sun. Their hair, in shades from deep brown to almost white, hung in varying lengths that touched wide shoulders and immense chests. Some of the warriors were shorter than Galen by several inches. Others might have been a bit taller. Old men. Young boys. Each very handsome in his own right.

One tall warrior with a bandage across his chest started toward her. Thea backed up a step, hesitated, then stood her ground. The warrior was almost directly before her when she heard someone call her name from behind.

Thea turned to find Mya, babe in arms, coercing another woman to come forward. Warrior forgotten, Thea gazed at the two small children clinging to the reluctant woman's skirt. Tears once again threatened to fill Thea's eyes.

"Do not be afraid, Abbith. This is Thea of Glacia. She brought my son back from certain death."

Thea's heart wrenched at Mya's words. How much did the people of Cree know about her?

The woman addressed as Abbith knelt before

her, head bowed. Thea grasped the woman by the shoulder. "Don't do this. Do not bow to me. Please."

The woman looked up. Thea's gaze locked with hers. Thea smiled to offer reassurance, then assisted the woman to her feet. The little girl, blond curls dangling beneath a bandage about her head, clung to Abbith's skirt and began to cry. The boy, whom Thea judged to have seen no more than six winters, hid his face in the folds of fabric, but kept his right arm firmly about his little sister's shoulders, offering all the protection he could give.

Thea went to her knees. She reached out for the little boy's hand and drew it from the girl's shoulder. "I won't hurt you or your little sister," she whispered. The boy pushed the fabric of his mother's skirt away and looked into her face.

Tears streamed down his dirt-smudged, pudgy face. "Karn can't see," he said. "The fire burned her, and her eyes won't work."

Thea bit her bottom lip to stifle the cry of anger that rushed to her lips, the waves of hatred that followed. Innocent children! Would Berezan stop at nothing to see his goals met?

Determination filled her breast. Thea looked up at the child's mother, then reached to pull the little boy from behind the protection of her skirts. When she noticed the sling about his small arm, her heart skipped another beat.

Swallowing hard to prevent her anger from turning into tears, Thea reached forward, placing her fingers gently under the boy's chin. "What's your name?"

"Olin," the boy responded softly.

"What happened to your arm?"

"Mother says it's broke."

Thea looked at the boy's mother for confirmation.

"Please . . . help . . . my . . . children . . ." The woman's words were broken by her tears.

Thea closed her eyes. A tremor of doubt raced through her. She desperately wanted to help these children, but she wasn't sure she had the strength. Broken bones were no problem. Thea had mended Nola's brother's arm when she herself was little more than a child, but damaged eyes?

She remembered a moment many moonrises ago when she'd first believed the warrior to be blind. She had touched his mind, found it in turmoil, and knew she could help him overcome his problems given time. But his sight?

Gustoff had always taught her that her powers were gifts, bestowed upon the Ancient Ones to help the people of the world. She had never doubted his teachings, but now . . .

Unmindful of the crowd of people gathered around her, Thea drew a deep breath and reached for the little boy. She carefully removed the sling from his arm, then ran her fingers along his limb to determine the position of the break.

"I won't hurt you," she whispered, then closed her eyes. Bright light burned once again inside her head. She could feel her arm twist, the bone bending in an unnatural way until it pierced the muscle of her forearm. Pain grew in intensity for a moment; then the light grew brighter, brighter still, until the sense of peace she had felt many times before overcame her.

Swaying back and forth on her knees, she groped for the boy's shoulder to steady herself and opened her eyes. The little boy was staring down at his arm, wiggling his fingers, bending his elbow.

His arm was healed, but the cost to Thea's weakened condition was great. She felt the tragedies and turmoil of the last few moonrises drain her energy. She ignored the astonished whispers and murmurs from the crowd and reached for the little girl. The young boy scampered away, whooping and hollering.

Thea carefully peeled the bandages from Karn's head, then dropped the cloths to the floor. She placed her hands alongside the girl's cheeks, raising her face higher. "Open your eyes for me, Karn. I promise I will not harm you in any way."

The little girl's lashes fluttered several times as if she felt pain from exposure to the light. Thea took this as a sign Karn's eyes had not been severely damaged and continued her perusal. She noticed the dried blisters around her small eyes and thin, scorched blond brows.

Thea looked once again to the child's mother. "The gift I possess will allow me to heal the burned tissues of her eyes, but I cannot restore her sight if any damage has been done beyond what we see."

The woman nodded in understanding.

Thea placed her palms over the little girl's eyes. She closed her own eyes, ignored the weakness that grew by the moment to siphon her energy, and concentrated on making the little girl whole again.

It took every ounce of stamina she had in reserve to open her eyes and draw an even breath, but the expression of tenderness in the woman's eyes as she stared down into her girl child's face was enough to garner the energy Thea needed to rise slowly to her feet.

"The tissue is healed, Abbith. Clean bandages should be placed back over Karn's eyes for several more days to allow the healing process to complete itself."

Thea turned to walk away, but found herself enclosed from all sides by other women, each carrying an injured child, all begging for her help.

She looked from one desperate face to another, closed her eyes, offered a swift prayer, then reached out to a woman who stood before her with an infant in her arms and one still growing in her belly.

Chapter Twenty-Two

"Take this."

Galen turned to find Kajar holding the emblem of the bronze sun he had taken from his father's neck. The same emblem Galen had rejected when he allowed his emotions to override his common sense and set out after Berezan many sunrises ago.

Galen held out his hand. Kajar draped the golden-linked chain across his palm. Clutching the chain firmly, Galen felt the warmth of the metal sear his flesh. It was his destiny to lead the people of Borderland. His duty to keep them safe, provide ample nourishment, medicine, shelter. A responsibility he had forsaken in his hour of grief.

He closed his eyes against the memories that tormented him, both the bitter and the sweet. Instead, he thought about what had befallen his people, what could still befall his people, and that there was little he could do to stop it.

He had witnessed firsthand the evil powers of Berezan, stood high above and watched as two men possessed with abilities he had never considered possible attempted to destroy each other. Abilities he nor his few remaining warriors could conquer or imitate.

For the last two hours, he and Kajar had walked through the many winding tunnels of *Naro*. During that time he had told Kajar of all he had experienced since leaving Cree. Kajar had, in turn, told him of all the events that had taken place in Cree since his departure.

They had discussed strategies they could have used *if* they were preparing to defend against a natural foe.

Much talk. But no solutions.

Now his best friend stood beside him, demanding he take his place as heir to Borderland, *regis* of a desperate race of people with little hope for the future.

Galen's hands trembled as he placed the medallion around his neck and felt the heavy disc fall against his chest. A strange warmth began to flow through his body, renewing his spirit, lifting him from the clutches of defeat that ridged his shoulders.

The blood of Shakara ran through his veins. A warrior's heart beat within his chest. The warrior's creed, something he'd forsaken many sunrises ago, echoed in his mind. Death with honor in defense of his own, no matter the foe, had been the war song he'd lived by, would go on living by until the last breath left his body.

"There must be a way to separate Berezan from

his army," Galen said. "From what we have experienced firsthand, those men fight as we do, with weapons we can defeat."

Kajar shook his head. "We are only a little more than a hundred strong, Galen. Our scouts report Berezan's army numbers in the thousands."

Galen paced before his friend. A hundred different strategies bounded around in his mind. He rubbed his chin, tried to place himself into Berezan's position. What if the men who made up Berezan's army were reluctant participants? Suppose there were those among the vast numbers who did not want to create the havoc on which Berezan seemed to thrive?

The warriors of Borderland had trained their entire lives to reach their state of physical accomplishment. To his knowledge, the men of Solarus had never been warriors. By all the accounts he had heard, the people of Solarus were farmers and herdsmen who eked out a meager living from the hot desert sands.

Berezan had obviously used the threat of his evil to turn docile men into a militia. Men who killed rather than be killed.

Would this fact work to Galen's advantage? Offer some firm ground on which they could fight?

"What do you know of this mysterious Sphere of Light, Galen? Why would it be so important Berezan would kill everyone in his path to obtain it?"

Galen looked at Kajar. His friend had leaned against the stone wall, crossing his arms over his chest, and stood watching, waiting patiently for an answer. "From what I learned from Gustoff of Glacia," Galen said, "the Sphere is an ancient talisman, handed down through the generations by a people the Glacians refer to as the Ancient Ones. This Sphere is supposed to protect the world from evil."

"Some protection," Kajar grunted. "If this talisman was supposed to be in Gustoff's possession at Glacia, why did Berezan invade Borderland, then from what we were told by the survivors, spend numerous sunrises searching for it among the destruction created by his army? Nothing fits."

Galen agreed. The more he thought about all Gustoff had told him in the corridor of Glacia, the less sense his words made. If Gustoff truly possessed some magical force that would destroy Berezan, why had he allowed the demon to wreak such havoc over the world? Why had Gustoff himself perished?

Kajar pulled away from the wall and paced three steps before turning. "If this Sphere is to protect from evil, why would Berezan want it? Seems to me something that destroys the type of magic Berezan creates would be the last item he would wish to possess."

Galen studied the anguished expression on Kajar's face and wished he had some way to ease his torment. But he had asked himself that same question numerous times over the past few sunrises. He still had no answer.

"This Glacian woman you brought home with you is also supposed to be able to control the Sphere and use it to destroy Berezan?" Kajar asked, confused.

Galen sighed heavily. "Thea has been taught the whole of her life to believe she carries special powers within her. Gustoff proclaimed it to be her destiny to wield the Sphere against Berezan and destroy him."

"Do you believe this tiny woman capable of such deeds?"

Galen closed his eyes, raising his hands to run his fingers through his hair. He remembered the battle he had witnessed in the tundra, the horrible aftermath that had left huge, charred pits in the snow.

Unbidden, Gustoff's words echoed through his mind. *All things in life have a purpose. Yours is to stand by Thea's side, to help her see her destiny through.*

Other memories followed. He saw Thea as she had been in the steam bath, beautiful, curious, and willing to share herself completely. Innocent, yet seductive. As clearly as if she were standing beside him, he felt her touch on his body. The effects of that remembered touch almost staggered him.

Galen recalled Thea as she had been in the alcove only hours ago. Her attempts to use her powers to save her mentor had depleted all of her strength, leaving her in a state of total exhaustion. When she had awakened briefly, staring into his eyes, he had read agony, confusion, pain. She had been too weak to leave her dream state for more than a few moments, but in that small space of time, he had sensed her feelings of betrayal.

He sensed it still.

To face Berezan is her destiny. Gustoff's words once again filled his mind. *She must be in Glacia to wield that power.*

A sharp pain jabbed into Galen's heart. Was it possible the old man had spoken the truth? Had he made a serious mistake in his attempt to protect the woman he loved? By taking her away from her homeland had he doomed them all?

"Well, do you?"

"I don't know. I have experienced some of her strange powers, Kajar. She immobilized me with the slightest touch of her fingers. I've seen her heal wounds, leaving no evidence they ever existed. And I've seen her disappear in a flash of light so bright it was near blinding. Yet no matter how hard I try, I cannot envision Thea striking another being to death with an arc of fire."

"Then you believe the tale told to you by the old man?"

Galen shook his head. "There is so little left to believe, Kajar. All we know has been taken from us by powers we never knew existed before Berezan invaded our world. Who's to say whether Thea, diminutive as she may be, might accomplish what the mighty warriors of Cree could not."

"Maybe we should do everything in our power to assist her towards her goal."

"A part of me says yes, another part no. I have been taught all of my life to protect the women left in my charge. Somehow, it seems if we allow Thea to proceed with what she believes is her destiny, she will be protecting us."

Kajar placed his hand upon Galen's shoulder. "This woman, is she your chosen mate?"

"She is to me what no other can ever be, my friend. I have made her mine, though I don't believe she would agree with me at this moment. Thea thinks I have betrayed her by bringing her to Borderland when the people of Glacia need her so desperately."

"Have you?"

Galen thought for several moments before

answering. "Perhaps, but at the time, I acted to save her life."

Galen reached down, grabbed the bronzed medallion dangling against his chest, and lifted it until the polished metal glistened in the sun. "Gustoff came to Borderland to seek my father's aid in forming an alliance to protect both Cree and Glacia from Berezan's wrath. In my pain, when he approached me with the same request, I adamantly refused him.

"But as I finally accept the responsibilities attached to this medallion, I acknowledge the old man's heart was true when he proposed a joint effort. The people of Borderland and the people of Glacia must unite to protect what they possess."

Galen closed his eyes and cursed Berezan's rotten soul to burn in eternal damnation.

"Thea is a very stubborn woman, my friend. Over the past few sunrises she has experienced more pain and frustration than many suffer their entire life. She is exhausted, but she will do everything in her power to get home. In her present condition, a hasty act will mean certain death."

Galen opened his eyes and stared into his friend's face.

"Nothing will be gained by making an unplanned march on Glacia. By the time we arrive, Berezan will have already committed all of the mayhem he is capable of. The only thing we will accomplish is to warn him of our retaliation."

Galen thought about the hidden doorway he had found on the lower level. He was still convinced the cold air that had seeped in around the door meant the entrance led outside of the keep.

An entrance that could be used to their advantage. "There are secret entrances into the Governing House of Glacia, ones I pray Berezan knows nothing about. A force as few as ours could sneak into the keep under the cover of darkness.

"I have had the opportunity to explore Glacia's Governing House over the last few mooncycles. I know where the best areas of defense lie.

"A rational, structured invasion would allow us to seriously deplete Berezan's army and increase our chances of victory. But our plans must be carefully drawn."

Kajar agreed. "We also need time to mass our warriors and to instruct them as to what they might expect when the warriors of Borderland finally come face to face with Berezan's wrath."

"I pray our warriors never come within a thousand spans of Berezan, Kajar," Galen whispered.

"Are you prepared to believe what you have been told about your woman?"

"Do I have another choice? All that's left is to convince Thea I have not betrayed her, to make her understand that alone she has no chance against Berezan and his army. But first, Thea must be given time to recuperate from her past ordeals."

Galen slapped Kajar on the shoulder. "Come, my friend. It is time you met the woman who has captured my heart."

Thea had no idea how long she had been functioning on willpower alone. She had stumbled from one ailing Creean to another, digging deeper and deeper into herself for the courage and strength it took to make another being whole. Hours ago she had lost count of the people she had touched. Yet hundreds more awaited her, desperately needing her help.

She leaned heavily on the strong arm of a warrior who had called himself Thorn, one she had touched to heal a festering wound in his chest created by one of Berezan's invaders. Since then, he had made himself her champion, supporting her as she walked, offering her food and drink, demanding she not tire herself further, then making sure the people who sought her aid were those with the greatest needs.

Thea found herself leaning more and more on Thorn's strength. She liked the big warrior, and though he bore little resemblance to Galen, she saw in him the same qualities of integrity and honor.

Through it all, every other sentence out of the warrior's mouth was praise for Galen.

"Another child, *reina* Thea."

He simply refused to call her Thea. *"Reina"* seemed to be a term of affection these people placed upon those females they held in great esteem, and Thea felt honored by their praise. All of her life she had been "Thea," daughter of Arlin, stepsister of Alec, a female in a society where a woman's worth was judged by the number of children she had or how she took care of her man.

A tiny voice in her mind argued that the people of Glacia never knew of the powers she possessed, but another voice stated emphatically that it would have made no difference. A female was simply a female under the *Articles*. No more, no less.

She looked into Thorn's deep brown eyes and

tried to smile. Nola's sweet face materialized, and Thea realized just how perfect this warrior would be for her lifelong friend.

Thea shook her head, chastising herself for such silly thoughts and blaming her sudden flight of fantasy on fatigue. She reached forward to touch the child in Thorn's arms. Fever burned like fire through the boy child's tiny body. He was weak, and from the appearance of his lips, looked to be dehydrated.

"Has this child been given no liquid?" she asked his mother.

A tall, dark-haired woman stepped forward. "I have tried repeatedly to force water past his lips, *reina*. It will not stay with his stomach. His fever burns hotter by the moment. Can you help my child as you have helped the others? Please, don't let my baby die."

"Thea!"

Thea turned to find Galen stalking furiously toward her. The crowd of people who had been standing near parted to allow him passage. She looked at the tiny child in Thorn's arms, then back toward Galen. Anger hovered about him like a cloud as each long stride brought him nearer.

Defiance welled within her. She took the baby from Thorn's arms. "Restrain him, Thorn. This child needs my attention and I cannot allow Galen to restrict my help."

"But, *reina*," Thorn protested.

She looked up into his eyes. "Please."

Thorn shook his head and walked toward the warrior whose presence in the cave reminded her of a renegade equox.

Forging beyond whatever what might be transpiring behind her, Thea closed her eyes and hugged the child to her chest.

Moments later, the last thing she would remember was falling exhausted into strong arms.

And those arms were not Thorn's.

Chapter Twenty-Three

Thousands of men, women, and children lined the ice-covered roadway that wound through the center of Glacia and approached the keep, but the silence was deafening. Even the wind, which blew constantly through the high mountain passes, was calm.

Nothing moved.

Berezan looked up. Thick gray clouds hung heavy in the air, obscuring the jutting peaks of the mountains surrounding the city, blocking out the sun.

The eerie creak of Berezan's saddle as he stood in his stirrups to survey all around him pierced the quiet like the shriek of a wild creature. Berezan looked into the faces of the people standing near, saw the terror he knew would be there, and smiled.

He had withstood two moonrises of unnecessary frozen travel for this moment, but every discomfort had been worth it. Glacia was his. Yet his victory was not complete.

Spurring his equox into motion, Berezan rode slowly through the winding streets, passing hundreds more frightened faces. He gazed about, taking in all he commanded. The houses, constructed from the silver-flecked granite so abundant in these mountains, were as he remembered them—tiny, no more than four rooms each. The roofs were several spans thick and woven from boughs of the mighty *piceas* that thrived in the snow-filled valleys below the city to the north. Windows, covered with wooden shutters, kept out the blinding light of the sun reflected off the snow and the howling winds usually present.

His party passed an intersecting roadway. Berezan stared at the huge metal vats that burned constantly on the corner.

The closer he came to the keep, the more familiar his surroundings became. As a young boy, he remembered running through the ironsmith's shop, watching in awe as the fires that burned in the pits turned heavy chunks of black ore into flaming spears of red. Clearly, he remembered the hissing of the steam created when the smith plunged the hot rods into a vat of cold water, the way it burned his eyes, his fingers if he got too close.

He closed his eyes. Vivid pictures came to his mind, images he had recreated over and over again for 25 years. There had been a time when he was a normal boy, able to run and slide along the icy passages with the other children of Glacia. He had been the cherished heir to all around him, loved by a mother whose face he could not remember, a father for whom he now felt only a deep hatred.

Bitter memories churned the fire in Berezan's blood. Arlin DeLan. The name burned deeply in Berezan's chest. His father, the one who had forsaken him. A man who had never searched for him, had forgotten he even existed.

Berezan opened his eyes and, this time, saw the city of Glacia in a different light. He pushed memories of the past far back into a hidden corner of his mind.

Glacia was his. *His!* On the eve of his thirty-second winter, all that had been taken away had been returned. Anyone who thought to oppose his destiny would perish.

"Rhem!"

Berezan turned to face the columns of men who stood at attention behind him—his army—thousands strong in flanks that lined the icy streets six deep and 500 spans in length. Men who would carry out his orders without question. They had no choice. Just as the people of Glacia had no choice.

Peasants, all of them. Men who aspired no higher in life than to dredge out a meager existence. He cared little that his army had been unequipped to transverse the miles of frozen wasteland, that their clothing, suited for warmer climates, had caused more than one death.

Berezan's purpose had been met.

He looked down from his position high atop the equox to stare into Rhem's face. "Disburse this crowd immediately. Send these people to their homes and post guards along the streets to see that they remain there. Anyone caught disobeying my orders is to be executed."

283

Moments later, the streets stood silent, deserted, except for the guards his commander had posted along the slippery walkways. Berezan spurred his mount, listening to the clopping of his beast's hoofbeats as they echoed off the mountainsides.

The wind reappeared, whipping through the passages, stinging his face. Snowflakes fell from the clouds. Berezan drew his emerald cloak around him.

"Master!"

Berezan looked ahead to find his commander standing on the street corner, back turned to the fire in the vat. Berezan pulled back on the reins.

"Master, your army freezes."

"Do you question my orders?"

Rhem shook his head. "No, Master. It's just that so many have already died from the cold, I fear our numbers will be weakened."

Startled by Rhem's comments, when in the past he had offered no voice, Berezan looked around and studied the men posted along the roadway. Each man hugged himself to ward off the cold, and attempted to brush away the snow that fast accumulated on their clothing.

"Send a party to search each house. Have them confiscate all warm clothing found and distribute it to my men."

"Thank you, Master." Rhem nodded and quickly set about his task.

Berezan once again spurred his mount and rounded the last bend that would take him home. He never tried to see beyond the blinding snow or to look up at the sight he knew would be just as he had left it so many years ago. The keep, positioned a hundred spans above the roadway, appeared as a natural formation in the mountainside. Berezan knew better.

He remembered each stone, carved to fit perfectly together to create the rounded surface of Glacia's Governing House. He could see in his mind each of the balconies that jutted away from the mountain, the deep crevice cut into the stone that formed a tunnel almost 50 spans deep, a tunnel lit by thousands of tiny lumastones. He could envision the ornate wooden doors at the end of that tunnel and what lay beyond.

He closed his eyes as his equox picked its way carefully over the icy bridge across the deep crevice that separated Glacia's primary mountain from the rest. He allowed his mount free rein, knowing the beast would seek shelter from the cold and snow deep within the tunnel.

His mind conjured up the vision of the first place he intended to visit. His flesh tingled in anticipation of a warm steam bath that would wash away years of sandy residue from his skin.

"Nola! Here!"

Nola turned in a circle, seeking the source of the voice that reached her above the howling wind. She pushed her fur-lined hood closer to her ears, covering all of her face except her eyes.

"Here, Nola!"

Nola squinted to make a out a dark figure huddling behind one of the houses that lined the avenue. Trusting her instincts to know it was Elijah, she hurried in his direction, careful to look over her shoulder to avoid the horrible soldiers who were moving from house to house, ordering everyone inside.

As if the people of Glacia needed to be told to stay

inside when the wind and snow reached blizzard proportions!

Nola blew out a disgusted sigh. "Elijah!"

"Come here, girl. You'll catch your death." Elijah grasped her around the arm and pulled her through a back doorway. He pulled the panel shut against the wind and cold, then ushered her over to a fire pit burning brightly at the room's center.

"I'd all but given up hope for you, girl. What took you so long?"

Nola shrugged out of her wrap and handed it to a woman standing near. She nodded thanks, then bent to warm her hands before the fire. "It wasn't easy sneaking out of the keep with all those hideous soldiers rumbling about. As it was, I had to use the exit we led Thea and the warrior to when they left the keep." She raised her warm hands to cup her cheeks.

Elijah tugged impatiently upon her arm. "Were you successful?"

"The keep is empty. The foodstuffs harvested over the past four moonrisings have been distributed among the households of Glacia. All members of the staff were able to get out before that demon's men got in." Nola turned to look Elijah in the eye. "I hope he finds it lonely in that big stone monster all by his evil self!"

"Here, dear. You need something warm inside you."

Nola looked over Elijah's shoulder to find a very pregnant blond woman holding a cup of something that steamed delightfully. Outwardly Nola smiled, but inside she hoped the woman didn't decide to give birth while they were confined to these tiny quarters.

Elijah stepped to the woman's side. "I'm sorry, Nola. This is my oldest son's wife, Willa. That's my only grandchild, Lemont, and my son, Julian."

A little blond boy Nola guessed to be no more than six winters huddled into the arms of Elijah's son. Nola placed her cup on the table, then walked across the room and dropped to her knees before the child. She reached out, attempting to touch the boy's face, but the boy turned and buried his head beneath his father's arm.

"Lemont is still upset over seeing all of those strange men in the streets of Glacia," Julian said.

"Aren't we all," Nola replied. She bowed her head, then rose. "I'm pleased to meet all of you."

She retrieved her cup and turned back to Elijah. "How about you, Elijah? Were you able to get Thea's message to the people outside the keep?"

Elijah nodded. "Julian and my other son Tomas helped me pass the word. I'm just sorry we didn't have time to flee into the mountains and go to Dekar."

"Do you think everyone will cooperate?" Nola brought the steaming cup of herb tea to her lips and drained the contents. She handed the empty cup back to Willa. "Thank you."

"I believe any doubts the people of Glacia had were set aside when Berezan and his army entered the city. I don't think anyone will want any part of him or his evil doings."

"Good. Now, all we have to do is wait for Thea or Gustoff to return and—"

Thump! Thump! Thump!

All eyes in the room turned toward the door.

Julian eased his son into his mother's arms and stood. He walked to the door, threw back the bolt, and opened it. A soldier stood huddled before the

287

door for shelter from the blast of cold air and snow.

"The Master has ordered that you relinquish all warm clothing to his army! You will do so immediately or we will search your home and take what we need."

Indignation swelled within Nola. She hurried around the room, gathered up all the cloaks, then walked to the door. "Here. Take these. The citizens of Glacia know better than to stand outside in weather like this! Now, leave this house!" She slammed the door in the soldier's face.

"Nola!"

Nola, realizing what she had done, turned sheepishly and stared into Elijah's eyes. "I'm sorry. I just . . . just . . ."

Willa hurried across the room and placed her arm about Nola's shoulder. "We understand, dear. Come. Make yourself comfortable. We are liable to be here for many moonrises to come."

Nola sighed. "I wish Thea and Gustoff were here!"

"We all do, Nola," Elijah whispered. "We all do."

Chapter Twenty-Four

Galen once again found himself watching Thea sleep. The hours had abated his anger, but the memories remained. Over and over he saw Thea stumbling around in the large cave, approaching one Creean after another, giving her healing touch to make them whole, while each effort took away more and more of her strength. Her face had been pale as death when she collapsed into his arms. The circles already present beneath her beautiful eyes had darkened from light purple to charcoal.

"Thea. Precious Thea," he whispered. "You give all that you have to help the others and save little for yourself." He bent his head to kiss the pale forehead nestled against his breastbone. "Gustoff said it was my destiny to stand at your side, not before you to shield you, but beside you as your strength." He shook his head. "I doubt when you awake you will accept any assistance I might offer."

Galen inhaled, drawing the fragrance that was Thea's alone deeply into his mind. Many times in the sunrises he had known her, he had doubted her, believed her to be Berezan's pawn. He had once spent a great deal of time trying to decide if Thea DeLan was truly as innocent as she seemed when she touched him.

Gustoff's words haunted him. He didn't want to believe Thea was all Gustoff claimed her to be, but with each unselfish act of kindness she performed, every evidence of the power within her he witnessed, the old man's words seemed more and more accurate.

A great tenderness foreign to his warrior's nature grew within him. Galen longed to tell Thea of his affection, to explain what she believed to be his betrayal had been the act of a desperate man attempting to protect the woman he loved.

But he could not. Too much still stood between them.

He stroked her arm, her shoulder, buried his hand in her hair, and caressed the back of her neck. He thought about the battle ahead, his people, Glacia's subjects, and Thea.

How many more would die?

Thea opened her eyes slowly to find her head pillowed against Galen's hard chest, her body stretched over the mounds of fur that made up his bed. She chewed her bottom lip to keep from groaning as she felt his large, callused hand glide over the exposed flesh of her arm, her shoulder, rekindling fires deep inside her she fought to douse.

Her eyes burned from the fullness of tears, but Thea refused to allow them to fall. Instead, she used the heat of his touch to fuel her only defense against his nearness. Anger. She had used him. He had used her. What had been between them could not be repeated. In the moonrises ahead she would miss the feel of his arms around her, the heat of his flesh against her own, his mouth, his hands.

She swallowed hard to subdue the groan that gathered in her throat.

"Thea?"

The sound of his voice rippled over her flesh, caused her heart to sputter. She drew a deep breath, raised her hand, placed it against the hardness of his abdomen, and pushed.

"Release me, Galen." The hand he had twisted in her hair fell away. Thea took advantage of her freedom and sat up. A wave of dizziness passed over her, then subsided. She kicked her feet, freeing them from the confines of the heavy fur, and swung her legs to the cave floor.

"Where is my clothing?"

She felt the furs move beneath her, and turned to see Galen reach to the floor and pick up her woolen robe. She snatched it out of his hand, pulled it over her shoulders, and drew three more determined deep breaths before she rose slowly to her feet. She dared not take a step for several seconds.

"You should get more rest before attempting to walk about, Thea. You have already expended too much energy over the past few sunrises."

Thea cast a glance over her shoulder to find Galen still seated on the fur pallet, clothed in the same taut leggings and tall leather boots so many of the other warriors of Cree wore. The dim glow of the fire glistened off the fine sheen of perspiration on his bare chest.

But something different had been added. A thick gold chain hugged the cords of his neck and dropped to his breastbone. Suspended from that chain was a bronze-colored object she could not identify. Curiosity almost caused her to ask what the object was, but she suppressed the urge. Since he had not worn it in Glacia, it apparently was some symbol of his authority in Cree—a symbol that brought their different destinies into sharp focus.

Thea swallowed hard. Galen displayed the powers bestowed upon him by his ancestors proudly on his chest. Hers were hidden deep within, but were no less binding, no less restricting to any wishes she might have otherwise. Fate had chosen a path for her life to follow, and she could not forsake her duty.

"I have no time to consider anything other than my people, Galen. I must return to Glacia immediately."

"You cannot."

She met his intense stare. "I will do what I must, Galen of Borderland." Before he could offer further argument, Thea hurried to the cave entrance, determined to be away from him before she collapsed and proved she was not strong enough to undertake the necessary mission.

"Thea."

She had not heard Galen stand or walk across the cave. The whisper of his breath over the side of her face caused her to shiver. She bowed her head, fighting familiar longings that, no matter how hard she tried, could not be conquered. Then, just as suddenly, she sensed he had stepped away. Thea turned to find Galen had crossed to the fire pit at the cave's center and looked down into the flame.

She studied his tall form. The flicker of the fire sent patches of light dancing over his muscular chest, defining the tension in his arms, the enlarged veins that protruded from the top of his hand as he clenched his fist.

"I cannot allow you to leave Borderland, Thea of Glacia."

His words were soft, final.

All they had shared had finally come to this. "Am I your prisoner, Galen? Have you brought me to Borderland to hold me against my will?"

Galen's bark of laughter sent another chill down her spine. "How could I possibly hold you if you are determined to leave?"

You could tell me you love me, Galen. Make me believe all that has gone on between us is real. Ask me to stay by your side. Say no matter what should happen in the future, we will face it together.

Thea betrayed none of her inner turmoil as she stepped to Galen's side.

"Each of us has responsibilities." She reached to touch the bronze medallion. "Your people need you. Mine need me. Just as your duties as new *regis* of Cree demand your attention, my destiny is also about to be fulfilled. I must meet Berezan in Glacia. I *must* do everything I can to see that his rein of terror ends. I have no choice."

She touched his arm, felt it tremble. Her heart ached, her mouth felt dry, and she had to make three attempts before her voice finally worked. "Galen."

He turned his head and looked down to meet her gaze. His features were distorted by firelight and shadow, but his eyes blazed with another unnamed emotion. Thea swallowed. "I must leave," she said softly. Before he could offer another objection that might chip away at her resolve, Thea dropped her hand to her side, turned, and walked toward the cave opening.

"Go. I cannot stop you."

Galen closed his eyes to the sight of her walking away from him. His tensed muscles ached, but he continued to hold firm, knowing if he weakened, if he gave in to the tremendous fury burning deep in his gut, he would be lost. His emotions ran rampant, churning with the intensity of the storms that raged through Borderland when the monsoons came.

He drew a deep breath and held it, listened to the pounding of his heart as it echoed against his brain. "Thea."

She stopped, but did not turn. He shook his head and crossed the space that separated them, pausing so close to her back he could smell her soft fragrance. His hand trembled as he laid it upon her shoulder. He felt her tremble in return beneath his touch.

Galen bent to place his face against her hair. "Thea."

"Please, Galen, don't do this."

He placed his other hand upon her shoulder, turning her until she faced him, their bodies separated by less than inches, but she kept her face averted. Galen released her shoulders, placed his hands tenderly beneath her jaw, and lifted her face. When he saw tears slipping through her clenched lashes, his anger disappeared.

"Thea, look at me."

Thea tried to shake her head, but his hands, the gentle pressure he applied, held her immobile. She didn't want to look at him, didn't want to see the man whose very presence stripped away years of training and left in its place only a raw desire to be in his arms.

"Look at me."

Thea bit her lip and tried to think of what lay ahead of her, but she could not concentrate, could not get past the anticipation twisting through her body, circling, swirling, racing through every nerve until her flesh tingled.

His hands slipped from her jaw to her neck, drawing her face closer as he bent his head. His mouth was less than a breath away, stealing her willpower, replacing it with a want, a need, far deeper than any mystical force that might lie within her. He gazed into her eyes, casting his own arduous spell, holding her in a sensuous web she had no desire to escape.

All sense of reality was lost when his mouth touched hers and began that motion so familiar, gently shaping her lips to his.

His tongue probed for entrance, found no resistance, and challenged hers to the same erotic dance they had shared many times before.

Thea slid her hands slowly up the muscled planes of his chest, past the medallion that built the final wall between them, wound her fingers in his golden hair. When his hand slipped beneath the folds of her woolen robe to caress the aching fullness of her breast, she leaned against his hard body for support.

She moaned in protest when his hand slid away. In response he deepened his kiss, asking, begging, demanding her total surrender. Galen's hand slipped lower to the juncture of her thighs. Thea welcomed his exquisite touch, arching her body so he might ease the ache within her.

She cried out when he pulled his mouth from hers, abandoning her lips to kiss the soft flesh of her neck and lower, to the wool-covered tautness of her breast. She clasped both hands, fingers entwined, behind his head and held him against her.

Galen slid quivering hands beneath the roundness of her buttocks to raise her from the floor, then silently cursed his own hunger when he heard Thea draw a startled gasp and grow stiff in his arms.

He tightened his embrace, holding her against him, breast to chest, her feet dangling above the floor. He buried his face into the hollow of her neck, inhaled her sweetness, and tried to still the raging force within himself, to conquer the urgency in his loins. He loosened his embrace. Thea slid slowly down the length of his body, torturing him with the softness and warmth he desperately needed to ease the aches of denial.

"Galen," Thea whispered, clutching at him for the support her wobbly knees failed to give. She panted for breath, needing a fresh supply of oxygen to restore the self-control Galen fast stripped away. She looked up into his eyes, saw the deep blue, and recognized the passion that burned just within the barriers of control. She dropped her gaze to his chest. She couldn't look at him, couldn't witness the same desperate need within him that she carried.

Thea closed her eyes, remembered the pledge she'd made never to allow the lovemaking they had shared in the past to be repeated. Her memories were already too vivid, too raw. She needed to leave Borderland, leave him. Destiny called her. She had to use all of her powers of concentration to meet the challenges of the future.

"We—"

He placed his finger over her lips, hushing her denial. Thea tried to slip away from him, but he refused to release her. She considered transporting from his embrace, but the safety of his arms was like a balm to her soul, a comfortable haven in a world of strife and turmoil.

"Spare me a few minutes before you leave Borderland, Thea. Walk with me."

Startled, Thea looked up at Galen. He released her from his arms and stepped back.

"Come." Galen held out his hand. Thea watched it for several heartbeats, waging a silent war with herself, one side demanding she take his hand, hold it to her heart, the other arguing this was her chance to sever the bond between them, to refuse and turn away, to distance herself, her heart, from the ties that secured her eternally to him.

She placed her hand into his.

Without another word, Galen led her from the cave, down the long corridor of stone that ended in the great cave where she'd met so many of his people, and beyond, through another set of winding, hot tunnels deeper and deeper into the mountain.

Thea followed in silence, listening only to their soft footsteps as they trod through yet another tunnel. They passed several people. Galen stopped to speak with each one. She ignored his words, studying instead the look of adoration on each

Creean's face, the forthright manner in which they spoke to their *regis*, the way Galen absorbed their every word before continuing.

In Thea's weakened state, their trek seemed miles. She looked ahead, beyond Galen's tall form, and found they traveled toward a bright light. As they grew nearer the light, Thea realized the source was an opening in the cave a hundred spans ahead.

Beyond the cave opening, Thea shielded her eyes with her free hand until they adjusted to the brilliance of the jungle sun.

They stood on a small plateau overlooking a clear pool of water shimmering in the dapples of sunlight that filtered down through the trees around it—trees unlike any Thea had ever imagined. Mammoth trunks, dark brown in color, reached to touch the heavens before displaying a profusion of leaves bent toward the ground longer than she was tall. Greens in shades ranging from almost black to a soft hue rustled softly in the light breeze that floated around her.

She followed the trunk of the tree closest to her, down its magnificent length to the base, to find yet another profusion of color. Leaves, hundreds of different shapes and sizes, in as many shades of brown, yellow, and green as there were species, hugged the jungle floor. Through this tangle of greenery, a multitude of tiny flowers grew, displaying a full rainbow of color. The breeze mixed the fragrances, filling her nostrils with a scent more enticing than anything she'd ever smelled.

Humid air swirled around her, warmed her flesh, and relaxed her muscles.

"This pool feeds an underground spring that flows through the middle of *Naro*. The fresh water you saw in the main cave begins here."

Galen's words shattered the spell that had captured her. Thea looked to find he had leaned against the side of the stone walkway, crossing his arms over his chest, and now watched her carefully, almost as if he were judging her impression of his homeland.

"It's beautiful, Galen. I never imagined such a display of nature could exist. Often I have thought of the magnitude of the snow-covered hills of Glacia, of the *piceas* with boughs bending to earth beneath their burden of snow and ice, and believed nothing on our world could equal that sight. I see I have been wrong."

Galen pulled away from the wall and walked to the patch of greenery and flowers she had studied. He pulled up a small bouquet and brought it to her hand. Thea couldn't resist bringing the tiny blossoms to her nose and inhaling several times to capture their fragrance, enclosing it tightly in her memory.

Thea looked up at Galen, watched his face, saw his blue eyes shimmer in the soft sunlight. Galen was in his element here. The warmth of the sun, the light wind that ruffled his golden hair magnified his personality. His muscular chest seemed a bit larger, swelled, she guessed, with pride in his homeland, his people. His handsome face bore none of the telltale signs of his recent stay at Dekar and the horror that had gone before.

"Come on. I have something else to show you." He held out his hand. She gladly accepted it.

Thea continued to follow Galen. She could not imagine where he might be taking her, but they

were climbing higher. Each bend in the stone
walkway they passed seemed steeper, the trees
less tall. She became aware of a roaring sound
that grew louder the higher they climbed.

Galen paused, looked back at her. "Are you all
right? I don't want to weaken you further."

All signs of her earlier debilitation had mysteriously vanished. She felt refreshed, eager to
discover whatever Galen led her towards. She
shook her head. "I'm fine. My curiosity is about
to get the best of me."

Galen chuckled and tightened his grasp on her
hand, pulling her along behind him.

They rounded another bend and Thea almost
cried out in awe. They stood on a rock balcony
that projected about ten spans from the stone
walkway. The pool was beneath her, and above
her was a spectacle the likes of which she could
never have imagined.

A great wall of falling water flowed over the
side of the mountain, pouring down hundreds of
spans to splash into the pool. Curtains of vibrant
flowers grew on each side of the falling water,
clinging to a base she knew to be solid rock.
Looking higher still, she saw the sky, unobstruct-
ed by the tall trees. Aqua, unblemished by even a
wisp of cloud.

Thea was acutely aware of a heart that beat too
fast within her breast, of breath that seemed to
whistle past her teeth, but she could not calm
herself. She looked down to the pool. Its color
mimicked the sky, yet it was so clear, so pure,
she could see a bottom as white as the new-fallen
snow that covered her homeland. She quickly
scanned the shoreline, the blankets of vivid col-
or that grew to the water's edge, then up again,

past the towering trees and sheer rock cliffs that cut this beautiful retreat away from the trouble beyond its walls.

Galen was forgotten by her side as she stood mesmerized by the spray that flew when the tumbling water hit the rocks below, sending cascades of water high into the air. Bright sunlight filtered through the sprays, causing prisms of light to rival a rainbow.

Galen leaned back against the stone wall rimming the balcony and watched Thea. He couldn't take his eyes from her face as she absorbed a world so different from the frozen plains and valleys of her ice-covered home. He thought about how he would like to keep her here, safe within the walls of *Naro*, to take her as his mate, to bear his children, to grow old with him, how he would like to lie eternally at her side when their lives came to an end.

"It's breathtaking. Thank you for bringing me here."

"There are many such sights in Borderland and beyond, Thea. Our world is as multifaceted as what you see before you. To the south, Solarus offers its own vast beauty, if you like leagues and leagues of hot, dry sand."

"I have often wondered about the world beyond Glacia. For as long as I can remember, I have dreamed of one world, one people. A place where one could travel freely from one place to another, experience the different cultures, learn new things." Thea slid slowly to the stone, wrapped her arms around her knees, and pillowed her cheek on her forearm. "Gustoff never discouraged my imagination. He saw it as a part of my training, persuaded me to test the limits of my imagination beyond the knowledge that I could acquire in Glacia.

"There are great scrolls and huge leather-bound books in Gustoff's towers that were passed on from the Ancient Ones. I spent every available hour studying them. Though I read about such spectacles as I witness here, nothing compares to seeing them with my own eyes."

She closed her eyes. "Do you know that before I touched Mya's child, I had never held an infant in my arms?"

A sharp pain shot through Galen's chest. He wanted to reach out to her, pull her into his arms, but he sat watching her, remembering the expression on her face when he had approached her in the center cave, the way she had clutched the fevered infant to her breast, refusing to release it even when she collapsed in his own arms. A great ache grew within him, magnified by the thought of all the simple pleasures denied Thea.

"My mother died giving me birth. I do not remember too much of my early childhood, except that Nola's mother was there for me, and Gustoff was always at my side, teaching me, guiding me, sheltering me. I don't recall when I realized I was gifted with powers beyond those of my servants.

"Each day Gustoff would take me to his tower. For hours he'd teach me of those who had gone before, telling me of their abilities, their beliefs. Each time we'd leave the tower, he would caution me to hold silent, to never tell anyone of the things we discussed. I trusted him completely and never thought to question his words.

"When I reached my second and tenth winter, Gustoff performed the ritual that would transfer the Sphere of Light into my care. Over the years that have passed since, I learned there were those who would destroy me to possess the secret I hold within."

Galen silently cursed Gustoff and her ancestors, those mystical people who had stolen Thea's soul, replaced it with a sense of purpose that would not give her peace until her destiny was fulfilled or her life forfeited.

He thought about his own life, how vastly different his childhood had been. He was heir to Borderland, but there had always been laughter, companionship, and love. He had had a loving mother to dote upon him, a father to guide and teach him right from wrong, to ready him to one day lead his people.

Gustoff's sole purpose in teaching Thea had been to meet and defeat any evil threatening the Sphere of Light, but beyond that he had given her no insight into normal life, into how to function as a complete person, separate from her Guardianship.

Thoughts of Gustoff rekindled the guilt Galen hid inside. He knew Berezan had left Borderland, had probably already reached Glacia. By this time, Thea would have realized it, too.

Thea needed time to regain her strength, time to understand there were others who would share her destiny. Galen prayed he could convince Thea to wait for the Creean warriors to go with her, for the plans he and Kajar had discussed to be placed into action.

Galen walked to her side, then dropped to his haunches. "We must go back now, Thea. You tire easily. After you have taken nourishment, we have much to discuss."

Thea looked up at him. Galen saw the fatigue that dulled her eyes, darkened the circles beneath. He wanted to take her into his arms, shelter her from all that would happen over the next few sunrises, but he knew he could not.

He stood and held out his hand. She placed her fingers into his, and he helped her to her feet.

Chapter Twenty-Five

Berezan climbed the stairs of stone. A thrill crawled along his legs and up his spine and centered in his chest with each pause, each step. He stopped at the landing of each flight of stairs, gazing down through the center spiral to the floors below, then up to stare in wonderment at the chandelier and its thousands of tiny lumastones, each burning brightly with its own eternal light.

His fingers skimmed the smooth granite rail, up the arches that supported every floor of the keep. His mind recaptured the many hours he'd spent as a young boy racing up and down these same stairs with all the vim and vigor of youth, then sped ahead to the hours he'd spent in the hot cave of Solarus with Elsbar.

The lumastones were one of the luxuries he'd missed most sorely. Mined in the granite peaks of Glacia and the foothills that passed through Borderland, the lumastones could not be obtained in the southern portion of the world. For light in that part of the world they used smelly tallow candles and lamps that burned oils taken from the stomachs of the oxum they killed for food and clothing.

It had taken him many moonrises to get used to having to ration water. Glacia's snows had always provided an abundance of fresh water with which to wash, to quench one's thirst. Solarus had no such luxury. Water was doled out from a central well located in the heart of the city. Guards were always in place to see that no one took more than their share.

The thirst within him had gradually eaten away at the little boy he had been and replaced him with a hardened youth, one willing to do anything to gain a measure of comfort. Elsbar took advantage of his youth and taught him that there were ways to have what he needed. By the time he'd reached his tenth year, Berezan was as proficient at thievery as he was at creating the dark magic that had rewarded him with Glacia.

At 27, he'd grown powerful enough to use his powers to overthrow the sovereigns of Solarus and move himself and Elsbar into the relative luxury of their abode, but he hadn't been satisfied. He'd hungered for Glacia. He'd hungered for vengeance, and he'd hungered to use the vast knowledge he possessed to take back all that had been taken from him.

Berezan considered Alec DeLan, the heir his father had designated to rule Glacia in his place. Alec's mother, Nadia, had been instrumental in placing young Alec under his control. In her thirst for revenge against the poor treatment she believed she had received by Arlin DeLan's hand, she had sent her young son to Solarus to meet with Berezan and form an allegiance.

Though Berezan had never confessed his true identity to the young man, it had been easy to befriend him, and after a few visits, even easier to manipulate him. Berezan had counted on Alec's assistance to help him locate the Sphere of Light when he arrived in Glacia, and was surprised to find the young heir missing. He suspect Gustoff's hand in Alec's absence.

Berezan shook away his thoughts and continued up the stairs. He found the wooden door to Gustoff's tower, and took great pleasure in opening the door that as a child had been forbidden. A hundred more creaky wooden stairs lay before him, up through a dark winding passageway to the tower room. Berezan fought back the urge to forgo the stairway and transport directly to the top. He wanted to climb these stairs, run his fingers along the cold stone, and know Gustoff had died to protect the secrets he believed the tower held.

Berezan closed his eyes, drew a deep breath. He had already spent the past two moonrises searching every inch of the keep for the Sphere of Light. Gustoff had not brought the Sphere with him when he met his death, and Berezan knew there was no place left in the world to shield its powers.

Anticipation stirred within him, but Berezan fought it. He took each step slowly, pausing after five to draw a deep breath. He listened to the sound of the wind that whirled around the outside tower walls and seeped through the cracks in the ancient stones. He inhaled the scent of musk, the aroma of stale smoke and ash.

Chills crawled along his flesh.

Berezan shook away the eerie feeling and continued, faster and faster, until he reached the last step. He stood for several moments in the darkness, watching the faint moonlight through the lone tower window. He closed his senses to everything around him, searching instead for any trace of power, no matter how weak, within the tower.

Cold air, nothing more, rippled along his spine.

Berezan held his hand in the air, fingers spread, and called forth a spark of fire to each fingertip to light his way. He touched a candle he found on a rickety table and watched the flame flicker. Shadows crawled over an old cauldron at the room's center. Ashes and bits of wood in the grate evidenced that it had been long unused. He walked to the cauldron and looked down into the liquid that lay smooth as glass. His reflection stared back.

Casting a glance over his shoulder, Berezan found a lumalantern on the shelf against the wall and walked toward it. He slid the lid open a fraction of an inch. A shaft of light touched his face. He stared into the light, looking even deeper, searching for the source of its power. He had never questioned the power of the stones, never asked what made them shine.

Anger flared within him. He threw back the lid, completely exposing the stone. Light as bright as sunshine flooded the tower to reveal a room about 30 spans in diameter and another 30 spans high. Along the wall on the opposite side from the window, bookshelves climbed to the ceiling. Hundreds of scrolls and ancient textbooks lined each shelf. Hundreds more had fallen to the floor.

He walked toward the shelves, bent, and picked up one of the scrolls. He opened the brittle paper slowly, watching several bits crumble and fall to the front of his tunic. He turned the scroll in his hands, holding it this way and that in an attempt to decipher the odd script, then crushed it in his fists in defeat moments later. Soon several more scrolls and a number of textbooks littered the center of the tower, and then Berezan vented his anger at his inability to understand them by setting them afire.

Berezan crossed his arms over his chest and watched the ancient writings go up in smoke. He inhaled, taking reassurance that the power within him was great enough that he did not need anything else.

Berezan turned slowly in the center of the tower floor, concentrating on every crack between the stones, each chink that might give him a clue to the whereabouts of the Sphere. He cursed Berezan, Elsbar, his father, and all those who had gone before.

He closed his eyes, concentrating hard once again to feel the power he knew the tower hid. Moments later, he opened his eyes and raised his hands. Arcs of fire streaked from his fingertips to fill the room. He raised his hands higher. The red arcs of fire shot toward the ceiling of the tower. A great rumble occurred; then the ceiling disintegrated, leaving nothing but smoking timbers exposed to the cold night sky.

He turned his wrath toward the bookshelves, the volumes lining the shelves, those on the floor.

Seconds later all were destroyed. The cauldron, the chair, the table and candle were next to feel his fury, but Berezan wasn't satisfied.

When the contents of the tower were no more than smoldering ash, he drew a deep breath and disappeared empty-handed in a flash of brilliant light seconds before the stone walls of the tower tumbled down the mountainside.

Chapter Twenty-Six

Thea looked around the central cave and studied each face, every smile. She touched the head of the small blond girl sitting beside her. The little girl looked up, casting a grin that exposed two missing front teeth, then back down at the tasty *domini* pear she had all but devoured.

Thea bent her head to study the sleeping form of Mya's boy child cuddled against her breast, and felt her face warm when she sensed Galen's eyes upon her. Thea raised her head slowly, meeting his gaze from across the fire that burned between them. A thin smile creased his lips. Her heart skipped a beat, and another deep ache like the one she'd experienced when this same child nuzzled her breast bore through her stomach. She turned away from Galen's eyes.

"*Reina* Thea."

The warrior Thorn had eased in between herself and the little blond girl. Thea looked into his smiling face. "Thorn."

"How are you feeling, *reina?* You scared me when you collapsed. I thought Galen was going to—"

"Thorn."

Galen's sharp voice cut off whatever Thorn was about to say. Thea wondered what that something might be. Instead of asking him to continue, sure at some later time the warrior would feel Galen's temper, she looked deeply into Thorn's eyes. "I'm feeling much better, Thorn. Thank you for your concern."

"Reina?"

"Yes?"

"I wonder if you would share with us something of your homeland. Few people of Borderland have seen snow. Please tell us of Glacia."

Thea cast a quick glance over the 30 or so people seated in the circle around the fire sharing their meal. Curiosity beamed from their faces. She looked at Galen. He nodded his agreement that the people of Borderland should hear of Glacia.

"Well, Thorn, today I have witnessed such beauty in your homeland that I hope my descriptions of Glacia do not disappoint you."

Several people murmured at once.

"The Governing House of Glacia sits high in the mountains on a plateau about four miles above the tundra. To reach the city you have to travel by equox or cart up a winding road that cuts through beautiful *picea* forests. The road itself is steep, and during a blizzard it can be treacherous, but our animals have been bred to withstand the climate and terrain."

Thea watched the eyes of the people as they listened to her tale. She saw them struggle for understanding. She knew unless one had felt cold, had had snowflakes touch one's cheeks, had seen the wind whip piles of fluffy white high into the dark night sky, had watched the moonlight catch each tiny flake and set it sparkling like a gemstone, one could never understand or form a mental picture of Glacia's beauty.

She thought about something Gustoff had taught her as a child that she'd not used in a number of winters. She looked down at the babe sleeping against her breast, crossed her ankles beneath her robe, and made a cradle in the opening of her legs for the infant before laying him down.

"I'm going to ask each of you around this circle to join hands." She reached for Thorn's hand and felt his callused palm; then his strong fingers closed around hers. She touched Mya's hand, squeezed it in reassurance, then looked across the fire to see Galen smile at her. Thea returned his smile, nodding for him to join hands with those on each side of him. He complied, and she nodded again. "Now, please close your eyes and trust me. I want you to concentrate on my voice."

Thea looked toward the little blond girl whose hand was hidden in Thorn's much larger one. She noted the girl had squeezed her eyes so tightly lines appeared on her forehead. She glanced slowly around the circle, pausing only to lock gazes with Galen before he closed his eyes. Then Thea closed her own eyes.

She concentrated hard on Glacia, described each detail as she saw the snow piled in drifts 20 spans high, the *piceas*, heavy with snow and ice, bowed in the afternoon sun. She mentally traveled up the steep roadway to the city, pausing several times to touch an icicle, concentrating on the cold upon her fingers. The sentry mountains of Glacia came into view, each reaching thousands of spans into the sky with snowcapped peaks sparkling in the sunlight. The houses, the people who walked the streets, even the cauldrons on every street corner filled her mind.

She stood on the frozen bridge, looking up at the keep itself, past each balcony to the icicles that hung from the roof hundreds of spans overhead. She then saw shadows fall and the sun pass beyond the peaks.

Night followed, bringing with it a sky full of stars and a full moon to light the snow and turn Glacia into a fairyland.

Several ooohs and ahhhhs broke her concentration. The images vanished. She opened her eyes. The spell was broken, but she could tell from the fascinated expression on each participant's face that they had seen what she saw, felt what she felt.

"It's beautiful," one woman whispered. Several more agreed.

"I want to go to your home," the little blond girl announced.

Thea smiled. "I would love to take you to Glacia, little one." She looked around. "All of you would be welcome in my home, just as you have made me welcome in yours."

"Does the snow ever go away?" someone across the circle asked.

Thea had no idea who had asked the question, so she addressed the group. "I have never seen the ground there in my twenty-two winters. I have never seen grass, nor water outside of the keep that was not frozen into hard ice."

"How do you grow your food?"

Thea smiled. She looked at Galen.

"I have seen the gardens of Glacia, my friend," Galen answered. "It's hard to describe to someone who has never witnessed such strange methods of cultivation, and I do not have Thea's wonderful gift of sharing what is in my mind." He winked at her, then went on to tell his people about the hydro gardens beneath the keep.

Thorn squeezed her hand. "You have no hordes of insects to destroy your crops?"

Thea thought about Thorn's question. "We have no insects I can recall. I guess they do not survive in our climate," she whispered, realizing she had never given any thought to the tiny creatures.

"As Galen told you, our crops are well protected within our mountains. Nothing threatens our food supply," she said, not adding that Berezan threatened not only Glacia's food supply, but its very existence.

Thea gazed about sadly at the faces of those around her, noting their expressions had changed dramatically. They were remembering all they had lost. She felt her eyes burn at the terrible ordeal these people had gone through, but she blinked the wetness away. These were a proud people, a race of warriors and strong females who would eventually rebuild their way of life. Their jungle homes would once again be filled with children's laughter. They would survive.

But if Nola and Elijah had failed in their mission, the people of Glacia were as helpless as innocent animals under Berezan's hand.

"*Reina* Thea." The small voice pulled Thea from those pain-filled thoughts.

Thea smiled at the little blond girl, who had scrambled across Thorn and now knelt before her. She released Thorn's hand and placed her fingers alongside the girl's cheek.

"Take me home with you," the little girl pleaded. "I want to see snow. I'm tired of living in this old cave."

The tears Thea had tried hard to hold back fell down her cheeks. "I must leave Borderland very soon, little one. My people need me as desperately as you and your people need Galen." She looked to Galen, then back to the little girl. "The same mean men that came to your home and caused you to live in this cave threaten Glacia. I must go and use these strange powers I possess to fight this evil and make all right with the world again."

The little girl started to cry. Thea wiped her tears away. "When I was only a little older than you, my greatest friend helped me to understand why I could do things others could not. You remembered how I touched those who were injured and they became well?"

The little girl nodded.

"Well, the ability to heal is but one of my gifts, just like the way I made you see my home."

A bright smile lit the child's face.

"Do you know what destiny is, little one?"

The child looked toward her mother, then back at Thea. After a moment she said, "They teach us that each person has a path to follow in life. Is that destiny?"

"Yes. My path was chosen for me just as your lifepath has been chosen for you. Some of us go through life not knowing where our destiny will lead. Mine has been clearly drawn. Because of this, I must return to Glacia and do whatever I can for the people I know as family."

"I'll miss you," the little girl whispered.

Thea leaned forward to kiss the little girl's forehead. "I shall miss you, too." She rose and walked away from the gathering, afraid if she stayed longer, she wouldn't be able to control the sobs that would accompany the tears she could no longer contain.

"Thea, wait!"

Thea turned to find Galen had followed her from the main cave. Thorn stood by his side. "Come with us, Thea." Once again he held out his hand, but this time Thea hesitated to take it. She had stayed too long with Galen's people, learned to love each one as she had never had the opportunity to come to love the people of Glacia.

"Please, Thea. This is very important."

Thea met Galen's gaze, and saw the emotions in his eyes. She placed her hand into his. She followed Galen as she had earlier through another set of winding tunnels. Thorn walked behind them.

Galen entered a cave, smaller than the main cave but larger than the opening she had slept in earlier. Thea noticed over a hundred warriors were seated around a center fire. They each bowed their head.

"Join us," Galen said, holding out his hand to indicate several vacant spots. She walked across the floor and joined the group at the fire. Galen sat next to her, Thorn next to the man she had learned earlier was Galen's second in command, Kajar.

"We welcome you to our meeting, Thea of Glacia," Kajar said.

"Thank you."

Galen grabbed her hand and held it. "Thea, these men are what's left of the Warrior Council of Cree. I've called this meeting to discuss something that involves you as well as the people of Borderland. I hope you will bear with us for a moment."

Thea nodded.

Kajar addressed the group. "It is the proposal of Galen, and myself, that we band our remaining warriors together and accompany Thea back to Glacia."

Thea felt Galen's hand tighten on hers. She concentrated instead on the loud murmuring going on around her. It appeared the warriors of Borderland did not agree with Galen and Kajar's proposal, and rightly so.

"No." The word had fallen from her lips before she realized it. All eyes turned toward her. "I cannot allow you to do this. Your people have suffered enough by Berezan's hand."

"Our people will continue to suffer by Berezan's hand if we do not destroy him, Thea," Galen said. "What happens if you fail in your mission? Do you think Berezan will be satisfied knowing the Creean people exist and, after his attack, are still not under his control?"

Thea glared at Galen. "I have no intention of failing."

"Even if you are successful in defeating Berezan, what about his army?"

Thea shook her head. "No, Galen. I cannot let you do this. I cannot allow—"

"Thea," Galen said, then turned away to look

at the other warriors about the fire. "We have no other choice. We cannot fight Berezan. We cannot use our weapons against his fire, but his army fights as we do with swords, clubs, and spears. We can destroy the backbone of Berezan's strength."

Thea chewed her lip, trying to find the words that would dissuade Galen's course. "There are so few of your people, Galen. I cannot let you sacrifice more lives for the people of Glacia."

"True, there are few of us left to carry on as our ancestors, but should Berezan decide to bring his wrath down upon us again, we will cease to exist. Our only hope of survival lies in destroying Berezan's evil before it destroys us."

"I agree." Several other voices echoed the same statement.

Thea turned to look into the faces of the warriors of Cree. All but a few were young men. She considered the women and children in the caves, the life they would lead if these men were killed. She shook her head.

"It's not possible, Galen."

Galen turned toward the warriors seated around the fire. "Do I have a unanimous vote?"

All voiced their approval.

"We march with you, or we march alone, Thea of Glacia."

"Oh, Galen, no," she cried, sniffing as he stood to stand before her.

Galen dropped to one knee and took her hands into his. "I am only a man, Thea," he insisted quietly. "I have no special powers other than those I have acquired by years of hard training. I can offer only my sword, my life, in your protection, but all I have is yours, all that I am is yours."

A hearty round of cheers erupted in the cave.

Thea could only blink back her tears and stare into Galen's beautiful blue eyes and at the emotions she believed she saw there. She could not be sure of Creean customs, but from the tone of his words and the response those words had created among his peers, she guessed he had just done something she had never thought he would do.

She touched his cheek. He stood and took her into his arms.

"I have just declared myself to be yours, Thea of Glacia. Do I get no words in return?"

Tears poured down her cheeks. She touched his brow, his cheek, the tiny cleft she loved in his chin. "I love you so much, warrior, I don't know what to say."

Galen scooped her into his arms and twirled her around the room. Cheers and laughter echoed off the walls.

"You have just said all there is to say, my heart, except . . ." He kissed her cheeks, the tears that wet her flesh, her eyelids. "Be my mate, Thea of Glacia. Bear my children. Love me the way I do you until my dying breath leaves my body, and beyond to whatever eternity brings."

"Children? Oh, Galen, I would love to have your children, to hold a little one like Mya's against my breast, but—"

Galen hushed her with a kiss.

Thea broke away. "Galen, please, you are embarrassing me."

Galen laughed. "The warriors of Borderland honor their females. We have no inhibitions about showing our affection to the one we have chosen."

A chorus of agreement followed Galen's words, then the chant: "Thea! Thea!"

Thea shook her head. "This is not right, Galen. We cannot celebrate our happiness when so much lies ahead. There may be no tomorrows to—"

"That's right, my heart. There may be no tomorrows, so today we rejoice and draw the strategies we need to meet and defeat our mutual enemy." Galen took her hand and led her back to her place before the fire.

Thea had a hard time concentrating on the words that passed around the circle, until Galen's voice rang clearly in her mind.

"There is a hidden entrance to Glacia's keep. I found it while exploring the hydro gardens. We could slip into the keep and remain hidden in the numerous hallways that intersect below the main floor until the time is right to strike."

Thea looked at the warriors. Each was clad in the same leggings and fur vests Galen wore. She studied their size, the muscles that crossed their chests and rippled down their arms.

"Galen." She touched his arm, drawing his immediate attention. "How long will it take an army afoot to reach Glacia?"

"Five sunrises."

"Then this is all impossible. I must return to Glacia immediately. Berezan—"

"Cannot do more harm than he's already done in a matter of sunrises, Thea. Besides, you need rest before you meet your destiny."

She looked deeply into Galen's eyes and saw his determination. He had given her little choice. To leave for Glacia now would be placing the warriors of Borderland into danger. To stay . . .

"Look at these men," she said. "Each one is as large as you. We cannot possibly find suitable clothing warm enough for them to wear across

321

the tundra. They would become sick and die in matter of days."

"We could have the women and children forage through the remains of the villages, bring back all of the furs and hides that are not damaged. With everyone working together, we could find suitable clothing," Thorn responded.

Several of the others nodded.

Thea shook her head. Agreeing to have the warriors of Borderland accompany her to Glacia was like sentencing them to death.

"Please, listen to me," she said, addressing the assemblage. "I cannot tell you how much I appreciate all you are offering, but you cannot do this. You can't place yourselves in danger for me."

Every man present shouted his disagreement.

Thea swallowed hard and nodded. "If you are insistent on doing this, you should know all." She looked at Galen, saw the strange expression on his face, and realized he thought she was about to disclose something he should have known long before.

Perhaps he should have, she thought.

"Before Galen and I left Glacia, I gave instructions to my most trusted friends to deploy in the event Berezan arrived before I returned. Nola and Elijah will have organized an evacuation of the village into Dekar Facility. If there wasn't time for an evacuation, they were told to instruct the people against any resistance to Berezan's will. If they are docile subjects, and no threat to his takeover, I don't believe Berezan will harm them."

"The people of Cree posed no threat to Berezan, but he murdered innocent men, women, and children," a warrior across the fire challenged.

"Berezan invaded Borderland because he believed the mountain *Naro* shielded the Sphere of Light. Your people were massacred because of something I hold inside me, something that was placed there by the man some of you met many days ago, Gustoff."

Kajar and several of the other warriors nodded.

Thea went on to explain about the Sphere, its origin, her destiny. Each warrior listened in silence to her tale. When she'd finished, many moments passed before anyone spoke.

"Do you believe you will be able to create these arcs of fire like Berezan used to kill Gustoff in the tundra?"

Thea sighed. "I don't know, Thorn. I have never used any of the powers within me to do harm. The Sphere of Light releases its power differently through each Guardian. Gustoff could not tell me what path my strength would take, but did all he could to prepare me for my destiny before he died."

"Do you feel this Sphere inside you?"

Thea looked first to Galen, then to the warrior who asked the question. "No."

"Then how can you be sure it truly exists?"

"I have to have faith. I must believe that the strange powers I have learned about and have used are but a fraction of the force that lies within me. I have to trust in my destiny, see it through, no matter what becomes of me." She once again looked into each man's face, pausing on Galen's. She spoke directly to him, needing to hear his answer above all others.

"Can you follow me into a battle knowing, when the time comes to meet Berezan face to face, I may fail?"

323

Galen captured her hand, brought it to his lips, and kissed her fingers. He looked deeply into her eyes. "My heart, many sunrises ago Gustoff told me that my place, my destiny, was by your side, no matter what that future might bring.

"I believe in my destiny as strongly as you believe in yours."

Chapter Twenty-Seven

The forays into the jungle to bring back the needed supplies became a celebration. The people were divided into groups. Women and children large enough to help them set out into the jungle at sunrise with three warriors to a group. Those children too young be taken away from the caves were brought into the center cave, and women carrying unborn children did their part by taking care of the young.

As the hours passed, the pile of furs and hides grew, as did a stack of discarded weapons left by Berezan's army. Warriors formed a hunting party, and the food gathered also grew. Another group of women prepared the food, saving out enough to feed the people who would be left behind and preserving a vast quantity for the warriors to consume on their trek through the tundra.

At each meal, Thea and Galen were toasted before the huge fire that lit the jungle through darkness and light for two sunrises. As each party returned, Galen supervised the refurbishing of the Solarian weapons. Thea directed yet another group of Creean women as they prepared the clothing to be used by the warriors of Cree. Using the supplies and clothing Thea and Galen had used to travel through the tundra as examples, hides were stretched, measured, and cut into long rectangles, then sewn together with heavy thread to make tents. Each warrior was carefully measured; then thick animal fur was cut to each man's size and sewn into warm clothing that would keep out the cold but not restrict movement.

At the twilight hour, when the exhausted children were placed on their pallets for the night, Thea walked among them, touched each one's hand, placed kisses on their foreheads, and wished them a good sleep. She then sat with the women around the fire, sewing as they sewed, before she fell into Galen's bed, too exhausted to think about what might lie ahead.

An hour before sunrise she would wake and find that Galen had joined her on the furs sometime during her sleep. She would kiss his lips tenderly, then begin another day.

On the fourth rising, Thea looked over her shoulder, expecting to find Galen sprawled out beside her. He was not there. She sat up slowly, stretching the stiff muscles in her back, rubbing her sore hands. She looked down at the blisters that had risen on her flesh from yesterday's labors, clasped her hands together, and concentrated, healing the abrasions just as she had for the last three risings. She drew a deep breath and prepared to face another day.

Thea drew herself unsteadily from the mound of thick fur and groped for the silky gown she had borrowed from Mya. She took a moment to experience the luxurious softness of the homespun cloth against her bare flesh, then belted a sash of the same fabric about her waist and walked to the cave exit.

Galen met her as she stepped into the tunnel.

"We are not going to the central cave today."

She glanced at the pouch he held in his hand.

"I have had food prepared for us. We will not return until sundown."

Thea looked at him strangely, wondering at the odd way he was acting, but did not question him as he captured her hand and led her down yet another tunnel that wound and twisted through *Naro*.

Thea was mildly disappointed when they stepped out of the tunnel opening. She looked forward to visiting the sparkling pool again and had hoped that was where Galen led her. Instead, their path appeared to be blocked by towering trees and dense shrub. Galen did not pause. He continued to lead, shortening his strides to match hers, to a path Thea had not seen before. They traveled along this winding pathway through the jungle for almost an hour.

Thea took advantage of their trek to study the many different species of plants and flowers that grew in abundance. She listened to the sharp cries of the multicolored birds that perched in the trees and the humming of insects, and tucked each sound into her memory for the mooncycles ahead, believing she might never pass this way again.

Galen paused. Thea was so intent on her surroundings she almost bumped into him. His chuckle sounded like music to her ears.

"Behold before you the City of Cree." He swept his hand wide. Thea's gaze followed the motion.

They stood in a wide-open area. To her left for about a thousand spans, the remains of tall stone houses captured her attention. Huge gaping holes where windows used to be absorbed the sunlight. The stone, the familiar gray granite she had seen all of her life, was marred by soot and ash. Not an inch of any wooden structure had been left unscathed.

Multicolored flower beds that lined the avenues between the houses were wilted from neglect. The vines and crawlers that crept down from the trees in the jungles nearby were blackened by the heat from the fires that had obviously destroyed this glorious city.

Thea looked at the ground to find the terrain had been swept clean, all evidence of those who had died here cleared away.

"Cree is many times larger than the other villages." Galen pointed to an open area ahead of them. "The farmers from the outlying villages used to bring their wares there to be sold."

Thea studied the area. If she concentrated hard she could visualize marketplace stalls where piles of burned wood and rubble now stood. Broken pieces of pottery, small portions of woven baskets that had escaped the fire, several old upturned carts, and some pieces of metal, for which she could fathom no use, littered the ground. Neither plant nor weed grew up through the ashes.

Galen touched her hand, recapturing her attention. "Since we have but two defined seasons, one hot and dry, the other hot and wet, the farmers and craftsmen of Borderland would bring their goods to market on the full moon of each month. The Creeans are people who seize any opportunity for a festival, and marketing day became just such an occasion."

Galen closed his eyes against the carnage, remembering life in Cree as it had been before Berezan's massacre. "It was such a day when our hunting party left Cree to go into the jungle."

The sadness in his voice tugged at Thea's heart. She placed her hand softly on his arm. "Galen, sometimes it's best to put the things you cannot change behind you and concentrate on those matters within your control."

He opened his eyes, looked down at her, and smiled. "There is much you should know before we leave Cree, Thea. Come with me." He placed his arm around her shoulder and led her away from the marketplace.

"This is the Temple of Cree."

Thea looked up at a structure miraculously untouched by the destruction around it. She recalled Gustoff describing this building to her. A moment's grief twisted in her chest as she studied the same three-story dwelling at least 50 spans wide. Her gaze climbed each of the stone steps that led up to an enormous pair of bronze doors, doors embossed with an emblem that matched the medallion on Galen's chest. She stared at the two huge beasts that stood sentry, wondering what they were, and more importantly, if they were modeled after a beast that roamed the jungle where she now stood.

"This temple was built in the time of Shakara. Those beasts, the *Tighra*, who guard the doors are said to have been my ancestor's pets. We see them as symbols of Shakara's great power."

"They are terrifying."

"Be at rest, my heart. No longer does the great beast of Shakara roam these jungles." Galen hugged her close to his body. He kissed her forehead, then sat down on the steps.

"Join me."

Thea sat by his side. Galen opened the pouch he'd carried from *Naro*, handing her a small section of bread, a chunk of cheese, and two *domini* pears. They ate their meal in silence, washed it down with water from his flask, then sat soaking up the afternoon sun for many minutes before Galen finally took her hand.

"There is much you should know about the events that took place before you found me in Dekar."

Thea only looked at him.

"When you brought me to Glacia and prepared to use me as an impostor for your stepbrother, I could have been more forthright with you and explained that even if I did resemble Alec, I could have never have portrayed him." He looked into her eyes.

"Berezan had seen my face, Thea. He would have known me the moment he stepped into the same chamber with me."

"H-how?"

Galen leaned back against the steps and closed his eyes. He told her of returning to Cree, of finding his village in ruin, his people murdered. He

330

described the agony that tore him apart inside when he found his father dead, witnessed his mother's death.

Thea wept.

"I allowed rage to consume my common sense. Kajar tried to tell me I should not leave Cree alone, but vengeance drove me. I refused this symbol of the station I suddenly held." He reached down and grasped the medallion in his hand. "Even now, I don't feel I am worthy to wear the badge of leadership," he said quietly.

"Nonsense, Galen." Thea touched his hand, brushed her fingertips over the bronze disc. "This is your heritage. You have trained all of your life to lead. No one is more worthy."

"In my anger, I did not place my people above my own need for revenge. I left them to fend for themselves and set out to destroy Berezan. At the time I had no idea what I might face. Then, to me, Berezan was only a man. I didn't know about—"

Thea touched his lips. "There was no way you could have known, Galen. Stop berating yourself for something over which you had no control."

"I should have had control!"

"Think back, Galen. Consider the words spoken to you by Gustoff many moonrises ago. Gustoff's vision foretold of your part in my destiny. Can you say with certainty that our paths were never meant to cross? That what we have found was never meant to be?"

He shook his head. "I don't know, Thea. I just don't know."

She entwined her fingers with his, holding his hand securely in her lap. "Tell me about your meeting with Berezan."

"I don't remember everything that happened before I was taken captive, but running through the jungle, hearing men shouting and equox hooves thundering closer and closer still creep into my dreams. The thing I remember most vividly is being held in Berezan's camp, secured by metal chains like an animal, subjected to painful torture.

"I don't know how long I was held captive. Pain obliterated all sense of reality. After a time, it became hard to breathe, hard to remain conscious. Lucid time escaped me, yet with each clear thought, I plotted a way to escape and to extract my own brand of revenge."

Thea touched his face. "There were no marks on your body when I found you in Dekar."

"Berezan has ways of inflicting pain that leave no scars, Thea. Just as you touched me to heal my wrists, Berezan touched me to set every nerve in my body on fire."

"No," she whispered.

"My escape is something that fades in and out of my memory. I know I overpowered my guard. I remember running and running, going nowhere. I recall the cold, the sting of the wind against my flesh. I also have vivid memories of feeling my skin catch fire, of heat so intense it seemed to melt the flesh from my bones, and the relief I felt when I stumbled and fell into something that blanketed my hot body in cold.

"My last coherent thought was that I would die and there was nothing I could do to prevent it."

Thea touched his cheek, his lips, the tiny cleft in his chin. She looked deeply into his blue eyes, wishing there was some way she could ease his pain. She allowed her fingers to drop to his chest,

332

felt the steady beat of his heart, the warmth of his flesh. "But you did not," she whispered.

She fell against his chest and his muscular arms closed around her. Thea buried the top of her head beneath his chin, speaking to the tiny pulse that thundered beneath her lips. "You awoke to find your escape had led to yet another capture."

He stroked her hair, her arms, the contour of her back. She arched into his touch, welcoming it, needing it, and in return offering solace with her lips as she placed tiny kisses against his flesh. She wound her arms upward, entwined her fingers into his golden hair, made many tiny swirling motions over the shell of his ears with her fingertips.

"My heart," he said softly, placing his hands beneath her chin to raise her face to his. His mouth cast that same wonderful spell it had many times before, drawing her away into bliss, dispelling any thoughts that were not directly related to this moment, this particular place in time.

Desire rode hard upon Galen's body, need burned deeply into his very being, but thoughts of what lay ahead, of what the tiny woman in his arms would face in the next few sunrises, ate away at him like a festering sore. He had faced Berezan's wrath, knew the pain he could administer. Thoughts of Berezan inflicting that same agony on Thea twisted like snakes inside his mind, drawing him away from the beauty around him.

He raised his hands to Thea's shoulders, pushing her gently away. The soft moan that slipped from her lips when their mouths parted tore away a piece of his heart. "We must leave this place, my heart. Darkness fast approaches. On the sunrise our journey begins."

Thea swallowed hard to relieve the lump that clogged her throat at Galen's words. The day she had trained for all of her life fast approached, but she was reluctant to leave the safety of Galen's arms. She clung to him, needing his strength, for hers was failing, needing his courage to fortify her will for the hours that lay ahead.

"Galen," she whispered in protest, snuggling closer to his chest.

"We cannot stay here. We are a great distance from *Naro*."

Thea's heart did a slow somersault in her chest. The many times she'd pledged never to lie with Galen again, not to experience the deep, binding emotions that his lovemaking would evoke, melted away like ice upon fire. Her very soul cried out, and she was determined it would not be denied.

"Take me to the waterfall again, my warrior. Give me one more chance to experience the magic of that place before I leave Borderland. Allow me to witness the unspoiled beauty of Cree before I meet my destiny." She kissed his lips urgently, wanting him to understand the need she could not express fully in words.

Galen held her against him, returning the fervor of her embrace, matching the erotic rhythm set by the motion of her tongue as it met and tempted his. Without severing contact with her warm flesh, he rose slowly to his feet, cradled Thea against his chest, and left the temple steps.

The sun had slipped below the tree line, casting long shadows in the dense jungle and cooling the air. Galen walked a path taken many times in his life, barely conscious of where he trod. By the time he reached his destination with his precious burden still in arms, twilight had come, bringing with it that strange gray glow that radiated from the frothing pool of water at the fall's base. Vapor caused by the rapidly cooling air and the warmth of the water rose like a specter from the surface, lending an ethereal quality to the beauty of the pool.

He placed Thea upon the bank at a spot where the flowers ended and a mossy green carpet grew down to the waterline, welcoming one more deep kiss before he pulled from her arms and stood to look down at a vision more beautiful than their surroundings.

Flowers of pale pink and lavender tangled in long tendrils of her auburn hair that spread over the moss like a silken blanket. The blue shift she had worn for three sunrises when her own woolen clothing became too warm to bare in the jungle heat molded sensually to every soft curve of her body.

Her face, pale and pure as the vapor around them, was highlighted by liquid brown eyes and feathery lashes that dusted the flushness across her cheeks. Her lips, still puffy from the kisses they had shared, were moist, enticing. His heart skipped a beat when she whisked the tip of her tongue over the fullness of her bottom lip.

Galen yanked at the laces that held his leggings taut about his hips, loosened them enough to roll the leather down his hips, and over his thighs, then discarded them along with his boots. He dropped to his knees beside her.

Thea watched each muscle in Galen's body as it stretched and relaxed, his hair, silver in the mist, swaying to and fro as he bent over her. She listened to her own heartbeat, accelerating until each thump overshadowed the steady roar of the nearby waterfall. A quivering began in her belly, radiating outward to her entire body. She twisted her fingers in the soft moss beneath her instead of following her heart's command to reach out for him, to hurry the ecstasy that had too long been denied.

Finally, when Thea thought she would scream from anticipation, she met his gaze, witnessed the dark passion in his eyes, and understood that he, too, fought to prolong their union, to draw out the few moments of privacy they would have for many tomorrows and beyond.

She reached out to him, entwined her fingers in his, and held his hand. She watched his eyes, and felt his gaze as it slipped slowly over her like the touch of a feather, leaving her tingling when he found another spot to explore. She dropped her hand to the moss when he slipped his fingers from hers and reached to untie the silky cord that belted her waist.

The broad expanse of his chest filled her gaze, drawing her fingers like a magnet to the hardened planes. She raised her arms, splayed her palms against his hot flesh, then grasped the chain of his medallion.

"Please remove this," she whispered, wanting nothing between them to dredge up silent memories of what lay ahead.

Galen looked down at the medallion in her hands, then raised his head to meet her gaze. He searched deep into her eyes, and found a sadness he did not want intruding on their lovemaking. He nodded, raised his hands, removed the chain, and dropped it atop his leggings.

"Please remove this," he countered, tugging on the hemline of her gown.

Thea smiled. She rose slowly from the moss to stand before her warrior. Her fingers were deliberate and slow as she loosened the lacings that held the neckline of the blue cloth closed. When enough of an opening appeared to slip the gown over her head, she bent, grabbed the hemline, and lifted the silky material gradually, exposing her flesh inch by inch to Galen's view.

Galen swallowed hard to dislodge the knot that threatened to choke him. The ache in his loins screamed out for release, but he held fast, using every ounce of his willpower to stay there on his knees, watching as Thea enticed him with her disrobing. His hands twitched with the effort it took not to reach across the scant span that separated them, grab the cloth, and tear it into scraps.

The light wind that rippled the leaves overhead joined forces with Thea to increase his torment by lifting the thin garment gently and flapping it around her, silhouetting her lush curves against the moon-drenched mist. His heart slammed against the walls of his chest when first her thighs, then the nest of auburn curls that shielded her woman's heat were exposed. He swallowed again as the filmy garment slipped up, until the edge caught against the fullness of her breasts.

He yearned to follow the path the gown had taken, thoroughly exploring every lovely inch of her flesh. He felt himself harden, harden again, until he throbbed with expectation. He almost cried out when the garment was quickly snatched over her

Trudy Thompson

head and discarded to flutter to the ground like a fallen leaf.

Thea dropped to her knees before Galen and looked up into his eyes. She leaned nearer, nearer still, until the heat radiating from his body captured her, drew her closer, teased her with promises of things to come.

She kept her hands clenched at her sides as his were, wanting to touch, to caress, but not daring to break the magic that surrounded them, not wanting to destroy the calm that fused their souls as they remained less than a breath apart locked in each other's gaze.

The splashing of the water, the roar of the falls, the night creatures that had come awake in an unmelodious symphony were overpowered by the pounding of hearts, the echo of breath drawn hastily over quivering lips. Swirls of mist, thickening as the night air grew cooler, closed in around them, lighting them in an ethereal glow as the moonlight reached down to illuminate the pool.

Thea had no idea who moved first. She was aware only of the moment she tumbled to the moss, buffeted by Galen's strong arms. She moaned in satisfaction as he took her mouth, opened her lips with his tongue, and touched her soul. She clung to him, digging her nails into the hard, sculptured contours of his shoulders, arching her body when his callused hand closed over her breast, spreading her thighs wide to accommodate him as he bore deep inside her.

Galen slid his hands beneath her hips to raise her. He felt the tiny muscles within her quiver, then tighten. Blood pumped furiously through his veins, and his breath, when he thought to draw it, burned his throat. Every muscle in his body ached, each tendon extended, contracted, extended again, leaving him trembling with the effort it took to hold on.

Thea thrashed her head back and forth against the moss, tangling bits of greenery into her hair. Light-headedness made the world around her move in slow motion. An eternity passed before her hand reached his hair and her fingers could gain a firm grip and pull his head down so she could capture his lips.

Another decade passed before his tongue entwined with hers, mimicking the carnal dance of his lower thrusts, charging, retreating, making her crazy, driving her wild. She moaned, groaned, cried out. He responded to her call by deepening his kiss, his conquest of her womanhood. She accepted his challenge, giving as well as she received, capturing his tongue as she captured his manhood, holding him to her until the last vestiges of her sanity slipped away, making her a prisoner of their passion.

Galen groaned and rolled onto his back, taking Thea with him. He arched his hips, filling her deeper, finding his own release as she reached ecstasy for the second time. He held her tight, fought to regain his wits, his breath. Thea lay still upon him, the length of her hair falling to cover his neck, his shoulders, and the spread of his hands over her buttocks. He kept from moving too soon, not wanting to give up the pleasure of holding her, of feeling himself still buried deep within her tender sheath.

Moments later, he arched his hips to judge her reaction and received a soft moan in response. He kissed the top of her head, slid his hands up the small of her back, and buried his fingers in her hair. She turned her head into the side of his neck. Galen felt a shiver run down the length of his body when her moist tongue touched his flesh.

He shifted his arms as he raised himself from the mossy ground, supported her buttocks, cradled her close, wrapped her legs around his waist, and stepped into the moonlight pool. Thrice more they reached one shattering wave of rapture after another, until they fell exhausted to the mossy bank and slept the darkness away entwined in each other's arms.

Chapter Twenty-Eight

"Thea."

Thea kept her eyes closed, resisting the intrusion of a new day, a day that would drastically change her life and that of those she had come to love and admire.

"Thea."

A soft kiss to each eyelid caused her lashes to flutter open.

"Thea."

Thea sighed. This rising they were to leave the safety of Borderland and travel across the tundra toward an uncertain future. No matter how much she might wish otherwise, her destiny called.

She opened her eyes to find herself lying on the thick fur in Galen's cave, the mystical darkness they had shared no more than a cherished memory. Galen had obviously been awake for a while. He was fully clothed, and his possessions

had been packed and stored neatly by the cave
entrance, waiting to be carried to his equox.

Thea offered a silent prayer that their journey would be safe, their battle successful, then
rose from the bed of fur. She carefully folded the
gown she'd borrowed from Mya, placed it upon
the bedding, then donned her own woolen robe
and tied it snugly about her waist. She gathered
her warm boots and the wool and fur cloak she'd
worn from Glacia, then walked to Galen's side.

"Thea—"

"No, Galen. There are no words to be said.
What must be done, must be done." She took
one more quick glance around the cave, remembered all she had learned about Borderland and
the people who had become so dear to her, then
left the cave.

Galen picked up his packs and followed her to
the central cave where his warriors waited.

Thea walked slowly among the people gathered
in the center cave. She looked deeply into their
eyes, read their sorrow, and felt it mirrored in
her own heart. She touched the tawny hair of
a small boy, smiled down at several young girls
who grasped her woolen robe, returned Mya's
hug, and kissed Deja's sleeping face.

The silence in the cave was unsettling. No one
spoke. The children were unnaturally still. A tremendous blast of thunder echoed through the
caves, scaring the two northern equox saddled
near the cave exit. Several warriors hurried to
calm the beasts, and the chilling calm was shattered.

Galen placed his hand upon Thea's shoulder,
and felt her tremble beneath the folds of her

woolen garment. He pulled her against his chest, and held her there for several heartbeats before he reached to lift her chin so he could look into her eyes.

"Thea," he whispered, leaning close to kiss her forehead.

She looked up at him, tears streaming down her cheeks. He wiped one away.

"I'm afraid," she said softly.

"We all are, my heart."

She smiled. "I love you, Galen."

"I love you, Thea of Glacia." He kissed her lips. A great cheer erupted in the cave.

Thea buried her head against his chest to hide her embarrassment, then drew a deep breath and faced the people of Borderland. "I shall miss every one of you," she said. Then, before the tears began to fall again, she walked to her equox and accepted Thorn's assistance into her saddle.

She closed her eyes, concentrated on the days ahead, and drew strength from all Gustoff had taught her. She did not hear Galen's parting words to his people, did not realize he had mounted and joined her at the mouth of the cave until he touched her hand.

"Destiny awaits us. Come." Galen spurred his equox and left the cave. Thea followed.

The impatient slap of his riding crop and the tap of his boot heels echoed off the stone walls as Berezan paced the meeting chamber. He strode through one of the archways that led to the balcony, pausing at the rail to look down over all he commanded.

The slippery streets were empty. Shadows from the mountains cast the tiny houses with smoke belching from stone chimneys into darkness. League after league of snow and ice crept up steep mountains with jagged, snowcapped peaks that reached the clouds and beyond. Hundreds of docile citizens huddled inside their tiny shacks, afraid to come outside, afraid to face him.

But his victory felt hollow.

He had searched every inch of the keep from the steam baths to Gustoff's tower and had not found the Sphere of Light.

Berezan shook his fist to the sky and damned Gustoff for the hundredth time since arriving in Glacia. He cursed Elsbar for never fully explaining all he would encounter in Glacia.

He closed his eyes and remembered the old man who had been more of a father to him than his own sire. Elsbar had been correct. Gustoff *was* a worthy adversary. Even in death, he protected the hiding place of the Sphere of Light.

Yet, it *had* to be in Governing House.

Or close by . . .

Berezan turned abruptly and entered the meeting chamber. He stomped toward the table. He hurled his riding crop to the table's center, then leaned forward to wrap his fingers around the edge of the carved wood. He tensed the muscles in his arms and hands, raised his head, and stared into the lumastone chandelier.

Incantations—strange, foreign—once again spilled from his lips.

His heart raced. His lungs burned. Every cell in his body tingled as Berezan placed himself into a seeking trance.

Cold air rushed past his face, stung his eyes. He looked down to the frozen ground, watched a black shadow—wings spread wide—sweep over

344

the snow. Three strokes of his powerful wings took him higher, above the frosted peaks, beyond the wispy clouds, to an altitude where the air was thin, the sunlight blinding.

He ascended higher. Higher still.

The village of Glacia, the keep, and the mountains filled the panorama beneath him.

Honing his senses, he concentrated on any power greater than his own and began to circle, each pass taking him lower, closer to his domain. He flapped his mighty wings to ease his descent, extended sharp talons to grasp the crumbled edge that remained of Gustoff's tower, settled his wings close to his body, then twisted his head in all directions.

Nothing!

His heart rate soared. Blood pumped frantically through his veins. A predator's vision caught the figures of a woman and child hurrying across the roadway.

Black rage consumed him. His wings extended, caught the wind that whipped around tower, lifted him from his perch. He collapsed his wings, talons extended, and dove.

"Master?"

Berezan jerked his head toward the sound of his commander's voice. Rhem ushered three old men toward the enormous table that took up almost the entire meeting room. Berezan clenched his fists harder to his sides to subdue the impulse to lash out at the three men in anger.

"This is Elder Faudrey, Master." Rhem pointed to the bent old man garbed in a white robe belted with gold. He was supported at each elbow by two other men in gray. "These are Messahs Thaddius and Jermaine." Rhem indicated the men cloaked in gray at the Elder's left and right, nodded, then stepped away to stand at attention before the chamber door.

Berezan strode across the chamber floor and paused before the men, looking down on them from his imposing height. He swallowed hard, vowing to control his fury until he had the answers he sought. He blew out a disgusted sigh. "You were summoned to arrive at Governing House three moonrises ago."

"We were delayed by the Elder's health, Master," the man introduced as Jermaine explained. "Elder Faudrey has been suffering from a weakening that has severely limited his mobility."

Berezan studied the old man under discussion. His face, pale as the robe the Elder wore and lined with wrinkles that resembled the parched deserts of Solarus after a season with no moisture, lifted slowly. Sunlight filtering in through the three draped archways defined each whisker in his sparse silver beard. Tiny bloodshot eyes of a color Berezan could not determine peeked through lids barely slitted, and his mouth, no more than a slash beneath an overlong mustache, seemed to be bent by pain.

"Why did you bring this old man to me?"

Jermaine bowed his head, exposing his bald pate. "W-we held a conference in the Temple of the Peaks, Master. The Elders searched their memories for any recollection of the item for which you search. None have any knowledge to offer you. Elder Faudrey has seen one hundred and forty-three winters. He alone remembers stories told by his ancestors of the Sphere of Light."

Berezan stepped forward and grabbed the old man by the front of his robe. "Tell me what you

346

know, old man. Your time is close, but I can make it that much closer if you deny me!"

The old man did not blink at Berezan's threat. He raised his withered hand and grasped Berezan's, digging his long, bent nails deeply into the exposed flesh. "I see much in your eyes, Berezan," he said with a raspy voice. "I see great hatred, and an evil so dark it consumes you. But even with all the powers you claim to have, you have no weapon to use against me. You cannot take from me what I refuse to give. If you insist on killing me, you will never know what secrets I carry to the ever after."

Berezan's hand shook beneath the old man's fingers. He choked down the rage that rose like bile in his throat, the instinct to kill that fired his blood. He had destroyed Gustoff's tower in search of the Sphere of Light. He had scrutinized each square inch of Governing House, sent his men into the villages to empty the contents of every house out into the snow, and moments ago he'd examined the mountains beyond. He had found nothing.

Nothing!

Now this old man stood before him, questioning the power he could wield.

Berezan closed his eyes, concentrated on the tips of his fingers, the old man's withered hand. Heat radiated from Berezan's fingertips, traveled up his fingers, across the back of his hand, burning the old man's flesh, his robe, the tip of his beard, before Berezan released the Elder's garment and spun to vent his ire on the vermillion draperies hung at the floor to ceiling windows that led to the balcony.

Arcs of red fire shot across the chamber, igniting the lengths of fabric. Fire charred the ceiling, the stone archways, then dropped with the burning material to the chamber floor.

Berezan watched it burn until nothing but ashes and smoke remained. He turned to find the Messahs gaping at the carnage. He stared at the Messahs, at faces gone as white as the Elder's robe. He watched their bodies tremble beneath the folds of their long gray garments, then gazed at the Elder. The old man had dropped his burnt hands to his sides, clenching his skeletal fists, yet he met Berezan's gaze without fear.

"Tell me what you know, old man, before I decide to cremate your companions," Berezan whispered.

The old man blinked, then raised his clenched hands. The Messahs reached to restrain him, but the Elder shook his head, forbidding their action. He took a step closer to Berezan.

He straightened his bent body and drew a deep breath. "I have heard the stories of your childhood you have spread since your arrival in Glacia, Berezan. Anyone who might doubt you are anyone other than who you claim need only to look into your face to see your father, Arlin DeLan. I understand how you could believe you have the right to claim your place as heir."

The old man shook his head. "But I look into your eyes, your soul, and see the evil Gustoff must have sensed when you were but a small boy."

"Old man—"

The Elder raised his hand. "I understand you have destroyed Gustoff." He pointed a twisted finger at Berezan. "By committing that crime, you have forfeited any right you might have had to govern!"

Berezan raised his hands. Jermaine and Thaddius stepped forward to shield the Elder. Fire flew from Berezan's fingertips, striking the Messahs, reducing them to ashes. The Elder looked down at the remains of his companions, then back at Berezan.

Tears streaked the old man's face. "I pray Gustoff will be forgiven in his afterlife for what he did to you as a child, but I am sorry he did not destroy you when he had the opportunity."

The Elder collapsed to the chamber floor, drawing his last breath and taking any secrets he might have disclosed with him into his next life.

Berezan's shouts of rage echoed off the chamber walls. He turned and stomped to the table, banged his fists against the wood, then faced his commander, who still stood at the door.

"I *will not* be denied!" he shouted, then disappeared in a flash of brilliant light.

Solarus . . .

Berezan drew his emerald cloak around him to ward off the chill. Darkness surrounded him. A cool, damp breeze blew in through the open window at the far side of the tower. The old boards in the floor creaked as he walked toward the window, paused, and looked up into the midnight sky. Raindrops splattered the windowsill, causing vapor to rise from the warmer stone. He held out his hand, captured a few drops of the moisture that fell so rarely from the sky over Solarus, closed his hand into a fist, and slammed it against the sill.

Turning, Berezan lifted his hand above his head. Sparks of light ignited his fingertips. He looked around, found a tallow, lit it, then grasped the holder. He shielded the flame with his hand. Shadows and faint light preceded him across the floor.

As he set the candle down on the table Elsbar had used for his maps and calculations, he noted the ink his mentor had used had spilled on the parchment, run in a snaking trail over the edge of the table, and dried in a dark puddle on the floor.

He circled the table. A dark form blocked his path.

Berezan reached for the candle, held it out before him, then cried out. The lifeless form of Elsbar lay on the floor, eyes wide open, as if he had died in fear.

Berezan dropped to his knees, touched the old man's cheek, and found that Elsbar's skin was as hard as stone. In his cold, twisted fingers, he still clutched the old quill he had used to etch out the strategies they had drawn to progress this far with Berezan's plans to reclaim his heritage.

Reaching forward with shaky hands, Berezan closed the old man's eyes. He sat back on his haunches, gazing out of the window into the dismal night.

The sense of being totally alone closed over him. He drew several deep breaths in an attempt to regain his composure, but memories got in the way. He saw the old man who had cared for him, helped a small boy survive when no one else gave a damn whether he lived or died. The old man who, no matter how much Berezan had ranted and raved and threatened, had deserved a comfortable life, which Berezan had planned to provide before he drew his last breath.

Berezan rose slowly to his feet, cast one final glance at Elsbar's still form, then searched the tower for additional light sources. He lit several more tallows, then stood in the center of the tower and searched for whatever Elsbar had been frightened by when he died.

The parchment on the table drew his attention. Berezan grabbed a tallow, moved it closer to Elsbar's work, and examined the etchings scribbled across the page. He bent closer, not believing the symbols and shapes so like those he had seen in Gustoff's tower. He touched the script, followed the flowing ink marks with the tip of his finger. He then studied the other marks about the parchment, and knew these foreign designs had not been made by Elsbar's hand.

Rage caused his body to tremble. He slammed his fist against the parchment, then crushed it in his hand.

"You were right, old man," he whispered to Elsbar's silent form. "Many times you warned me, but I did not believe you." Berezan closed his eyes. The parchment within his grasp went up in flames. "Gustoff could not be trusted, could he, old man?"

Berezan raised his arms above his head. He spread his fingers wide. Arcs of red fire danced between his fingertips, jumped from hand to hand.

An ancient chant spilled from his lips. Berezan swayed back and forth, breathing slowly, deeply, speaking the words Elsbar had taught him so long ago. He opened his eyes and watched as a bright glow filled the tower, as Elsbar's body shimmered in the light, then disappeared.

He looked up into the darkness of the ceiling. "You have tried to take away everything I have ever needed, Gustoff of Glacia. But you have not won."

He rose, turned, and looked for a final time at the tower.

Thunder rumbled across the night sky.

Berezan raised his fist, shook it. *"I will not be defeated!"*

Lightning flashed through the empty tower.

Chapter Twenty-Nine

Thea huddled deeper into the mounds of fur. She drew her knees to her chest, crossed her booted feet, and raised her hands to press the thick hood that covered her head closer to her ears to block out the sound of the wind howling beyond her tent and blowing in through the seams she and the other women had stitched, causing the tiny fire at the tent's center to sputter.

Thea wished for Borderland's heat to still the trembling of her body. Sighing, she recalled she had been warmer in Borderland than she'd ever been in her life, and free from the restrictive layers of clothing that did little to hold out the cold of the tundra.

She silently cursed the chattering of her teeth, not welcoming as she had on her first journey through the tundra the sound that echoed in the wind. She needed sleep, blessed oblivion that would chase away the cold, the memories, the thoughts of what lay ahead. Sleep would fully restore her powers for her confrontation with Berezan.

Thea agonized over the time it took to travel from Borderland to Glacia, and the people she had left without her protection.

Day blended into night. Had it only been four sunrises ago when they had left Borderland? She remembered their departure from Cree, the gallant way the warriors of Borderland marched through the jungles, the crystal-clear springs that flowed up from cracks in the earth along the thaw line, the way the air grew cooler, the vegetation more sparse the farther north they traveled.

Galen spent more and more time with his men, leaving her alone in their tent. At first she had welcomed the privacy, using the time to remember all the lessons Gustoff had taught her, all he'd told her of Berezan, and what she had seen take place with her own eyes in the valley of ice.

Now the hours of loneliness bred doubts, and doubts bred fear.

Be strong in your convictions, Thea DeLan, Last of the Ancient Ones. Hold true to your feelings. . . . See your destiny through. . . .

Gustoff's words haunted her. Thea missed the old man deeply, wished he had confided his plans to her before he left Glacia and met Berezan alone in the valley. She swallowed and squeezed her lashes against the tears that threatened to fall, fearing the moisture would freeze on her face.

Moments passed. The wind continued to howl. The fire sputtered. Thea tossed restlessly, attempting to find a comfortable position to sleep. After several minutes and no success, she struggled into a sitting position, crossed her booted feet before her, and shook her head.

It was no use. Until Galen decided to return to their tent, she would never be able to relax enough to sleep, or to be warm enough. Over the past three moonrises they had shared each other's heat, cuddled close during the long night hours, but little more. Thea missed the touch of his hand upon her flesh, the feel of his big body pressed intimately against hers, the taste of him.

Thea groaned. She thought about Elijah and Nola, the plans they had made before she and Galen left Glacia, and prayed her friends had been successful in their efforts to evacuate as many of the people of as possible to Dekar before Berezan's arrival.

Thea visualized the battle she had witnessed between Berezan and Gustoff. She wiggled her hands free from the long sleeves of her cloak, held them over the tiny fire for added warmth, then raised them above the fire to stare at the tips of her fingers.

She whispered incantations Gustoff had made her recite over and over again as a child. Warmth flowed from her shoulders, down her arms, her hands, to the end of her nails. Tiny sparks of blue flame danced on the tips of her extended fingers. She wiggled her fingers. The flames swayed back and forth, disappearing when she closed her hands.

She opened her hands, recalling the spell that came quickly to her now. The flames ignited again. Stiffening her fingers, curling them like talons, she concentrated harder. The height of the flames was neither increased nor diminished by her efforts.

"It's no use," Thea whispered in frustration. "I can light a fire, a candle, warm hands. But what good will this do against Berezan? If I only knew what form the power of the Sphere would take with me."

The tent flap opened. A cold gust of wind blew across her face. Galen huddled in the doorway, snow and ice caked in his hair, across the bridge of his nose, in the fur that hugged his neck. She looked away, unable to face him, unable to explain her failure.

"Thea."

She shook her head, listening while he crawled into the tent, secured the flap, then shook the snow away when he removed his outer cloak.

"Thea," he whispered.

She bowed her head. "I cannot create anything more than a flicker of light. I've tried, but I don't—"

His cold fingertips touched her lips. "Don't do this to yourself. Perhaps it was never meant to be that you meet Berezan with his own magic." He grasped her hands, kissed each trembling digit. "You told me Gustoff explained there was no way to know how the Sphere would react with each different Guardian."

Galen smiled. "You punish yourself needlessly, my heart."

"I know, but—"

Galen hushed her with a kiss. "Gustoff was adamant in his belief you would succeed. He never doubted you, Thea. You should not doubt yourself." He pulled her close, held her against his chest.

"I believe there is a power within me that will destroy Berezan's evil. Gustoff would never have left me to this task alone if there was any chance I might fail." She raised her hands, spread her palms against his cheek, and called forth her inner fire to warm his flesh.

"I have faith, but I'm still terrified, Galen," she whispered against his neck.

Galen kissed the top of her bent head. He pulled her with him as he lay down on the thick fur that made up the tent floor, covered them with another fur, slid her into the curve of his body to shield her from the cold, then lay awake long after her trembling had subsided and her breathing had become slow, regular.

He didn't dare think of what the future might bring, nor plan or dream beyond their journey to Glacia. Instead he thought over the strategies he and the other warriors had discussed earlier, reconstructed the keep in his mind's eye, saw each corridor, doorway, and alcove his army might use for a hiding place while they awaited the opportunity to strike Berezan's forces.

He couldn't consider Thea's part in the upcoming confrontation. Hearing the frustration in her voice was enough to send his heart into palpitations. His anxiety turned quickly to anger. He cursed fate, Gustoff, and himself for placing Thea in danger, for taking such a delicate creature and demanding she destroy or be destroyed.

Galen choked down his anger, cuddling Thea closer. He smelled her hair, remembering the first time he'd inhaled the mysterious fragrance that enticed him more and more as each day passed. He stroked her arm, her side, and finally cupped the fullness of her breast. Swallowing hard, he buried his lips in the wild tangles of auburn at the crown of her head. "I love you, Thea of Glacia. I will do all within my power to protect you from harm."

Thea wrapped her cloak more tightly around her and climbed to the top of a small ice-covered hill. She stood unmoving for several moments, feeling the cold breeze swirl up under her heavy woolen skirts and circle her legs. She looked down upon their camp, wondering at the peace that settled over the tundra as the warriors took to their beds. Turning, she studied the higher peaks of Glacia in the moonlight, the snowcaps that glistened pearly white, the black night sky, the countless stars in the heavens.

Coming home touched her deeply. Warmth grew within her, reaching outward to heat the tips of her toes, her fingers. She thought about the people of Glacia, those she had never come to know. Were they safe? Had Berezan's arrival in Glacia changed their simple lifestyles?

Her thoughts turned to the women and children left behind in the caves of *Naro*. She remembered each trusting face, every smile. Her heart beat a little faster. Another glance toward the camp below caused it to pound against the walls of her chest.

Galen and the warriors of Borderland were trained and ready to give their lives to insure the safety of their families.

The few gentle men she knew in Glacia, so different from the proud men who slept below, came to mind. How many had died if they had refused her command and engaged in efforts to save their own from Berezan's wrath?

Tears flooded over her lashes. Thea let them fall.

"Thea."

She had not heard Galen approach. She raised her hand, hastily wiping at the tears that wet her cheeks, not wanting him to witness any more weakness on her part. His arm draped around her shoulder, drawing her nearer, offering strength and warmth. She fell against him, accepted his offerings, listened to the thundering of his heart.

Thea closed her eyes, remembered his pledge given on an eve that seemed so long ago. His sword, his heart, his life.

Could she offer him any less?

"We should reach the keep by moonrise tomorrow," he whispered.

Thea swallowed hard. They had one plan, one opportunity to reach Berezan and put an end to his tyranny. If they failed . . .

"Come." Galen steadied her steps down the hillside, led her to their tent, then cradled her body for long hours before Thea finally closed her eyes.

"It *has* to be here!" Galen ran his fingers over the rough stone, feeling for the doorway he knew had to be located in this area. He stepped back, studied again the wall of granite that filled the ravine on the southernmost side of the keep. Glacia's Governing House was built inside the mountain. The abandoned tunnel he had found was but one of the numerous caverns and corridors that twisted away from the center of the keep.

He looked up. The stone climbed upward for 50 spans before disappearing again into the side of the mountain. He then glanced over his shoulder toward his warriors huddled in the shadows created under the full moon.

"The moon will be directly overhead soon, Galen. Our cover of shadow will be lost," Thea whispered. "Perhaps we should use the exit Elijah led us to when we left the keep."

Galen looked up into the sky again, then around at his warriors standing near. "There's no time to circle the mountain and enter through another passageway."

Thea stepped forward and touched the cold stone. A flicker of recognition flared to life inside her. She ran her palms over the rough surface, pausing a moment when the strange feelings within her grew sharper, moving on when they faded. "Something *is* here, Galen," she whispered. "I think . . ." She retraced the stone she had just passed. "Gustoff!"

Galen touched her shoulder. "What is it?"

"Gustoff has been near, Galen. He's touched this stone. I can feel his essence, though it is very weak." She trailed her finger down to the snow-covered ground, then up again, outlining a perfect doorway in the stone. "This is an illusion, Galen. What appears to be solid rock is not." She stepped back, raised her hands into the air, and uttered several strange words.

After a moment, she shook her head. "I cannot undo whatever he did."

"But if it's an illusion . . ."

Thea reached up, touched Galen's temples. "Concentrate. Look at the wall. See only what you wish to see, not what your mind tells you is there."

"The doorway . . ."

"Reach out. Touch it. Feel the seams with your fingers."

Galen did, then turned to Kajar. "Give me a pike." He placed the hard steel edge into the seam he had visualized, applied all of his strength, and bit his cheek to subdue his shout when the stone moved.

Kajar stepped quickly forward, adding his strength to Galen's. Within moments a gaping rectangular hole stood in the surface of solid granite.

The warriors of Borderland wasted no time on awe. They gathered their packs, hurried into the dark, cold corridor, took seats along the stone wall, and awaited further instructions.

Thea walked among the warriors uncapping the ancient lumalanterns that lined the walls. Bright light filled the corridor, illuminating each face, each pair of eyes. She listened as Galen once again explained his strategies, studying the acceptance in each man's expression. She looked to the far end of the corridor, at the old wooden door shielding them from the lower level of the keep, and wondered what went on beyond that door.

Thea found a vacant spot along the wall, sat down, and closed her eyes. She concentrated on Berezan, believing she could sense his evil presence no matter where he might be inside the keep.

Three deep breaths calmed her heart rate, slowing the blood flow through her veins. She exhaled slowly, counting to ten. Images of the steam baths, the bedchambers, the hydro gardens, and Gustoff's tower flooded her mind.

Chills crawled over her flesh. Every cell tingled.

Concentrating on the interior of the keep, she opened her eyes and found herself standing at the head of the circular stairway, the chandelier of lumalights dangling 30 spans below her. She focused on each closed door, searching beyond to find empty chambers. One after another, she searched the corridors and passageways of Glacia, finding no trace of Berezan or his army.

Thea closed her eyes again, visualizing Gustoff's tower. She almost lost control when she opened her eyes to discover the destruction that had taken place around her. The enormous bookshelves which had held Gustoff's cherished scrolls and ancient books were destroyed. Bits and pieces of wood were strewn about the interior of the stone chamber.

She looked up. Moonlight poured in through what had once been a wooden roof. Great piles of ashes littered the stone floor. Only scraps of the primitive leather bindings remained of thousands of years of recorded history.

Thea felt herself weakening. The tower room began to fade. Cold crept along her limbs. She inhaled deeply, drawing more strength from the energy within her, wanting to hold on for a while longer—

"Thea!"

Thea jumped. Galen's hands were on her shoulders, shaking her. She blinked several times to clear the fuzziness from her head.

"Thea!"

She stared into his face, gasped a deep breath, and held it to slow the thundering of her heart. "Berezan's not in the keep," she whispered.

Galen's face was pale, his movements frantic. "Thea, what's wrong? Are you ill?"

She swallowed and forced a weak smile. "I'm fine, warrior. Please." Thea shrugged her shoulders beneath his hands. "You are bruising my arms."

Galen looked down, realized he was holding her too tightly, and dropped his hands. "You were so pale, so cold."

Thea closed her eyes, remembered the destruction she'd seen, the emptiness she'd felt, and prayed the keep was vacant because Elijah and Nola had been successful. "I've searched the keep, Galen. Berezan is nowhere to be found."

"H-how?" he stuttered.

"Someday I'll explain," she said, reaching to touch his face. "The keep is empty, warrior. No one is about, not even Berezan's army. From what I can determine, the hydro gardens have not been tended in many days. Vegetables have rotted on the vines."

Galen's brow arched in confusion. "If Berezan is not here, where is he? What happened to the servants of Glacia?"

Thea sighed, then reached to stroke his cheek. "I pray the absence of Glacians in the keep means Elijah and Nola were able to warn the people before Berezan arrived. As to Berezan's whereabouts, I wish I knew."

Galen sat down beside her and drew her into his arms.

"He has destroyed Gustoff's tower," she said softly. "All of Gustoff's books, his scrolls, have been burned. Thousands of years of recorded history have been lost."

Galen started to speak. Thea hushed him with a finger to his lips. "Later." She leaned her head into his shoulder, closed her eyes.

363

"Galen?"

Galen looked up into Thorn's concerned eyes. He shook his head. "There are many things I still don't understand about my woman."

Thorn chuckled, then took a seat at Galen's side. "If Berezan is not here, what do we do now?"

Galen placed his hand upon Thea's back, leaned his head against the stone wall, and closed his eyes. "We wait."

Chapter Thirty

Thea sat straight up out of a dead sleep. Her heart raced, her pulse pounded, and perspiration dampened her forehead. She drew several slow breaths to calm herself. She looked down the darkened corridor, over the warriors asleep along the walls, and studied each one carefully in an attempt to identify what had awakened her so abruptly.

Galen shifted at her side. She glanced at him. His big body was bent in an unnatural position, but he appeared to be in a deep slumber.

She closed her eyes, searched within for an answer to her question. When it came the answer sent chills along her spine and caused her whole body to tremble.

Berezan!

Thea could sense him, feel his evil crawl over her flesh like static. She grabbed two handfuls of her woolen robe to keep from digging at her skin to ease her discomfort. She concentrated on his essence, choking on the malevolence that radiated from his being and filled her every pore.

She disappeared in a flash of light.

Thea opened her eyes to find herself standing in the enormous meeting room her father had used to conduct Glacia's business. She looked around, noting the smoke-darkened stone surrounding the three open archways and the ashes on the floor. She gazed up at the lumalights suspended overhead, remembering Gustoff in this same room, the Messahs, the hundreds of times her father had sat at the head chair.

Something moved in the shadows at the other side of the chamber. Thea held her breath, knowing the time had come to face her destiny. She braced herself, clenching her hands so tightly her nails dug into her palms.

A man stepped from the shadows and paused about 30 spans away. The lumalight reflected off a long emerald cloak that swayed around his booted feet, but stopped short of revealing the man's face. He took another step. Light flooded his features.

Thea gasped. Her father's essence filled the chamber, reached out, drew her closer. She took a hesitant step. The man took another. She looked into his eyes, into pools of brown that mirrored her own. The light reflected off streaks of red in his brown hair. Thea glanced down at a tendril of her own hair resting against her breast, at the color reflected by the light, then up again to study his face, wanting to find her father's familiar smile, the mustache of auburn she had touched as a small child, but finding none of her father's kindness.

The man brought his hand to his head and rubbed it through his hair, apparently analyzing her as she studied him. She noted his fingers were not wrinkled with age, but were long, strong, and straight.

Another chill raced up her spine, freezing her foot in place as she prepared to take another step closer.

"Who are you?" she whispered.

A familiar evil laugh filled the chamber.

"Ah, a little sister."

Thea gasped. It could not be—it had to be an illusion. This could not be the same man who had faced Gustoff in the valley of the tundra. "No. You cannot be—"

"Your brother?" Berezan crossed his arms over his chest, spread his booted feet wide. "Why not? Do you not believe it possible to have a brother you knew nothing about? I certainly had no idea you existed."

Thea shook her head, denying what her eyes told her was true. It couldn't be. Her father would not have designated Alec as his heir if—

"It's not possible. Gustoff would have told me about you."

Berezan's evil laugh once again filled the chamber. He took a step closer, completely out of the shadows so Thea could get a good look at his face, his body. "Gustoff," he growled. "That wonderful old man who stole a child of six from his bed and sent him to the deserts of Solarus to meet his death."

Thea shook her head adamantly, not knowing how else to respond to the ridiculous accusations this man, her brother, cast at the mentor she had known and loved her entire life.

She watched him tap his fingers against his biceps, noting that his facial expressions were those she remembered from her father. The hair. Those eyes. Tiny seeds of doubt sprang to life in her mind. Why would Gustoff lie to her about Berezan? Why had her brother's name never been mentioned during her childhood?

"Come closer. Let me get a better look at you."

Thea took two steps back, resisting the mesmerizing quality of his voice that attacked her willpower. He was a tall man, almost Galen's height, but his shoulders were not as wide, his legs not as muscular. He stood with his shoulders squared, his chin held high, his hands once again planted firmly upon his hips.

"Do not be afraid of me, dear sister." He held his left hand out to her. "I would harm only those who stand in my way as I claim the destiny denied me so many years ago."

Thea turned away, refused to look at him. "I don't know you."

"Of course you do. Look at me."

Something touched her, sent a chill over her body, forced her to do his bidding. Thea struggled against his hold, but she had no will of her own. She met his gaze.

"I am Berezan DeLan, son of Arlin and Dimetria." Berezan raised his hands into the air. "Behold all that is around you, sister. Know it is and shall always remain mine!"

No matter how hard Thea tried, she could do little more than stare into his eyes. She trembled. Fury flashed through her nerves like lightning. She gasped for breath, held it, counted to ten, and repeated the ritual three times. It didn't help relieve her temper, nor did it settle her nerves. "You have no right, Berezan. You are evil. You have destroyed and killed. Glacia will never belong to you!"

Berezan shook his head. "Is it evil to try to reclaim all that has been taken away from me? I think not." He stroked his hand through his hair again. "Besides, I have an army a thousand strong awaiting my command in the village. No other power in our world is strong enough to defeat me or say nay to my claim as leader."

Thea closed her eyes, blocking out Berezan's words. She thought about Gustoff, Galen, the people of Glacia, of Borderland, anything that would distort the visions her brother's words planted within her mind. It took every ounce of willpower she possessed to overcome the mysterious hold Berezan had over her, but she persevered.

Galen's face appeared along with those of the warriors of Borderland huddled in the hidden corridor. *Galen! Please hear my voice! Berezan's army is in the village. Go there, my love. See your mission through!*

Galen came awake with a start. He pushed past the wild palpitations of his heart and concentrated on the words that replayed in his mind. Thea's voice. He heard her words as clearly as if she had been standing next to him.

"Kajar!"

His warriors were immediately on their feet, weapons at ready. They stood at attention, awaiting their orders.

"It's time, old friend." Galen drew his sword

369

from its sheath, then grasped Kajar's arm. "Come."

Galen led his warriors to the exit Elijah had shown him when he and Thea had left Glacia days ago to follow Gustoff. They flooded out into the streets of Glacia, taking Berezan's warriors by surprise. At the sight of the warriors of Borderland, fully armed and ready for battle, many of Berezan's men turned and fled down the slippery roadway.

"Kajar!"

Kajar turned to engage the soldier charging toward him. Galen stepped to his flank and raised his sword to do battle with another of Berezan's soldiers.

Thea opened her eyes to stare into eyes like her own.

"Your beloved Gustoff stole me from my bed, told our father I had died in my sleep, and paid a servant woman to take me into the deserts of Solarus and dispose of me." Berezan paced back and forth under the lumalight.

"Fortunately, the servant was greedy and sold me to an old hermit for six crystals." He stopped pacing, placed his fisted hands upon his hips, and stared into her eyes. "You have been the fortunate one, little sister. Since you grew up in luxury, there is no way you could know how it feels to be abandoned by a father you loved, cast out into the desert where your thirst was never quenched, your flesh never clean."

Berezan turned, paced again. His emerald cape billowed out behind him as he walked. "My one stroke of good luck was that the man who purchased me, Elsbar, treated me kindly, and taught me all he knew of the arts of the Ancient Ones."

Berezan stood with his head held back, his hands at his sides. "Glacia is mine, little sister. I am the rightful heir to all around us!"

He turned, folded his arms over his chest. "Gustoff used the magic of the Ancient Ones to kill Elsbar, little sister. He murdered a defenseless old man!"

Thea thought about what Berezan had told her of Elsbar, of the dark magic he obviously possessed, and knew Gustoff had not murdered a defenseless being. He had destroyed a part of Berezan's evil.

"The Ancient Ones never used their powers for evil, Berezan. This old man Elsbar spoke false."

"Did he?" He raised a dark brow. "Perhaps your limited knowledge has been tainted by Gustoff's words, little one. Elsbar once believed he and Gustoff were the last in the world to carry the Ancient Ones' powers, but he was wrong. When Elsbar saw in me what had caused Gustoff to cast me out, he knew I was destined for higher things."

You are wrong, Berezan! There is yet another chosen one left!

Thea had to bite her lip to keep from hurling her thoughts at Berezan. Instead, she searched deep inside her heart, waiting for some spark, some hint of the affection she felt should be present for one of her kin. She saw only the city of Cree, the sad faces of the people of Borderland, the destruction this man had left in his wake as he journeyed to reclaim his heritage.

She shuddered, thinking the same thing could happen to Glacia, remembering a sample of his malevolence in Gustoff's chamber, the battle that had taken place between him and Gustoff in the valley of ice.

In the place of a kinship, she found evil, an evil she knew she must destroy.

But how? Gustoff had tried and failed.

The passing of the Sphere of Light gives you the knowledge of the Ancient Ones to be hidden in the depths of your mind until the demand for such knowledge surrounds you. When needed, a voice will come, whispered through thousands of years and by generations.

Cherish the truths and confidences you have been taught, for if you allow doubts and uncertainties to fester and grow, the power of the Sphere will be weakened.

Bless you, Thea, daughter of the Ancient Ones.

Gustoff's voice filled her mind, speaking words she remembered hearing him speak before. The warmth of his love flowed through her. "You are the one who's wrong, Berezan. Glacia will never be yours," Thea hissed, and listening to the foreign words that whispered in her mind, she repeated the sounds, forming her tongue to create the garbled tones.

She raised her hands into the air, felt the energy within her flare and grow, heating her flesh, her hands, surging through every blood vessel, every nerve. Her fingers filled with a brilliant white light, pulsing, growing, encompassing her hands, her arms.

Berezan cursed himself for a fool thrice over. He listened to his sister speak words in the tongue of the Ancient Ones, watched as her eyes grew almost twice their normal size. His hands shook, his body trembled, every inch of his flesh tightened and contracted.

He dug his fingers into his hair, closing his eyes against the light that grew stronger and brighter with each word passed from her lips. He reached deep within, summoning the dark power that would destroy this weak girl and allow him to possess what was rightfully his.

Galen clutched his side, staring down at the warm stickiness that flowed over his fingers. He pressed hard against his torn flesh to stem the blood flow, then wiped the blood of the Solarian who had given him the wound off his sword on the dead soldier's clothing.

He turned, stumbled as the frozen ground shook beneath his feet, and looked up at the keep a hundred spans above his head.

Galen tried to keep a tight rein on his nerves, forcing himself to look back at the battle going on around him instead of overhead to where his love might forfeit her life to fulfill her destiny. He ignored the constant spasms in his stomach, the feel of cold sweat running in torrents beneath his woolen tunic, the ache between his shoulder blades, the pain in his heart.

Kajar stepped to his side, drawing his attention. "Hundreds of Berezan's soldiers have fled down the mountain roadway, Galen."

Galen looked at the carnage strewn over the icy main street of Glacia, with 50 or so men still locked in mortal combat. Hundreds of bodies littered the snow. Blood froze in pools that shimmered in the sunlight. Discarded weapons lay where they were dropped or had been kicked aside in the heat of battle.

Thankfully, though his warriors had suffered many wounds, none seemed serious.

"Galen!"

Galen turned and engaged swords with another member of Berezan's army. He lunged, locking hilts with the soldier's bloody sword, pinning it back against the stone of the mountain, while he grasped a knife protruding from the interloper's belt with his free hand and slashed upward across the man's exposed throat.

"What's happening?" Kajar shouted, his voice barely audible over the howling of the wind.

Thunder rumbled overhead. Shadows crossed the ice, blocking out the sun. Galen looked up. Thick black clouds reminiscent of the ones he'd seen over the ice valley where Gustoff and Berezan had met filled the sky. A strange red glow flashed like lightning through three arched windows, reflected from the dark clouds.

The thunder grew stronger. The ground quaked beneath his boots. Wind whipped over his body, picked up energy, wound through the streets, between the stone houses, whistled through his hair.

Galen brushed the hair from his eyes. His heart did somersaults in his chest; his blood ran like iced water through his veins. "Thea!"

Kajar grabbed his arm. "Go to her!"

Arcs of red fire sprang from Berezan's fingertips, streaked across the chamber toward Thea. She braced herself for the impact, held her hands higher to shield her face, not knowing or understanding the power she held in her palms.

The Sphere of Light absorbed Berezan's fire and grew larger.

One after another, red arcs crossed the chamber, collided with the stone wall behind her, burned craters in the granite, upon the floor at her feet. The walls shook. The floor vibrated, making it extremely hard for Thea to maintain her balance.

Thea's hands trembled. She didn't know how much longer she could hold on, how many more of Berezan's evil strikes she could withstand. She offered a silent prayer, seeking Gustoff's guidance, listened for his words of instruction, and found only silence.

"Give that to me! It is mine! You have no idea how to control the Sphere! It will destroy both of us!" Berezan's voice echoed around the chamber.

Thea could do no more than shake her head at his demand.

"The Sphere is mine! Give it to me! Now!" Berezan began a chant of his own, speaking words Thea did not understand. The red arcs of fire spewing from his fingertips grew stronger, merging together to form a huge burning globe that encompassed half of the chamber.

The chamber became unbearably hot. Perspiration dripped into her eyes, blurred her vision. Heat siphoned more of her strength, weakened the muscles in her arms, burned through to the very marrow of her bones.

Thea swallowed hard. She shook her head. She needed to lower her hand, wipe the moisture from her eyes. But she held strong. "No! Gustoff passed the Sphere to me for safekeeping, Berezan! I will not allow you to possess it! I will see it destroyed before it falls into your hands!"

Several more arcs of red fire were absorbed by the Sphere.

Berezan cursed, shaking his fists in the air. "Give it to me, sister, or I shall destroy all of

Glacia and every living soul who lives within these mountains!"

Tears poured from Thea's eyes, but she could not release the Sphere to wipe them away. She could only stare into the white light in her hands, feel her body quake, and hold her arms out.

Another barrage of red fire filled the chamber, this time aimed not at her but at the chamber walls. Horrendous blasts of thunder echoed over her head, shaking the walls, dislodging mortar, sliding the stones from alignment. The floor trembled more violently beneath her feet as large blocks of granite fell one atop another, crumbling the walls, breaking away huge chunks of the ceiling.

The floor split beneath the weight of the fallen stones, leaving a gaping chasm that grew wider and wider. She heard Berezan's evil laughter over the noise of his destruction.

The floor shifted again. Thea fell to her knees, tearing her flesh on a chunk of stone. She shifted her legs to support her weight, disregarding the debris that fell around her, the smaller pieces of rock and mortar that struck her arms and jostled her hold on the Sphere.

As she watched all that she had grown up with and loved disintegrate before her eyes, a great anger grew within her. She allowed the energy flowing through her to feed on her anger. The Sphere pulsed within her grasp, growing larger, brighter, until its luminescence filled the chamber. Suddenly she became multidimensional, her essence no longer contained within the shell of her flesh.

Thea stared through the white light, the red blaze that shielded Berezan, into the evil that poured so freely from Berezan's eyes, and saw the elation he felt at the destruction he created.

Thea met Berezan's gaze, held it. "No! You will not do this! You will not destroy Glacia!"

The sound of his laughter once again crawled over her flesh.

"I shall destroy all I cannot have, sister of mine!"

"You will *not!*"

"Stop me!"

Thea raised her arms above her head, spread them wide, splayed her fingers. A strange blue light weaved itself through her fingers, over her palms, down her arms. "With the power entrusted to me by the Ancient Ones to wield the Sphere of Light, I destroy you, Berezan DeLan, Son of Evil!"

The light emanating from the Sphere of Light turned a deep yellow, blinding Thea with its glow, hiding the sight of Berezan's flesh being torn from his bones, his body sagging to the floor in a blaze of yellow fire, then disappearing.

Thea fell to the floor unconscious.

Chapter Thirty-One

Galen hesitated, looking over his shoulder at his warriors still locked in battle with the men of the south. His heart gave another lurch, and the desire for revenge and blood evaporated.

"Go!" Kajar shouted.

Another soldier blocked his path. Galen surged forward with a roar, sword held high, prepared to dispatch the man who barred his flight to Thea.

"Listen!" the Solarian soldier cried.

Galen halted his sword in mid-swing, stopping only inches short of cleaving off the man's head. He jerked his head around, stared up at the keep a hundred spans above.

"The thunder has stopped," the man whispered.

The silence was deafening. Galen looked around.

All of his warriors stood with their weapons limp by their sides. Those who remained of

Berezan's army had dropped their weapons to the ground and fallen to their knees.

Hearing no more than his own heartbeat, Galen quickly searched the faces of the Solarian soldiers, hoping for some plausible reason for their withdrawal from battle.

None came.

He raised his head, watched the archways high above, and noted that not only the thunder but the bright light that had emanated from the arches had passed.

A knot twisted in his chest.

"Thea!"

He dropped his weapon to the frozen ground and ran, slipping and sliding over the bridge that crossed the creviced entrance to the keep. He did not turn to investigate the footfalls he heard behind him, nor consider what might lie ahead inside the stone structure.

"Gustoff?"

Gustoff stood before Thea enshrouded in mist. The brilliant purple robe she remembered well seemed lavender, translucent. It blew in gentle ripples around his frail body, but Thea could feel no wind. She looked into the glassiness of his eyes, studied the opalescence of his flesh, and understood Gustoff was not with her in body, but in spirit.

"Come with me, my child." The old man held out his hand.

Thea entwined her fingers with his, felt no substance, only the warmth of his love. "Where are we going, Gustoff?"

"To a place where you will learn everything I have not had time to teach you."

379

"But Berezan—"

"Is destroyed. Come. There is much to tell you and little time."

Thea concentrated on placing one foot before the other. Gustoff led her toward a light. She followed eagerly.

"Why did you not tell me Berezan was my brother, Gustoff?"

Gustoff looked over his shoulder at her. The light breeze rippled through his beard, fluffed his white hair. "It would have served no good. You could not have faced your destiny knowing you must destroy your own brother."

"But, Gus—"

"Berezan was my mistake, Thea. His malevolence grew out of his hatred for me and the things I took away from him. I should have destroyed him. Instead, I exiled him. I will pay in the afterlife for my weakness, but I could not pass my misdeeds on to you." He turned away, refusing to offer more.

The light suddenly grew nearer, brighter. A hundred faces filled her path. Thea reached out, tried to touch one, but her hand passed through the image.

"Explain this place to me, Gustoff."

"Listen to the voices, my child. Concentrate and hear what is your true destiny."

Gustoff's image faded away. "Remember, I will always love you, Thea of Glacia. Go in peace."

"No! Gustoff! Come back. Don't leave me," she cried, but Gustoff was no more.

The hundred voices spoke as one within her mind.

"Child of destiny. Hear our words. Know these as truths that shall be honored for all times."

Thea turned about, watching the ghostly images float all around her. A mysterious calm filled her, soothed her.

"The Sphere of Light you have been given to hold has but a simple purpose. When the Sphere is possessed by good, all things evil will be destroyed. Should it ever fall into the hands of evil, all that is known as good in our world will forever perish.

"Your life must be spent protecting the Sphere until the time comes when you shall pass it on to its next bearer, the male child who grows within your womb."

Thea dropped her hand to her stomach, but was distracted by the next words that filled her mind.

"The Sphere has completed its task. Speak the words. Call it back into yourself, hold it dear."

Thea listened in awe as strange words fell from her lips, words that were familiar but that she could not remember ever hearing used. She looked down, saw the Sphere draw its brilliant yellow light back into itself, watched it shrink until it became no more than a pulse of light in her hands.

"Place your hands upon your breasts, child. Feel the warmth that flows through your body."

Thea followed the directive of the strange voice. She watched in awe as the Sphere disappeared, leaving no more than a warmth in the region of her heart.

She closed her eyes and succumbed to the darkness.

Galen took the stone stairs three at a time, never pausing. He slid to a halt before the meeting chamber door, looking about to find no evidence of the destruction he'd heard from below.

Vermillion draperies at the three archways flapped in the light breeze that blew through the openings. The table, the floor, the walls, all glowed in the light of the luma chandelier that hung over head.

His heart turned over in his chest at the sight of Thea kneeling as if in prayer at the far end of the chamber. He hurried to her side, dropping to his knees beside her.

"Thea," he whispered, watching as she drew herself from a trance and looked up at him.

Galen knelt within a hand's span of her, his blue eyes paler than Thea had ever seen them, and so filled with his emotions her heart beat wildly within her breast. His distraught face was streaked with blood. His woolen shirt clung to his flesh like a second skin. Blood seeped through the cloth at his waist, darkening the beige fabric to almost black. His hair, that glorious flow of blond and platinum that hugged his muscular shoulders, was matted and wet. He had never looked more handsome.

Thea swayed forward another inch. Galen's arms were around her, clinging to her tightly. She melted against the muscles of his chest. Her sob of relief was smothered as his mouth crashed down upon hers, his kiss deep, ravaging, eager as her own.

Thea lifted her lips from his. "Galen. It is done."

Galen did not release his grasp, or break his hypnotic gaze, nor did the heat of his embrace cool to offer her any reprieve. He whispered her name over her flesh. Then his lips once again met hers, stealing every memory but one from her mind.

"Bless you, my lady."

Galen pulled away reluctantly and looked over his shoulder to discover one of Berezan's soldiers standing at his back. He watched in awe as the man dropped to his knees before Thea, reached to touch the hemline of her gown.

"Bless you," he repeated.

Galen withdrew one hand from Thea's back, placed it upon the man's shoulder, and shoved him away. "What are you doing here?"

Rhem met his gaze. "Surrendering, my lord."

Galen looked at Thea, then back at the man still kneeling.

"I was Berezan's commander, my lord. Many sunrises ago, the people of Solarus lived in peace. Then Berezan killed the rulers of Solarus and the lives of every person of the desert changed. We, the members of Berezan's army, followed him not because we believed in his cause, my lord. We had no choice. Families and homes were threatened, livestock destroyed. Our livelihoods were taken away."

Rhem bowed his head. "I beg you for the lives of my men. I pledge myself to see that the army of Berezan is disbanded if you will allow us to go home to our land, our families, and live once again in peace."

"Galen."

Galen turned to Thea, stared into her beautiful eyes.

She reached forward, touching the bronze medallion that hung against his chest. "It is your decision whether these men live or die. By right, you not only rule Borderland, but the whole of our world."

Galen grasped her hand, pulled it from the disc, then raised it to his lips. He kissed her fingers. "No, Thea. The right to rule Glacia is yours."

Thea shook her head. "I cannot. The *Articles*—"

"Will be changed," Galen finished.

"The Elders—"

"Were not here to protect Glacia from Berezan, nor were they in Borderland, or Solarus. Those who would call themselves leaders, yet stand by and relinquish their beliefs to the evil of Berezan, have no say in anything that shall happen from this day forward."

Rhem cleared his throat.

Galen turned to the soldier of the desert. "Do you have a family who awaits your return?"

"A sister and her children."

"Would you return with the army to Solarus, then gather a delegation of trusted men? And women?" he added with a smile. "Have them travel to Glacia with you for a celebration that shall take place at the next full moon?"

Rhem bowed. "I would be honored, my lord." He looked at Thea. "My lady."

The shuffle of boots drew Thea's attention from Galen and Rhem's conversation. Thea gazed over Galen's shoulder to find Kajar and Thorn standing in the center of the chamber. She raised her hand, beckoned them forward.

"Galen," she said softly. "Kajar and Thorn are here." She smiled up at the two warriors. "I would ask you to join us, but my legs have lost all feeling."

Galen immediately understood. He stood, bent, and picked Thea up in his arms. "See that this man

384

gets adequate provisions for the men of Solarus to make a safe journey home."

Thea chuckled and ducked her head into the side of Galen's neck when she witnessed the startled expression on the two large warrior's faces.

"I have given Berezan's army my leave to travel home in peace."

Kajar nodded.

Galen clasped Rhem's hand. "Go in peace."

Thorn stepped forward. "Any orders for me, *regis?*" he said with a smile.

"See that the people of Glacia know it is safe to come out of their homes, return to the keep with Kajar, find chambers for my warriors to rest, healers to take care of their wounds, then seek me out at sunrise and I will fill you in on everything that's about to take place.

"But for now, Thea is exhausted, and I intend to do everything in my power to see that she receives a proper rest."

Without a backward glance, Galen left the meeting chamber, cradling Thea in his arms.

Galen took the stairs two at a time, pausing before the huge carved door of the chamber he had used many sunrises ago. He positioned Thea so he could open the door, then walked inside and dropped her in the middle of the high poster bed.

"You should now use my father's chamber, *regis*," Thea whispered.

Galen shook his head. "I happen to like this chamber just fine," he answered, then walked across the floor to loosen the cord that held the tapestries open. The fabric swished together, shutting out the light, leaving only the faint glow of one lumastone to guide him back to the bed. He shrugged out of his woolen shirt, slipped the medallion from his neck, dropped both to the floor, and bent to slide his taut leather leggings from his hips and discard his boots.

"Galen." Thea held out her hand to him, touching his side, healing his wound. "I have had a strange vision."

Galen looked to his side, then back to Thea. "Tell me about it later. I have waited too long for this moment, my heart."

Thea shook her head. "But I remember something I think you should know."

"Later." He fell upon the bed, upon her, twisting her over until she lay on top of him. He made quick work of her woolen gown, then changing positions, smothered her with his body, placing warm kisses on every inch of her accessible flesh.

"It's cold in here, Galen," she murmured against his ear.

"Not for long."

Hours later, Galen stirred, pulling the thickness of the fur coverlet about his shoulders. "What was it you wished to tell me earlier?"

Thea twisted in his arms until she faced him. "What type of celebration do you plan for the next full moon?"

"Hmmmm?" Galen had already been distracted. Positioned as she was, with all of her glorious charms readily within reach, he had forgotten he'd even asked a question. He stroked her arm, her side. She arched to meet his touch. He raised his hand, stroked her bare breast gently, then eased his way down to the heat that burned between her thighs.

"Galen." She squirmed beneath his touch.

"Hmmmm?"

"What type of celebration do you have planned for the next full moon?"

Galen sighed. "As you heard, I've invited a delegation from Solarus to hear our plans for a lasting peace."

"Will Borderland also send a delegation?"

Galen nuzzled the tender flesh of her neck. "Of course."

"Women and children, too?"

"Thea!"

"Answer me, Galen. It's important."

"Every last person of the jungle is welcome to our celebration, Thea of Glacia." Galen gave up, realizing Thea wasn't about to allow him another bout of lovemaking until he answered *all* of her questions. He flipped over to his back, staring up at the dark ceiling.

Thea watched him in the faint lumalight. He had closed his eyes. His mouth was pressed in a taut line. All that glorious hair was tangled about his head, teasing her fingers. She leaned across his body, kissed the hardened plane of his chest, and licked his breastbone, his nipple.

"Good. Now, tell me what type of celebration you have in mind," she said between kisses that worked their way slowly down the length of his body, nearer and nearer the part of him that gave her such pleasure.

Galen groaned. He grasped her by the shoulders, pulling her back until they were almost nose to nose. "A joining, Thea of Glacia. I plan for a great feast to celebrate our joining!"

"Perfect."

He tangled his fingers into her flowing hair, pulled her face closer.

"I wouldn't want our babe to be born a bastard."

Galen bolted upright, dislodging Thea, who sprawled to her buttocks beside him on the soft mattress. He turned, reached to place one hand on each side of her body, and stared deeply into her laughing eyes.

"A child?"

Thea raised her hand, placed her splayed fingers upon his shoulder, and pushed the mammoth warrior over as if he weighed no more than a feather. She scrambled up, spread her legs over his chest, then slid lower and opened wider to welcome the thickness of him that claimed her heat.

She sat straighter, undulating her hips in an erotic dance that caused the ends of her hair to sweep his rippled abdomen. Reaching down, she traced each band of muscle, the arrow of dark blond hair that grew downward to where their bodies joined, then lifted her hands and spread them over her own belly.

Galen reached up, entwined his fingers into the wild tangles of her beautiful hair, then drew her down. He used his lips, his tongue, his body to express all of the words of love his mind failed to offer, all the promises he would make to her and his unborn child to keep their world safe, to reunite the three regions into one, and to join with her in protecting the Sphere of Light.

He skimmed his hands over the warm flesh of her breasts, the slim contours of her back, her buttocks. He held her, embraced her as the ripples of ecstasy washed over their bodies, fusing them together as one in this and life for whatever came after.

Epilogue

Thea stood on the balcony and watched the sun slip slowly behind the peaks and streaks of gray and purple gather in the sky. She wrapped her arms around her waist to ward off the chill that increased with the coming darkness.

She looked down upon the multitudes of people gathered in celebration on the icy streets, their faces lighted by the thousands of lumastones decorating the houses and shops of Glacia. The people were garbed in warm clothing befitting Glacia's climate, and she could not tell Creean from Solarian or Glacian.

Joining Day. A day that would remembered in history, for not only had she taken her warrior as mate, but the boundaries of their world had been dissolved. The people now were free to travel as they would, experience all the wonders each region had to offer.

"Thea?"

Warm arms wrapped around her waist and pulled her back to rest against a solid chest. Large, callused hands slipped to cradle her still flat belly. "Your subjects await you, my heart."

Thea smiled. "*Our* subjects, *regis.*"

Galen bent his head closer to savor the fragrance of Thea's beautiful hair. The responsibility he had been given weighed heavy upon his shoulders, but with Thea by his side and the Sphere of Light under their protection, his child would grow up in a world of peace—a world where evil no longer threatened.

He kissed the crown of her head, looked down into the streets at the different cultures gathered there, and smiled. "Is that your Nola by Thorn's side?"

Thea eased forward, glancing toward the couple standing before the smithy. "Yes, I suppose it is," she whispered, then snuggled tighter into her warrior's arms. She would never confess she had sent Nola to Thorn's side for answers to her numerous questions about Borderland.

Galen nuzzled her ear. "Do you suppose we could skip the celebration for a few hours?"

"Do you have something more important in mind, warrior?"

Galen stepped away and held out his hand. "Walk with me, Thea." He led her into the chamber and closed the tapestries tight against the night air.

Futuristic Romance

Love in another time, another place.

CIRCLE OF LIGHT

NANCY CANE

"Nancy Cane sparks your imagination and melts your heart!"
—Marilyn Campbell, author of *Stardust Dreams*

Attorney Sarina Bretton deals with hard, cold facts, not fantasies of faraway planets and spaceships. Then a daring stranger whisks her to worlds—and desires—she's never imagined possible. Despite her yearning to boldly explore new realms with Teir Reylock, destiny appears to decree that Sarina shall fulfill an ancient prophecy in the arms of another man. Besieged by enemies, and bedeviled by her love for Teir, Sarina vows that before a vapor cannon puts her asunder she will surrender to the seasoned warrior and his promise of throbbing ecstasy.

_51949-6 $4.99 US/$5.99 CAN

LOVE SPELL
ATTN: Order Department
276 5th Avenue, New York, NY 10001

Please add $1.50 for shipping and handling for the first book and $.35 for each book thereafter. PA., N.Y.S. and N.Y.C. residents, please add appropriate sales tax. No cash, stamps, or C.O.D.s. All orders shipped within 6 weeks via postal service book rate. Canadian orders require $2.00 extra postage and must be paid in U.S. dollars through a U.S. banking facility.

Name _____

Address _____

City _____ State _____ Zip _____

I have enclosed $_____ in payment for the checked book(s).
Payment <u>must</u> accompany all orders.☐ Please send a free catalog.

Futuristic Romance

Love in another time, another place.

New York Times Bestselling Author
Phoebe Conn writing as Cinnamon Burke!

Lady Rogue. Sent to infiltrate Spider Diamond's pirate operation, Drew Jordan finds himself in an impossible situation. Handpicked by Spider as a suitable "pet" for his daughter, Drew has to win Ivory Diamond's love or lose his life. But once he's initiated Ivory into the delights of lovemaking, he knows he can never turn her over to the authorities. For he has found a vulnerable woman's heart within the formidable lady rogue.

_3558-8 $5.99 US/$6.99 CAN

Rapture's Mist. Dedicated to preserving the old ways, Tynan Thorn has led the austere life of a recluse. He has never even laid eyes on a woman until the ravishing Amara sweeps into his bedroom to change his life forever. Daring and uninhabited, Amara sets out to broaden Tynan's viewpoint, but she never expects that the area he will be most interested in exploring is her own sensitive body. As their bodies unite in explosive ecstasy, Tynan and Amara discover a whole new world, where together they can soar among the stars.

_3470-0 $5.99 US/$6.99 CAN

TIMESWEPT ROMANCE
TEARS OF FIRE
By Nelle McFather

Swept into the tumultuous life and times of her ancestor Deirdre O'Shea, Fable relives a night of sweet ecstasy with Andre Devereux, never guessing that their delicious passion will have the power to cross the ages. Caught between swirling visions of a distant desire and a troubled reality filled with betrayal, Fable seeks the answers that will set her free—answers that can only be found in the tender embrace of two men who live a century apart.

_51932-1 $4.99 US/$5.99 CAN

FUTURISTIC ROMANCE
ASCENT TO THE STARS
By Christine Michels

For Trace, the assignment should be simple. Any Thadonian warrior can take a helpless female to safety in exchange for valuable information against his diabolical enemies. But as fiery as a supernova, as radiant as a sun, Coventry Pearce is no mere woman. Even as he races across the galaxy to save his doomed world, Trace battles to deny a burning desire that will take him to the heavens and beyond.

_51933-X $4.99 US/$5.99 CAN

Futuristic Romance

Love in another time, another place.

Golden Conquest

Patricia Roenbeck

Strong willed and courageous, Aylyn fears nothing—until a faceless man begins to haunt her dreams. For the golden-eyed beauty knows that the stranger from a distant planet will never fall under her control. Only when the visions become reality, and hard-muscled Kolt rescues her from a devious kidnapper, does Aylyn surrender to his embrace. But before they can share their fiery desire, Kolt and Aylyn must conquer an unknown enemy bent on destroying their worlds and turning their glorious future into a terrifying nightmare.

_3325-9 $4.50 US/$5.50 CAN

Three captivating stories of love in another time, another place.

MADELINE BAKER
"Heart of the Hunter"

A Lakota warrior must defy the boundaries of life itself to claim the spirited beauty he has sought through time.

ANNE AVERY
"Dream Seeker"

On faraway planets, a pilot and a dreamer learn that passion can bridge the heavens, no matter how vast the distance from one heart to another.

KATHLEEN MORGAN
"The Last Gatekeeper"

To save her world, a dazzling temptress must use her powers of enchantment to open a stellar portal—and the heart of a virile but reluctant warrior.

__51974-7 *Enchanted Crossings* (three unforgettable love stories in one volume) $4.99 US/
$5.99 CAN

TIMESWEPT ROMANCE
TIME REMEMBERED
Elizabeth Crane
Bestselling Author of *Reflections in Time*

A voodoo doll and an ancient spell whisk thoroughly modern Jody Farnell from a decaying antebellum mansion to the Old South and a true Southern gentleman who shows her the magic of love.

_0-505-51904-6 $4.99 US/$5.99 CAN

FUTURISTIC ROMANCE
A DISTANT STAR
Anne Avery

Jerrel is enchanted by the courageous messenger who saves his life. But he cannot permit anyone to turn him from the mission that has brought him to the distant world—not even the proud and passionate woman who offers him a love capable of bridging the stars.

_0-505-51905-4 $4.99 US/$5.99 CAN